Three Princess Series

BOBBY CINEMA

authorHOUSE®

AuthorHouse™
1663 Liberty Drive
Bloomington, IN 47403
www.authorhouse.com
Phone: 1-800-839-8640

Published by AuthorHouse 4/30/2014

ISBN: 978-1-4969-0809-4 (sc)
ISBN: 978-1-4969-0810-0 (e)

Contents

Introduction: Three Princess Series are three stories from three different princess from the modern time. The First story is called The Princess and the Angels a story about a princess who is a member Albanian royal family and second heir to the throne of Albania. Her name is Serena who lived in America during her high school years and went to a public high school in Anaheim California. Her family and her friends don't know she is a princess. She is a die hard Anaheim Angels fan and wants go to college in UCLA to become a broadcast journalist in baseball. She meets one of the Angels players who is a ten year veteran of the Angels John Mackey. John Mackey is jewish pitcher and nerdy nice guy who is never arrogant or egotistical like all the players in baseball. Serena who is eighteen sees John and it's love at first sight. Her parents visited Anaheim and tell her that her sister is getting married and they'll have the wedding in Diplomatic mansion where Serena has been living at for four years. Serena is about to graduate in three weeks and their going to have her sisters wedding in a few days after graduation. Their parents tells Serena that they expect her to move back to Albania and attend the university their after your royal duties. That's another word for, they find a potential suitor for her to marry when she goes back. Serena spent three weeks with John and fell in love with him, even though he has a lot of money. But he's not noble blood, she wants to stay in America and go to U.C.L.A. and continue dating John. She has a choice go back to Albania with her family and carry on her royal duties and marry a rich noble jerk her parents pick out or stay in America and go to college in UCLA and continue dating John. The second Princess Series is about Princess Amy from London England who father is the Duke of Granwich. The Duke is the Queen's cousin and twentieth line to the throne of England. Her father owns a billion dollar oil company that his great grandfather struck oil in 1890 and built a billion dollar company. Nivel the Duke of Granwich is been losing money from his oil company for a nearly a year because his oil wells been dried up. His main competitor Lord Randall Alden might be the one who is stealing oil from his wells, no proof that's he behind it. Nivel made a deal with Lord Randall Alden, who went to Oxford University with her daughter Amy, to sign a merger agreement that can save his company and all the people who work for him. Their was a clause in the contract, that his daughter has to wed Lord Alden after the merger agreement is signed and she refused, her father will have to 800 million dollars to buy his company back since Lord Alden owns 50 million shares of the voting stock of Nivel's company. But Lord Alden gave him a ultimatum, he's got two weeks either buy his stock back and they could nearly bankrupt him and his daughter or his daughter will have to marry Lord Alden to save his father's company. Nivel explains this to his daughter and he saw how sad she is that she has to marry this jerk, Nivel had a bigger problem that he had a heart attack and rush to the hospital. But he's fine, it was a mild heart attack. Nivel tells his daughter, she has two weeks to make a decision. Whatever she decide, he'll support her no matter what. Back home Amy read online about Abda Electronics in Mountain View, California nicknamed Silcon Valley. It is Electronics and computer city of the world. Abda Electronics just closed an account with British Knights shoes, a billion dollar shoe company that we will help advertise for the company. They're about to close the account in a week and looking for investors to invest in the company. Amy decides go to Mountain View, California and start investing two hundred million dollars Abda Electronics, if she invest the stocks will hit the roof and make enough money to but Alden stock back. While she was in Palo Alto, Amy hasn't figure out what to do, until she stops by Mountain View Public Library and meets a librarian named Robbie Champberg, a nerdy fat jewish librarian who has a Bachelor's degree Palo Alto University in computer science and help her make the right decision to invest in what company. Robbie used to work as a computer programmer Abda electronics. They fired him six months ago, he messed up a billion dollar account for the company. End up working in a library since he minored in library and science. Robbie and Amy fell in love at first sight, but their in different worlds. Robbie is a middle class geek whose father works in a pencil factory assembly line and works in a library since he got fired and uses all his savings to use a start up computer company with his best friend Jaleel. Princess Amy is about to marry Lord Alden, is handsome, british lord who is about to take over her father's company and take his duke title from him. They gotta a bigger problem, while Princess Amy trying to investigate about the stolen oil from her wells and doesn't have any proof that Lord Alden is behind this. She gets help from Robbie and his friend Jaleel who works in the library with him, to track down who stole that oil. I think somebody in Abda Electronic works for Lord Alden and trying to stop her from making that investment to save her father's company. Can Robbie and Amy stop Lord Alden from stealing his father's oil and bigger plan that he is using with that oil. Can Robbie and Amy be together after this huge adventure together and Robbie telling Amy who he is. Only time will tell. Third and Final Princess Series of the Four Princess Series is called the Princess of the Water. Opens up with a flashback of JACK KOUFAX as a nine year old boy in Los Angeles. It is during this flashback that the audience learns about his tight knit family and the heroism of Jack's DAD, a rescue swimmer for the Coast Guard.

The story then moves to present day New York City where a twenty-something Jack is now head librarian at the New York Public Library. Misfortunate in love, Jack tries repeatedly to woo the opposite sex, but to no avail. BOBBY ROMANO, Jack's best friend since youth teases Jack about his failed romantic endeavors, but he and his wife SARAH ROMANO want to see Jack in a happy romantic situation. Bobby Romano mentions to Jack that he has won free swimming lessons for two weeks at the Lorelai Rosenberg Recreation Center. Unable to attend the lessons due to a meeting with a party planner, Bobby gives the lessons to Jack. Jack goes to the swimming lessons, hesitatingly, until he meets the Olympic gold medalist and supermodel LORELAI ROSENBERG, his swim instructor for the next two weeks, a striking woman in her late twenties and wealthy.

They call her the Princess of the Water, she scored a few gold medals in Swimming in the Olympics and she makes more money in Endorsements and modeling gigs than no swimmer ever had. Jack is instantly intrigued. After Jack's first lesson there is a flashback to Jack as a nine year old boy. The flashback is of the telephone call that Jack's MOM received telling of her husband's death during a heroic rescue attempt. This flashback explains Jack's fear of the water. After the flashback the story returns to the present day, to the Lorelai Rosenberg Recreation Center where Jack is taking swimming lessons. Very interested in Lorelai, Jack asks her out on a date for ice cream. On this date he learns that she is engaged. Nevertheless they have a great time and end up planning a double date, in spite of the fact that Jack does not have a girlfriend. It is on this date that Jack meets COLIN, Lorelai's fiancé. After the double date, Jack continues his swimming lessons. After one of his lessons, Jack asks Lorelai to dinner with him, Bobby, and Sarah at the Ritz-Carlton Atelier, much to the chagrin of Colin. Jack finally reaches the final lesson and says goodbye to Lorelai. The story then moves to the anniversary party of Bobby and Sarah at the Ritz-Carlton. As this scene is unfolding the story cuts to Lorelai's wedding day. As Lorelai prepares for her wedding too her fiance Colin. Will Lorelai will take the plunge and marry Colin, for somebody she is not in love with or decide to take the plunge and be with his true love Jack. Only time Will tell. Three Princess stories in one book, I hope you guys enjoy reading them.

Princess and The Angels

Plot Summary: King Rufus and Queen Esmeralda, rulers of Albania who has two daughters, their first daughter is getting engaged to a royal British duke and their other daughter who is the baby of the family Serena lives in America to get an education by their parents. Serena is a beautiful tall brunette who attends the Anaheim High School and it's her senior year in that school against her parents wishes. Since Serena attended this school, since she was fourteen, she dropped her Albainian accent and tries to talk more like an american girl and is like a beautiful tomboy. She's the star of her softball team and trying to get a scholarship in UCLA. She wants to major in broadcast journalism and someday do play-by-play to any major league baseball teams ever. Serena is a die hard Angels fan, goes to the locker room to get an autograph, all the players is unaware she is the princess of Albania and second heir to the throne after her sister. She meets one of the Angels players who is a ten year veteran of the Angels John Mackey. John Mackey is jewish pitcher and nerdy nice guy who is never arrogant or egotistical like all the players in baseball. Serena who is eighteen sees John and it's love at first sight. Her parents visited Anaheim and tell her that her sister is getting married and they'll have the wedding in Diplomatic mansion where Serena has been living at for four years. Serena is about to graduate in three weeks and their going to have her sisters wedding in a few days after graduation. Their parents tells Serena that they expect her to move back to Albania and attend the university their after your royal duties. That's another word for, they find a potential suitor for her to marry when she goes back. Serena spent three weeks with John and fell in love with him, even though he has a lot of money. But he's not noble blood, she wants to stay in America and go to U.C.L.A. and continue dating John. She has a choice go back to Albania with her family and carry on her royal duties and marry a rich noble jerk her parents pick out or stay in America and go to college in UCLA and continue dating John.

Once upon a time, their was a king and queen named Rufus and Esmeralda who is the ruler of Albania and they have two daughters. Their oldest Marissa is the heir to the throne of Albania and is planning on marrying her fiancé Andrew who is twelfth Duke of Lancaster. Marissa is the heir to the throne of Albania and King Rufus and Esmeralda has a second daughter, the baby of the family is Serena. King Rufus and Queen Esmeralda are in their late fifties. Rufus Royal Advisor enters the throne room and sees Rufus and Esmeralda who are sitting in their thrones and goes over talk to them. Rufus Royal Advisor is in his early thirties, a little bit chunky and is really serious about his job. Rufus royal advisor wishes Rufus, hello your majesty. Hello Donald said King Rufus. Queen Esmeralda ask Donald, what brings you here. Donald tells the royal couple, I have the wedding invitations finished your heinous. You want me to mail them today? King Rufus tells Donald, not today. We have to figure out where we can have this wedding, because we never figure out where to have it. Esmeralda ask her husband, I thought we already agreed that we'll have it here in the royal ballroom. King Rufus explains to Esmeralda, do you remember honey. That the royal ballroom is being remodeled and Serena is still in school and her finals won't be done in the end of two weeks and we have to be at her graduation in two weeks. Since the ballroom remodeled, we can't have the wedding here. I been trying to figure where to have the wedding at? Donald suggest to King Rufus, what about the church. Nobody is using it in a few weeks, if it was booked, they'll never say no to you if you call the archbishop. Rufus tells Donald, actually the Pope will be coming to the church in six weeks and everybody in the church getting everything ready for the Pope to arrive. So we can't make any reschedules. Esmeralda is thinking for a minute, okay we can't use the church or the ballroom. Their has to be someplace they haven't used. Donald tells the royal couple we can't use the ballroom at the Rogner Hotel Europapark it's already booked up for the pope in six weeks. Since we waited in the last minute for the royal wedding princess Marissa. I guess we'll have to find another location in Tirana. King Rufus is thinking for a minute, we'll have to find someplace to find a place for the wedding. Donald, go to the computer room and find us a place where to have the wedding. Donald tells King Rufus, yes your majesty. Donald was about to leave the throne room, until King Rufus stops him for a minute and tells him something. King Rufus tells Donald something, Donald! Donald stops for a minute and turns around. Donald ask King Rufus, yes your heinous. King Rufus tells Donald, find us a location for my daughter's wedding, if you can't find one. I'll be jamming my crown right down your throat, if you can't find us a place. Donald panics for a minute, didn't see the centerpiece that's on the table and bumps into the table and Donald falls down on the floor and breaks the centerpiece and the table. Donald is still panicking and just hopes King Rufus is not mad for a minute. Donald tells King Rufus, sorry your majesty. King Rufus yells at Donald, will you get out of here, before I break that centerpiece that you call a face. Donald is still panicking for a minute, gets up from the floor and exit's the throne room. King Rufus tells Esmeralda, why did we pick our court jester as our royal advisor. Esmeralda tells Rufus, we drew straws and he was selected. King Rufus tells Esmeralda, I wish Lukas didn't publish his book and gone to the book tour. How I miss him. Esmeralda, tells King Rufus I know Donald is a little rough around the edges but he is a good advisor. You never know, he could surprise us. King Rufus tells Esmeralda or worry us. Just hope this castle is still one piece if the wedding is set. God help us. Donald is in the computer room, trying to find a place to have the wedding. Donald is searching for a place in Albania. While searching for a place to have it, Donald's cell phone rings for a minute that's on his table and Donald grabs his cell phone and picks it. Donald answers his cell phone and says hello. The person on the phone is Serena. Serena is King Rufus second daughter and the baby of the family. Serena tells Donald, Hey Donald, it's me. Donald tells Serena, hey Serena how are you doing? Serena answers, I'm good. How are you. Donald tells Serena, Not so good for me, I have to pick a place to have the wedding for your sister. You know she's getting married in three weeks. Serena answers, yeah tell me about it. She's been on the phone all day about how rich George is and how big George estate is and how much power he's going to have when he runs for Prime Minister in a few years. Trust me, I think Marissa is getting a swell head. Donald answers to Serena, any bigger and I think her head will explode. I was going to ask, how's school over in California? Serena answers to Donald, Cornelia Connelly School is the toughest school to attend. I never have to worry about the teachers chewing me out. But, it's my headmistress whose chewing me out for being on time in class. I may have a straight A average. But being on time in class, one thing she's always chewing me out on. Donald ask Serena, is their any reason why you're late for class? Serena tells Donald, it's a big school. It's hard to find any classes in that school. Donald tells Serena, you've been in that school for four years, when you told your parents that you wanted go to school in America. How hard is it to find your classes in that school. Serena tells Donald, I couldn't find it in a map or a GPS. It's one of the main reasons why Ms Lawley is giving me detention for it. I already have five tardies this week that results for a detention. So, I spent all afternoon with her chewing me out being late. Donald tells Serena, well at least you have three more weeks before graduation. Serena tells Donald, just hope Mom and Dad don't set me up with some guy whose has a royal background that I hate and end up marrying this guy. It was okay for them to set up George for Marissa. But not for me. Donald tells Serena, you may want to hear this. But I think you're father is considering setting you up with one of the princes for you to date or marry in a few years. Serena, tells Donald, I'm really upset right now that they have to stop butting in my life. I love my parents, they have to stop setting me up with these royal jerks they want me to marry in a couple of years. It's time, they should let me make my own decisions. Donald tells Serena, well good luck with that. I have to go finish searching for a place for the wedding, bye Serena. Serena tells Donald, bye Donald. Say hello to my parents for me. Donald tells Serena, sure thing. Serena tells Donald, if you're looking for a wedding, you should have it in my house that my parents bought me if when I stayed in Anaheim. Man, Alan is the toughest butler ever, I can't believe my father had to pick him look after me. Donald, tells Serena he's the only guy your father would trust to look after you. Serena, tells Donald I know my mansion is a diplomatic house in Albania and Alan is like Rambo when he tries to protect me from bad guys. Donald tells Serena, a guy like that is doing his job. Protecting the royal family is his job, bye Serena. Serena tells Donald, bye Donald. Donald hangs up his phone and Donald puts his phone back on the table. Donald is thinking where to have the wedding. Donald tells himself, can you believe what Serena said, that they should have the wedding at her mansion in Anaheim. Donald snaps his fingers for a minute and has an idea. Donald tells himself, I have an idea where to have the wedding, thank you Serena. Donald picks up the phone and makes a call . Donald calls Serena's body guard and chauffer Alan and tells him, Alan listen I need a favor. Serena's mansion where the princess is been living at for four years, when she wanted go to school here. Her mansion is gated and goes up to top window where Serena's room is at. Serena's room is huge, she's wearing a robe hanging up her phone calling Donald, her father's royal advisor and her friend. Serena is sitting down in her chair, while she hangs up her phone and Serena is about eighteen, a beautiful brunette whose about 5'8 or 5'9 and looks like a supermodel. Serena gets up from her chair and sits down on her bed where the tv remote is on and turns it on. Serena is watching Chuck on tv tonight. Serena starts laughing for a minute, until her door is knocking. Serena tells the person, come in. The door opens and it's Alan. Alan is 6'3 tall man who looks tough on the outside and good man in the inside who has a soft side for Serena. Alan is also her chauffer and her royal advisor go to. Alan tells Serena, hey Serena. Serena tells Alan, hey Alan. You're still on that Angels game tomorrow. Alan tells Serena, of course I got the box seat tickets today. It's a good thing you bought those season tickets before opening day. Serena tells Alan, I've been Angels fan, since you took me out to the ballpark. I always heard about the team and watched it at home in the castle. But, I never seen the game up close. When you bought those season tickets for me. You must have been psychic. Alan tells Serena, you mention talking about watching the game for a hundred times when I first took the job. So, I thought I could make it interesting and probably get in good with you. Serena tells Alan, I appreciate that. That's the reason, why you've been my favorite bodyguard for four years. Alan tells Serena, I'm your only bodyguard. Serena tells Alan, I know and you're my best friend. Alan tells Serena, I'm here to tell you, you better set your alarm clock at seven. You have school tomorrow. Serena groans for a minute, Man, I wish I didn't have school today. Even though, I only have three weeks left before graduation. I don't even know why my parents want me go to Cornelia Connelly School in the first place? Alan tells Serena, it's the only school that you're parents approve of you going, if you want to get an education here in California. Serena, tells Alan too bad they don't know, I really attended Anaheim High School instead of Cornelia Connelly School for four years. Alan tells Serena, they don't know you go to a public high school and your principal is Ms Lawley. Who was also your friend and mentor of the school who let you come here and keep your identity a secret from this school. So no student will want something from you. Serena tells Alan, of course. I want people to like me for who I am, not what I can offer. I had lie to Donald and tell him, that Ms Lawley was a tough principal who was riding my back for four years. I had to make a tough bodyguard, too fool Donald and that way my parents will know I'm miserable that way they won't pull me out of the school. Alan tells Serena, how come you didn't tell your parents that you wanted go to a public high school here in California. Serena, tells Donald they would never let me go their. They don't want me go to place with regular kids and luckily for me I gave them address here to mail our tuition and school supplies here. Instead of this school. Besides, just once I want to be a regular kid. Not some mindless princess who has to live a certain way. Alan tells Serena, what are you going to tell them, when they arrive to graduation to a school you don't go to and if you do send them an address where your graduation is. They'll know it's in Anaheim High School. Serena tells Alan, I'll tell them before they come here, they will be upset at first, but they will be okay when they come. If that means, they'll either they cut me off or they'll take me back home so I can attend the school here. Or have a bodyguard that's worse that I actually attend their school their. But, I'll deal with it. Alan tells Serena, I think they might cut you off. When you tell them what you school you went too. Serena tells Alan, I think so. But I'll be okay with it, luckily for me I avoided the paparazzi every step when I first came here. Alan tells Serena, how did exactly avoid the paparazzi here? Serena tells Alan, I tipped them off and tell them I go to school at Cornelia Connelly School and luckily for me I have a decoy who I hired that help me cover the paparazzi tracks. Like going inside the school and come out. Because I always have one step ahead of them. Even though this might be your last three weeks before your parents send you back to Albania or if you get your acceptance letter to UCLA. Once you tell them, you're going their and they'll cut you off for good. Serena, tells Alan I know. Even thought I would tell my father, he would've been upset at first, but he would be okay with it. But my Mom, is another story. She would be totally upset what happened, I thought I would be cut off or go back to Albania for university where they can keep an eye on me and have a security detail 24/7. So, those are the obstacles I have to take. Alan tells Serena, just remember set your alarm at seven you have school tomorrow and you don't want to miss the Angels game after school. Serena tells Alan, no way I don't want to miss that. But, maybe I don't have to worry about my parents coming to my graduation. Ms Lawley owes me a couple favors since I donated money for the music room and a new wing for the library. She owes me. I think I have a way, to keep my savings and you can still stay as my bodyguard and continue living here. Alan tells Serena, what is that your heinous. Serena tells Alan, I'll tell you tomorrow. Good night, Alan. Alan tells Serena, good night Serena. Alan exits Serena's bedroom and closes the door. Serena continues watching Chuck on tv. The black SUV van is parked right across the entrance of Anaheim High School and the passenger door opens and it's Serena. Serena is wearing ray ban sunglasses, jeans and a t-shirt and carrying a book bag on her shoulder. Serena exit's the van and closes the door. Alan exit's the van and tells Serena something before he leaves. Alan tells Serena, I'll pick you up right after softball practice. Bye Serena. Serena tells Alan, see ya, Alan. Alan gets back in the car and starts the car and exit's the school main entrance. Serena goes inside the school and heads to her first class. Serena walks to her hallway and sees her best friends Mona and Warren. Mona is the same age as Serena and she is attractive but nerdy and her boyfriend Warren who is also nerdy and lovable. They're both loyal to Serena. Serena sees them and tells them hi guys. Both of them say, hey Serena how you doing? Mona tells Serena, you pumped up for the game. We have a big match with Grant for the district championship in two weeks. Warren tells Serena a lot important college scouts will be at the game, especially UCLA. Serena tells Mona and Warren of course I don't want to miss the game for good. This is my chance to get that softball scholarship and who knows I'll be wearing a bruins uniform next year. Warren tells Serena you've been telling us for the last four years you wanted go to that school and major in broadcast journalism. Mona tells Serena UCLA has the best broadcasting journalism program in California. Serena tells them maybe I'll be doing play-by-plays for the Angels when I graduate. Mona tells Serena, well good luck. If we don't win that championship. The only college we might go to is community college. None of our families are rich enough go to those schools. Serena laughs a little, tells them yeah, I know what you meant. Mona tells Serena, we've been best friends for four years I'm sure they give you that scholarship. Serena whispers to herself, I hope so. Warren tells Serena, we have to hurry we don't want to be late for American history. Mona tells Serena, we'll see you in class bye Serena. Warren tells Serena see ya! Warren and Mona exit's the hallway and head to class. Serena tells her friends, bye guys. Serena looks at her watch and realize she doesn't want to be late for class. Serena tells herself well I better hurry up, I don't want to be late for class. Serena exit's the hallway until she bumps into her rival from who was carrying books and drops them. Serena stops for a minute and realize who it is starts groaning for a minute. Serena rival tells her well well if it isn't princess geek. You lost you're heinous. Serena tells her rival no Jenn the only person who is lost is you. Shouldn't be at your school right now, what are you doing here. Jenn tells Serena I have to speak to the freshman softball team about good sportsmanship and since I used go to this school when my father transferred to Bel-air last year for his job and moved to better school when people need me and I don't have to look at losers like for the rest of my school year. So, how is my old team doing anyway. Serena tells Jenn were doing okay we have that district championship in two weeks against Grant. You may have been star of the team three years in a row and all state. Since I'm the captain, that's going to change when I take this team to the championship against Grant. So, why don't tell the freshman softball team how much of a jerk you always been to me and to everybody in this school. Jenn tells Serena, what was the full name of the school that you're competing against. Serena tells Jenn it's Ulysses S. Grant Prep why do you ask? Jenn tells Serena that's my school you're competing against and I'm the captain and the star of my softball team you're facing. Serena panics a little and says aah man! Jenn tells Serena enjoying Anaheim community that's where you will be attending after I defeat you guys in the district championship. Enjoy defeat loser. Jenn leaves the hallway and starts laughing for a minute.

Serena looks a little upset right now and tells herself, I love to shove the softball right down her throat. Serena heads to class and leaves the hallway. Serena is on the baseball field with Mona who is practicing the game against Jenn's team. Serena and Mona are warming up playing catch. Serena throws the ball and Mona catches it in her glove on her right hand. Serena tells Mona I can't believe were taking on Jenn's team. You know it was bad enough she always has to show on the field and act like egotistical jerk in front of this team like she's owns the place. Mona tells Serena I know you were her back up for this team and she always rubs it in her face how great she is. She always tries just to push us around. I know she was homecoming and prom queen and she dated the star quarterback of this school and was class president of this school. I don't think you should let that get to you Serena. She just transferred to Grant Prep she has to start all over in that school. You have nothing worry about. Serena tells Mona she doesn't have to start over her popularity in that school. She was already was flaunting her money to her classmates, became captain of the softball team in one year when their old captain broke her knee during their first practice. Their was a rumor that Jenn started it. Anyway she homecoming and prom queen and dated the star quarterback of her school all over again. Mona tells Serena it's like she never left. Anaheim High Softball Coach blows his whistle and tells his players all right girls batting practice. Serena you're up. Mona tells Serena good luck. Serena tells Mona I don't need luck. Serena heads to the batting cage, grabs her bat and wait for the Anaheim high pitcher throws the ball hard and Serena swings her bat and hits it out of the park. Anaheim high pitcher throws the ball hard again and Anaheim high pitcher throws the ball hard and Serena swings her bat and hit's the ball out of the park again. Anaheim high pitcher throws the ball hard again and Serena swings her bat and hit's the ball out of the park again. Mona goes over to Serena for a minute, Serena tells Mona like I said I don't need hard just hard work and practice that's all. Mona tells Serena I'll remember that. Serena looks at her watch for a minute and tells Mona I better hurry up I don't want to miss the game. Mona tells Serena what team the Angels are playing against today. Serena tells Mona they're playing against the Orioles today. I don't want me and Alan miss the game. Mona tells Serena Alan you're uncle right. Serena tells Mona, yeah my uncle. Mona tells Serena you know Serena I met your uncle and me and

Warren never came over to your house. Neither does the rest of the team. I wanted to ask maybe if it's okay with you that me and Warren can come over to your house and see you. If it's okay with you. Serena tells Mona I'll have to think about it. Mona tells Serena yeah you have to think about it. Mona is really disappointed. Mona tells Serena are you ashamed of me and Warren being seen in your house. Serena tells Mona no of course not. Me and Uncle Alan are busy doing spring cleaning for people coming over three weeks. So we have to keep the place ship shape. So, I'm kind of busy for the next three weeks. So, I can't have any guest right now. Mona looks disappointed. Mona tells Serena yeah you're busy. You're always busy too ashamed for me and Warren come to your house. Serena tells Mona, I have to go bye Mona. Serena exit's the baseball field and head to her locker room and Mona is still disappointed that Serena won't invite her to his house. Serena and Alan enters Angels stadium and walks to their seats in the stadium. Serena and Alan has seats front row on the baseball field and Serena was amazed how great the field is. Serena sees the Angels players warming up. Serena also sees John Mackey a ten year veteran who pitches for the Angels. John is warming up his pitches and Serena sees a 2002 world series ring on his finger. John doesn't have any luck pitching right now. His pitching wasn't he used to be. John Mackey is 6"4 is Jewish and a nerdy lovable nice guy and doesn't have a superstar status like his teammate Troy Glass. Troy Glass was Al MVP in the American league championship, ten time all-star and won five golden gloves. Even though Mackey is a one time all-star, makes eight million dollars a year and been nominated for the Cy young award in 2002. But his pitching game never came back after the world series. So, he spent most of his time trying to get his pitching game back, but no avail. Alan tells Serena, I'm going to get some food in concession stand want anything Serena. Serena tells Alan dog with ketchup and mustard, bottle diet pepsi, cracker jacks and nachos. Alan tells Serena, let's say the usual. I'll be right back. Serena tells Alan, thanks Alan I appreciate it. Alan tells Serena hey no problemo. Serena sits down in her chair and the game starts with John as a starting pitcher. Angels broadcaster Vince Rawlins announces the game and tells Angels fans, welcome Angels fans where the Angels will be taking on the Baltimore Orioles on a five game trip this week. Starting pitcher of this game John Mackey he's 3-17 and his E.R.A. 4.50. His game hasn't been the same after the world series when his old rival Troy Glass shows up him in the world series. Left Fielder Ron Vent is up to bat, John Mackey makes the pitch. John throws the ball hard and Vent sees the pitch and hit's the ball out of the park. Vince tells the fans, Vent hit's the ball way out of here and makes the score Baltimore one nothing. Serena and Alan continues watching the game and Serena finishes her hot dog and continues watching the game. Vince tells the fans it's top of the sixth and Baltimore is leading six nothing. Mackey is struggling with Johnson. Mackey is 3-0 to Johnson and two men are on base and Mackey makes the pitch. Mackey throws the ball slowly and the ball is way over the plate and the umpire makes the call. Vince tells the fans and the ump calls it and it's ball four. Johnson takes his base. The fans are really disappointed in that call. Serena sees the game and feels a little sympathy to John. Serena tells Alan, aah man another walk. Look, I know Mackey lost his game for a long. But I think he still has it. Alan tells Serena, Serena Mackey's game hasn't been the same after the world series. Serena tells Alan, I know. Way deep down he still has potential to get this team back to the world series. All he has to do is get this team to win the pennant and he's back on top again. Alan tells Serena, The Angels have twenty more games if they reach the Al championship. They can't lose any games right now if they want get to the pennant. Serena tells Alan, don't worry about it I'm sure John still have some pitching power back like he used to. Vince tells the fans, well looks like Angels manager Nick Brawny coming out of the field and he's going to take John out of the game. Brawny heads to the mound and with the Angels catcher Hank Lewis joining talk to John. Brawny tells John, sorry John I have to take you out. John tells Brawny, look Brawny I know my pitching hasn't been the same like it used to be. But I can still throw hard. I think I can finish this game. Brawny tells John, I know you can and you're doing a great job Mackey. But, I think you're done for the day. You pitched a great game. John tells Mackey, okay but I did everything I could. Brawny tells John, well take a seat and will get Ryan out for you. John tells Brawny okay good luck. Vent who is up to bat and sees John going back to the dugout. Vent tells John, Go back to the dugout wuss boy. You been humiliating yourself this time for a long time. John heard and goes back and face Vent. John tells Vent what did you say to me. Vent tells John, you're not washed up Mackey. You're a has-beened. You're watching your old teammate Troy

Glass taking all your glory. Let's just face it Mackey you don't have the pitching power like you used to have. I don't even know why they let you on this team. John is very upset and tells Vent you better watch it Vent. You'll be waking up with a black eye. Vent tells John, I like to see you try. John tells Vent watch me, Brawny and Lewis goes over to John and tries to break up this fight and separate them. Brawny tells John, Mackey this guy is not worth it. Unless you want to be fined 500 for brawling with Vent. I say, you should go back to dugout and sit down. Mackey sees Brawny's face and decides to back down. Mackey tells Brawney, okay I'm sorry Skipper. Brawny tells Mackey, I'm proud of you, you did the right thing. John was about to leave the baseball field, until Vent pushes his buttons again. Vent tells John, I always knew you never had to guts to face me. You're still a loser Mackey. That's the main reason why guys your age are washed up at age thirty. John is now upset and doesn't care about the fine. John tells Vent, I'll show you whose washed up you jerk! John goes over to Vent, punches him in the face and Vent falls down on the floor. Vent gets up from the floor and starts brawling with John. Vince tells the fans, take a look at this sports fans. It's looks like World War 10 out their with John Mackey versus Ron Vent. The umpires, the players tries to break up Mackey and Vent. Brawny separates Mackey out of that fight, the umpire makes the decision. The home plate umpires sees Mackey goes over talk to him and makes the call. The home plate umpire tells Mackey, Mackey you're out of here. Mackey tells the Umpire, you're kicking me out. I'll kick you out you dorkhead. The Umpire tells Mackey, I said you're out of here now. Mackey tells the umpire, You're kicking me out fine I'm out of here. I'm leaving not because you tell me too. You fat moron. The umpire tells Mackey, I dare you say to me again. Mackey tells the umpire I won't because you're not worth saying. The umpire tells Mackey, I told you were a gutless wuss. Mackey tells the umpire You're a gutless fat moron. Mackey punches out the umpire and the umpire starts brawling with Mackey. Vince tells the fans, not only Mackey was fighting with Vent. He is also brawling with the umpire. Brawney separates Mackey with another fight and tells him to go back to the locker room. Brawney tells Mackey go back to the locker room or you're suspended. Mackey tells Brawney yes sir. Vince tells the fans, looks like Mackey going back to the locker and watches the game. Brawney has a soft spot with this kid, but I hope he get

Mackey's act together or he's going to be sent back to the minors or being thrown out of here. Serena sees the brawl and tells the Ump come on Ump let him stay and he's a good pitcher don't throw him out. Vince tells the fans and Mackey is going to watch the game back in the locker room. In another note the Angels wins the game 4-3 against Baltimore with Troy Glass hitting two homeruns in the game and relief Pitcher Don Manning makes the save in this game. Serena and Alan watches the game and feels kind of bad for John. Alan tells Serena, poor Mackey he was a great pitcher. But doesn't have the speed like he used to have. Serena tells Alan, I wish we could help him get his game back. I always looked up to him when I was a kid. Alan tells Serena, I wanted to ask Serena, of all the players in that team how come you root for a guy like John instead of a guy like Troy Glass. Serena tells Alan, John is a good guy inside and he doesn't show off and acts like an egotistical jerk in front of anybody. This guy cares about people, not about fame and fortune. Alan tells Serena, it sounds like you more than a fan to this guy. Serena tells Alan, Alan I'm just a fan that's all I am. Alan tells Serena, we better get home you have go to school tomorrow. Serena tells Alan, we go home later. I caught this foul ball and I wanted to see if John Mackey wants to autograph my baseball. Alan tells Serena, I just hope he doesn't charge you a hundred dollars for this baseball. Serena tells Alan, I hardly doubt it. Luckily for me, I know where the locker room is. John stars changing his clothes and he's wearing his jeans and t-shirt. John is also looking at Troy interviewing the press about his win. Manning sees John and goes over talk to him. John tells Manning, thanks for saving my game Donnie. Manning tells John, hey, no problemo. I always thought this was your day to get your game back. John tells Manning, I struck out five batters in Game 1 and four batters game 4 in the world series. I was nominated for the cy young award and been in one time all star and my game hasn't approved back then. Manning tells John, your game hasn't been the same since Diane died. You ever thought talking to anybody about her besides me. John tells Manning, I don't think so. This conversation is between me and you. I only talked about her only once and that's it. Manning tells John, you only talked about Diane how she died. You never talked about how she lived. John tells Manning, I don't want to talk about it anymore. Manning tells John, well at least try to move on. You know we should go to that Red Club tonight and see if we can find us a date for the weekend. John tells Manning, I hardly doubt it. I'm just going to stay home and watch a rerun of Psych tonight. Manning tells John, okay but you're going to miss out finding a perfect woman. It's too bad you're not going. When Troy goes their millions of women are over him. John tells Manning, because Troy is a superstar he's always acts like an egotistical jerk in front of us. The guy rubs our faces how great of a player he is. Manning tells John, just because the guy is Al MVP in the American league championship, ten time all-star and won five golden gloves. And he's dating Miss USA doesn't make him a jerk. Troy finishes his interview and sees John and Manning talking and goes over talk to them. Troy tells John, hey dorkey lose another game huh. How many players did you walk? John tells Troy, I think I walked eight players and I have five players who were hit by a pitch. You'll be next, when I throw the baseball over your head. Troy tells John, forget it Mackey your pitching hasn't been the same for along time. It's too bad were in the same team, I always thought Brawney should dump you in the minors right now. The way you pitch. John tells Troy, well Troy he hasn't dumped me in the minors. He and I are great friends he and I were like this. So, he's not going to dump me. Troy tells John, I don't even know why I'm on this team that's this close to be in last place. The only main attraction on this team is me, because I'm the star that sell out the crowds. Too bad when the crowds sees you, you're more like court jester than a player. Because I'm the king of this stadium. John tells Troy, you don't like this team so much why are you still here. Their a five top teams want to take you and their offering a lot of money that the Angels can give you. Troy tells John, there is one reason why I haven't taking any offers. Because I like humiliating you. I always hit five hundred homeruns over your head when we practice. If I was traded for another I can hit another homerun over your head anytime. John tells Troy, at least I can get dates more than you could. Troy starts laughing for a minute and stops. Troy tells John, yeah right you haven't dated for a long time. I always thought you were gay. John tells Troy, I am not gay I just suck with women. Troy tells John, you have that right. Let's face it Mackey, you're a total geek and I'm the popular jock. Let's face it, you're always going to be losing out to guys like me everyday. It's too bad you won't be going to the red club tonight. Because I can get a date in that club in a heartbeat. John tells Troy, what about Miss USA that the girl you wants brag about dating. Troy tells

John, I cut her loose yesterday. She was getting to clingy I have to break up with her. But she took it really well. John tells Troy, let me guess she was sobbing all day and still pining for you. Troy tells John, it's hard to lose a great guy like me. Let's face it Mackey, I'm perfect and I always get the girls. Let's face it you don't have what it takes to get a date. That's the main reason, why I always been a great power hitter and I always hit a homerun over your head when I hit a homerun over your head in practice. John looks upset and sees a bat and grabs it. John looks like he wants to smash Troy's face right now. John tells Troy, why don't we start batting practicing why don't I use your head as a ball when I hit it out of the park. Troy starts laughing for a minute, very funny Mackey. You never could, but if you ever do pitch against me. I will hit a homerun out of the park right now and I can watch you being humiliated in front of the whole world on tv. When they laugh you're head out. Oh by the way, the skipper wants to see you and he doesn't look pleased about your performance. I know I haven't. Excuse me, ESPN likes to see me right now. Later geek face. Troy starts laughing for a minute and exit's the locker room Troy looks upset right now and wants to smash his face with his bat. John tells Manning, man I like to use his head with this baseball and hit a homerun off his head. Manning tells John, too bad Troy's head is attached to it. Even if his head cut off, it probably filled with slime or blood. John tells Manning, you got that right. John and Manning laughs for a minute. Serena and Alan are outside the locker room and sees a security guard guarding the locker room. Serena and Alan goes over to the locker room and talks to the security guard. Security Guard sees Serena and Alan for a minute and talks to them, Angels security guards tells Serena, hi can I help you folks. Serena tells the Security guard were here to see John Mackey and I want to see if I can get his autograph from him is he here. Angels Security guard tells Serena, yes he is, he's inside the locker room right now and I'll go inside and see if he wants to get an autograph from you. Serena tells the Angels security guard, thank you I appreciate that. Angels security guard tells Serena, I appreciate that. The security guard opens the door, goes inside the locker room and talk to John. Serena and Alan enters the locker room to see if he can John Mackey to sign her autograph. Serena sees John for a minute and he was about to exit the locker room. Serena goes over to see John for a minute. Troy sees Serena and is totally attracted to her. Troy goes over to Serena and talk to her. Troy tells Serena, hi sweet thing I'm Troy Glass I wondered if you're here for an autograph or ask me out on a date. If you ask me out, I will say yes. Serena was kind of disgusted about Troy's actions about asking her out and finding out he's an arrogant jerk. Serena tells Troy, excuse me Troy I am here to get an autograph from my favorite player and it's not you. If I wanted to ask you out on a date, I rather lick a bag of ice than going on a date with you. Troy ask Serena, if you're not here to get an autograph from me, than who are you want an autograph from. Serena tells Troy, that guy right their. Serena points out to John Mackey and puts her arm down. Troy starts laughing for a minute and stops. Troy tells Serena, Mackey trying dating guys who are eligible to make the hall of fame instead guys who get rejected from their first try. So, why that dork? Serena tells Troy, because he's a good guy and I don't date arrogant jerks like you. Now excuse me, I'm here to get my autograph from my favorite if you don't mind. Serena and Alan goes over to John. Troy starts laughing for a minute, too bad that girl is so way out of my league. It's a good thing she's not eligible to date a hot guy like me because she's cramping my style. Since, there are a lot of eligible candidates to date me, instead of that geek. Serena and Alan goes over to John and talk to him. Serena tells John, excuse me, Mr. Mackey. John sees Serena for a minute and tells her hi, can I help you. Serena tells John, Mr. Mackey I'm a great fan of yours I wondered if I can have your autograph. John tells Serena, Troy Glass is right over their and he still here in the locker room and I think you still have some time to get his autograph. John points out where Troy is and puts his arm down. Serena tells John, I'm not here to get an autograph from Troy Glass. I'm here to get an autograph from you. Alan takes out a baseball and pen out of his left pants pocket and gives it to Serena. Serena grabs the baseball and pen out of her right hand and observes it for a minute. John tells Serena, I beg your pardon. Serena tells John, I wondered if you can autograph my baseball Mr. Mackey. John tells Serena, why would you want to have my autograph. You do realize I'm not a superstar in this team or this league. Mostly I always thought girls like you would want to get an autograph from Troy Glass not me. Serena tells John, You're my favorite player, guys like Troy Glass are egotistical jerks who only care about money and fame. Troy Glass, is a guy who cares about himself and he's like one of high school jocks wearing letterman jackets where they run this school with an iron fist. That's exactly what Troy is like, he thinks he can run this team and this league with an iron fist. Thanks, but no thanks I would never date that jerk. John smiles a little and really likes her. John tells Serena, tell me about it. Serena tells John, that's the reason, why I respect you love the game and you don't care about who you are and still think about the little guys who don't have a swell head. John smiles for a minute and tells Serena I appreciate that. Here let me sign that ball for Miss…? Serena tells John, Serena Albania. Serena gives the baseball and pen to John and John grabs the baseball and pen to sign her baseball. John tells Serena, it's a pleasure to meet you Serena Albania. John looks at Serena for a minute and finds her attractive. John is really attracted to her and don't know what to say. John tells Serena, Serena there is something I wanted to ask you. Serena tells John, sure go ahead. John tells Serena, I wanted to ask how old are you? Serena sarcastically tells John, too old for me. John laughs for a minute. Serena tells John, I'm eighteen and I go to Anaheim High School. I'm finishing high school in three weeks. John tells Serena, Serena I wanted to ask would you like to go on a date with me on Friday. It's okay if you say want to no to me, if you want. I'm not exactly the type that women usually date. Serena starts laughing for a minute, I love to go out with you. John is really excited for a minute, finishes signing his autograph and gives the baseball and pen to Serena. John tells Serena, here you go. Serena grabs the baseball and pen from Serena and observes it for a minute. Serena takes out her phone number from her right pants pocket and gives it to John. Serena tells John, here you go. John grabs Serena's phone number and observes it for a minute. Serena tells John, here's my phone number you can call me tomorrow and I'll give you the address where you can pick me up on Friday. John tells Serena, I appreciate that. Serena tells John, hey no problemo. Bye John. John and Alan head to the door. John is love struck for a minute and tells himself, bye Serena. Serena and Alan exit's the locker room and Alan tells Serena, excuse me you're majesty are you sure you want go out with John Mackey. Serena tells Alan, yeah I'm sure Alan why do you ask. Alan tells Serena, you know John Mackey is not exactly the kind of guys you usually date. The guy looks like a geek and he's way out of your league to date you no offense. Serena tells Alan, none taken. That's what I'm looking for a guy. Not a good looking guy who passes me around like a trophy. I want a nice nerdy guy who likes me for who I am not what I can offer. Besides this is my first date like ever. I really like this guy. Alan tells Serena, are you sure you want to date him there is a lot of hot guys who would love to go out with you. Why this guy, he's not exactly a type your parents would never approve of. Serena tells Alan, I know, but he's exactly the guy I want to date. Like I said, I want to date a guy who likes me for who I am. Trust me, John is exactly the guy I want to date. Alan tells Serena, if you say so you're heinous. Serena tells Alan, come on Alan let's go home. Alan tells himself, well good luck on the date John. Heaven help you now. John is about to leave the locker room, until Brawny calls him up. Brawny tells John, Mackey in my office. John heads to his office, until Glass tells John. Probably might be your bonus. John is a little upset and tells Troy, very funny. The door opens and it's John. John goes into Brawny office and talks to him. John closes the door. John tells Brawny, you wanted to see me skipper. Brawny sits down in his chair and tells John, Yeah, sit down Mackey. There is something I want talk to you about. John sits down in his chair and talks to Brawny and it doesn't look good. Brawny tells John, I spoke to the GM. He's fining you 500 for fighting with Vent and the umpire. John tells Brawny, they started it. Brawny tells John, well it doesn't matter who started it. He wants to fine you 500 for the fight. John tells Brawny, what about the ump and Vent are they going to be fined too. Brawny tells John, no just you. John tells Brawny, I can't believe it. They started the fight and I'm the only one get the shaft. Brawny tells John, I stick up for you from the front office and the commissioner. But I lost, they have no choice to give you the fine. John tells Brawny, thanks Brawny trying to stick up for me. I always knew you have my back. But I'll pay the fine. If that's everything else, I'll get my wallet to pay it. You guys take Visa. John was about to leave, until Brawny stops him and tells him, one more thing. John tells Brawny, what is it. Brawny tells John, they're suspending you for one week. John is a lot more upset right now, one week isn't that a little harsh. Brawny tells John, actually suspending you for a week is my idea. John tells Brawny, what! Brawny tells John, you're game hasn't been the same for a long time John. If you take a week off and relax and probably practice your pitching game. You probably have a great chance to get your game back and we might have a chance go to the pennant. John tells Brawny, I thought you were on my side. But being suspended that's harsh. Brawny tells John, those are my terms. The club wants to release you and that's a word for being fired. They're planning on releasing you if you don't get your game back. John is still upset about this decision, tells Brawny I can't believe they're going to fire me. I still have a five year contract and I'm trying to get ten mill so that can set me for life. I won't even have that, if I get released. Brawny tells John, I checked the contract the front office has authorization to trade you, send you to the minors or release you. But I talk to them and made a deal with them. If you can get your game back, get this team to the pennant. They'll null and void for being released and you will get your ten million with your new contract next season so you can finish out your career with the angels. John tells Brawny, so I don't have a choice. I have to accept this suspension and have to work hard to get my game back. If I don't get my game back or don't get this team to the pennant. I'm fired. Brawny tells John, you betcha. Not just you, but me. John tells Brawny, let me guess they're going to fire you too if we lose. So both of our jobs is both our on the line. So our jobs is directly on my hands. Brawny tells John, you betcha. If we lose our shot in the pennant. We can kiss our career in baseball goodbye. John tells Brawny, don't worry skip. I won't let you down. Brawny tells John, that's the go-to-attitude I'm looking for Mackey. I'm proud of you kid. Go work on your game. John gets up from his chair and shakes Brawny's hand. John tells Mackey, Yes sir. John let's goes of Brawny's hand and let go. John heads to the door, opens it and exit's Brawny's office. John closes the door. Serena comes out of the bathroom and wearing a beautiful black low cut dress for her date with John. Serena goes to her mirror and puts on some lipstick. The door is knocked for a minute. Serena tells the person who knocked, come in. The door opens and it's Alan. Serena tells Alan, hi Alan. Alan tells Serena, hey Serena I guess you're ready for your big date with John. Serena finishes with her lipstick and goes over to John and talk to him. Serena tells Alan, I hope Alan is not a show off where he has to take me to this fancy restaurant. Just to impress me. Alan tells Serena, I hardly doubt he will impress you. He already knows you're not rich and you like him the way he is. Plus, the guy has money and he might impress you with a fancy restaurant to take you. Serena tells Alan, I hope not. Because one thing I hate about a guy. That he has to show me off like a trophy by taking me to a fancy restaurant. The reason why I like John, because he doesn't have to impress me. I want him take me to a simple restaurant where I can eat that I can pronounce. Alan tells Serena, I'm sure he won't do that to you. Alan hears the door bell ringing. Alan tells Serena, I better get that. You're heinous, if you don't want John to impress you go to a fancy restaurant. I don't think you should wear a fancy dress just to impress him. Serena tells Alan, you got a point Alan. I'll guess I'll change. Distract him for me. Alan tells Serena, yes you're majesty. Alan comes down from the stairs and gets the door. Alan opens the door and it's John. Alan tells John, hello Mr. Mackey please come on in. Prin...? Almost gave away Serena's identity. Miss Albania will be expecting you. John tells Alan, thank you aah...? Alan tells John, Alan sir. John tells Alan, thank you Alan. John enters the mansion and Alan closes the door. John looks at this place and it's really expensive. John tells Alan, this place is really expensive what does Serena parents actually do here. Alan has to come up with a lie and got one. Alan tells John, Serena mother is the maid here. They moved out here when her father died. John tells Alan, so where's her mother. Alan tells John, the master gave her a couple weeks off and she went on vacation in Maui. John tells Alan, that sounds cool. Alan tells John, why don't you have a seat in the living room and I'll tell Miss Serena, you're here. John tells Alan, thank you Alan. John heads to the living room and Alan calls for Serena. Alan shouts at Serena, Miss Serena Mr. Mackey is here. Serena yells over at Alan and tells him, I'll be right their in a minute. John takes a look at this living room and looks impressive. John sits down in the couch and sees some of Serena's picture on the stand. John tells himself, I guess the owner makes Serena a part of the family. He must have been a great guy. Serena comes down the stairs and wearing jeans, t-shirt and a leather jacket talk to Alan. Serena tells Alan, is John here. Alan tells John, He's in the living room I'll go get him. Serena tells Alan, you haven't told him about who I am. Alan tells Serena, you're safe and I told him you're mother was a maid and worked here for four years right after your father died. Serena tells Alan, it's going to be hard to tell him that I'm a princess and both of my parents are alive and I own this house. Alan tells Serena, I know you like him you're majesty. But maybe it's time to find out to let him know the real you. Serena tells Alan, I wanted John to like me for who I am. Not what I can offer. Alan tells Serena, I think he does like you for who you are? He said yes to you. No man like John would say yes to anybody whose mother works here as a maid and he's waiting for you right their. I think this might be a test to see if he likes you or your royal title. Serena tells Alan, I think you're right Alan. Maybe it's time I test him to find you if he likes me for me. Or my royal treasure. Alan tells Serena, if you do tell him. Maybe he wasn't right person for you. Serena tells Alan, one way to find out. Wish me luck. Serena leaves the main entrance and heads to the living room. John is waiting for Serena, Serena enters the living room and goes over talk to John. John looks at Serena, smiles for a minute and has a crush on her. John gets up from her couch and goes over talk to Serena. John tells Serena, hello Serena. Serena tells John, hello John. John tells Serena, shall we. Serena giggles a little, tells John if you insist. John and Serena exit's the living room and head to the front door. The front door opens and it's John and Serena. Serena closes the door and they head to John's 2011 Mercedes-Benz E-Class. Serena holds John right arm and cuddles with him. Serena and John goes over to his Mercedes and stops. John tells Serena, shall I open the door for you mi-lady. Serena tells John, it's okay I got it. Serena let's goes of John's arm and opens the passenger door by herself. Serena enters the passenger car and gets inside. John tells Serena, shall I. Serena tells John, I think I can make an exception. John tells Serena, okay if you insist. John closes the door for her. John heads to his door opens it and gets inside his car. John closes his door, starts his car and exit's the mansion. John enters the Cubic Steakhouse and John parks his car in the parking lot. Both of them exit his car and closes their door. John and Serena enters the restaurant and goes inside. Serena tells John, this place is something. Are you sure the paparazzi won't find you here. Even if thought this is a two star restaurant. John tells Serena this is a four star restaurant and I hardly doubt the paparazzi will find me here. Serena tells John, how come? John tells Serena, I'm not exactly a superstar athlete here. Mostly Troy is the superstar here, not me. I hardly doubt the paparazzi will take pictures of a has-beened athlete like me. Serena is relieved to hear that. Serena tells John, good thing or we never get any privacy. Serena and John are inside the restaurant and the waiter escort them to their private booth. The waiter tells them, right here sir and Madame. John tells the waiter, thank you garcon. Serena sits down in her chair on the booth and John was about to sit in his chair, until the waiter tells John something. The waiter tells John, excuse me Mr. Mackey I wondered if I could get your autograph. John tells the Waiter, do you have a pen and paper. The Waiter tells John, hold on sir. The Waiter grabs his notepad and pen out of his left pants pocket and gives it to John to sign. John tells the Waiter, who should I make it out too. The Waiter tells John, to my best friend Richard. John signs his autograph and he's done. John gives back the notepad and pen to Richard. John tells Richard, here you go Richard. Richard grabs the pen and paper from John and observes it for a minute. The Waiter tells John, I'll be back in a minute to see what you guys want to order and dinner is on the house today Mr. Mackey. John tells Richard, thank you Richard. Richard tells himself, I gotta call my father and tell him I got an autograph from John Mackey. Richard exit's the table and John sits down in his chair and talk to Serena. Serena tells John, I thought nobody recognize you here and you told me you were a washed up athlete. John tells Serena, I lied but the paparazzi won't come here that's the truth. Because I tipped them off and told them that I was going to Spago's to have dinner tonight and that's the truth. Serena is a little upset right now. Serena tells John, great somebody might recognize you and tried to get my picture and they'll alert the paparazzi. John tells Serena, I think the paparazzi has better plans to see me eat in a four star steakhouse here with my date. Even if they did, so what. You're my girlfriend and I'm not ashamed to admit it to them. Serena tells John sarcastically, if they find out I'm your girlfriend and I'm sure they'll respect my privacy. If they find us here. John tells Serena, relax remember what I told you. I tipped off the press that I'm at Spago's. So, they have better things to do than watching me eat lunch in a five star restaurant. Serena tells John, I guess that's fine. Serena and John starts eating their dinner. Serena and John are eating their steaks medium well and drinking their Dr. Pepper. Serena tells John, how old were you when you decided to make baseball your career. John tells Serena, I always loved the game when I was a kid. My father died when I was one and it was me and my Mom. Serena tells John, I'm sorry. John tells Serena, it's okay I barely remember him. My Mom told me he used to pitch for the minor leagues and he never made it to pro. But I did. Serena tells John, fascinating. John tells Serena, my mom and I were Angels fans. She and I always go to the games together and she taught me how to pitch before. Serena tells John, she did. John tells Serena, yeah. She played softball in high school and was state champion. My mother was an excellent athlete and really beautiful. Serena tells John, I'm sure she was. Did she ever played in college. John tells Serena, yeah she did. She played in the college world series 1982 before I was born. I was born in 1983 and I was eighteen when I got called up in the majors in three weeks. I was the youngest player to play in the world series. Serena tells John, you were all star in one year and your game hasn't been the same in years. What happened to it. John tells Serena, I haven't told anyone about this not even Brawney. My Mom died after I won the world series. She died of pancreatic cancer after my team won. I left the celebration early and told my Mom the good news. She died when before I got their. I never said good-bye and I went to the funeral. But I never visited her in the grave before to say good-bye. I couldn't say some kind words to her in the funeral. It was too much to watch. That's one of the main reasons why I couldn't play again. Serena tells John, pretty soon the league is about to be released me. Not yet, but soon if I don't get my game back. Serena tells John, man that bites. John tells Serena, that bites. John tells Serena, it gets worse I'm already suspended for one week. Serena tells John, let me guess that fight you had with Vent. John tells Serena, you betcha. Serena tells John, I can't believe they suspend you for that fight. I thought they would let you pay a fine. John tells Serena, I did pay a fine. For my last my fight with the umpire and fighting against Vent other times when he gets in my face in the field. I been suspended eight times for beginning of the season because of him. My pitching game hasn't been the same since my Mom died. I guess I don't blame the organization to release me. Serena tells John, if you're pitching good. They won't release you. John tells Serena, Of course not and if I get that team to the pennant. I might get my ten mill a year that would set me for life after my career is over. Serena tells John, I know how. Since you have a free week, you can train yourself hard to get my pitching game back. John tells Serena, I do have a free week. But even I train myself to get my pitching game back. I don't have a pitching coach to help me. Because my pitching coach is busy with other players this week and the team is on the road this week. Serena tells John, maybe your pitching coach can't help you this week. But I know a pitching coach that can help you this week. John tells Serena, Me and my coach will help you get your game back. John tells Serena, wait a minute your coach the one who coaches your high school softball team. Serena tells John, you betcha. John tells Serena, can you tell me who he is and does he have any experience on coaching baseball. Serena tells John, plenty of experience. He took this team to ten district championships and one state championship and his name is Woody Riker. John tells Serena, are you sure your coach could give me my game back. Serena tells John, you never know if you don't try. Serena was awaiting to kiss John, until John tells Serena, there is also something you don't know about me on a date. Serena tells John, what's that? John tells Serena, I don't kiss in the first date. Serena giggles a little and tells John, you truly are a gentleman ball player. John tells Serena, let's just say I'm kind of a white knight. Serena tells John, how many dates do you think we should have until we kiss. John sarcastically tells Serena, I wondered if you like to wait for an eternity to make out. Serena hits John in the arm, John starts laughing for a minute and stops. John tells Serena, just playing with you, I always think the fifth date would be appropriate to make out. Serena tells John, I think I can wait for that. John tells Alan told me about your parents. Serena looks a little worried for a minute and tells John, he did. What exactly did tell me about my parents. John tells Serena, your mother was a maid and she started working in that mansion after your father died. Serena is a little relieved for a minute and tells John, it's true. My father four years ago, we didn't have a lot of money back then and my Mom got the job in the employment agency that their was an opening for a maid job in that mansion and the rest is history. John tells Serena, Alan told me your Mom is on vacation and I can guess she won't make it to graduation. Serena tells John, she won't make it to my graduation. But she'll make it to my party. John tells Serena, I hope you're coach could help me getting my pitching game back. Serena tells John, he will if you're willing to work for it. Come by at three at Anaheim High School will help you get your game back. John tells Serena, I hope so. My career is on the line here. John looks at Serena and knew he's in love with her. John takes Serena home in his car and parks his car next to the front door. John and Serena exit's the car and John escorts her to her house and head to the front door and stops. John tells Serena, I'll see you in the afternoon. How do I find you in the school, it's a big place. Serena tells John, come by the main entrance and I'll take you to the field. John thinks about kissing Serena, Serena is about to kiss him again but he stops himself and tells Serena, good night Serena. John shakes Serena's hand and let's go. John leaves the front door. Serena is blinded by love and tells herself, good night my handsome prince. John heads to his car and tells himself, man I can't believe I missed the kiss. I have to bang my head in the car door for missing it. But like I said, I don't kiss in the first date. I wish I wasn't born nice. I can see why nice guys like me finish last. Serena goes inside and Alan sees her upstairs and tells Serena, you're majesty you're okay. Serena tells Alan, I'm fine Alan good night. Alan tells Serena, good night. Serena tells herself, I hate my life. Back in Albania where King Rufus advisor Donald enters the throne room and goes over talk to King Rufus. While King Rufus is sitting down in his throne reading his book. Donald tells King Rufus, hello you're majesty I have some news for you. King Rufus puts his book down and tells Donald, what is it Donald? Donald tells King Rufus, I have our pilot ready and our private jet fueled up on our way to California. The royal wedding planner is on his way to Los Angeles to coordinate the wedding at your estate their, Sire. King Rufus is really happy to hear this and tells Donald, Excellent work Donald and what about the invitations? Donald tells King Rufus, it's mailed out sir and where to have the wedding. I already send out the plane tickets and hotel reservations to our guest sire? King Rufus tells Donald, Esmeralda will be pleased to get everything ready for our daughter big wedding after our daughter's graduation. It's a good thing to have the wedding in a couple of days right after Serena's graduation. I always been worried about her when she wanted go to school a thousand miles away in California. Donald tells King Rufus, well Sire it's part of growing up. She would've left here and go to school a thousand miles anyway not right now but soon. King Rufus tells Donald, I know Donald. It's hard to let go but I had to. When she graduates at least she'll come home and start going to university where we can see more of her. Donald tells King Rufus, I'm sure you are, don't worry sire about Serena, we arranged everything with her before she left to school and have somebody like Alan look after. He was the best body guard too look after her. King Rufus tells Donald, you have that right lad. Donald, you have everything ready for Marissa and George. Donald tells King Rufus, Yes sire. They'll be in California in a couple days earlier, so they can spend some time with Serena and spend some time vacationing before the wedding starts. King Rufus tells Donald, Well, I guess everything's ready. Well be leaving to California before Serena graduation starts. Donald tells King Rufus,

Everything's ready then. King Rufus tells Donald, let's get started and we have a lot of work to do, before we leave. Donald call the coordinator and tell him if he found a caterer in California yet. Donald tells King Rufus, Yes sire. I'll call him and find out. King Rufus tells Donald, Okay then and that's everything. Good-bye Donald. Donald, good-bye Sire. Donald exit's the throne room and King Rufus goes back to reading his book. Serena is waiting for John to arrive in the main entrance of high school. John sees Serena and goes over talk to her. John tells Serena, hey baby. Serena goes over to John and hug him. Serena tells John, hey honey. John let's goes of Serena for a minute and tells Serena, where do we meet your Coach at? Serena tells John, follow me. John follows Serena to meet her coach. John and Serena head to the high school baseball field and see Serena's Coach and her best friend Mona their. Serena tells John, here he is. High School softball coach, hello Serena so this is thee John Mackey. Serena tells her Coach, yes sir. John Mackey. Serena high school Coach tells John, It's a pleasure to meet you kid. Serena's coach shakes hands with John for a minute, John tells Serena's Coach it's a pleasure to meet you sir. Serena's coach let's goes for a minute and tells John, I wondered if I could have your autograph. I remember the 2002 series where you struck out Barry Bonds twice. What game was that? John tells Serena's Coach, it was Game 1 sir. Serena's Coach tells John, I'm a die hard Angels fan. You're one of my favorite pitcher in baseball. John tells Serena's Coach, I appreciate that sir. If you give me a pen and paper, I'll sign your autograph for you. Serena's Coach tells John, I appreciate that kid. My pen and paper are on the dugout, so I'll get it later after practice. John tells Serena's coach, okay, no problemo. Serena tells John, well anyway John this is my Coach, Coach Parker and this is my teammate and my best friend Mona Pax. She's going to help us practice. Mona is shell shocked when he sees John, she shakes John's hand for a minute. Mona tells John, it's a great to meet you Mr. Mackey. When I was a kid, me and my father stayed up late watching 2002 world series, we was rooting for you and the team back then. John tells Mona, I appreciate that Mona and please call me John. Mona tells John, okay John. Mona let's goes of John's hand for a minute and ask John, John I wondered if I could have your…? John interrupted Mona for a minute, I give you an autograph after practice. Serena tells everybody, let's get to business, Coach you know why I called you about a favor you owe me on the phone. Coach Parker tells Serena, yeah I remember. One week private practice, don't worry the championship is not until next week. John tells Coach Parker, thank you for helping me out for this. If I do well, I tell my Manager to hire you as a new pitching coach. Their's an opening slot in the coaching staff. Mona tells John, what happened to the old pitching coach? John tells Mona, he took the manager job in Salt Lake. Serena tells John, that's the minor league area. John tells Serena, you betcha. Coach Parker tells John, I'll be happy take the offer, if I do a good job with you. Mackey. I have a uniform in the dugout box about your size, suit up and get on the mound and see what you got. John tells Coach Parker, sure thing Coach. Before John heads to the mound, he talks to Serena and ask her what's the favor you gave him to do this private session. Serena tells John, I gave him a few Angels tickets to some of the games from my season tickets. John tells Serena, it actually worked? Serena tells John, the seats were in the luxury box. John tells Serena, pretty cool. Serena tells John, hit the mound. John suits up and wearing high school baseball uniform and carrying his glove. John sees Mona as the catcher and wait for her signal. Mona gives her the signal and Serena is up at bat at home plate. John throws the ball slowly, Serena swings her bat and hits it out of the park. Serena tells John, try to throw hard this time. John throws the ball hard and beams Mona in the head with a catcher's mask. Mona falls down on the ground and John tells Mona, sorry. Coach Parker looks at the radar gun and sees Mackey's pitch. Serena tells Mona, Mona you okay. Mona gets up from the ground and tells Serena, I'm fine. Luckily for me I was wearing a catcher's mask. Serena looks at Coach Parker for a minute and ask him, how much. Coach Parker, tells Serena 81. Serena tells herself, not good. John throws a few more pitches hard, but the balls ends up hitting the fences. John throws the ball slowly three times, Serena ends up hitting them out of the park. Coach Parker goes over to John and talk to him. Coach Parker tells John, Mackey are you sick or something? John tells Coach Parker, no sir. Coach Parker tells John, what are you waiting for, the next train to Albuquerque. Mackey, you're a good pitcher. I feel like you're losing your focus. It's like your mind is somewhere else. John tells Coach Parker, of course I am coach. I have a lot riding me, I have my old rival Ron Vent is pushing my buttons and a lot worse than Troy Glass. My manager is going to release me from this league if I don't get my game back. I have a lot riding me on this, that's the reason why I can't pitch anymore. Coach Parker tells John, their has to be something that's making you lose your focus? John tells Coach Pakrer, right in front of my girlfriend, because it's personal. Coach Parker tells John, let's head to the dugout and you can tell me what's losing your focus. John tells Coach Parker, okay follow me. John and Coach Parker head to the dugout box and they start talking about John's problem. Mona sees John and Coach Parker talking in the dugout and ask Serena, what are you think they're talking about in the dugout. Serena tells Mona, whatever it is, it must be personal. Coach Parker tells John, you're going to be okay. John tells Coach Parker, I'm fine. Coach Parker tells John, talking about it always helps. Remember, look up in sky and pray to Diane I want to pitch. John tells Coach Parker, I will sir. Coach Parker tells John, you will have to talk to Diane about her. John tells Coach Parker, I know. It's going to be hard. Coach Parker tells John, you'll be fine son. Let's get back to pitching. John is back on the mound, looks up on the sky and pray's to Diane. John tells himself, Diane I want to pitch. John looks back to Serena whose up at bat. Serena tells John, hey batter hey batter let's see what you got. John tells himself, I'll show you. John throws the ball hard and Serena swings her bat and misses. Serena gets a first strike when the ball hits Mona's glove. Mona tells herself, ow! Coach Parker sees the radar gun and John's pitching is up to 92. Coach Parker, come on kid you can do better than that. John throws the ball hard and Serena swings her bat and gets another strike. John throws another ball really hard and gets another strike from Serena when she swings her bat. John throws the ball hard and gets another strike from Serena when she swings her bat again. Coach Parker sees his speed on his radar gun again. The target speed is up to ninty-nine. Coach Parker tells himself, close but no cigar. We have a long way to go. John runs laps on four bases. John is drinking Gatorade in the dugout box. John is cardio training with dumbbells and Serena is counting. John is spiking a volleyball near Mona where she is the catcher. The volleyball hits Mona's catcher's mask. John spikes the volleyball three times and Mona tries to catch it. But gets hit in the head in the catcher's mask and falls down on the floor. John does twenty pushups and Coach Parker is counting. John drinks more Gatorade in the dugout box again. John and Serena are running in the park, John is tired but Serena isn't. John is still drinking Gatorade still taste bad and continues drinking it. John is still exercising with dumbbells and running four bases in the field. John still does twenty more pushups. John is still spiking the volleyball and Mona caught it. John does thirty sit ups and Coach Parker is counting. John does twenty more reps in the dumbbells and Coach Parker is still counting. John is still running the four bases and when he gets to home plate. He slides through fourth base with Mona tagging him out and Coach Parker is the umpire and tells John he's out. Ten more laps. John groans a little and start doing ten more laps on the four bases. John is reading a guide to pitching book and still drinking Gatorade. John takes some notes in the book. John slides through home plate and after doing 10 laps in the four bases. John slides through home base and Mona doesn't tag him this time. Coach Parker makes the call and tells John, you're safe. John tells Coach Parker, Is that mean, I'm done running laps. Coach Parker tells John, no we just started your condition, ten more laps come on. John tells himself, I hate my life. John finishes his baseball test in the dugout box and gives it to Coach Parker. Coach Parker takes a look at the test and gives him a thumbs up that he's ready. John spikes the volleyball again and Mona catches it again. Coach Parker gives him a thumbs up. John slides through home plate again and Mona doesn't tag him out and Coach Parker tells John, safe. You're done. John gets up from the ground and smiles at him and sees him giving him a thumbs up. John is in good shape running through the park with Serena and he's done. Serena stops and she is exhausted. Serena tells John, time out! John stops for a minute and goes over to Serena and talk to her. Serena tells John, I think that's it for the day. John tells Serena, not yet!. Serena tells John, I beg your pardon. John makes out with Serena for a minute. John tells Serena, now I'm done. Serena smiles for a minute and tells John how many miles did we ran. John tells Serena, I think twenty. Serena tells John, Actually it's five miles. John tells Serena, how many more miles to go? Serena tells John, five more miles. John starts groaning, I hate my life. John and Serena starts jogging again from the park. John and Serena are in the high school baseball field and waiting for Coach Parker and Mona to come. John and Serena are in the pitcher's mound. Serena ask John, are you ready. John tells Serena, I don't know. I've been training really hard, I haven't figured out if pitching game is back. Serena tells John, before Coach Parker and Mona arrives. Coach told me about Diane. John groans a little, tells

Serena I guess he told you about her. Serena tells Diane, not a lot. He told me you used to gone out with her. Who was Diane. John tells Serena, my fiancé I was about to marry her right after I called up in the majors. Serena tells John, what happened to her? John tells Serena, we used to gone out in our freshman year in high school, right after I got drafted by the Angels. I asked her to marry me and she said yes. Anyway, we were about to get married right after I got called up. She died in her sleep before I was going to see her and tell her the news that I'm in the majors and we were going to set a wedding date. Serena feels bad for John and tells him, I'm sorry. John tells Serena, it's okay I'm fine. It's been a long time I told about her. Serena tells John what happened to her anyway. John tells Serena it was pancreatic cancer, she's been having it for months and the virus already spread. She was unaware she had it, until yesterday before she died. She was about go to the doctor to find out what happened, she died before he saw her. Serena tells John, that really bites. John tells Serena, yeah it did. I guess you're my first date ever since she died. You're the second person I told about her. Serena tells John, I guess John was the first. John tells Serena, you betcha. Serena and John were about to kiss when she was comforting him, until she sees Coach Parker and Mona arriving. Coach Parker is carrying his radar gun. Serena snaps her fingers and tells John, Coach Parker and Mona arriving. John tells Serena, Oh sorry about that. I was just out of it for a minute. Serena tells John, sure you were. John tells Serena, funny cute but funny. Coach Parker and Mona goes over to Serena and John and talk to them. John tells Coach Parker and Mona, hi guys! Coach Parker and Mona, hey Serena, hey John. Serena tells Coach Parker and Mona, hi guys. Coach Parker tells John, well Mackey you been training really hard and let's test out your pitching power to see if you're ready to play tomorrow. John tells Coach Parker, were about to find out Coach. John is on the mound and ready to pitch. John sees Coach Parker with his radar gun to test his pitching speed to see if he's ready and Mona as a catcher. John throws the ball hard and hits Mona's glove hard. Coach Parker sees the target speed and sees 89 on the radar gun. Coach Parker tells John, good but a little harder. John sees Mona's glove, puts his game face and whispers to himself, Diane I need your help. John throws the ball hard. Back at Angels Stadium around tomorrow, Tampa Bay Devil Rays batter swings his bat, misses and gets. The home plate umpire calls it,

Strike! You're out. Vince broadcast the game and tells Angels fans, Well ladies and gentlemen Mackey strike out All Star MVP Clewood out the third time. That Mackey tenth strike at this game. I don't know what happened, but his game is been approving since his week suspension. I thought the rumors that the club would release were practically false. Coach Parker, Serena, Mona, Warren and Alan sitting in their luxury box. Coach Parker tells Serena, I knew that coaching would pay off. Serena tells Coach Parker, well not yet it hasn't. Were in top of the ninth, all John has to strike out his next player and he's back. Warren sees John pitching the Tampa Bay Devil Rays next batter he's pitching for. Warren tells everybody, Mackey is 0-2. One more strike and we win. Vince still broadcasting the game and tells the fans that John makes the pitch. John throws the ball hard, Tampa Bay Devil Rays batter swings his bat and misses and gets a strike. The home plate umpire makes the calls and tells the fans, Strike Three You're Out. Vince tells the fans, it's over Angels 1-0 with a miracle shut out game by John Mackey. This is his 11 strike out for the game, Mackey's last game of the Angels was all a façade. Congratulations Mackey! Coach Parker, Serena, Mona and Warren celebrates in the luxury box. John and his team celebrate in the locker room, where his team is congratulating him. Brawny goes over to John and congratulate him too. Brawny tells John, congratulations John, I'm proud of you. John tells Brawny, thank you skip! You weren't serious releasing me from this team. You know I got my game back, I'm pitching well so please don't kick me off this team. Brawny tells John, relax John I'm not releasing you. I told you, to clean up your act and I won't kick you out. You did, I'm proud of you son. John tells Brawny, thank you sir. About our deal…? Brawny interrupts John for a minute, actually I'm not releasing but the deal is still secured. If you can take this team to the pennant, you'll get your ten mill that you'll be set for life when you retire from this team. But the GM still want you get this team to the pennant, to get your ten mill or they would release themselves. You still have a long way to go. John tells Brawny, I guess I have to practice hard if I want to stay on this team or get a better contract deal. Brawny tells John, good because you have a lot of work to do. John, there is something I want to talk to you about? John tells Brawny, what is it? Brawny tells John, It's about Troy Glass. Brawny tells John, what about him? John tells Brawny, he's been traded to the Orioles. John tells Brawny, what? Brawny tells John, they offered him a better contract that's worth 15 million with a six year guarantee. The Orioles is favorite to win the pennant this year, they been after him for months. He took the deal. John tells Brawny, I'm glad we don't need him, we can win this pennant with or without him. Brawny tells John, good because we need to win 16 more games to win the pennant. John tells Brawny, you can't count on me sir. Brawny tells John, I know you could. Remember you'll be starting the next game in two days. John tells Brawny, sure thing. One more thing Brawny. Brawny tells John, what is it? John tells Brawny, if I get this team to the pennant, I need a favor you can help me with. Brawny tells John, sure what is it? John tells Brawny, not now I'll tell you when we win. Brawny tells John, just hope we win. I'll own you any favor you want. All right, I have to go bye Johnny. John tells Brawny, see ya skip! Brawny exit's the locker room and heads to his office. Serena enters the locker room, goes over to John and hug him. Serena tells John, hey honey. John tells Serena, hi baby. Serena kisses John and let's go. Serena tells John, we should celebrate tonight you think we should go to Cubic Steakhouse. John tells Serena, I don't think I can go tonight. I think Brawny is going to start me in 16 games. I think I really need Coach Parker train me if I want to take this team to the pennant. I'm going to call him if he can train me tomorrow at the field in school. Serena looks a little disappointed, but understands. Serena tells John, if you call him, I think he'll help you out. You owe him a favor to get him that pitching coach job next year. He'll do whatever it takes to get the job. John tells Serena, I know. If I want to get that ten mill or stay in the Angels. I have to concentrate on my career. So we can't date in a few weeks. Serena tells John, hey I understand. John tells Serena, actually I was going to ask if you want to help me practice. If we both practice, it could help both of us out. If you win the championship, you'll get your scholarship to UCLA. If I get my team to the pennant, I can stay in the Angels and get a better multimillion dollar contract. Serena tells John, I got one thing say to you. I'm in. Come on, we better make a call to Parker and tell him we have a lot of work to do. John tells Serena, you betcha. Serena and John start practicing in her high school baseball field where Coach Parker and Mona are watching. John is doing reps with dumbbells and Coach Parker is counting. Coach Parker tells John, eight, night, ten. Serena does twenty sit ups and she is sweating. Coach Parker swings his bat, hit's the ball where Serena can catch it in the centerfield. The ball hits centerfield and Serena catches it. Coach Parker is pleased about that. John starts doing ten pushups and starts sweating. John also practices his pitching where Warren is the catcher and Mona is batting. John throws the ball hard, Mona swings her bat and misses. Warren felt that when the ball hits his hand and Warren throws the ball back to John. Coach Parker sees the speed on his radar gun, it's up 98. Warren makes ten more pitches and Mona strikes out ten times. Coach Parker sees his radar gun, it's up to 99 now. Coach Parker smiles for a minute and gives him a thumbs up. Serena and John drink nothing but protein drinks in the school kitchen where Coach Parker making in the blender. Coach Parker pours the protein drinks in their glasses and John and Serena starts drinking them. John and Serena drinks them, Serena tells Coach Parker, yuck! Coach Parker tells Serena, I know. Another one. Serena tells herself I hate my life. Serena and John, head back to Serena's home and John closes the door. John is dressing casually for their date staying in tonight. Serena tells John, make yourself at home. I'll be down in a minute while a change. John tells Serena, okay. Serena goes upstairs and starts changing and John heads to the living room. Serena is in the hallway and sees Alan for a minute. Alan tells Serena, hello you're heinous you had a nice practice. Serena tells Alan, I think I'll be ready for the championship game tomorrow. Alan tells Serena, sounds amazing but you're majesty we have a problem. Serena tells Alan, what's the problem Alan? Alan tells Serena, open your bedroom and I'll show the problem is. Serena and Alan head to her bedroom and opens it. Serena and Alan enters her bedroom and sees Marissa and George sitting down in their bedroom. Serena tells Marissa and George, Marissa, George what are you guys doing here. Alan tells Serena, that's the problem I wanted to tell you. You're sister and her fiancée here. Marissa sees Serena and goes over to Serena and hug her. Marissa tells Serena, hello sis how are you doing? Serena tells Marissa, I'm good big sis. Marissa let's goes of Serena for a minute. Serena tells Marissa, what are you guys doing here. Your wedding is not going to start until next week. Marissa tells Serena, mother and father let us come in early, so we can hang out together and so is our royal wedding planner so he can help us coordinate the wedding. Serena is a little shocked for a minute, how great. Marissa ask Serena something, so sis that's amazing american accent you have there. Where did you learn it. Serena tells Marissa, I watch a lot of 90210 and Psych. Plus, Alan taught me how to speak with an american accent for a few months. George tells Serena, the wedding planner is in the living room and we have a couple of weeks until the wedding starts next week. Marissa tells Serena, we have to pick up Mother and Father next week on Monday before the wedding starts. Marissa looks at her room and sees Anaheim Angels, LA Lakers, Anaheim Angels, Superman and Batman memorabilia in her room. She also sees Psych, Chuck, Buffy the Vampire slayer, Superman Returns and the big bang theory dvd's in her room. Marissa tells Serena, your room is interesting it's like a comic book store and a sports memorabilia store. Serena tells Marissa, I can explains this. Marissa tells Serena, if Mother and Father sees this, they would throw a fit. What's going on, it almost like living a nerd's bedroom. Serena tells George, why don't you give us a moment. George tells Serena, okay I guess I can watch tv in the living room. I wondered if One Tree Hill is on tv. George and Alan exit's Serena's room, Alan tells George. No, but the big bang theory is on. George tells Alan, I don't want to miss Howard striking out with another girl. George and Alan are in the hallway and Alan closes the door. Back in Serena's room, where Serena is explaining her situation to Marissa. When Serena looks at Marissa for a minute and it doesn't look good. Serena tells Marissa, that's it. Marissa is upset at Serena, tells her so you spend Mom and Dad's tuition and room and board in this mansion so you can have a fancy education in a public high school with regular kids. That haven't been vaccinated yet. Serena tells Marissa, I know how it sounds. But I wanted go to school here and I wanted to be a regular kid for one day. I didn't want to spend the rest of my life, like planning parties, doing royal dignitaries and state functions for the rest of my life. I didn't want Mom and Dad pick a suitor for me like they did that for you. Marissa tells Serena, why didn't you tell Mom and Dad what you wanted back then. Serena tells Marissa, you think I wanted to tell Mom and Dad, I wanted go to regular high school that doesn't care about social standings, how you look and how much money you have. Or I play for my high school softball team and wanted go to a regular college so I can be a broadcast journalist. Do play-by-play commentary for Major league baseball. You think I wanted to tell them that. Marissa thinks for a minute and tells Serena, no I don't think they would approve. I don't think they would approve of

George. Serena tells Marissa, why don't you think they wouldn't approve of George. I thought he was rich duke in England. Marissa tells Serena, because George isn't a duke or have any noble blood. Serena tells Marissa, if George doesn't have noble blood or is not a duke, than what is he? Marissa tells George, his father drove a truck for Chanel and his mother work as a perfume salesman in Macy's in London. Serena is a little shocked for a minute, tells Marissa no way. How did George end up in Oxford and how did you know what his parents were doing for a living. Marissa tells Serena, George got a Rhode scholarship to Oxford and he told me himself when we start dating when I asked him out in history class. Serena tells Marissa, so you lied to Mom and Dad about George's background and so they can let you marry him. Marissa tells Serena, yeah, I know them. They wouldn't approve. Serena tells Marissa, welcome to my world. Serena, Marissa, George and Alan sits down in their chairs discussing about Serena's situation. Marissa ask Serena about John, so who is this pro ball player you're seeing. Serena tells them John Mackey he...? George interrupts Serena for a minute and tells Serena, Angels pitcher who pitched in world series 2002 and nominate for Cy Young Award last year. He was also a one time all star. Serena tells George, how did you know that George. George tells Serena, around. Everybody stares at George for a minute. George tells them, my family has a satellite and we have Angels and Dodgers game in american channels. Everyone says oh. Marissa tells Serena, you haven't told him who you are? Serena tells Marissa, I want him to like me for who I am. Not what I can offer. George tells Serena, what about your friends from school do they know. Serena tells George, yeah they do and Coach Parker who is my favorite teacher in school. Marissa tells Serena, how did they knew who you were? Serena tells Marissa, I invited them to the mansion for school function and Coach Parker, Mona and Alan accidentally mentioned I was a princess when he called me you're heinous. I explained everything to them the rest is history. They also helped me cover my tracks from my parents. Coach Parker has a friend in Cornelia Connelly School to help me out. Alan tells Serena, you know when they do come for graduation, it's going to be hard to tell them that the Connelly School never heard of you. Serena tells Alan, I know that. They probably disown me or probably make me move back home and have a tutor with me twenty-four hours for college. George tells Serena, so what are you going to do. Serena tells George, I'm going to tell them when they get here from graduation. Marissa tells Serena, when are you tell him who you are? Serena tells Marissa, we have a date tomorrow after the district championship. I'll tell him then or probably dump me for lying to him. George tells Serena, if he doesn't. Serena tells George, I don't know, George. I just want him to like me for who I am. Not what I can offer. Alan tells Serena, you never know if you don't take a chance. He may surprise you. Serena tells them, we'll see. Tomorrow, I have the championship game tomorrow. I have to be at practice tomorrow morning at six. Marissa tells everybody, me and George has a date with the wedding planner tomorrow. So, we got a lot work to do. Alan ask Marissa and George, I wondered if you guys need help with the wedding. I love weddings. George tells Alan, it's okay with me. Marissa tells Alan, me too. Alan tells them, thanks guys, because I know a good caterer. George tells Marissa, this is going to be a long day. Marissa tells George, tell me about it. Serena is in the high school baseball field with Mona and Coach Parker who are the only one here for softball practice. Coach Parker tells Serena, I just got your message on the machine. So, how's your sister and you're future brother-in-law doing Serena. Serena tells Coach Parker, they're good. We may be graduating next week before my sister wedding starts. I'm worried about one thing. Mona tells Serena, what's that Serena? Serena tells Mona, I don't know how I'm going to keep my parents out of bay before graduation. It's going to be tough time, that I'm graduating from a public school where commoners go to. Mona tells Serena, Namely us. Serena tells Mona, that's not only the problem that I have to deal with right now. Coach Parker tells Serena, worse than you're parents finding out you go to a public high school. Mona tells Serena, what would happened if you're parents find out you go where. What could they do to you? Serena tells them, worse than being disowned. I probably have go back to Albania, have security detail 24 hours a day and go to college in the palace. What do you think? Mona sarcastically tells Serena, I always thought they would cut you off. Serena tells Mona, yeah if you want to put it like that. Mona tells Serena, we know you're not talking about your parents. Serena tells Mona, you mean John. That's the reason I have a hard time telling him about this. Coach Parker tells Serena, what are you going to do? Serena tells Coach Parker, well Coach I'm just going to tell after the championship. It's better off he hears this from me, than from somebody else. I'm just afraid he won't see me anymore after this. Coach Parker tells Serena, if he doesn't maybe he's not the right guy for you. Serena tells Coach Parker, thanks Coach I appreciate that. Coach Parker, hey no problemo. Come on, we better practice the championship game is going to start at five. We better get ready. Serena tells them, sure thing. I'm ready to take on Jenn's team. If I lose she probably rub it in my face for the rest of my life. Mona tells Serena, well were not going to let that happened. Troy overheard what Serena, Coach Parker and Mona said on the field. Troy was hiding behind the bench of the dugout box and heard everything. Troy tells himself, I knew their something about this girl I knew about. Their was no way, I'm going to let Mackey beat me in the Al championship. A little tip of the press and a little international incident from Albania would ruin Mackey's career and boost mine. When I beat him in the Al championship. This will teach her not to reject me, no one rejects me. Serena is practicing hard for the championship game. Serena hits five homers out of the park. Mona pitches another one to Serena, Serena swings her bat and hits it out of the park. Troy exit's a few miles out of the ball park and takes out his cell phone from his right pants pocket and makes a call. Troy tells himself, it's a good thing their was an open gate from the baseball field or I would never get out or they would've spot me. Troy calls his agent from his cell phone and tell him, Eddie I need a favor. I need you to call a couple of newspapers from Albania and LA Times. Tell them there is a Albanian princess dating a major league baseball player and going to public high school in Anaheim. Thanks. Troy hangs up the phone and tells himself, looks like I hit this one out of the park. Mona sees Serena ready for another pitch for batting practice, Mona throws the ball hard and Serena swings her bat and hits it out of the park and the championship game is going on. Where Serena runs through four bases with two of her teammates. Jack the broadcast journalist doing the play-by-play championship high school game, Jack tells softball fans it's out of here. That's two homers for Serena Albania for this game and Anaheim is one run behind Grant High for the championship. Jack still broadcasting and he tells the softball fans, top of the six and the score 3-3. Mona watches the signals and she's ready. Mona throws the ball hard, Grant High batter swings her bat and hits it near left field wall. Jack broadcast it and tells the fans, Mona makes the pitch and Gerber hits it near left field. This could go all the way. The ball is out of the park, but it hits the foul line. The home plate umpire makes the call, foul ball. Jack broadcast it, the ball is foul and it's strike one. Mona throws the ball hard again, Gerber swings her bat and hits it out of the left field. It could go all the way out of the park. Jack broadcast it and tells the fans, Mona makes another pitch, Gerber swings it and hits it out near left field. This could go all the way. The ball almost go near out of the fence, but Serena who is playing left field runs all the way to the fence, leaps up and catches the ball. Everybody is cheering about Serena's catch. Jack broadcast it and tells the fans, it could go all the way and it's in fair territory and Albania near the left field fence, leaps up and caught the ball. Jack still broadcasting the game and tells the fans, it's down and Jenn Lindley is up to bat. She is an excellent pitcher, with 15 strikes outs during the game and she's 13-0. A lot of college scouts wanted to sign her, even UCLA wants to sign her too whoever wins this game. Remember Jenn hit two homers in this game too. Jenn tells Mona, you're wasting your time Mona I'm going to hit this baby out of the park again before you make that pitch. I just hope the homer lands on Serena's head. Mona tells Jenn, well see about that. Mona throws the ball hard, Jenn sees the opportunity to hit the ball out of the park. Jenn swings her bat and hits it out of near left field. Serena sees the pop fly and dives down on the grass and catches the ball. Jack still broadcasting the game, tells the softball fans Mona makes the pitch and Lindley swings and it hits near left field. Albania got the good grip on the ball and dives and caught it. That retires the side. Bottom of the seventh and one out in this inning. Looks whose up to bat. Marissa, John, George, Alan and Warren are in the bleachers and watching Serena up to bat and cheering her on. John cheers for Serena and tells her, come on Serena, Come on. Serena is up to bat, heads to home plate and ready to bat with Jenn pitching. Jack still broadcasting, tells the softball fans and Serena is up to bat and Lindley sees her important rival getting ready to get her out. Their been bad blood between these two. Jenn is ready to pitch, sees Serena in home plate and ready to bat. Jenn tells Serena, just think Serena all you need is a homerun to win the game. Too bad you're wasting your time, I know you. You always choke under pressure. Serena tells Jenn, throw the ball you airhead and I'll show you who chokes under pressure. Jenn throws the ball, Serena swings her bat and hits it in left field near foul line and its out of the park in the foul line. The home plate umpire calls it and tells the softball fans, foul. Serena points out to the right field fence. Jenn sees it for aminute and tells Serena, what are you crazy. You calling your shot, what is this world series 32 where Babe Ruth calls his shot. You really think you can hit the right field fence. Serena tells Jenn, throw me another ball and I'll hit it in the right field fence. Jenn tells Serena, I hope you enjoy community college, that's where you going to be in four years. While I'm riding high in UCLA. Serena tells Jenn, just throw the ball and well see who gets into UCLA. Jenn throws the ball hard, Serena swings her bat and hits the ball out of the park. Grant High outfielders head to right field to catch the ball near right field. The ball hits it out of the park in centerfield. Jack still broadcasting and tells the softball fans, Jenn makes the pitch and Albania hits it out of the centerfield wall. Anaheim High wins, Anaheim wins district. Jenn kicking the dirt and is really upset about the game. Serena runs all the way to four bases and steps on home plate. Serena sees Jenn who is still upset losing to Serena. Jenn tells Serena, I can't believe I lost out to you. Serena tells Jenn, next time you play with fire, you get burn. Enjoy community college, you airhead snob, that's where you going to be in four years. Jenn is still upset. The crowd exits the bleachers and starts hugging Serena and so does Serena's teammates. Alan, George and Marissa congratulates Serena for a minute. Marissa tells Serena, I'm proud of you sis. George tells Serena, Me too sis. Alan also congratulate her too and tells her, you did good kid. Serena tells Alan, thanks Alan. Alan tells Serena, hey, no problemo. UCLA scout goes over to Serena and tells her, Miss Albania. I'm Rick Layfield, the assistant coach of UCLA Softball, we love to offer you a full scholarship to play on our softball team next year. Serena tells Coach Layfield, well Coach Layfield I got one thing to say to you. I'll be honored to play for you next year. Coach Layfield tells Serena, I appreciate that. You'll get my letter in the mail next week, you'll love playing for the Bruins. I'll see you in September kiddo. Serena tells Coach Layfield, sure thing Coach. Serena shakes Coach Layfield hand and let's go. Serena exits the baseball field and sees John behind the trees waiting for her. Serena goes over to John and talk to her. John tells Serena, so Miss Bruin how does it feel having all your dreams come true. Serena tells John, their is something missing in my dream. John smiles a little and tells Serena, what's that. Serena tells John, you! Serena and John start making out, until a couple of paparazzi photographers come out of nowhere and takes pictures of Serena and John. Photographer 1 tells Serena and John, You're majesty give us a smile. The photographers takes a lot of pictures of Serena. John tells Serena, come on guys how did anyone know I'm here. It had to be Glass, I knew he still holds a grudge on me. The photographers still taking pictures of Serena and tells Serena, a couple more you're heinous. John tells the photographers, what's going on. Serena tells John, the paparazzi are not here for you, their here for me. John tells Serena, what. Serena tells John, come on let's get out of here, I'll explain everything. Serena and John exits the field and hideout in the school gym where they can find them. John tells himself, what's going on and why did those photographers call you you're heinous. Serena tells John, John I haven't been honest with you in the beginning. John tells Serena, I beg your pardon. Serena tells John, I'm a princess. John tells Serena, princess of what? Serena tells John, Albania. I know you don't believe me, but the paparazzi are telling the truth and you saw the mansion. It's diplomatic and Alan is my bodyguard and royal advisor. John tells Serena, wait you're a princess. You don't have an accent. How did you talk american. Serena tells John, I watch a lot of tv and Alan taught me the language. John tells Serena, does any of your friends know about you. Serena tells John, yeah they do. John tells Serena, I'm the last person you know. I got to get out of here. A lot of girls always use for wanting something from me and you're a lot worse. Serena tells John, when I came here for four years ago, I wanted to be a regular kid. So I lied my way in and fool my parents that I went to prep school. So, I can hang out with real kids who like me for who I am. I fell in love with you on the side. John tells Serena, why couldn't you just tell me you're a princess. Serena tells John, like you said a lot of people want something from me. I want you to like me for who I am, not what I can offer. You would want something from me or trying to boost your image dating me. John tells Serena, I don't even know who you are. I'm sorry. John exits the gym and Serena is crying a little and stops. Marissa, George, Mona and Coach Parker. Marissa goes over to Serena and tell her, you okay. Serena tells Marissa, no it's not. It's just got worse. Serena exits the gym and still crying a little. Back in the Albania castle and King Rufus is sitting down in his throne in his throne room. Donald enters the throne room and goes over talk to the King. Donald is carrying a newspaper from

Albania about Serena. Donald tells the king Rufus something, you're majesty we have a problem. King Rufus tells Donald, what is it Donald. Donald tells King Rufus, You're majesty have you seen what's in the paper? King Rufus tells Donald, no I haven't. I never gotten my paper today. Donald tells King Rufus, no but I have. Donald gives King Rufus the paper, King Rufus grabs it and observes it for a minute. Donald tells King Rufus, it's about your daughter Serena. King Rufus reads the paper about her daughter dating Angels ballplayer John Mackey. King Rufus looks upset right now. King Rufus tells Donald, tells me this isn't true. Donald please tell me this isn't true. Donald tells King Rufus, I afraid it's true you're majesty. King Rufus tells Donald, call Esmeralda that were going to California today and were going to have a word with our daughter about this incident. Donald tells King Rufus, yes sir, but I'm sure this is a misunderstanding. King Rufus looks upset and that is not another word to be quiet. King Rufus tells Donald, Donald call the pilot and tell him get the plane fueled up. Were going to America today. Donald tells King Rufus, yes, you're heinous. Donald is a little scared for a minute, exits the throne room. Serena is a little upset and she's in the living room watching the Angels game. Vince commentates the game on tv and he tells the baseball fans, this top of the ninth and it's two down. Mackey is 0-2 to Gerard, Mackey strikes Gerard out. The Angels will win against the Athletics. Mackey throws it, Gerard swings and misses and it's strike three. The Angels win 3-0 to the Athletics. They have 18 more games to reach the Al championship. Serena grabs the remote the coffee table and turns off the set. Marissa enters the living room and goes over talk to Serena. Marissa tells Serena, sis we have a problem. Serena tells Marissa, what is it? I can't deal with another crisis right now. It's bad enough John broke up with me. Right now, Mom and Dad see my picture in the paper. They're not going to be thrilled what they're going to read. Marissa tells Serena, it's going to get worse. Donald called, they seen the paper. Father is not exactly happy right now. Mom and Dad are coming to LA and they want to talk to you and they might ask you to come home. Serena tells Marissa, you know what I have something to tell them. I'm not going home, if they want me to cut me off or give up my crown, if I'm dating a commoner like John or going to public school in California. Let's them do it, I don't care anymore. You can call them on a plane, I want nothing do with them anymore. I love John, I'm going after him. Plus, I'm staying in Anaheim High and I'm graduating three weeks. Marissa tells Serena, well good. But, no matter what you do. You can't give up who you are, you maybe american but you still have royal blood inside you. Are you willing to give that up for John. Serena tells Marissa, yeah I do. They can ask me abdicate my throne, but they can't abdicate who I should date. Marissa tells Serena, Okay, that's what you wish. Serena tells Marissa, but if you tell Mom and Dad about George, maybe they can take the heat off me for a minute. Marissa tells Serena, if I did that they could make me choose the throne or fiancee. Serena tells Marissa, I understand. But, it's your choice. Marissa tells Serena, whatever happens were in this together. They can kick both of us out of throne, they can't kick out who we love. Serena tells Marissa, thanks Marissa I appreciate that. Marissa tells Serena, hey no porblemo. Marissa hugs Serena and let's go. Marissa tells Serena, I'll call them on the phone and see when they're going to land. I guess we can kiss our boyfriends and your scholarship to UCLA good-bye. Serena tells Marissa, I may have the scholarship. But all I ever wanted to do, is become Serena. Not Princess Serena who is the second heir to Albania. Marissa tells Serena, when Mom and Dad get here. You won't be Princess Serena, you will be Serena. I better go call them and see when they land. Wish me luck. Serena tells Marissa, were going to need it sis. Marissa tells Serena, tells me about it. Marissa exits the living room, takes out her cell phone from her right pants pocket and starts dialing. Marissa makes the call on her cell phone, hi Father. Their is something I wanted to tell you and mother. Please don't be angry with me or Serena, please. In the Angels locker room, where John is interviewing with the press. The ESPN reporter tells John, so you been in a slump for the last few years. How are on earth did you ever get your game back? John tells the ESPN reporter, it was hard work. I met a high school coach name Coach Parker who helped me get my game back. But one person I ever admired that inspiring to never give up was a girl I met few weeks ago here name is Serena. ESPN reporter tells John, speaking of Serena. You do realize, that you were dating Princess Serena, King Rufus daughter of Albania. You think you pissed off the country and create an international incident for dating his daughter. John tells ESPN reporter, no I never did. I guess I was unaware about who she was, plus she never told me herself that she was royalty. ESPN reporter tells John, how come she never told you who she was? John tells ESPN reporters, same reason with me. I guess she wants me to like her for who she was. Not what she could offer. That's what I felt too, if I was in her situation. A lot people want something from me, for Serena they want something from her. I guess I didn't blame her. ESPN reporter tells John, so John what happened between you two? John tells ESPN reporter, I guess we broke up. It's bad enough I was just a high profile athlete. I guess when I found out she was a high profile princess, were a high profile couple. We kind of broken up. Or I broke up with her, I already have enough paparazzi in my face, a little more if I date her would get worse. So, I end things with her. ESPN reporter tells John, it's because you were protecting her from the press or you broke up with her she lied to you for who she was. That's the main reason, why you split. John tells ESPN reporter, I guess that's the million dollar question I can never answer. That's enough for me for now. I'll see you next game. See ya. ESPN reporter tells John, bye John. John exits his locker and goes to the soda machine to get a drink. Brawney sees him and goes over talk to him. Brawney tells John, Mackey I need to see you in my office. John looks kind of worried, this doesn't look good. John goes to Brawney's office and talk to him. John enters Brawney's office, closes the door and talk to Brawney. John tells Brawney, you wanted to see me skipper. Brawney tells John, their something we need to talk about. John tells Brawney, it's not bad is it. Brawney tells John, of course not. I wanted to ask, I over heard about what you talk to the reporter in the locker room. Their is something I wanted to ask you, just between us. John tells Brawney, what is it? Brawney tells John, about Serena the princess of Albania you been dating for the last couple weeks. John tells Brawney, what about her? Brawney tells John, do you love her? John tells Brawney, I did. When I find out who she was, I ended it. Brawney tells John, was it really have to do with her being princess, she lied to you about who she was or you're scared of moving on. John tells Brawney, I don't know. When I found who she was. I thought she lied to me about she is, I was angry that I was the last person she told and about her background. That she grew up as a maid's daughter. Why couldn't she just told me who she was, I would understood. Brawny tells John, this has nothing to do with about her royal background. You would've understood in a heartbeat, if you were in a same situation as her. You want somebody to like you for who you are, not what you can offer. John tells Brawny, I guess I understood I was upset at first. I handled it wrong. The worse thing, I broke up with her that has nothing to do with her being royalty. Brawny tells John, I think I know why. You got too close to a person you were in love with and you feel like you were going to lose her. You were going to find a way to break up with her, it wouldn't be the press. It would've been something else. That would make you dump her. John tells Brawny, I guess you're right skip. It wouldn't be the press, finding out about Serena royal background. It would've been something else. Ever since Diane died, I guess I could never move on. I did for a minute, when I spend a day with Serena. I fell in love with her and I didn't want to lose her. Brawny tells John, I think you should go after her. If you don't, you're going to lose true love forever. Trust me, Diane would want you to go after her. Because I do. She's an amazing girl. John tells Brawny, you're right. I'm going after her. Thanks Coach. I was going to ask, how did that press found about me and Diane? Brawny tells John, I think I knew who? It all starts with a word that has a another name for cup. John tells Brawny, Glass. I knew he had it in for me, but Serena. I like to get him back someday. Brawny tells John, you will on the field. But remember what I told you...? John interrupts Brawny Go after Serena. Brawny tells John, Go! John heads to the door, opens it and closes the door. John exits the office and go after Serena. King Rufus and Queen Esmeralda enters the house with Donald and Marissa comes down the stairs and greets them. Marissa tells her father and mother, hello Mom, Dad. Listen remember the stuff I told you on the phone. I know you're upset, but if you give me and Serena a chance too...? King Rufus interrupts her daughter for a minute. King Rufus tells Marissa, that's enough Marissa. I want you and Serena in the living room. Especially George, go call him. Serena, Marissa and George sits down in the couch and waiting for their parents to arrive in the living room. Marissa tells Serena, this doesn't look good. Serena tells Marissa, me neither. George tells Marissa, I might have go back to England and work in my father's job. I always knew you're parents would never approve of me being a commoner. Serena tells George, what about me. I lied to them, about me going to school at Cornelia. So they let me go to California by myself and dating an american commoner whose a major league baseball player who they never would've approve of. Marissa hears their parents coming for a minute. Marissa tells them, worry about that later, because here they come. King Rufus and Queen Esmeralda enters the living room and talks to their daughters. Serena tells her parents, father, mother before you start yelling at me. I wanted to tell you, I'm sorry about lying to you what school I was going too and dating an american commoner that you never would've approve of. Whatever you're decision is, I'll happily take full blame for the outcome for the last four years. Don't blame Marissa or George about this, they deserve to have a wedding. Even though you would never approve of George or me dating a commoner. King Rufus tells Serena, that's enough Serena. Marissa told me everything. I have to say I'm very disappointed both of you. Marissa tells her parents, I'm sorry. Serena tells her parents, me too. Queen Esmeralda tells them, Marissa you never I never would approve of you marrying a commoner like George. You lied to me about George's background and why didn't you explain to him about who he was. Marissa told her mother, you would never approve, father would've. But you wouldn't. Queen Esmeralda tells Marissa, no I wouldn't. King Rufus tells Serena, I'm disappointed in you, for lying to us about what school you were going too for four years. Why didn't you just tell us you wanted go to Anaheim High School. Serena tells King Rufus, father you would never approve, because you never let me bond with commoners. I had to life, so I can have real friends who like me for who I am. King Rufus tells Serena, kind of like dating this baseball player that I saw in the paper. Serena tells King Rufus, yes, I know you wouldn't approve of me dating him. I know you would ask me to abdicate the throne for John and me going to UCLA Marissa tells her parents, I knew you would've done the same thing with George. But I love him. Serena tells her parents, I love John too. Even though we broke up because of this paparazzi mess. But I still love him, I'm going to graduate high school with my friends and go to UCLA on a softball scholarship you would never approve of. So, go ahead and abdicate us. Marissa tells her parents, were not leaving them for the throne. You could find another heir if you want, but we don't want it. If we have to give up what we love. King Rufus tells her daughters, girls I have one thing say to you. Would you give up your seat on the throne for these two men you're in love with. Marissa and Serena tells their parents, yes. Queen Esmeralda tells her daughters, so be it. But I have one thing say to you, were not going to ask you leave the throne. Marissa, if you love George. We can still have the wedding this week. George you have our blessing. George tells her Queen Esmeralda, thank you you're majesty. King Rufus tells Serena, Serena we want you to be happy. I guess I understood why you lied. You're not just a princess with royal obligations. You're a person and regular kid. You deserve to make your own choices. I can see why you love this man, I can see why you like to give up to be with him. That's what it takes to be a good princess or future queen if anything happens to Marissa. Serena gets a little teary. King Rufus finishes telling Serena, you can graduate with your friends and play softball in UCLA. Like you wanted and you can have part-time royal obligations on the way that way you don't interfere in your studies. Queen Esmeralda tells Serena, I think you should go after this man and don't lose him. George tells the King and Queen, I don't get it. I always scared you reprimand us. King Rufus tells George, I guess we never told you about how we met. I was a commoner too, I used to work in a bakery and I met your mother. It was love at first sight. I knew her father wouldn't approve. Queen Esmeralda tells her daughters, he made a choice for me, the throne or love. Serena tells her parents, how did you keep both. Queen Esmeralda, we found a loophole. Your father had to speak the constitution of Albania to parliment and that was that. That's what you have to do George. If you want to marry my daughter. George tells the Queen, I'll do that. King Rufus tells George, good because parliament will be here and you can read the constitution to them. Before you marry my daughter. Serena tells her parents, luckily for me I still have it in my room. I'll go get it. Mom and Dad, for understanding. Marissa tells her parents, me too. King Rufus, we were in love too. We knew how you guys felt. Serena go get the book. Serena tells King Rufus, sure thing Dad. Serena gets up from her couch and heads upstairs. John parks his 2011 Mercedes-Benz E-Class outside the front door. John exits the car, heads to the door and starts ringing the door bell. The door opens and it's Donald. Donald tells John, Hi, can I help you sir? John tells Donald, I'm here to see the princess? Donald tells John, which one? John tells Donald, Serena. Is she here? Donald tells John, yes she's in the living room and you're John Mackey. It's a pleasure to meet you. Donald shakes hands with John. John tells Donald, it's a pleasure to meet you. Who are you? Donald tells John, my name is Donald. I'm the king's royal advisor. John let's goes of Donald's hand. John tells Donald, how did you know who I was. Are you Angels fan? Donald tells John, I saw the paper yesterday about you dating the Princess. John tells Donald, I forgot about that. Donald tells John, come on in. The King and Queen is expecting you. John tells Donald, this doesn't look good. John enters Serena's mansion and Donald closes the door. John enters the living room and sees George and Marissa reading the Albania constitution for the wedding with Serena, Alan and Serena's parents. John tells Serena, Serena! Serena tells John, John what are you doing here? John tells Serena, I've been looking all over for you. I just wanted to tell you I love you. I don't care about who you are or what the press say about us. King Rufus and Queen Esmeralda looks at John for a minute, not exactly the guy that their daughter would date. King Rufus tells Serena, this is thee John Mackey you were talking about. Serena tells King Rufus, yes dad that's him. King Rufus goes over to John and talk to him. King Rufus tells John, so John tell me what brings you here. I already know about you dating Serena. Don't deny anything. John tells King Rufus, hello you're heinous and your majesty, I'm John Mackey I pitch for the Anaheim Angels. I love your daughter, sire. I really care about her, it was a mistake breaking up with her. When I found who she was. It wouldn't be the paparazzi, that would break us up. It was me, I was scared to move on. I been in a relationship and it ended badly. i didn't want go through that again. When I met Serena, she saved my life and brought me back to the guy I used to be. I don't want to lose her, I like her for who she is, I don't care if you abdicate her from the throne. I love her and I'm not losing her for anything. King Rufus tells John, well John it took a lot of guts about what you said. Me and Esmeralda definitely would approve of you dating my daughter. You have our blessing. John tells King Rufus, thank you you're heinous. King Rufus tells John, you know Serena invited us to a couple of games in the stadium. I would've love to see you get that Al championship back. If you like to have me and my family to have us come to your game. John tells King Rufus, I'll be honored you're majesty. John shakes hands with King Rufus and let go. John hugs Serena's mother and let's goes. John greets the rest of the family. John and Serena exit the living room and John wants to tell her something, you would've give up the throne for me. Serena tells her, if I have too. John tells Serena, I love you Serena. Serena tells John, I love you too John! John makes out with Serena. Marissa and John's wedding starts in the back yard of Serena's mansion. John finishes reading the constitution to parliament and puts the book down on the floor. Marissa and John get married, where the priest marries them with Serena and Mona as a bride's maid. John, Warren and Coach is the best man and Serena's parents sitting in the audience crying in the wedding and so is Alan and Donald. Serena, Mona and Warren have their high school graduation in Anaheim High, where Serena grabs her diploma and wears a valedictorian medal. Serena's parents are in the audience taking photos with Alan, Donald and John. Five months later, John is pitching against Troy Glass for the Al championship. Serena, Mona, Warren, Coach Parker, King Rufus, Queen Esmeralda, Marissa and her new husband prince George watching the game in front row near the Angels dugout. Vince broadcast the game and tells the baseball fans, Mackey is 0-2 to Glass. One more strike and the Angels win the pennant. Glass is batting in home plate and ready for the next pitch while John is on the mound. Glass tells John, let's face it Mackey you'll never get me out. I'm going to hit this baby out of the park. John tells Glass, well Glass it's your choice. You can hit it out of the park and be a hero or the goat. By the way, nice try to expose me for dating Serena. Glass tells John, just because you're dating the princess means you're a hotshot. Even if you married her and become a prince. You still would be nothing, you'll be prince of nothing. Trust me, Princey, you're going to choke. Trust me, you will and so will your career and your little princess. John tells Glass, well see about that. Serena sees John for a minute and tells herself, strike this bum out. John throws the ball hard, Troy swings his bat and misses. Vince broadcast the game, calls it Mackey throws and Glass swings and misses. It's over Angels win the Al championship. Angels win the pennant. I guess it's a long career for John Mackey. Serena, Mona, Warren, Coach Parker, King Rufus, Queen Esmeralda, Marissa and her new husband prince George starts cheering for a minute. Serena tells them, he did it. I told you he could do it. They exit their seats to congratulate John. Glass is really upset, tells John I hate my life and kicks the dirt off the ground. Glass keeps telling himself he hates his life and really upset he lost out to Mackey. The team and Brawny always congratulates John too. Brawny tells John, well Mackey we made a deal. It's time I keep my bargain. You're going to playing with this team for a long time and ten million deal too. Don't worry, I talk to Parker he will be the new pitching coach next season. Thank you sir. John hugs

Brawny and let's him go. Serena sees John and tells her, I owe it all to you. Thank you, how do you do it. Serena tells John, magic and never stop believing about who you are. I love you, Serena. Serena tells John, I love you too Johnny. John takes off his Angels cap and puts it on Serena. Serena and John start making out for a minute and stop. The Angels carries Serena and John on the shoulders to cheer them on. Serena and John continuing making out and they live happily ever after.

The End

Princess of Silicon Valley

Plot Summary: Princess Amy, is the daughter Nivel the fifth Duke Granwich in the UK. Her mother died at a young age. Nivel Greenly made a huge fortune in the oil business, when his great grandfather struck oil in 1890. That made him a billionaire and never accepted a royal allowance from her cousin the Queen of England. Nivel's oil wells been dried up for a year, Scotland yard been investigate it and they figure out somebody is stealing oil from his pipelines. They don't have any proof who stole it. Nivel made a deal with Lord Randall Alden, who went to Oxford University with her daughter Amy, to sign a merger agreement that can save his company and all the people who work for him. Their was a clause in the contract, that his daughter has to wed Lord Alden after the merger agreement is signed and she refused, her father will have to 800 million dollars to buy his company back since Lord Alden owns 50 million shares of the voting stock of Nivel's company. But Lord Alden gave him a ultimatum, he's got two weeks either buy his stock back and they could nearly bankrupt him and his daughter or his daughter will have to marry Lord Alden to save his father's company. Nivel explains this to his daughter and he saw how sad she is that she has to marry this jerk, Nivel had a bigger problem that he had a heart attack and rush to the hospital. But he's fine, it was a mild heart attack. Nivel tells his daughter, she has two weeks to make a decision. Whatever she decide, he'll support her no matter what. Back home Amy read online about Abda Electronics in Mountain

View, California nicknamed Silcon Valley. It is Electronics and computer city of the world. Abda Electronics just closed an account with British Knights shoes, a billion dollar shoe company that we will help advertise for the company. They're about to close the account in a week and looking for investors to invest in the company. Amy decides go to Mountain View, California and start investing two hundred million dollars Abda Electronics, if she invest the stocks will hit the roof and make enough money to but Alden stock back. While she was in Palo Alto, Amy hasn't figure out what to do, until she stops by Mountain View Public Library and meets a librarian named Robbie Champberg, a nerdy fat jewish librarian who has a Bachelor's degree Palo Alto University in computer science and help her make the right decision to invest in what company. Robbie used to work as a computer programmer Abda electronics. They fired him six months ago, he messed up a billion dollar account for the company. End up working in a library since he minored in library and science. Robbie and Amy fell in love at first sight, but their in different worlds. Robbie is a middle class geek whose father works in a pencil factory assembly line and works in a library since he got fired and uses all his savings to use a start up computer company with his best friend Jaleel. Princess Amy is about to marry Lord Alden, is handsome, british lord who is about to take over her father's company and take his duke title from him. They gotta a bigger problem, while Princess Amy trying to investigate about the stolen oil from her wells and doesn't have any proof that Lord Alden is behind this. She gets help from Robbie and his friend Jaleel who works in the library with him, to track down who stole that oil. I think somebody in Abda Electronic works for Lord Alden and trying to stop her from making that investment to save her father's company. Can Robbie and Amy stop Lord Alden from stealing his father's oil and bigger plan that he is using with that oil. Can Robbie and Amy be together after this huge adventure together and Robbie telling Amy who he is. Only time will tell.

Once upon a time, there is a big town called Granwich England that's twenty miles in London. It's been a happy place to raise your kids at and everybody treated like equals. In Granwich, there is a Princess named Amy, whose father Nivel Maston is the fifth Duke of Granwich, who rules over a peaceful town called Granwich. Princess Amy mother passed away when she was five and it was just her and her father. They get along really well, but he is worried about her. They made a fortune in their town, when they're great grandfather found oil in their property and strike it rich in 1890. They made themselves a lot richer and making them and their town rich. Nivel net worth is twenty billion dollars and he always invest in five hundred million dollars for the royal treasury for the Queen of England every year. Nivel always been a honest business man, he pays his taxes, his bills, his insurance and he puts his money in bearer bonds. So, he doesn't squander his fortune. He always makes good business decisions and doesn't invest in their business. They're always risky. Nivel is a kind hearted philanthropist, who gives money to the poor. Nivel is a middle age duke in his late fifties and wears a beard. Nivel was getting up from bed wearing his pajamas and went downstairs in the kitchen in his palace for breakfast where he is going to meet his daughter. They call his palace Nivel Palace, it's been in his family two generations. While Nivel was about head to the kitchen he sees a picture of his wife Hermoine, she is really beautiful and looks like his daughter. Nivel always loved her and tells himself, "hey Hermoine I love you. I wish you were here with me. It's not the same without you here." Nivel picks up the picture from the nightstand and kisses it and puts it back on the nightstand. Nivel exits his room and his royal advisor Newton Langley is waiting for him. Newton tells Nivel "Good morning, you're majesty. How are you this morning." They both head downstairs to the kitchen Nivel tells Newton, "Not really well, Newton. My oil wells is still dried up. Did the foreman figured it out yet, what happened to it." Newton tells Nivel, "He's still working on the problem sir. The Oil well is been dried up for nearly a year, You're well is supposed to be running three hundred years. I don't know why it's stop running." Nivel tells Newton, "I don't know what happened to it, it's like somebody hi jacked my oil or something. It's costing me a lot of money. I might have to shut down the rig." Newton tells Nivel, "If you shut it down sir, you're going to put a lot of people out of work, sir. They love working on that rig. You put the city of Granwich on the map, because of our oil rig, you're great grandfather found in 1890. Nivel tells Newton, "I don't want to put people out of work, I never fired anyone in my life. I really care about this people they work for me. I maybe been born as a royal duke, but that oil rig that my great grandfather built late nineteenth helped out

England and this town really well. But I have no choice to shut it down and sell it to Lord Arden." Newton tells Nivel, "You're majesty, you actually going to sell the rig to Lord Randall Alden. Nivel tells Newton, "Exactly!" Newton tells Nivel, "Lord Randall is like a one man wrecking crew. He maybe a British lord and member of parliament and a front runner to run for Prime Minister. This guy, likes to buy companies and tear it down like a wrecking ball. Our people who work for us in that rig, will be out of work in days. Nivel tells Newton, "I don't have a choice Newton, if I don't sell the rig. I can lose a lot of money. I still have two billion dollar in a savings account. But that rig is losing me money, I won't have enough money for Amy or keep the palace running. I can't be around forever. Nivel tells Newotn, I understand sir, but you are a Duke and Amy is a princess. Don't you guys have a royal allowance and move anywhere you want. Besides you're are the Queen fifth cousin and a member of Windsor Family who is twentieth line to the throne of England." Nivel tells Newton, "Amy is twenty-first line of the throne too." Newton tells Nivel, "So sir, what do you have to worry about. You have plenty of money around and you can give the rig to the government. We can be okay and save people's jobs. Nivel tells Newton, "I never except any money from the royal treasury. I have my title and my royal duties, but I never accepted royal allowance from my cousin the queen. Me and Amy are still heir to the thrones of England. But my bread and butter was the oil rig. It's already too late to ask my cousin for a royal allowance or give the rig to her government. I already signed a contract, that all my wealth will go to my oil rig but will not except any money from royal allowances in the near future. That my great grandfather made. But the good side is, the queen can tear off the contract anytime she wants since my great grandfather is dead and only him cannot not only except any royal allowance. But his family can, anytime they ask the king or queen. Newton tells Nivel, "Why didn't you ask the Queen for money?" Nivel tells Newton, "I don't want to look like a failure in front of her. She may never let me live it down." Newton tells Nivel, so what are you going to do you're majesty? Nivel tells Newton, I'm going to talk to my daughter about this and ask her advice about what to do?" Newton tells Nivel, so what can she do? Nivel tells Newton, I don't know, but I'll ask her." Nivel was about head to the bathroom, until Newton stops him for a minute and tells the Duke, "excuse me, you're majesty. Nivel tells Newton, what is it Newton?" Newton tells Nivel, "Their is a way to save our financial troubles on our oil rig?" Nivel tells Newton, "And that is!" Nivel tells Newton, Lord Randall Alden, also owns an oil rig in Westchester England, it's about twenty miles from here and he is making billions in his oil business. He is been asking to merge and invest in our company for years and maybe we can take in his offer." Newton tells Nivel, "Are you crazy, Lord Alden is my toughest competitor, he's been trying to put my oil company out of business for years. I also heard he is a front runner for the Prime Minister election. Planning on ruining me and trying to steal my title if I don't sign over his company to him." Newton tells Nivel, "I know that, Alden is been putting trying to take over the company, if we talk to him and make a deal to sign over a merger. Maybe we can still keep the company going and have enough money to leave Princess Amy something, before you kick the bucket someday." Nivel tells Newton, "It won't be tomorrow, but I have no choice. I really do love me daughter, I don't leave with nothing. Newton go to my den, call Alden's office on the phone and tell him to give me a call in a hour. I want to make a deal with him." Newton tells Nivel, "Yes, you're majesty." Nivel tells Newton, "I'm going to get ready and have breakfast with my daughter." Nivel heads to the bathroom and get ready. Newton heads to The Duke's office and make the call to Lord Alden's office. Nivel is in the dining room and eating his breakfast. He's eating his pancakes with syrup, bacon, scrambled eggs, sausage links and drinking water. Newton heads to the dining room and sees Nivel eating his breakfast and dressed in his casual clothes. Newton is carrying the duke's cell phone in his right hand and talks to the duke. "Excuse me, you're majesty." Nivel tells Newton, "What is it, Newton." Newton tells Nivel, "I got Lord Alden on the phone. He's reading to speak to you." Nivel tells Newton, "Okay then, give me the phone Newton. Me and Randall have a lot to talk about. By the way, is Amy coming down." Newton tells Nivel, "Yes sir, the princess is getting ready. She'll be down in a few minutes." Nivel tells Newton, "Excellent, I promise her that we go motorcycle riding in the country today. That is one of her favorite things to do after breakfast." Newton tells Nivel, "You sure have a great bond with your daughter sir." Nivel tells Newton, "I do, Newton the phone." Newton tells Nivel, "Yes sir.! Newton hands over The Duke's cell phone and Nivel talks to Lord

Alden on the phone." Nivel talks to Lord Alden on the phone, "Hello, Randall." Lord Alden is in his office in London talking to the Duke on the phone, "Should I address you as You're majesty or I'll just call you soon to be broke and take your oil fields Maston." Back in The Duke's dining room, Nivel is a little upset what Lord Alden said and tells him on the phone, "Very funny, Randall! Let's just stick to business. I want talk to about the merger. What are you intentions?" Lord Alden is in his office and talks to the Duke on the phone and tells him, "Simple you think are you sign this merger, that I will lay off your workers, steal your crown and be your boss. I was considering about doing it. But I won't, besides the only way I would take your dukedom, if I married your daughter and you would have heart problems and you have one month to live. To take your title, that's ridiculous." Nivel is on the phone with Lord Alden in his palace and starts laughing for a minute. Nivel tells Lord Alden, "Yeah, it is funny. It's true, but their is another way to get my crown, if I abdicate the crown and give it to you since you are noble born and you are member of the house of Windsor. Since you are and thirtieth line of the throne of England. That would be crazy, because you are not a member of the house of windsor." Lord Alden is still talking to the Duke on the phone in his office and tells him, "That is a joke, I am a member of the house of Windsor, since Edward VIII was my great cousin. I am noble born, so here's the deal, you are going to sign that merger with me and I will own sixty percent of the voting stock in your oil company. I will make a lot of changes in your company." Nivel is still on the phone with Lord Alden and he doesn't like what Alden is doing. But he still hearing him out what his plans are. Nivel tells Lord Alden, "What changes!" Lord Alden is on the phone with Nivel and tells him, "You were right about one thing, I will lay off your employees. Those guys are cramping my style and slowing me down. Since they are lazy and fat and totally weak." Nivel is still upset what Alden said. Lord Alden is still on the phone with, "1 I might think about drilling in the West End lake of that land to make more money when I drill that oil. Since you guys own it." Nivel is furious about what Alden is doing and he tells Alden on the phone, "I'm not going to let you lay off my workers, because they are weak and lazy? Lord Alden tells Nivel on the phone, "But you gotta admit one thing Nivel, that these guys are totally weak and you're paying them too much. Nivel tells Alden on the phone, "I'm paying them a fair amount and they're good men. Who has families and homes that need to be taken care of. I care about them, I don't what happens to me. But these guys who worked for me. I want them to be feel safe and secured when they work for me." Alden tells Nivel, "You got me their, but I don't think you have a choice in that matter. I'm your only chance to save your company and keep your dukedom." Nivel tells Alden on the phone, "Their is no way, I'm abdicating my crown or give my company to you. The deal if off." Alden tells Nivel, "Relax, I was just testing you. You don't have to give up on anything. You can still keep your crown and your company and your workers. The only thing we can do is sign a merger and I'll just invest in your company as a silent investor. Nivel tells Alden, "You were just testing me.! Alden tells Nivel, "Of course, I just want to make you squirm." Nivel tells Alden, "You're really are a funny guy, Randall." Nivel laughs for a minute and stops. Alden tells Nivel, "I thought so, come to London tomorrow in my office, will sign the merger agreement. Nivel tells Alden, "Okay, but remember. No funny business. If you double cross on anything. I'm coming after you." Alden tells Nivel, "Relax, you have my word. On everything you said. I won't double cross you. Nivel tells Alden, "Okay, I'll see you tomorrow to sign the merger agreement. Bye! Alden tells Nivel, See ya, you're majesty! Alden hangs up his phone and his assistant enters his office and talks to him. Lord Alden assistant tells him, "My lord what are you really up to. I know you want to take over that company. Not save it!" Lord Alden tells his assistant, "Of course I don't want to save it Patrick. I'm still going to take over the company and lay off the duke's workers and take his crown. Patrick tells Alden, "but Lord Alden you told the duke you were just going to be a silent investor when he's going to sign the merger agreement with him tomorrow in your office." Lord Alden tells Patrick, "Of couse I give him my word and I won't double cross. But I still have one trick in my sleeve. To get that company and something that the duke cares about more than anything. Patrick tells Lord Alden, "Whose that, sir." Lord Alden tells Patrick, "Somebody I been waiting for, since she and I went to St Andrews together. Patrick looks at Lord Alden and I think he knows who he is talking about. Patrick tells Lord Alden, "Ooh, I think I know what you are talking about." Lord Alden tells Patrick, "Patrick make the agreements, I want the duke really comfortable tomorrow. When I give him my little surprise." Lord Alden starts laughing for a minute. Patrick tells Lord Alden, "Yes, my lord!" Patrick heads to the door and exits Lord Alden's office. Lord Alden stops laughing. Nivel and his daughter Princess Amy are riding motorcycles in their huge backyard. Princess Amy is twenty-one and a very attractive girl who is a comic book fan girl like Superman and Batman and video games. She is like an attractive nerdy girl. Nivel tells Princess Amy, "looks like I win again." Princess Amy tells her father, "I let you win. I could've had Henry to spruce up the V8 engine too beat you." Nivel tells Princess Amy, Henry our chauffer could build engines, that's hard to believe." Princess Amy tells Nivel, "Father, their is a lot of stuff about Henry you didn't know. Nivel tells Princess Amy, "What is that." Princess Amy tells her father, "That he used to be on a pit crew on formula one racing team." Nivel tells her daughter, "My mistake, Amy you would have actually beat me with a spruce up V8 engine that Henry made." Princess Amy laughs for a minute and stops. Princess Amy tells her father, "I'm just kidding Dad, I just want to watch you squirm for a minute." Nivel tells Amy, "You're funny, baby." Nivel and Amy still laughing for a minute and stops. Princess Amy tells her father, "Once more on the willow trees." Nivel tells her daughter, "One more time in the Willow trees, we have to hurry back. I have to be in London in an hour." Princess Amy tells her father, "How come?" Nivel tells her daughter, "I have to meet Lord Alden in his office, I think I'm considering his offer." Princess Amy tells her father, "What offer is that, Dad?" Nivel tells Princess Amy, "I'm thinking about signing his merger agreement that could help my oil company." Princess Amy tells Nivel, "Look Dad, I know how much you love your oil company and it meant a lot to you. Are you sure you can trust, Lord Alden?" Nivel tells Princess Amy, "I don't. He's up to something, I have no choice and my oil rig is been dried for a year. I feel like somebody is stealing my oil from my rig." Princess Amy tells her father, "Who do you think would steal our oil from our rig. It's like somebody is trying to put us out of business." Nivel tells Princess Amy, "I don't know who, but I already got Scotland Yard trying to investigate it for a year." Princess Amy tells her father, "Do they have any leads?" Nivel tells her daughter, "None that I know of. Scotland Yard had their top guys investigating it. They couldn't find anything who stole my oil." Princess Amy tells her father, I bet you it had to be Lord Alden. He was your biggest competitor, he would do whatever it takes to put us out of business and trying to steal your crown for years." Nivel tells her daughter, "My oil wells been dried up for months, I am losing money with these wells. I don't want go to my cousin for money problems." Princess Amy tells her father, "I thought we are doing okay?" Nivel tells her daughter, "We are, we still have a lot of money for us. But my oil well is kinda dry and I never needed money from my cousin the Queen. It's not us, it's the people that work for us. I don't think I can afford to keep that Rig going and keep the people that are working for me, if my oil well is dried up." Princess Amy tells her father, "What's going to happen? Nivel tells her daughter, "If it's drying up. I may have to let go of my workers, who have families, bills and mortgages to pay and shut down the rig." Princess Amy tells her father, "Are you sure you're going to let that happened, put a lot of people out of work who were a friends and family if you can't keep the rig going." Nivel tells her daughter, "Of course not, but I might find a way to keep my company going." Princess Amy tells her father, "how are you going do that?" Nivel tells her daughter, "I have to meet Lord Alden, I might not have a choice that I have sign a merger agreement with him." Princess Amy tells her father, "What kind of merger agreement are you talking about?" Nivel tells her daughter, "It means if I sign the merger agreement, he will buy 10 or twenty percent of my oil stock. Alden will control ten or twenty percent of the voting stock of my company and he can use his oil continue make a profit and keep a lot of jobs for my workers. Princess Amy tells her father, "You are going to trust him with this agreement?" Nivel tells her daughter, "Like I said, I don't have a choice and money is tight with my company." Princess Amy tells her father, "Daddy, you are not answering my question with this merger agreement?" Nivel tells her daughter, "No, I don't. I think he might up to something." Princess Amy tells her father, "He is up to something, I went to Oxford with him. He is like a human wrecking ball, he buys company like this that are in trouble and he tears it down piece by by piece. Our oil company will be gone in a few days." Nivel tells her daughter, "We don't know for sure and yes you told me he's been in love with you since, you went to Oxford University together and he's been asking you out for years. But you always turn him down, because you thought he was arrogant and vile. But I'm sure that is in the past, I'm sure he changed." Princess Amy tells her father, "Dad, people like Alden don't change. They become worse when they're older. I think it might be a trap. I just want you to be careful what you're stepping into. Nivel tells her daughter, "Honey I'm going to be fine. I'm going go to London tomorrow and meet him in his office and see what my options are with him." Princess Amy tells her father, "What happens if you don't like the options that he is giving you?" Nivel tells her daughter, "I think I'm standing in a no win situation, if I don't sign my workers will be out of work and I have to close the company. If I do sign for him, he might be up to something and I won't like how he will run my company or go back in his word and put my workers out of work. Princess Amy tells her father, "Like I said, no win situation." Nivel tells her daughter, "Let's not worry about it today, let's just concentrate on having fun today and will worry about tomorrow." Princess Amy tells her father, "So what do you want do today? Nivel tells her daughter, "How about once more around the yard and we can go to Mcdonald's after that." Princess Amy tells her fahter, "Okay, loser buys the next the double cheeseburgers, fries and diet coke." Nivel tells her daughter, "You're on. Just to be fair, I'm going to have a head start. Starting now! Nivel starting riding his motorcycle gets a head start once around the back yard first. Princess Amy yells at her father, "No fair, I was supposed to go first." Princess rides her motorcycle and tries to catch up with her father. Outside of Lord Alden's office and the limousine parked right outside Alden's office. The Limo driver exits the limo and heads to back of the limo door and opens the door for Nivel. Nivel exits the limo, carrying his briefcase and talks to the limo driver, Nivel tells the limo driver, "Well Stephen, wish me luck. I heard this Alden guy is tough." Stephen tells Nivel, "He's not tough, you're heinous, this man is rock solid. He is sneaky and ruthless, just be careful of Lord Alden sir." Nivel tells Stephen, "I think he should be worrying about me right now, since he wants my oil wells and probably would do anything to get it." Stephen tells Nivel, "I think that's the other way around sir. I think you would do anything to get him to sign that agreement, since he is holding the contract like a doggie treat and he'll make you beg for it like any other dog." Nivel tells Stephen, "You right about that Stephen, I wish he didn't hold that contract like a doggie treat. Well, here goes nothing." Nivel is about head to Lord Alden's office, Stephen tells the Duke, "Good Luck sir! Nivel tells Stephen, "Thanks Stephen, I'm going to need it!" Nivel goes to the door and opens it and goes inside Lord Alden's office. Lord Alden is in his office working. Lord Alden is the same age is Princess Amy and he is handsome, rich and power hungry. Lord Alden hears the door knock for a minute and tells the person, "Come in!" The door opens and it's his secretary. Alden's Secretary talks to Lord Alden and tells him, "Excuse me, my lord Duke Nivel Greenly here to see you." Lord Alden tells his secretary, "Send him in Flora." Flora tells Lord Alden, "Yes Sir!" Flora who is outside the main entrance to Lord Alden's office and tells the Duke, "Lord Alden is ready to see you now, you're dukeship." Nivel tells Flora, "Thank you, madam." Nivel heads to the door and opens and closes the door. Nivel enters Lord Alden's office and Alden exits his chair and starts to greet Nivel. Nivel shakes Lord Alden's hand and let's go. Lord Alden tells Nivel, "Hello, you're majesty it's good to see you." Nivel tells Lord Alden, "Good to see you, Randall. Let's get on to business! Lord Alden tells Nivel, "Before we get onto business you want anything?" Nivel tells Lord Alden, "No, I'm good" Lord Alden tells Nivel, "Are you sure, I have some coffee you want any." Nivel tells Lord Alden, "I don't drink coffee, but do you have any hot chocolate? Lord Alden tells Nivel, "I think so. Flora!" Flora enters the office and talks to Lord Alden and Nivel. Flora tells Lord Alden, "Yes, Lord Alden?" Lord Alden tells Flora, "Do you have any hot chocolate?" Flora tells Lord Alden, "Yes, we do?" Lord Alden tells Flora, "Get some for the Duke Greenly? Flora tells Lord Alden, "Yes, my lord" Flora leaves Lord Alden's office and get some hot chocolate for him. Lord Alden tells Nivel, "Have a seat, you're heinous and will wait for Flora get your chocolate and get on with business." Nivel tells Lord Alden, "Okay, but I thought we can get on business right now." Lord Alden tells Nivel, "In a minute, I want to wait until you're hot chocolate arrives. Besides we can drink anything on a empty stomach." Nivel tells Lord Alden, "You got a point their? After a few minutes when Nivel is drinking his hot chocolate for a minute and sitting down in his chair. Lord Alden is ready get to business. Nivel tells Lord Alden, "What are my options?" Lord Alden tells Nivel, "Simple, I send you a contract and you look it over a couple of days and if you agree with it. You can sign the contact and start a merger and you can connect my oil pipelines to your rig. We both can make some money and you can keep you're workers." Nivel tells Lord Alden, "That sounds like a fair deal, what are you really up to Randall. I know guys like you, like to destroy failing companies and not keep it going?" Lord Alden tells Nivel, "I know up to something? I just want to help you're company keep going. True, I was a tough competitor back then. I used to love it when I crush little companies like yours and destroy it. But no more, so I want to save you're business? Nivel tells Lord Alden, "That sounds like a fair deal, where do I sign?" Lord Alden tells Nivel, "Not yet! Nivel tells Lord Alden, "I beg your pardon?" Lord Alden tells Nivel, "Their is another option you should look at? Lord Alden tells Nivel, "What other option are you talking about?" Lord Alden tells Nivel, "This option?" Lord Alden opens his drawer and opens a contract and put it on his desk. Lord closes his drawer and shows it to Nivel. Lord Alden tells Nivel, "I think you should read it and weep." Nivel looks at the contract for a minute and he gets a little upset for a minute. Lord Alden tells Nivel, "Right now, when you read that!" Nivel tells Lord Alden, "It says here, you own fifty percent of the voting stock of Greenly Oils." Lord Alden tells Nivel, "So here are my options, I own fifty million shares of your company, I can destroy it or I keep it going. Mostly for me, if I tear it down, their will be no competition for me. Because I like making people like you squirm. Nivel is a little upset for a minute and wants to tear Lord Alden head off for a minute, but he is keeping it under control. Not losing his temper. Lord Alden continue telling Nivel, "But these are my options, you can buy my stock back of fifty percent of my stock that I own is worth 800 million dollars. I'll bet it will take half chuck of your 1.2 billion dollars to pay for it to keep it going. If you pay that amount, you couldn't keep your manor and your servants going once you pay me and your company will be out of my business if you buy my stock back. You and your daughter will be out of on the streets. My second option that you sign the merger in two weeks, you get to keep your company and your workers and your mansion. But since I own fifty percent of the voting stock of your company, I have control, I may considering laying off all your workers or half of them. So, what do you think, you're majesty?" Nivel tells Lord Alden, "I think you're an arrogant jerk and you probably weren't breastfed when you were a kid." Lord Alden tells Nivel, "First of all, very funny. I probably ignore that remark, since I'm that close to take your company away from you. So, I probably think you better think about your options, I'm about to give you." Nivel tells Lord Alden, "So this is a no win situation, I sign the merger company, you control my company and you could lay off my employees who were family to me or I risk paying nearly half of my money to buy your stock back. I have control back, but I will lose my company and my rig and my home since my oil wells are dried up. So, another word to you, it's a no win situation for me." Lord Alden tells Nivel, "Exactly, so I think you better look at your options closely Nivel, you don't have a choice in this matter." Nivel tells Lord Alden, "How long do I have to think about this?" Lord Alden tells Nivel, "You got two weeks, you better sign that merger agreement with me or you better pay me my 800 million dollars to buy my stock back. I'm that close to close your business in a minute." Nivel tells Lord Alden, "You really are a totally jerk Randall." Lord Alden tells Nivel, "I know that, but before you think about it in a couple of weeks, their is another clause you should read? Nivel tells Lord Alden, "What clause? Lord Alden opens his desk drawer and takes out a magnifying glass and closes the drawer. He uses the magnifying glasses and shows the clause on the contract to Nivel. Lord Alden tells Nivel, "This clause right here. Read and weep, old bean?" Nivel looks at the clause for a minute and starts reading it. Nivel reads the clause to Lord Alden and tells himself, "After you sign the merger agreement. You will also arrange Princess Amy Greenly, daughter Nivel Greenly the third Duke of Granwich to wed Lord Randall Alden for wedded bliss after this event." Nivel can't believe what he is hearing and tells Lord Alden, "What I can't believe what I'm hearing this. You expect my daughter to marry you just for a business arrangement?" Lord Alden laughs for a minute and tells Nivel, "Yes,. I can. You see, I'm in love with her, I've been love with her since I first saw her and she would have make a great trophy wife for me. If I running for Prime Minister pretty soon. Since I don't have a strong following to run, I got something else that bigger is your daughter and something bigger than the prime ministership." Nivel can't believe he is still hearing this and tells Lord Alden, "Don't tell me, my Dukedom." Lord Alden tells Nivel, "Exactly, you'll be giving that to me in a minute. Since when I have your crown, I will be heir to the throne of England pretty soon." Nivel tells Lord Alden, "I'm twentieth line to the throne of England. You will have to wait for a long to time until you'll get that crown and besides. You're not a member of the Windsor family to qualify for the throne anyway." Lord Alden tells Nivel, "Actually I am, even if I married your daughter or not, with your dukedom title and my family background where my Grandfather was Edward VIII fifth cousin removed and qualifies me to be a member of the

Windsor family. Since I'm thirty-fifth line in the throne, like you said I might have to wait forever to get that throne. That's when you're duke title, will get me to move up to sixteen spaces for the throne." Nivel tells Lord Alden, "What makes you think I'm going along with this?" Lord Alden tells Nivel, "If you don't sign that merger agreement, you will owe me 800 million dollars to buy your stock back and it's going to net worth. I don't think you have enough to keep your life of luxuries going. I really love to see you and your pathetic crew out of on the street" Nivel tells Lord Alden, "This is blackmail and extortion, I can sue or press charges with the Crown Prosecution for this." Lord Alden tells Nivel, "You won't, but they don't have a case and it's iron clad. You forgot I was a crown prosecutor, before my father died and inherited his seat in Parliament. So, that contract you're reading their is iron clad and fairly legal. If you play golf, this is where I hit a hole in one." Nivel tells Lord Alden, "You are a total arrogant jerk, Randall." Lord Alden tells Nivel, "Thanks Nivel, I appreciate that." Lord Alden smiles a little, like an evil smile. Lord Alden tells Nivel, "Like I said, that agreement when you sign that merger not only saves your company, but also getting your hands of my oil wells that will make a rich man. Nivel tells Lord Alden, "And my daughter?" Lord Alden tells Nivel, "If she doesn't agree to marry me in two weeks, even after you sign the merger agreement. Not only will you lose the merger agreement with my company. You will have to pay me 800 million dollars to buy my stock back, and nearly leave you guys nearly in debt." Nivel tells Lord Alden, "Like A Dowry?" Lord Alden tells Nivel, "Yes it is, you're majesty." Nivel tells Lord Alden, "What century is this and this is legal." Lord Alden tells Nivel, "It is when you read that contract and it's iron clad. You don't have a choice." Nivel tells Lord Alden, "How long do I have to agree to this? Lord Alden tells Nivel, "You got two weeks to think it over, if you don't sign that agreement, you still would owe me 800 millions if you want to get your company back. In a way, it's a win-win situation." Nivel looks at Lord Alden for a minute and wants to punch him, but he did one noble thing. Nivel got up from his chair and heads to the door talking the contract with him from Lord Alden's desk. Nivel is about head to the door, until Lord Alden tells Nivel, "You're dukeship, you better get my money quickly or talk your daughter to me. Either way, I'm about to take both of them. Without you knowing it!" Nivel exits Lord Alden's office for a minute.

Outside of Lord Alden's office where Stephen is waiting for the Duke, outside his limousine. Nivel exits Lord Alden's meeting and really upset about his options that he made with Lord Alden. Stephen tells Nivel, How it go, You're heinous? "Nivel tells Stephen, "Let's say I made a deal with Satan Jr and he gave me options that I can't refuse." Stephen tells Nivel, "That bad, huh." Nivel tells Stephen, "I really need talk to Amy, maybe she could help me out of this. She was a business major and I could use her advice right now?" Stephen tells Nivel, "If you want to talk to her about this agreement, you have to talk to her in her favorite place." Nivel tells Stephen, "I know exactly the spot? I'll give her a call and meet me their in a minute. But I need to be alone first. Before I talk to her." Stephen tells Nivel, "So, where do you want to go you're majesty?" Nivel tells Stephen, "How about a drive around London for a hour, before we meet her." Stephen tells Nivel, "Sure thing, you're majesty" Stephen opens the door and Nivel gets inside the limousine and Stephen closes the door. Stephen goes to his driver seat and exits Lord Alden's office. Stephen is waiting for Princess Amy at her favorite place to go is McDonald's. It's her favorite place to eat and so is Nivel. Princess Amy enters McDonald's and sees her father waiting for her. Princess Amy goes over to her father, where he is sitting and sits down and talk to him. Princess Amy tells her father, "So, what happened today?" Nivel tells her daughter, "I spoke to Randall and gave me his options about how to save my company." Princess Amy tells her father, "Whatever it is, it doesn't look good. I know a guy like Lord Alden can't be trusted." Nivel tells Princess, "You got that right, honey." Princess Amy tells her father, "So what are your options?" Nivel tells Princess Amy, "I can buy my stock back from him?" Princess Amy tells her father, "That doesn't sound bad." Nivel tells Princess Amy, "Randall controls fifty percent voting stock of my company." Princess Amy doesn't like what she is hearing. Princess Amy tells her father, "Fifty percent of the voting stock?" Nivel tells Princess Amy, "In Wall Street talk, he owns fifty million shares of my company, I have to pay 800 million dollars to buy the stock back out of my own pocket." Princess Amy tells her father, "That nearly bankrupts us, plus we can't afford to pay our servants or keep Greenly Manor." Nivel tells her daughter, "That place is been with our family for years." Princess Amy tells her father, "So, you're willing buy back our stock back, father." Nivel tells her daughter, "Baby, even if I buy that stock back. I have control of my company again. But my oil wells are dried up and I could still put my company ruin if I buy it back." Princess Amy tells her father, "It could put all of us out of work pretty soon." Nivel tells her daughter, "Their was another option, that Alden gave me, I don't think you're not going to like this idea." Princess Amy tells her father, "What is it?" Nivel tells her daughter, "I think you better read this contract for a minute." Princess Amy tells her father, "Later, I can't ready anything with an empty stomach." Nivel tells her daughter, "That goes double for me" Princess Amy tells her father, "So dad the usually." Nivel tells her daughter, "2 double cheeseburgers Large Fries, Hot Fudge Sundae and a Large Diet Coke." Princess Amy tells her father, "You remember!" Nivel and Princess Amy are eating their two double cheeseburgers, large fries, hot fudge sundae and drinking their large diet coke. Princess Amy reads this contract for a minute and doesn't like what she is hearing. Princess Amy tells her father, "I have to marry him." Nivel tells her daughter, "I'm afraid so honey, even if I signed the merger agreement and that could save the business and keep our estate. If you don't back out, even if I signed. I still have to pay 800 million dollars like a dowry. Princess Amy tells her father, "A dowry, what century is this? Is this even legal? Nivel tells her daughter, "I'm afraid so, it's iron clad. I got two weeks to decide. I'm going to let you decide. Whatever your decision you make, I'll support you whatever you decide. Princess Amy tells her father, "Thanks Dad, I appreciate that. I don't ruin our family estate that our great grandfather built. I don't have a choice in this matter, I might have to do this. Even if I don't want to." Nivel tells her daughter, "Look honey, I know you would do anything to help me. But like I said, it's your choice." Princess Amy tells her father, "Even if I have to marry this jerk, just to save our business. That's pratically low for me. But like I said, I don't have a choice." Nivel grabs his double cheeseburger and starts eating for a minute. Princess Amy tells her father, "If I say yes, I'll end up one of Randall's trophy wife and while he's out their dating other girls behind my back in his harem. I'm not going to live like this, sometimes I wish I wasn't this attractive to attract a man like Randall Alden. But I guess their is no other way, if there was a sign out their telling me I can't marry him. I hope they can give me one." Nivel finishes his double cheeseburger while his heart is pounding in his chest really. Nivel who is not feeling well tells her daughter, "Honey, before you make any decision. I have one decision for you right now." Princess Amy tells her father, "What is it Dad?" Nivel tells her daughter, "I thought you better call for some help right now. I think I might need it." Princess Amy tells her father, "I don't get it?" Nivel collapses on the floor from his chair and drops his double cheeseburger. Nivel is having a heart attack and Princess Amy is scared. Princess Amy goes over to her father and checks his neck and his chest to see if he's breathing. Princess Amy tells her father, "Dad, dad! Oh no, somebody get some help now! Get an Ambulance now? The McDonald's counter looks at Nivel and tells his colleague, "Get an Ambulance now. We have a man down with a heart attack. Go!" The second man from the McDonald's counter tells his colleague, "You got it!" McDonald's counter guy heads to the phone and calls an ambulance. Princess Amy tells her father, "Come back Dad, speak to me. Don't worry, help is coming. Somebody help! Please somebody help! The Ambulance heads to Royal London Hospital. Princess Amy and Stephen are in the waitng room waiting for the doctor to see if Nivel is okay. Newton arrives in the waiting room and sees Princess Amy and Stephen in the waiting room. Newton talks to Amy, "Hello, you're heinous. I just heard the news, I got here as fast as I can." Newton is still pacing from running all the way to the hospital here. Newton tells Princess Amy, "How is he doing?" Princess Amy tells Newton, "The doctor hasn't arrived yet, so we don't know. Thanks for coming Newton, he appreciate it." Princess Amy hugs Newton for a minute. Newton tells Princess Amy, 'I know. I can't picture our life without him here. He made Greenly manor a great place to live. It was liking in Disneyland their." Princess Amy tells Newton, "I know." Princess Amy let's go of her butler and they both sit down in their chairs with Stephen and waiting for the results. Newton tells them, "I can't picture my life without the Duke, he was more than boss and employee. He was my best friends and like a surrogate brother to me." Stephen tells them, "I know he was a like a second father to me. I just hope he's okay." Princess tells them, "I hope so, too. I can't picture my life without my father. I love him and he always supported my dreams no matter what." Newton tells Princess Amy, "Don't worry, you're majesty I'm sure the Duke Greenly will be fine." The doctor arrives at the waiting room and goes over talk to Princess Amy, Stephen and Newton about Nivel's condition. Newton tells himself, "I hope!" Princess Amy talks to the doctor and tells her, "Dr Wesley, how is my father?" Dr Wesley tells Princess and the others, "You're father just had a heart attack. But luckily for us, it's a mild heart attack he's fine." Everyone is relieved that he is okay. Princess Amy tells herself, "Thank goodness." Dr Wesley tells Princess Amy, "Mostly his mild heart attack came from a lot of stress. He has to take it easy for a few days." Newton tells Dr Wesley, "Will the Duke be out soon." Dr Wesley tells Newton, "He's going have to stay here for a week to recuperate before you take him home. You're majesty, I suggest you get him some clothes and some things for him before he leaves." Princess Amy tells Dr. Wesley, "Okay, can we see him right now!" Dr Wesley tells Princess Amy, "I'm afraid not, he's in recovery right now. So, you can't see him until tomorrow morning. I suggest you guys head on home and you can see him tomorrow." Princess Amy tells Dr Wesley, Okay!" Princess Amy looks at Newton and tells him, "Newton, get some clothes and stuff for him while we visit him tomorrow." Newton tells Princess Amy, "Yes, you're heinous." Princess Amy tells them, "Come on, guys let's go home and come back tomorrow morning." Stephen tells Princess Amy, "I get the limo, it's double parked outside." Princess Amy, Newton and Stephen exits the waiting room and head to the lobby to go home. Princess Amy is in her room at Greenly Manor watching Chuck marathon on tv. Princess Amy tells herself, "You know Chuck, you surprise, I hope someday I have an adventure like that someday." Princess Amy thinking for a minute. Princess Amy tells herself again, "I wish how I can save my father's business and not marry Lord Alden. That guy is a total jerk! I wish their was a get out of this. I am not going to let my father to die for nothing, their has to be a sign to get out of this." When Princess Amy sees Chuck working on a computer and pauses the screen with her remote. She sees something she never saw before. Princess Amy tells herself again, "If my father went back in time and invested in Microsoft back them, we would have never worry about money again or be stuck in an arraigned marriage with Randall." Princess Amy sees a laptop that Chuck is fixing in the Buy More and that gives her an idea. Princess turns off her tv set and goes to her laptop and sit down in her chair for a minute. She is searching for computer companies in her laptop. Princess Amy tells herself, "Come on, come on it has to be here somewhere." Princess Amy found what's she is looking for in her computer. Princess Amy taps on the screen and found what's she looking for is Abda

Electronics. Princess Amy tells herself, "Bingo, this could solve my problem." Princess Amy sees the intercom button on her phone and turns it on. Princess Amy calls Newton and tells him, "Newton, I have some news." Newton on the intercom tells Princess Amy, "What is it, you're majesty?" Princess Amy tells Newton on the intercom, "Not now, I'll tell you on the way when we meet my father in the hospital." Newton tells Princess Amy, "I beg your pardon?" Princess Amy tells Newton on the intercom, "In the hospital. Call Stephen and get the limo ready." Nivel tells Princess Amy, "I don't know what's going on?" Princess Amy tells Newton on the intercom, "You'll find out soon enough." Princess Amy turns off the intercom button and starts printing out information on Abda Electronics. Nivel is lying down in his hospital bed getting his rest, until he hears a door knock. Nivel tells the person behind the door, "Come in!" The door opens and it's Princess Amy and Newton. Princess Amy and Newton enters Nivel hospital room and goes over talk to him. Nivel tells Princess Amy and Newton, "Newton, Amy it's really good to see you." Princess Amy who is carrying a briefcase, hugs her father for a minute. Princess Amy tells her father, "Dad, you give me a scare their. I thought I lost you." Nivel tells Princess Amy, "I know I thought I lost you too." Princess Amy let's go of her father and Newton tells Nivel, "Hello, you're majesty it's good to see you." Nivel tells Newton, "It's good to see you too Newton. Come on give me a hug." Newton tells Nivel, "Are you sure, sir?" Nivel tells Newton, "I'm sure of it. Were two friends hugging each other, not in that way. If that's what you're thinking?" Newton tells Nivel, "No sir, I wasn't thinking that." Newton goes over to hug Nivel for a minute and let's go. Princess Amy tells her father, "So Dad, how are you feeling?" Nivel tells her daughter, "Hospital is not bad, but the worse thing where I have to come home too if I lose my oil company or Greenly Manor if I buy Alden stock back." Princess Amy tells her father, "I think I have an idea to solve our problem." Nivel tells Princess Amy, "What is it?" Princess Amy puts her briefcase on the chair and opens it. Princess Amy takes out the information of Abda Electronics that she printed a couple of hours ago and shows it to her father. Princess Amy gives the information of Abda Electronics to her father and he takes a look at this information for a minute. Nivel tells her daughter, "Abda Electronics, I never heard of this place." Princess Amy tells her father, "It's one of the top computer companies in Mountain View?" Newton tells Princess Amy, "Where is Mountain View?" Princess Amy tells Newton, "It's in the States in California. It's part of Santa Clara County that's near San Francisco." Newton tells Princess Amy, "Santa Clara County, that's Silicon Valley." Nivel tells Newton, "What is Silicon Valley, Newton?" Newton tells Nivel, "It's the Computer Capital of California when you enter San Francisco." Nivel understands what Silicon Valley means, "Oh that Silicon Valley. Honey, what does Abda Electronics can help us?" Princess answers her father's question and tells him, "Simple Dad, they just locked in a huge account in British Knight Shoes. The account is worth three hundred million dollars and they are looking for investors to invest in Abda Electronics." Newton tells Princess Amy, "Still, how does it help us get us out of this merger agreement with Lord Alden." Princess Amy tells Newton and her father, "They are looking for investors, with this big account with British Knight Shoes the stocks will hit the roof and make them a fortune whoever invest. So I thought if we invest in one hundred million dollars with that company, once B.K. shoes close the deal with Abda. The stock will rise and we can make a fortune enough to buy our stock back to Lord Alden and make extra money on the deal." Nivel tells her daughter, "That doesn't sound so bad, what about our oil company and our workers. Even if we invest in Abda Electronics and buy the stock back." Princess Amy tells her father, "I already figure that out, simple I read Abda Electronics is looking for software building and shipping companies being build in Europe, since were going to invest in the company. I already emailed the chairman of the board about who we are and I told them about our oil company. He's willing to put a new factory in Granwich and gives a thousand workers to transfer from the oil rig to the computer plant." Nivel tells Princess Amy, "That doesn't sound so bad, are you sure it's going to work Amy?" Princess Amy tells her father, "Trust me, it's going to work. With this investment, we can buy back our stock and double the money our net worth. Save a lot of jobs for our workers that need it." Newton tells Princess Amy, "You're majesty when are they going to close this deal with British Knight Shoes and look for investors?" Princess Amy tells Newton, "Friday night at seven at the Ritz in San Francisco." Nivel tells Princess Amy, "That's like four days ahead. I don't think I can get out of this hospital for four days and make that deal." Princess Amy tells her father, "You can't, but I can. I go in your place and make that deal." Nivel tells Princess Amy, "Are you sure you want to do this honey? Their are a thousand people depending on us for those jobs if we make that investment." Princess Amy tells her father, "I can Dad, I know how much those people who work for you depend on you. I won't let you down. I just need your signature on the check and we can make the deal Abda Electronics." Nivel tells Newton, "Newton start making the arrangements and you know where you want to stay Amy?" Princess Amy tells her father, "I know where I want to stay, but I won't stay in a hotel." Newton tells Princess Amy, "Why not, you're majesty." Princess Amy tells Newton, "Too many distractions, I need some alone time to think." Nivel tells Newton, "Newton you will go with her and help her make this deal." Newton tells Nivel, "You're majesty, are you sure about this?" Nivel tells Newton, "I don't want her go to the city alone, she'll have plenty of freedom to walk about. But I don't want her to be alone. I need somebody to watch her back. Since I read, you were in the special forces in the British Army?" Newton tells Nivel, "I was a war hero and awarded the medal of honor by the Queen herself." Nivel tells Newton, "Then it's settled, Newton start making the arrangements tomorrow." Newton is a little reluctant at first, but he doesn't have a choice. Princess Amy tells Newton, "Don't worry Newton, you're going to love Mountain View and San Francisco." Newton tells Princes Amy, "I hope I can stay in one piece their. Come on, you're majesty let's go home and I'll make the arrangements." Princes Amy tells Newton, "Sure thing, Newton." Princess Amy kisses Newton on the cheek and exits her father's room. Newton tells himself, "I know the Princess is ready go to Silicon Valley. I wondered if Silicon Valley is ready for her." The limousine enters London Runway and sees the private jet with a red carpet waiting for Princess Amy and Newton. Stephen exits the limo and opens the back door for Princess Amy and Newton. Princess Amy and Stephen exit the limo and sees their private jet. Princess Amy is a little thrilled about going to America. Stephen opens the trunk and get the luggage out for the Princess and Newton. Stephen grabs their luggage and tells Princess Amy, "Well you're majesty good luck out their." Princess Amy tells Stephen, "I know, I'm going to need it. Bye Stephen." Stephen puts their luggage down and hugs Princess Amy for a minute. Stephen tells Princess Amy, "Bye you're heinous. Don't worry Saturday will come soon for your return." Princess Amy tells Stephen, "I know!" Stephen let's goes of the Princess and hugs Newton for a minute. Princess sees her luggage and grab it and take it onto the plane herself. Stephen let's goes of Newton for a minute and tells him, "Good luck sir!" Newton tells Stephen, "I'm going to need it." Newton grabs his luggage and they both goes inside their private jet and since they like they can do things for themselves. The Private jets flies off the runway and head to the States. Inside the private jet where Princess Amy and Newton are sitting down in their chairs and discuss what they're going to do when they get their. The female flight attendant goes over to Newton and Princess and ask them what they want to drink. The female flight attendant talks to them, "Excuse me, you're majesty is their anything you like to drink?" Princess Amy tells the Flight Attendant, "I'll take a diet Pepsi with a can and some pretzels." The female flight attendant tells Newton, "What about you sir?" Newton tells the flight attendant, "Pretzel and a bud light." The female flight attendant tells them, "Okay, coming right up." The female flight attendant head to the kitchen and get their drinks. While Newton and Princess Amy are drinking their Diet Pepsi and his Miller Lite and pretzels, they're are discussing about this deal with British Knight Shoes. Newton tells Princess Amy, "You're majesty when is your appointment of the Chairman of the board." Princess Amy tells Newton, "Tuesday morning at ten." Newton tells Princess Amy, "Are you going to worry about Lord Alden if he knows what were up to?" Princess Amy tells Newton, "Lord Alden, what is that have to do with anything what's going on?" Newton tells Princess Amy, "If he knew about our deal with Abda Electronics, he'll do whatever it takes to block that investment deal." Princess Amy tells Newton, "I don't think we have anything to worry about Newton, he doesn't know were here." Newton tells Princess Amy, "Will have to be careful, he might have spies everything trying to stop us." Princess Amy tells Newton, "We have nothing to worry about, I hardly doubt he has any spies watching us. Besides this week will be smooth sailing." Newton tells Princess Amy, "If you say so, you're majesty." The female flight attendant looks at Princess Amy and Newton talking and goes back to the kitchen and sees her laptop for a minute. The female flight attendant starts typing her email to an anonymous source. The female flight attendant typing on the computer says, the fish is taking the bait. You want me to keep an eye on them more." The Anonymous person reads the email and starts typing the email and says, excellent and don't worry you did your job and leave everything up to me. The Anonymous person clicked on email and starts laugh and sees it's Lord Alden who was spying on Princess Amy and Newton on the plane. Lord Alden turns on the intercom button and calls her secretary. Lord Alden tells her secretary on the intercom, Flora book me a flight to Mount View California. I got a little business to do up their in a week." Flora on the intercom tells Lord Alden, "Yes, Lord Alden." Lord Alden turns off his intercom button for a minute. Lord Alden tells himself, "Wait until they get a load of me." Lord Alden starts laughing for a minute. The Private Jet lands on Moffett Federal Airfield and Princess Amy and Newton exits their plane and carrying their suitcases. Their limousine just arrived on time and they head to Mount View, California. The limousine takes a tour around Mount View and the window opens and it's Princess Amy. Princess Amy sees the city of Mount View and it's really breath taking. Princess Amy sees the view for a minute and closes the limo. Inside the limo Newton and Princess Amy are talking about where are they going to stay. Newton tells Princess Amy, "You're majesty ask me again, where is this place were staying at and how come we can't stay in a hotel?" Princess Amy tells Newton, "Like I said, Newton. I need to concentrate on this deal for a minute. I don't need a little distractions. Besides the place that I rented out for a week is almost their." Newton tells Princess Amy, "So, how did you find this place anyway?" Princess Amy tells Newton, "I found this place online." Newton tells Princess Amy, "How do you know this place isn't a dump?" Princess Amy tells Newton, "Trust me, Newton you're going to love this place." Newton tells Princess Amy, "That's what I was of afraid of." Princess Amy see the house after the limo stops for a minute. Princess Amy tells Newton, "Were here!" The house that Princess Amy rented out is a two story house and it's really beautiful. The man who owns the house is an African American guy who is in his late twenties and nerdy sees the limousine and goes over talk to the people who is renting the house this week. Princess Amy and Newton exits the limousine and sees the house for a minute. Princess Amy looks at Aawed when she saw this house and it's really beautiful. Newton tells Princess Amy, "I gotta say, you're majesty. You have great taste finding living arrangements." Princess Amy tells Newton, "I appreciate that Newton." Newton looks at the owner for a minute and tells Princess Amy, "You're majesty who is that guy." Princess

Amy tells Newton, "That must be the owner of the house, he is the one that's letting us stay in his place." The owner of the house goes over talk to Princess Amy and Newton. The Owner of the house tells them, "Hi, you guys are the ones renting my house for a week." Princess Amy tells The Owner of the house, "Yes, we are. I'm Prince---?" Princess Amy wanted to tell them who we are, they need to keep a low profile. Princess Amy continues telling the Owner of the house, "I'm Amy Greenly and this is my uncle Newton Williams." The Owner of the house shakes Princess Amy hand and kisses it. The Owner of the house has a little attraction on Princess Amy since she is beautiful and let's go. The Owner of the house shakes Newton's hand for a minute. The Owner of the house tells them, "It's a pleasure to meet you guys." Newton tells The Owner of the house, "It's a pleasure to meet you too." The Owner of the house introduce himself and tells them, "Let me introduce myself, I'm Jaleel Brown, I'm the owner of this house. I owned this baby for two years ago. I can say, it's really good you that guys answered my ad house swapping website before I go on vacation." Princess Amy tells Jaleel, "Where are you planning on going?" Jaleel tells Princess Amy, "Actually, I'm not going anywhere. You see my vacation was cancelled today, because of the book fair." Newton tells Jaleel, "What book fair?" Jaleel tells Newton, "In Mountain View Public Library, I'm a librarian their." Newton tells Jaleel, "You can afford a house like this, in a library salary." Jaleel tells Newton, "The pay is great and I inherited this house from my Uncle estate in my freshman year in college in Stanford." Princess Amy tells Jaleel, "Since, you're not going on vacation I guess we can go somewhere else to stay." Jaleel tells Princess Amy, "Hey, whoa whoa guys. Since you guys are here. You guys can stay here for the week as my guest." Newton tells Jaleel, "We don't impose." Jaleel tells Newton, "Hey it's okay, I'm a nice guy and judging from the accent. I think you guys traveled a thousand miles to stay here and not go back for nothing." Princess Amy tells Jaleel, "Thanks Jaleel, we appreciate that." Jaleel tells Princess Amy, "That's a beautiful accent their, is it Irish." Princess Amy tells Jaleel, "Actually, it's British. Were from London." Jaleel is a little shocked for a minute and tells Princess Amy, "London, like in England home of James Bond and Harry Potter movies and Queen Elizabeth II?" Newton tells Jaleel, "That's the one." Jaleel tells them, "Can I take your bags, my lady" Princess Amy tells Jaleel, "It's okay, we got it." Jaleel tells them, "I'll show you guys your room and I'll give you the tour." Princess Amy tells Jaleel, "Okay, lead the way Jaleel." Jaleel goes inside the house, Newton tips the limo driver and Princess Amy and Newton grab their luggage and goes inside the house. The door opens, inside Jaleel's house where Jaleel, Newton and Princess Amy enter inside the house and Jaleel tells them, "First you guys can leave your luggage here and you guys come back to it in a minute. Right after I give you guys the tour." Newton tells Jaleel, "I don't have for any tour right now, maybe tomorrow. I'm kind of tired right now, I flew in a couple of time zones so I'm tired." Jaleel tells Newton, "Okay, I'll show you to your room right now. Miss Greenly, if you are not busy right now. I can give you the tour of the house right now?" Princess Amy tells Jaleel, "No, I'm not busy. You can give me and Jaleel call me Amy." Jaleel tells Princess Amy, "Okay Amy. Follow me Newton, you're room is upstairs." Newton grabs his luggage and head upstairs to Newton's room. Princess Amy looks at the house for a minute, "Wow, this is some house, I wondered if it has a swimming pool." Jaleel already show Princess Amy the swimming pool, the kitchen, living room with a huge flat screen tv and a computer room where Jaleel usually goes. Jaleel and Princess Amy head back to the living room. Jaleel tells Princess Amy, "That's it for the tour." Princess Amy tells Jaleel, "You have an amazing house Jaleel., so what did your Uncle do in the business afford a house like this." Jaleel tells Princess Amy, "Let's say he made a couple of good investments and that's how I get to inherit this place?" Princess Amy tells Jaleel, "He invested in Intel back in 1981 and Abda Electronics." Princess Amy tells Jaleel, "Abda Electronics I read about them, I heard it's a billion dollar and they're about to close a deal with British Knight Shoes for a close to three hundred million dollars." Jaleel tells Princess Amy, "Yeah, I read about that. I heard looking for investors to invest in their stock market. Whoever invest in their stock, it's going to hit the roof after they close the deal." Princess Amy tells Jaleel, "That's why I'm here." Jaleel tells Princess Amy, "I beg your pardon?" Princess Amy tells Jaleel, "I'll explain later." Jaleel tells Princess Amy, "If that's everything, you can grab your luggage. I'll show you to your room and then I have to go." Princess Amy tells Jaleel, "Where are you going?" Jaleel tells Princess Amy, "I have go back to the library and get back to work. My boss let me have an hour off. Too show you guys my house where you guys are staying and I have to head back right now." Princess Amy tells Jaleel, "I hope I didn't get you in trouble with your boss?" Jaleel tells Princess Amy, "It's okay, he's a nice guy and understanding. He wouldn't care if I'm little bit or a lot late. As long as I do my part in the library." Princess Amy tells Jaleel, "If it's okay with you, I like to see you where you work. I always wanted to see what an American library looks like." Jaleel tells Princess Amy, "You never seen an American library before?" Princess Amy tells Jaleel, "It's my first trip to the states." Jaleel is a little bit attracted to her, but the way he looks at her and I think he would love to be her tour guide. Jaleel tells Princess Amy, "Okay, first let me show you to your room and I'll show where I work. Follow me!" Jaleel shows Princess Amy to her, but first she grabs her suitcase and head to her room. Jaleel drives his 2012 Chevy Trailblazer to the library with Princess Amy in the front seat. Inside the 2012 Chevy Trailblazer where Jaleel is driving his car and talking to Princess Amy in the front seat of his car. Princess Amy tells Jaleel, "This is my first time sitting in the front seat." Jaleel tells Amy, "You never sit in the front seat before?" Princess Amy tells Jaleel, "I always ride in limos or SUV VANS in the back seat. "Jaleel tells Amy, "Ride in the back seat, you are one weird girl, you sound like some rich chick." Princess Amy tells Jaleel, "I am a rich chick?" Jaleel was totally shocked and tells Princess Amy, "Wow, I can't believe it. You don't look like rich chick or act like one." Princess Amy tells Jaleel, "What do you mean?" Jaleel tells Princess Amy, "Rich girls are snobby, selfish and mean. Like Paris Hilton type who only care about dating hot guys, wear fashionable clothes and be seen trendy night clubs." Princess Amy tells Jaleel, "Trust me, I'm no Paris Hilton. I hate everything she stands for. Besides I'm like Ivanka Trump, she and I both work hard for our money like I did." Jaleel tells Princess Amy, "That explains a lot about you. Were almost their, you should meet my boss. Not only he is the head librarian of Mountain View Public Library, he is my best friend." Princess Amy tells Jaleel, "Any friend of yours is a friend of mine." A lot of people coming and going in the Mountain View Public Library. Inside the library where the head librarian is reading to the kids. This head librarian is a fat nerdy guy who wears glasses and wears jeans and a t-shirt and a leather jacket. This head librarian is in the children reading room reading to the little kids. The head librarian is reading a batman book to the children and tells the kids, "They say Batman was surrounded by the joker venom, he thought this was the end of them and sees the Joker laughing his head on top of the second floor where the door goes to the second floor. But Batman has his own trick inside his own sleeve, when he had an automatic gas mask in back of his cowl and cover his mouth to protect him from the Joker Venom. Batman chases the Joker the second floor that heads to the roof with his grappling hook." While the head librarian is still reading the book to the kids, Princess Amy and Jaleel enter the children reading room. Both of them see the head librarian reading to the kids and Princess Amy looks at the head librarian and he's not exactly what she is expecting. Jaleel tells Princess Amy by whispering, "That's him right over their reading to the kids." Princess Amy tells Jaleel by whispering, "Why are we whispering?" Jaleel points out to the kids for a minute and Princess Amy understands. Princess Amy tells Jaleel by whispering, "I hope New--" Princess Amy looks at Jaleel and forgets she is not supposed to tell him who Newton is. Princess Amy tells Jaleel by whispering, "Uncle Newton, that I'm fine. I don't want to worry him all day." Jaleel whispers and tells Princess Amy, "Don't worry, he's a sleep all day. Plus I left him a note in his bedroom, before we left and tell them where we are. In case he ever wakes up." Princess Amy tells Jaleel by whispering, "Thanks, who is this head librarian guy anyway?" Jaleel tells Princess Amy by whispering, "That's him reading to the kids in the kids reading room right here. His name is Robert Champberg, but we call him Robbie." Princess Amy tells Jaleel by whispering, "How long have you known him?" Jaleel tells Princess Amy, "I worked and known him for three years. We been best friends ever since." Robbie finishes reading the Batman book to the kids and tells the kids, "The Batman catches the Joker and Commissioner Gordon commended Batman for catching Gotham Most Wanted Criminal, the end!" The kids start applauding and all of them get up from their floor and their seats. Robbie starts greeting the children and a little boy tells Robbie, "That was an excellent story Robbie, when do you think the new Batman book will be done?" Robbie tells the little boy, "It won't be out until next week. Be here in story time next week Roy and you'll get a front seat when it's out." Roy tells Robbie, "Okay, I can't hardly wait to read it." The kids exits the reading room and Jaleel and Princess Amy has a chance speak to Robbie. Jaleel tells Princess Amy, "Okay, now is a good time for me to introduce my friend." Princess Amy tells Jaleel, "Are you sure, I don't want to disturb that guy." Jaleel tells Princess Amy, "Are you shy around him and don't tell me, you have a crush on him. Robbie is not exactly the kind of guy girls usually date." Princess Amy looks at Robbie for a minute and tells Jaleel, "No, of course not. He's not exactly my type." Jaleel tells Princess Amy, "Okay then, here we go." Jaleel and Princess Amy goes over talk to Robbie. Jaleel tells Robbie, "Hey Robbie!" Robbie hugs Jaleel for a minute and let's go. Robbie tells Jaleel, "Hey Jaleel, how are you doing buddy." Jaleel tells Robbie, "I'm good. How's that book fair going?" Robbie tells Jaleel, "Were about to stock up the displays in a hour. We got some time in our hands." Jaleel tells Robbie, "That's good!" Robbie tells Jaleel, "Look, I'm really sorry you had to cancel your vacation. I would've gone some help with my other librarians, you didn't have to stay and help me." Jaleel tells Robbie, "No, it's okay man. I wanted to help you. I wouldn't leave my friend with all the work." Robbie tells Jaleel, "I appreciate that." Robbie looks at Princess Amy for a minute and has a crush on her. Since she is really beautiful and lovely. Robbie tells Jaleel, "So, who is the girl. Don't tell me you and Louise broke up and she is your new girlfri...?." Jaleel interrupts Robbie for a minute and tells him, "No, of course not. You know me and Louise are still together and no I'm not cheating on her." Robbie tells Jaleel, "That's not what I was thinking." Jaleel tells Robbie, "You know she's in Paris for a week for her sister's wedding." Robbie tells Jaleel, "So who is she?" Jaleel tells Robbie, "That's the girl who is staying in my house for a week. You remember that house swapping ad that I sent online." Robbie tells Jaleel, "Yeah, I remember that." Jaleel tells Robbie, "She answered my ad when I was supposed go to Louise sister wedding anniversary in Paris this week." Robbie tells Jaleel, "But you chose to stay here, because of the book fair." Jaleel tells Robbie, "Yeah, when I found out their from England, they traveled a thousand miles to stay in my house for a week and I couldn't send them away since they're already here." Robbie tells Jaleel, "Wow, that was nice of you." Robbie looks at Princess Amy for a minute and is about to drool for a minute. Robbie tells Jaleel, "So who is she anyway?" Jaleel tells Robbie, "Her name is Amy Greenly, she's from London England and she is in town in business." Robbie tells Jaleel, "What makes you think she is in town in business, not on vacation." Jaleel tells Robbie, "I saw her briefcase and she and her Uncle Newton came to my house in a limousine." Robbie tells Jaleel, "Her Uncle Newton?" Jaleel tells Robbie, "Yeah, that who is she's with and I think he might be her financial advisor, they're were about invest in nearly a hundred million dollars for Abda Electronics tomorrow afternoon." Robbie tells Jaleel, "I heard about that company they just landed a big account for British Knight Shoes. I heard they're looking for investors to invest in their stock this week." Jaleel tells Robbie, "The British Knight Shoes account is worth about 300 million dollars, once they close that deal this week. The stock will hit the roof and the people who invest in Abda Electronics will make a fortune." Robbie tells Jaleel, "This girl is about to invest in one hundred million dollars in that company. I think it's a bad idea, since they're rival company might have a corporate spy trying to block that deal." Jaleel tells Robbie, "I know Abda called us to find this corporate spy. We got one week to find this spy and this rival company before they close this deal with British Knight Shoes. Trust me if they lose this deal by this unidentified rival company. The company might go bankrupt, since they're rival company is been stealing deals and trade secrets from Abda for a year." Jaleel tells Robbie, "I just hope Amy Greenly isn't a corporate spy for this rival company, trying to throw us off the track, when were trying to find the rival company." Robbie tells Jaleel, "I know she is rich, she and her Uncle came by limousine and I think that the rival company is footing the bill to spy on us." Robbie tells Jaleel, "I hardly doubt it, I think she might be a investor and I think she got that money by inheritance by a dead a relative and she is trying to invest in Abda Electronics. We can't let her invest in that company, since they're is a corporate spy out their." Jaleel tells Robbie, "Like you said, this corporate spy can block their deal in a minute and people who invest in a lot of money." Robbie tells Jaleel, "We better warn her not to invest anything." Jaleel tells Robbie, "You think we should tell her who we are?" Jaleel tells Robbie and tells him, "I think not." Robbie is thinking for a minute and tells Jaleel, "Actually, I think we can trust her. We can tell her." Jaleel tells Robbie, "I don't know, having her to help us is kind of dangerous." Robbie tells Jaleel, "I know, but we won't let her in the action. She'll just help us on research and look for information." Jaleel tells Robbie, "We can also make her an honorary member of our team." Robbie tells Jaleel, "You got that right, let's go talk to her." Jaleel tells Robbie, "Okay?" Jaleel and Robbie goes over talk to Princess Amy, Jaleel tells Princess Amy Greenly, "Hi Amy." Jaleel tells Princess Amy, "Hey Jaleel!" Jaleel tells Princess Amy,

"Amy this is my boss and my best friend, Robbie Champberg." Robbie grabs Princess Amy hand and kisses it and tells Princess Amy, "I'm the head librarian of this library." Princess Amy tells Robbie, "It's a pleasure to meet you, Robbie. Jaleel told me a lot about you." Robbie tells Princess Amy, "I hope good things." Princess Amy tells Robbie, "Nah just the unusual like you're a potential bed wetter and you sleep with a stuff bunny." Robbie laughs for a minute and tells Princess Amy, Funny, cute but funny." Robbie whispers to Jaleel, "You promise not to tell anyone about that." Jaleel whispers to Robbie, "I didn't, she's joking around I think." Princess Amy looks at Robbie for a minute and knows she has a crush on him. Trust me, Robbie isn't the type of guy that girls like Princess Amy date. Robbie tells Princes Amy, "Listen Miss Greenly--" Princess Amy interrupts Robbie for a minute and tells him, "You can call me Amy if you want." Robbie tells Princess Amy, "Okay Amy, listen their is something me and Jaleel want to talk to you about." Princess Amy, "Really what is it?" Robbie tells Princess Amy, "Not here, but I'll know a place we can talk and trust me it's really important that me and Jaleel talk to you about that's life and death." Princess Amy tells Robbie, "Whatever it is, it doesn't sound so good." Robbie tells Princess Amy, "Follow us." Princess Amy follows Jaleel and Robbie into the elevator, so they can take her to their secret place. So they can tell her about Abda Electronics. Princess Amy, Jaleel and Robbie head to the elevator and Robbie pushes the elevator button and the elevator door opens. They both goes inside the elevator and pushes the third floor. Princess Amy tells Robbie, "The third floor, what's on the third floor?" Robbie tells Princess Amy, "You'll see!" While the elevator goes up to the third floor, Priness Amy is thinking about her father and looking at these guy who are librarians. Princess Amy could she really trust these guys with her life. Their was something about these guys that she doesn't know and she is about to find out, when she heads to the third floor. The elevator rang and it's up to the third floor. Princess tells them, "So what's on the third floor here?" Jaleel tells Princess Amy, "You're about to find out right now." The elevator door opens and Princess Amy, Robbie and Jaleel exit the elevator and head to the third floor. Their in the main entrance and the door is locked that opens to the main room. Robbie takes out his key from his left pants pocket and opens the door. Robbie tells Princess Amy, "Come on in." Robbie, Princess Amy and Jaleel enter the main room and sees computers, a meeting room and shooting gallery for target practice, training room and it also has a candy and a soda machine. Princess Amy looks at this place and is kind of totally awed for a minute. Robbie tells Princess Amy, "Well Amy, welcome to the FBI secret room. We call this place the Secret Room." Princess Amy tells Robbie, "Why is it called the Secret Room." Jaleel interrupts Robbie and tells Princess Amy why is called the secret room, "A place that is top secret nobody ever seen or hear about this place." Robbie tells Princess Amy, "This is our main headquarters for the FBI, we were here for a month from Washington D.C. to track down a drug kingpin whose here to make a heroine deal with some corrupt British Lord." Princess Amy tells them, "You guys are FBI agents, no way." Robbie and Jaleel takes out their FBI Badges from their left pants pocket and shows it to Princess Amy. Princess Amy tells them, "Nice badges, what kind of toy store did you get those badges from?" Robbie tells Princess Amy, "Can a toy store buy you this." Robbie takes out a Beretta M9 gun out of back of his pants and shows it to Princess Amy. Robbie tells Princess Amy, "I dare you to touch, unless you want to shoot your own foot off." Princess Amy looks at Robbie's gun and feel like he's telling the truth. Princess Amy tells Robbie, "I believe you." Robbie and Jaleet put their badges back in their pockets. Robbie puts his gun back in back of his pants. Princess Amy tells them, "So, you guys are FBI agents and this librarian job is a cover." Jaleel tells Princess Amy, "You betcha, since you know who we are, maybe you can tell us who are you?" Princess Amy tells Jaleel, "What are you talking about?" Robbie tells Princess Amy, "The real reason why we told you our secret, Jaleel told me about your investment deal with Abda Electronics and judging from the foreign accent, the limo you came from and the guy that was with you isn't your uncle." Jaleel tells Princess Amy, "Which I told Robbie about." Robbie tells Princess Amy, "I think you're not some rich chick whose here on business, I don't think you didn't come all the way to England just for a business deal. So, who are you anyway?" Princess Amy tells them, "You guys trust me about your secret and this place. I'll tell you, not here. But if you have a computer, I'll print out my file and tell you who I am." Robbie tells Princess Amy, "Well Amy, since were going to read your file. You can read our file too, once we printed it out. I think you can trust us. Because were the good guys and were on the same side." Princess Amy tells them, "Okay then, let's print out our files." Jaleel tells Princess Amy, "Just want you to know that Robbie really likes you, when he first saw you. I would date you myself but I have a girlfriend" Princess Amy smiles for a minute and tells Robbie, "What?" Robbie smacks Jaleel in the arm and tells him, "Hey that was a supposed to be a secret." Jaleel is a little bit embarrassed and tells him, "Sorry Robbie, I thought we were all sharing secrets. Forget about the last thing I said." Princess Amy tells Jaleel, "What last thing, Jaleel" Jaleel tells Princess Amy, "Never mind, let's go to the computer room and print out our files." Robbie and Jaleel head to the computer, print out their files and tells them who they are. Princess Amy is about to follow him, but sees Robbie for a minute and whispers to herself, "I really like him a lot too. I wish I could tell Robbie that." Princess Amy goes over to the computer room and print out her file and tell them who they are? Lord Alden and two of his men exiting the San Francisco Airport. Lord Alden Assistant tells Lord Alden, "Excuse me, my lord. Why are we in San Francisco, shouldn't we be in Mountain View California right now." Lord Alden Assistant 2 tells Lord Alden, "Even if we leave now, it's thirty-seven miles from here. So, why are we stopping in San Francisco?" Lord Alden tells his Assistant 2, "I'll tell you why, Alberto. Were going to Fisherman Wharf today. We have go to the Harbor and make sure everything goes great on our deal. We have a huge important deal on Saturday night and we got to make sure everything is ready." Lord Alden Assistant 1 tells Lord Alden, "What deal is that, Lord Alden?" Lord Alden tells Assistant 1, "Rutherford, give me that travel book for a minute?" Rutherford tells Lord Alden, "Sure my lord, you want to see what restaurants we want to eat here." Lord Alden tells Rutherford, "Something like that." Rutherford gives the travel book to Lord Alden smacks Rutherford in the head five times and tells him, "It's an important deal. Were shipping a first rate package of heroine to a huge supplier who is willing to pay top dollar for it. I been stealing the Duke's oil from their wells for nearly a year. I used some of the money to buy a heroine lab here in fisherman wharf to make a huge profit from the company whose willing to pay a lot of money for this baby. I've been waiting for a year to get this heroine deal ready and we don't have time make mistakes. If we mess this up, not only am I going to lose this deal. I can lose my life with some angry clients whose going to make this heroine deal with me on Saturday night." Rutherford tells Lord Alden, "Sir, who is they company were going to make a deal with?" Lord Alden tells Rutherford, "The same company, that my love of my life is purchasing. She thinks this company, will help save her father's company if she makes a huge investment in the first place." Alberto tells Lord Alden, "How are you going to stop Princess Amy from making that investment from this company were dealing with?" Lord Alden tells Alberto, I have a man in the inside from the company whose going to help me block that deal." Alberto tells Lord Alden, "My lord what about Mountain View California, we are still going their pretty soon for business isn't that what you said?" Lord Alden tells Alberto, "Were not, because our heroine deal is San Francisco and our clients have a company in Mountain View California and they live their. Were doing our business deal with them in Fisherman Wharf on Saturday night." Albert tells Lord Alden, "That makes sense Lord Alden." Lord Alden tells Alberto, "You know what else makes sense Alberto?" Alberto tells Lord Alden, "What's that my lord?" Lord Alden tells Alberto, "This." Lord Alden smacks Alberto in the head really hard and punches him in the stomach. Alberto fells the huge effect on being punched in the stomach. Lord Alden tells Alberto, "Come on were going to fisherman wharf right now" Alberto tells Lord Alden, "Yes sir." Lord Alden, Alberto and Rutherford head to the limo and the limo driver takes them to Fisherman Wharf. Back in Mountain View Public Library on the third floor. Robbie, Jaleel and Princess Amy are reading their files about who they are and I think they're about to be finished. Robbie tells Princess Amy, "So, it's true you really are a princess." Princess Amy tells Robbie, "Yeah Robbie, it's true. My father is a duke and he's 20th line of the throne of England." Jaleel tells Princess Amy, "You also forget he is the Queen's cousin." Robbie tells Princess Amy, "So, what's the queen like, you're majesty." Princess Amy tells them, "She is a nice person and guys, I'm a princess, doesn't mean you have to bow to me or call me you're heinous. I'm just like everybody else. So, just treat me like anyone else." Jaleel tells Princess Amy, "It's hard to do that, since you're a princess and were federal agents. Since you have our protection." Princess Amy tells Jaleel, "Look Jaleel, I can take care of myself." Jaleel tells Princess Amy, "We know that and were just testing you." Robbie tells Princess Amy, "Instead of you're heinous, what should we call you. Because we never actually came close to royalty. We hardly doubt we ever met the President, more than royalty." Princess Amy tells Robbie, "Well Robbie, just call me

Amy." Robbie tells Princess Amy, "Okay Amy." Princess Amy tells them, "I read your file, you guys went to Caltech, got degrees in Computer Engineering and join the army after graduation and became green berets and awarded the bronze star for rescuing ten POW's in Iraq prison camp and discharged as rank of First Lieutenant. After the army, you got recruited to join the FBI, because one of the POW you saved, was the FBI director nephew. He's the one that got you into the FBI academy and the rest is history." Jaleel tells Princess Amy, "You got that right." Princess Amy tells them, "This is an outstanding resume, you guys were with the FBI for a year, you busted twenty drug labs and have 30 arrest on drug dealing gangs. You guys were also awarded FBI medal of honor and FBI bronze star." Robbie tells Princess Amy, "You also forgot recognition from the FBI director too." Princess Amy tells them, "You guys been here for a month on a drug deal?" Robbie tells Princess Amy, "We figure out from our source, that their was a British Lord who owns an oil company here in San Francisco has a heroine lab somewhere around in Fisherman Wharf and is planning a drug deal pretty soon." Jaleel tells Princess Amy, "That this British lord guy is selling the drugs here to a company in Mountain View. We haven't figured out which company is it. Until you came in and gave us a huge tip which company this British lord is selling his heroine too." Princess Amy tells them, "Let me guess Abda Electronics." Robbie tells Princess Amy, "Exactly." Princess Amy tells Robbie, Are you saying a British Lord might be involved in this drug deal?" Robbie tells Princess Amy, "Yeah, but we don't know who he is or when or where he is going to make the deal?" Princess Amy tells Robbie, "So Robbie, why is it taking you guys a month to bust this British lord?" Jaleel tells Princess Amy, "I can answer that question, I had a tip from my source that he might make this drug deal in a month. So, me and Robbie decided to take jobs as librarians and rented out a house for a month and look for this drug dealer for a month. We haven't found anything and SAC is pulling us out of this case for a week if we don't find this guy or this drug bust. So, I stayed on undercover for nearly a month to find him and I haven't found anything." Robbie tells Princess Amy, "So, I came in two weeks and start helping him out. We were about to pull ourselves out of this case. Until you showed up and maybe you could help us find anything." Princess Amy tells them, "Maybe I do have something, if I might be the same guy who is putting my father's oil company out of business and trying to force me into marriage to sign the merger agreement." Robbie tells Princess Amy, "If you say no?" Princess Amy tells Robbie, "My father will pay a 800 million dollar dowry if I back off this marriage and that's how much would it cost to buy the stock back. If my father bought the stock back, my father company would go in debt and we have no choice to sell the company since my oil wells are dried." Jaleel tells Princess Amy, "That's not good. If your father's oil wells are dried up, you guys would end up broke and maybe out on the street." Robbie tells Princess Amy, "Or even worse, maybe ending up giving up your crown." Princess Amy tells them, "Exactly, that's why it's not going to happen and maybe Abda Electronics may bail my family out." Robbie tells Princess Amy, "That's what we have to warn you about. Who is this British Lord whose force you into marriage and do I have to kick his face in three seconds." Jaleel smacks Robbie in the arm and tells him, "Robbie will you knock it off." Robbie tells Jaleel, "Sorry!" Princess Amy tells them, "It's Lord Randall Alden, he's the guy who is putting my father out of business." Robbie knows who that guy is and tells Princess Amy, "Amy, I think I know who he is?" Princess Amy tells Robbie, "You heard of him?" Robbie tells Princess Amy, "I've been after him for a year, I had nothing on him. At first when we found out a British lord might be involved in a drug deal. My first instinct was him, since he was in a oil business and our source gave us a tip about his description was involved in heroine dealings in San Francisco." Jaleel tells them, "So, I think we were right that Alden might be involved in this heroine dealing. Since our boss didn't believe us and we were back at square one for nearly a month." Princess Amy tells them, "Not anymore, now you guys have me." Robbie tells Princess Amy, "Listen Amy, I thought you can help us research. This stuff we do is very dangerous. We just don't want you to get killed because of us." Princess Amy tells them, "You guys can count on me, I'm a survivor. I'll be fine. I've been involved since Lord Alden stole my father's oil and I want payback for what he did. if we have enough evidence to bust him with this drug deal, we can put him away and take back all the oil he stole from us to save my father's business." Robbie tells Princess Amy, "Okay, well Princess Amy Greenly. Welcome to the Secret Room." Jaleel tells Princess Amy, "Before we start our investigation on Lord Alden, their is a release forum you have to sign. Don't ask what it is?" Princess Amy tells

Jaleel, "I wasn't planning on it, Jaleel?" Jaleel tells Princess Amy, "Were going to see how good you are?" Robbie tells Princess Amy, "If you're good enough, you can join in the action with us. If you don't you can still join us. Since you're already signed the release forums." Princess Amy tells them, "Okay, what do I do first?" Jaleel tells Princess Amy, "Were going to the training room, but first you have to change clothes. Luckily for us, we have some workout clothes for you and some with your size." Princess Amy tells them, "You have some workout clothes for me, where do I change?" Robbie tells Princess Amy, "Their is a locker room for you in the workout room." Princess Amy tells them, "So what do I do first when we go their?" Robbie tells Princess Amy, "Hand to hand combat. Come on, will take you to the changing room. Follow us?" Princess Amy, Jaleel and Robbie get up from the stairs and show her the workout and changing room. Robbie, Jaleel and Princess Amy are in the workout room teaching her hand to hand combat. Princess Amy is wearing a black tank top and tight black pants. Robbie tells Princess Amy, "I'm going to show you a few moves. I hope I don't hurt you this much." Princess Amy smiles a little and tells Robbie, "I don't think you have to worry about Robbie." Robbie punches Princess Amy, but she blocks the punch and knees him in the stomach. Princess Amy also flips him from the mat. Jaleel is carrying a fake knife and tries to stab her in back, Jaleel attacks and Princess Amy turns around and blocks the knife . Princess Amy punches Jaleel in the groin and flips him from the mat. Robbie is a little hurt, but tries to get up, but Princess Amy kicks him in the face and he falls down on the floor. Jaleel is a little soar from that attack from Princess Amy, he tries to get up from the floor and head butts from the face and flips him from the mat. Princess Amy kicks him the stomach also. Robbie gets up from the floor and tells Princess Amy, "Okay time out time out." Princess Amy stops for a minute. Robbie tells Princess Amy, "Like I said, I hope we don't hurt you that badly." Princess Amy tells Robbie, "Not at all!" Princess Amy punches him in the ribs and flips him down on the mat again." Robbie still hurting and looks at Jaleel hurting on the mat and tells him, "Remind me to call a doctor, when were down." Jaleel tells Robbie, "Ditto Pal." Princess Amy tells them, so what's next?" Robbie, Jaleel and Princess Amy head to the shooting gallery. It looks like a live action video game with a toy gun. Robbie tells Princess Amy, "Welcome to the FBI shooting gallery. Here we test every agent, how good they are with a total shot. So Amy ever used a gun before?" Princess Amy tells Robbie, "Maybe a little!" Jaleel tells Princess Amy, "Well let's see how good of a shot are you." Princess Amy grabs the toy guy and the video screen is in a harbor where she bad guys are shooting in the harbor. Princess Amy fires her toy gun, shoots the eight bad guys in three seconds. Princess Amy also used a real guy and starts target practice in the real shooting gallery. She fires her guy and five bullets hits the target and hits the bulls eye. Princess Amy fires her toy gun and shoots eight bad guys in a warehouse. Princess Amy fires her real gun, hits the bulls eye again with six bullets fired from her gun. Princess Amy fires her toy gun again, shoots six bad guys in the harbor again. She also fires her real gun again and hits the bulls eye again and eight bullets fires out of her gun. Robbie and Jaleel sees her target practice and tell each other, "She's good." Back in the meeting room where Princess Amy, Jaleel and Robbie sit down at. Princess Amy finishes signing her release forums to join them in this case. Robbie tells Princess Amy, "Wow, you're really good. Hand to hand combat, where do you learn how to fight like that." Princess Amy tells Robbie, "I'm a second degree black belt in Taekwondo and highly trained in Krav Maga when I was in Oxford?" Jaleel tells Princess Amy, "You studied martial arts in Oxford." Princess Amy tells Jaleel, "It was one of my electives I had to take if I want to graduate." Robbie tells Princess Amy, "Amy where did you learn to fire a gun like that anyway?" Princess Amy tells Robbie, "Nintendo Duck Hunt." Robbie tells Jaleel, "That explains a lot." Jaleel tells Princess Amy, "Okay maybe we can get started to see what Lord Alden is up to?" Robbie tells them, "Let me see if I get some files on him on the computer." Robbie gets up from his chair and heads to the computer room. Princess Amy sees Robbie leaving the meeting room. Jaleel took notice on Princess Amy on looking at Robbie and tells her, "So Amy, you really like the guy don't you" Princess Amy blushes for a minute and tries to deny it to Jaleel. Princess Amy tells Jaleel, "Jaleel, what are you talking about?" Jaleel tells Princess Amy, "Robbie, you sound like you have a crush on him when you first saw him." Princess Amy tries to deny this to Jaleel and tells him, "I don't have a crush on him. I think you're seeing things. Robbie isn't the guy I usually fall for." Jaleel tells Princess Amy, "You're a princess and he is fat, nerdy guy that will never grow up." Princess Amy tells Jaleel, "I don't think that's not true, I think he's adorable." Jaleel tells Princess Amy, "Whatever you say, You're Majesty." Princess Amy tells Jaleel, "Besides Robbie isn't my type anyway?" Jaleel tells Princess Amy, "Okay, besides he is no prince charming anyway. Girl like you, is looking for Prince Charming not Jack Black." Jaleel looks at Princess Amy and knows she is lying. Jaleel whispers to himself, "She's lying." Robbie heads back to the meeting room, Princess Amy looks at him and does have a crush on him. But is afraid of getting hurt if this didn't work out. Robbie tells them, "All right, I got the file. Did I miss anything?" Princess Amy blushes a little and tells Robbie, "No, not at all." Robbie sits down in his chair and shows the files to Jaleel and Princess Amy. Princess Amy reads the file on Lord Alden and tells them, "That's funny, it says here Randall was been suspected of heroine dealing by Scotland Yard for a year. but they never found anything." Jaleel tells them, "They had a search warrant from one of his warehouse to search for the drugs. But they couldn't find anything and he sued the police for a lot of money for harassment and he won." Robbie tells them, "How much did he win?" Jaleel tells Robbie, "Five point five million dollars and Scotland Yard decides to close investigation on him." Robbie tells them, "Here's an interesting fact, the warehouse that Scotland Yard investigated found no drugs, but ten barrels of oil and a pipeline where they pump it." Princess Amy tells them, "Robbie what was the address of the warehouse that Lord Alden owned?" Robbie looks at the address on the file and tells her, "515 West Chancy Street." Princess Amy snaps her fingers and got the answer. Princess Amy tells them, "That warehouse is close to my father's oil well. He said all the oil barrels from his warehouse came from his pipeline?" Robbie tells Princess Amy, "That's what it said, Amy." Princess Amy tells them, "Now I know how Randall did it?" Robbie tells Princess Amy, "Stealing oil from your father's oil well that has a pipeline and some of Lord Randall's guys use their plumbing skills to put your father's oil pipeline to go to Alden's oil well." Jaleel tells them, "So, he can pump up his oil well by stealing oil from your father and make a fortune." Princess Amy tells them, "My father said that his oil well been dried up for nearly a year. Since the oil pipeline was hi jacked by Alden's well. He has a shutoff switch from his well to turn it on or off. So he can make my oil well dry." Jaleel tells them, "Amy, why is Alden shutting off his own oil well. He can still make a fortune for pumping up your father's well." Robbie tells them,

"I don't think it's about money that Alden want. Their is something else he wants." Jaleel tells them, "Besides Amy hand in marriage." Princess Amy tells them, "Guys, please I'm trying not to relive that moment." Robbie looks at the file and tells them, "I think he found something bigger than money or his heroine dealing?" Jaleel tells Robbie, "What is that Robbie?" Robbie tells Jaleel, "Jaleel, it says here that Alden was trying to run for Prime Minister. He was a perfect candidate and qualified to win." Jaleel tells Robbie, "What happened?" Robbie tells Jaleel, "He didn't have a lot of endorsement deals and a lot of support to run. People didn't want to see him run this country. They rather have Queen Elizabeth more than Lord Alden than himself." Princess Amy remembers something and tells them, "Of course the royal family is not exactly his favorite type person. He is not exactly popular with them." Jaleel tells Princess Amy, "Why is that?" Princess Amy tells Jaleel, "They know he would turn this country into a Nazi war camp. He'll make Hitler like a wimp. That's how he lost his shot on his candidacy because the royal won't support or endorse him as Prime Minister." Jaleel tells them, "Alden might be ticked off right now. If he can't run for Prime Minister, what do you think a guy like Lord Alden would do to make head of state, if he can't run for prime minister." Robbie tells them, "The only has a bigger power than the prime minister is the royal family." Jaleel tells them, "The only way he can be part of the royal family is to marry one of them." Princess Amy tells them, "That leads to me and why he is forcing my father into bankruptcy. If I marry him to save my father's company and he will become a prince after he marries me." Robbie tells Princess Amy, "You told me yourself, that your father is Queen's cousin and he's twentieth line of the throne." Jaleel tells Princess Amy, "And you're twenty first line of the throne." Princess Amy tells them, "You got that right." Jaleel tells Princess Amy, "Well you have nothing to worry about Amy. If he marries you, I hardly doubt he will inherit the throne. It will take him forever to get to head of the line." Robbie tells them, "He may not have to. The royal family does have diplomatic immunity. But they can be humiliated by a huge scandal or could be bumped off one by one." Princess Amy tells them, "Lord Alden maybe power hungry and a total jerk, but killing the royal family is way beneath him." Jaleel tells Princess Amy, "You got a point, Amy. Killing the royal family is not exactly his style. Plus Interpol and Scotland has the best CSI team that can spot him in a heartbeat." Princess Amy tells Jaleel, "You got a point Jaleel, except he might have a CSI team or any federal investigators in his payroll. Including Interpol." Robbie tells them, "I hardy doubt he can make it look like an accident." Princess Amy tells them, "Their is always a scandal, how would he get the royal family to step down from the line of throne." Robbie tells them, "He can plant drugs anywhere that is owned by the royal family, give the tip to Scotland Yard and turn it into a royal scandal." Jaleel tells them, "Trust me, they have diplomatic immunity. But the press, will destroy their career and Parliament might have to force them to resign for shaming the country." Princess Amy tells them, "I think you guys might be onto something. He doesn't need to kill them, he just needs a smear campaign to destroy their reputation." Robbie tells them, "Planting illegal drugs into one of their places will create a scandal and force them to resign." Princess Amy tells them, "I don't think he has time to run a smear campaign on the royal family. First, I think he might concentrating on his drug deal first. Before he destroys the royal family reputation." Robbie tells them, "I think you got a point Amy. If he was in town to make a huge drug deal. It has to be a company that he's selling the drugs too." Jaleel tells them, "The only company we figure out might be involved in this heroine dealing with Alden is Abda Electronics." Princess Amy tells Robbie, "Robbie who owns Abda Electronics anyway. I never had a chance too look up who the chairman or the CEO is when I do business with them tomorrow." Robbie tells Princess Amy, "It's Carmelo Abda Jr is the Chairman and CEO of the company." Princess Amy tells Robbie, "What do you know about him?" Robbie reads Carmelo's record and tells Princess Amy, "His father built the company in 1982 with a sonic drive screen that he built for computer screens. He turned that company into a billion dollar company in two years. Carmelo Senior died of brain cancer last two years and left the company to his only son." Jaleel is also reading Carmelo's file and tells Princess Amy, "He has a degree in computer science in M.I.T. and a MBA from Harvard." Princess Amy tells them, "I know Abda Jr is about to close a huge account British Knight Shoes that his stock will hit the roof. Once he finishes the deal, that's why he's looking for investors to invest in this British Knight Shoe Account." Jaleel tells Princess Amy, "When were you supposed to meet Jr Amy?" Princess Amy tells Jaleel, "I'm supposed to meet him in ten in the morning."

Princess Amy looks at them and tells them, "You think Carmelo might be involved with Alden's drug cartel. I read about him, he doesn't look like the drug dealing type. He runs a honest corporation and he and his father run a huge philanthropy for their company." Robbie tells Princess Amy, "I know that, I know he has nothing do with this heroine business with Lord Alden. Plus, he is a nice guy. But their is somebody in his company might be involved in his heroine dealing with Alden." Princess Amy tells Robbie, "I'm supposed to meet Mr Abda tomorrow morning, maybe he can tell us who might be involved in this drug dealing and you maybe right about one thing Robbie." Robbie tells Princess Amy, "What is that, Amy?" Princess Amy tells Robbie, "I think this person is might be on Alden's payroll, I think he might block the account to put him out of business. Or has a dummy company to buy huge shares and control the voting stock to fire Abda Jr and run the business himself." Jaleel tells Princess Amy, "Even if we believe you, Amy. Could Alden's guy who is a corporate spy for Abda Electronics could by a dummy stock to take over Abda's company." Robbie tells Princess Amy, "Actually he could. I took a business course that I audited in CalTech, Alden's guy could buy a dummy stock. Since Abda Electronics is a public company and anyone could invest in controlling stake of his company. Jaleel tells them, "Amy is meeting with Mr Abda, tomorrow and maybe we can explain the whole thing to him tomorrow and tell him if anyone is suspicious to take over his company." Robbie reading the file and tells Jaleel, "Good theory Jaleel, but lame. Besides, Mr Abda won't be in the office all week. He has a business conference call in Chicago, so he will be out all week." Jaleel tells Robbie, "Robbie, whose looking after the company since Mr Abda away in a business conference all week." Robbie reads the file and couldn't read his name right and tells them name, "I don't know if I read this correctly. I think his name is Con. Connie, Constel or Contel. His last name is hard to pronounce." Princess Amy tells Robbie, "Let me look at the name on the file. Maybe I could pronounce it right." Robbie tells Princess Amy, "Here you go, Amy." Robbie gives the file about Carmelo Abda Jr to Princess Amy and starts reading the name. Princess Amy starts reading the name and tells them, "Here it is, Contel Yorkshire." Jaleel tells Princess Amy, "That's a weird name." Robbie and Jaleel are doing british accents and Robbie does an impression of a British guy and tells Jaleel, "Good day, sir. I think I like to have some tea and with crumpets with that." Jaleel also doing a British accent and tells Robbie, "How would like your tea sir, with one lump of sugar or two?" Robbie continues doing a British accent and tells Jaleel, "I'll take two please and don't forgot the scones my good man." Jaleel continues doing a British accent, "Coming right up and Jolly good sir." Princess Amy starts laughing for a minute and tells them, "Nice English impression and where do you learn it from Downton Abbey?" Jaleel tells Princess Amy, "We watch a lot of James Bond movies." Robbie does a good James Bond accent, "The name is Champberg, Robert Champberg." Princess Amy continuing laughing and tells them, "Well, you guys are good. You ever thought about doing a James Bond impression on Open Mike night in a comedy club." Robbie tells Princess Amy, "Me and Jaleel do open mike night it every night at Friday in Laugh Factory Club. Princess Amy tells them, "Laugh Factory Club where is that at?" Jaleel tells Princess Amy, "It's about a few blocks from the library." Princess Amy tells them, "Anyway back to business, I recognize Yorkshire somewhere?" Robbie tells Princess Amy, "You might know who he is?" Princess Amy tells them, "Yorkshire was Lord Alden was his campaign manager when he tried to run for the Prime Minister. Not only was he a campaign manager, he was also suspected of being a traitor for MI6 for selling trade secrets for Israeli Drug Lord who was on MI6 most wanted." Jaleel tells Princes Amy, "What kind of trade secrets are they?" Princess Amy tells Jaleel, "It had some kind of deadly plants that scientist found somewhere around Jerusalem." Jaleel tells Princess Amy, "Like heroine." Princess Amy tells Jaleel, "Something like that Jaleel and they said that plant won't just make drugs. It can also happen to make some kind of explosive." Robbie tells Princess Amy, "Of course I have a friend in MI6 and told me that plant is almost more explosive than TNT." Jaleel tells Princess Amy, "Like Dynamite." Robbie tells Jaleel, "Exactly, their were one hundred plants near Jerusalem. MI6 was going to send a team and scientist from Oxford needed to dispose the plants before it goes in the wrong hands. But all the plants were gone. Like it was stolen and nobody in MI6 could track it down. Anyone terrorist who carry that plant could start a war and invade a country with those deadly plants." Princess Amy tells them, "Whoever stole those plants might be connected to Yorkshire, I think he might been the guy who sold those secrets to Israeli drug lord." Jaleel tells Robbie, "So Robbie anything about this Israeli drug lord or we know who it is?" Robbie tells Jaleel, "The FBI doesn't have a lot of information on him or MI6. It could be anyone running heroine dealing in Israeli." Jaleel tells Princess Amy, "Amy what about Yorkshire, was he ever charged for selling trade secrets to that drug lord." Princess Amy tells Jaleel, "No, MI6 didn't have any proof that he was ever linked to selling those trade secrets to that Israeli drug lord. After that incident, he left the agency and work for Alden who was a friend of the family. They became fast friends and became his campaign manager and the rest is history." Jaleel tells them, "That explains why Lord Alden was never linked in heroine dealing or figuring who selling the drugs too. Because his friend Yorkshire, who used to work for MI6 helped him cover his tracks and give him his contact with his drug runner." Princess Amy tells them, "If Alden is running his drug business with his business partner Yorkshire. They might be selling the drugs pretty soon to the Israeli drug lord. It might be here, where he is selling it." Jaleel tells Princess Amy, "I hardly doubt he would sell his heroine in Mountain View, he needs a bigger city to sell it to. His drug dealing has to be somewhere that's dark and dank and has to be a bigger city." Robbie tells them, "Like San Francisco. I bet somewhere he has a drug lab their to. But one thing." Princess Amy tells Robbie, "What's that Robbie?" Robbie tells them, "His heroine lab and his drug deal could be anywhere in San Francisco. It could take us nearly a couple of weeks to find it." Jaleel tells them, "By that time. The drug deal will go through as planned and Alden and Yorkshire will disappear with the money and cover his tracks like last time." Princess Amy tells them, "Pretty soon my father will lose his business and me and my father will have to face bankruptcy and leave the palace pretty soon." Robbie tells them, "I wish we knew when or where they selling their heroine at?" Jaleel tells them, "Or who they're selling it too." Princess Amy tells them, "Were going have to look Interpol or FBI most wanted terrorist to find out who is he selling it. It has to be somebody Islamic terrorist team that is connected in drug dealing." Jaleel tells them, "You think Amy meeting Yorkshire for an investment is out of the question." Robbie comes up with an idea. Robbie tells them, "Wait, I want Amy to meet Yorkshire. Amy, you still kept your appointment with Yorkshire tomorrow morning?" Princess Amy tells Robbie, "I never cancelled it, I am about to when I find out, he might be suspected selling heroine to number one middle east drug runners with

Alden." Robbie tells Princess Amy, "Don't cancel it, tomorrow morning were going to meet Yorkshire and ask him about this heroine dealing with Lord Alden and when he is going to meet his clients pretty soon." Princess Amy tells Robbie, "Robbie if we ask him that, he'll probably will deny everything and will be back at square one. How come we can just arrest him and question him about his heroine dealing with Lord Alden?" Robbie tells Princess Amy, "We can't we don't have any proof that he and Alden are connected to the heroine dealing or selling to Islamic terrorist team. If we collar him and interrogate him, he's going to get his high price lawyers and sue the agency for harassment. Me and Jaleel could lose our jobs and he'll be out in a minute, when his lawyer arrive." Jaleel tells Princess Amy, "So, the only way we can do that is to piss him off." Princess Amy tells them, "That sounds better, so how are we going to pull this off?" Robbie tells Princess Amy, "Simple Yorkshire will expect you to be their. I'm going to go with you as your accountant and financial advisor. So, I'm going to be the master of disguise." Princess Amy is a little bit impressed and tells Robbie, "Pretty cool huh. I really like it when you do that." Robbie tells them, "Here's the plan! Jaleel, me and Amy will go to Abda Electronics and meet with Yorkshire and ask him about his heroine dealing with Lord Alden." Jaleel tells Robbie, "Robbie, you think Yorkshire might suspect anything or figure out were Feds." Robbie tells Jaleel, "Not right now, but soon. But will worry about that later. Jaleel, you go to the library and find any information on the Islamic terrorist team that Alden and Yorkshire is going to do business. We got one week track down Alden's drug deal, his laboratory and his Islamic clients and put these guys away. Or were sunk." Jaleel tells them, "Our jobs and Amy's father crown and his fortune are on the line in here." Princess Amy sarcastically tells Jaleel, "Thanks Jaleel, really a great motivation speech their." Jaleel tells Prncess Amy, "Thanks Amy." Robbie tells them, "We got one week to do this. Let's do it!" Princess Amy and Jaleel tells Robbie, "Let's do it. Yeah!" All three of them do a fist bump together and let go. Robbie, Jaleel and Princess Amy heads back to the first floor and Robbie tells them, "You guys want to get some lunch. We been researching this case all day." Jaleel tells Robbie, "I'm kind of hungry." Princess Amy tells them, "Me too." Robbie tells Princess Amy, "Amy, me and Jaleel always go to Mcdonald's to eat during lunch hours and after work. I don't know if you want to go with us or not. Because it's way beneath you since you are a princess?" Princess Amy tells Robbie, "Do they still have a the double cheeseburgers in the U.S.?" Robbie tells Princess Amy, "Yes." Princess Amy tells Robbie, "Let's go. I'm hungry." Robbie and Jaleel looks at Princess Amy for a minute. Robbie sees Princess Amy head to the exit and tells Jaleel, "I never seen a girl like that ever go to McDonald's and scarf a double cheeseburger." Jaleel tells Robbie, "I wonder what her secret is that made her so skinny." Robbie tells Jaleel, "Search me, I think I'm in love." Robbie and Jaleel head to the exit. Newton is sleeping in his bed, until he hears a door knock. Newton tells the person behind the door, "Come in." The door opens and it's Princess Amy. Newton sees Princess Amy and tells her, "You're Majesty, what brings you by here?" Princess Amy tells Newton, "Well Newton, I think I might have a chance to save my father's company." Newton tells Princess Amy, "I beg your pardon." Princess Amy tells Newton, "I think I might have some evidence that Randall is being stealing oil from my father's oil wells. Not only that, I think he's using my father's oil to hide heroine inside his oil barrels." Newton tells Princess Amy, "You're Majesty, are you saying Lord Alden is a drug dealer." Princess Amy tells Newton, "Not a drug dealer, a drug kingpin. I think he is planning on selling his heroine to Islamic terrorist." Newton tells Princess Amy, "You might know who this terrorist are, who Newton is selling the drugs too?" Princess Amy tells Newton, "Not yet, but I will look into it. If I can find some evidence I can put him away and get proof that he was stealing my father's oil. We can reimburse all the money that he made pumping up our oil and save my father's company." Newton tells Princess Amy, "Princess Amy, even if you have evidence to get proof that Lord Alden was stealing your father's oil and selling heroine to a terrorist drug runner. That won't be enough to put him away." Princess Amy tells Newton, "What do you mean Newton?" Newton tells Princess Amy, "You're majesty, Lord Alden has connections U.N. Delegacy and the Consulate for enough to give him Diplomatic Immunity. So he can't be arrested or prosecuted, if you have the evidence on him." Princess Amy tells Newton, "That's what I though about, if we get some proof that he's selling drugs to a terrorist drug runner. If might revoke his diplomatic immunity card and have enough evidence to put him away." Newton tells Princess Amy, "I guess you have a point there. So, you have been researching online about this." Princess Amy tells Newton, "Not exactly." Newton tells

Princess Amy, "What do you mean?" Princess Amy tells Newton, "Jaleel the guy who is letting us stay here. You know he is a librarian and he gave up his vacation to help his boss for the book fair. So, I ask him if I can show me where he works and he said yes." Newton tells Princess Amy, "You're majesty, I don't think you should go anywhere without me. It could be dangerous and you are a princess to the Duke of Granwich. The Duke would have gotten a second heart attack and you went by yourself." Princess Amy tells Newton, "Relax Newton, I'm fine. Thanks for worrying about me, I goanna be fine by myself." Newton tells Princess Amy, "Sorry about that you're heinous, I was just worry about you." Princess Amy tells Newton, "I appreciate that Newton. Anyway Jaleel showed where he worked and he introduce me to his boss." Newton tells Princess Amy, "So who is Master Jaleel boss?" Princess Amy tells Newton, "His name is Robbie Champberg, he is the head librarian of Mountain View Public Library. But that job is cover." Newton tells Princess Amy, "What do you mean the job is a cover?" Princess Amy tells Newton, "Their actually FBI agents." Newton tells Princess Amy, "FBI, like Federal Bureau Investigation in Washington. That FBI!" Princess Amy tells Newton, "Exactly!" Newton tells Princess Amy, "So how did you figure out they were federal agents?" Princess Amy tells Newton, "They told me, when they figure out that I was making a huge investment to Abda Electronics." Newton tells Princess Amy, "You're majesty why are two federal agents are interested in billion dollar electronics company." Princess Amy tells Newton, "The acting CEO is working with Lord Alden with his heroine dealing with Islamic terrorist." Newton tells Princess Amy, "Oh boy." Princess Amy tells Newton, "They showed me some files on Alden's partner. His name is Contel Yorkshire, who is looking after the business while Mr. Abda is on a business conference in Chicago all week. So Yorkshire is the acting CEO while he is away." Newton tells Princess Amy, "I heard about him, wasn't he Lord Alden campaign manager for Prime Minister?" Princess Amy tells Newton, "He was for a while before Alden didn't have enough votes to be a front runner for the Prime Minister race." Newton tells Princess Amy, "How did soem guy like Yorkshire who was Lord Alden campaign manger ended up being acting CEO of a billion dollar computer corporation." Princess Amy tells Newton, "He used to be an MI6 agent who was suspected of being a traitor for selling trade secrets for Israeli Drug Lord who was on MI6 most wanted? Newton tells Princess Amy, "Was Yorkshire ever charged for selling those trade secrets?" Princess Amy tells Newton, "No, MI6 never had any hard evidence that Yorkshire sold any trade secrets to a Israeli Drug Lord. After that he left the agency, he went to worked for Lord Alden and hired him as his campaign manager? Since he was an ex secret agent, has excellent computer hacking skills to cover his tracks and his employer. So, Scotland Yard or MI6 could track them down in drug dealings around the world." Newton tells Princess Amy, "Let me guess Lord Alden." Princess Amy tells Newton, "You got that one right Newton, he's the one who is pulling all the strings all a long." Newton tells Princess Amy, "This heroine dealing has to be the same drug runner that Yorkshire is selling the trade secrets too." Princess Amy tells Newton, "Exactly, if we can find this drug deal and catch Alden, Yorkshire selling heroine to Israeli drug cartel. We have enough evidence to put them away and save my father's oil company." Newton tells Princess Amy, "We don't know when or where Lord Alden going to have this heroine dealing, it could be anywhere?" Princess Amy tells Newton, "That's the reason, why me and Robbie are going to pay a visit to Yorkshire tomorrow." Newton tells Princess Amy, "Like I said, it could be dangerous." Princess Amy tells Newton, "Relax Newton, I'll be fine I promise." Newton tells Princess Amy, "What about Yorkshire, are you worried he might recognize you?" Princess Amy tells Newton, "Relax Newt, I am a master of disguise." Newton looks at Princess Amy and realize he is not buying it. Princess Amy tells Newton, "Plus he never met me. My cover will be in tact." Newton tells Princess Amy, "Now that is a good answer." Princess Amy tells Newton, "Don't worry me and Robbie make it in and out of his office in a few minutes." Newton tells Princess Amy, "You sound like you really like this guy," Princess Amy is blushing a little and tells Newton, "No, I don't. I swear I just like him as a friend really." Newton tells Princess Amy, "Okay, I was just checking. By the way, I think he really likes you too." Princess Amy tells Newton, "Really, did he say that." Newton tells Princess Amy, "I thought so, besides I never met him. So, how do I know. I'm going to get some sleep good night, you're majesty." Princess Amy tells Newton, "Good night Newton." Princess Amy leaves Newton's room and closes the door. Princess Amy is at the hall way and tells herself, "I really hope Robbie really likes me." Princess Amy heads to her room and go to bed. The next day started and it's morning at Jaleel's rented house. Princess Amy and Newton exits down in the kitchen wearing their pajamas. They see Newton eating some glaze donuts and coffee in the kitchen. Newton is also wearing his pajamas and sees Princess Amy and Newton comes down the kitchen. Jaleel tells them, "Morning guys." Princess Amy and Newton tells Jaleel, "Morning Jaleel." Jaleel tells Newton, "Listen Newton, me and Amy talked last night about this investment deal with Abda Electronics. I told her it was not a good idea for her to make an investment in that corporation since we found out that company might be involved some illegal operation. So, I told Amy, she and I will pay a visit to the CEO today and tell them were not going to make any investment on....? Newton interrupts Jaleel and tells them, "Master Jaleel, I know you're an FBI agent and I know everything." Jaleel tells Newton, "Let me guess Amy told you everything." Newton tells Jaleel, "Even about you being a potential bed wetter." Jaleel is a little bit confused and tells him, "What?" Newton starts laughing for a minute and tells Jaleel, "I'm only kidding." Jaleel starts laughing and tells Newton, "Funny Newton, cute but funny." Newton tells Jaleel, "You're partner Robbie Champberg, where's he staying since you guys been undercover for a month tracking down this heroine dealing with Yorkshire and Alden?" Jaleel tells Newton, "He is staying Four Corner's Hotel in the Presidential Suite." Princess Amy tells Jaleel, "Four Corner's Hotel that must cost a fortune. How does a guy with a FBI salary get to afford an expensive suite in a five star hotel like Four Corner's Hotel?" Jaleel tells Princess Amy, "He has a good deal on the room." Princess Amy looks at Jaleel and I don't think she is buying it. Jaleel tells Princess Amy, "One of the guys we stationed with in Iraq, his uncle owns the hotel. He saved his life once and owes him his life and he got to stay in his hotel for free." Princess Amy tells Jaleel, "That explains a lot." Jaleel tells them, "Well guys, I like to offer you some breakfast. I usually eat out and the only thing I have here is some Dunkin Donuts and some coffee. If it's okay with you. If you don't, I can order something from the iHOP." Princess Amy tells Jaleel, "What kind of donuts you have?" Jaleel tells Princess Amy, "I have glaze?" Princess Amy tells Jaleel, "My favorite. I really love this house." Newton tells Princess Amy, "Mine too!" Princess Amy, Jaleel and Newton sit down and eat some donuts and drink some coffee. A few minutes later Jaleel, Princess Amy and Newton are eating donuts and drinking their coffee.' Newton tells

Jaleel, "So, I guess making that investment deal with Abda Electronics is out of the question." Jaleel tells Newton, "Since Mr Abda is out of town on business, Yorkshire is running the company know. He could destroy Abda's deal with British Knight Shoes account. That account would help his company. Now, it's dangerous since Yorkshire is running his heroine business with Alden." Newton tells Jaleel, "Master Jaleel, I am worried about having the princess working on this huge case with you and Master Robbie. It is still dangerous to have a royal heir to the throne involved in a huge drug bust that could get her killed." Jaleel tells Newton, "That's what I thought first after talking to Princess Amy about this. She will help us with the case, but were going to keep her out of the action. We don't want her involved like this if this is going to get her killed." Newton tells Jaleel, "I appreciate that Sir!" Princess Amy tells them, "Guys, I can take care of myself. I can handle myself fine. First of all, Newton. I'm the twenty-first heir to the throne of England. It will take forever for me to get that crown. So is my father." Newton tells Princess Amy, "Oh, my mistake. I'm sorry about that you're heinous." Princess Amy tells Newton, "It's okay, Newton. I know you were just looking out for me." Newton tells Princess Amy, "I promise your father to keep you safe. I'm going to make sure I do that." Jaleel tells Newton, "Don't worry, Newton. The princess will be fine. I'm glad she is helping us. We couldn't find anything on our drug kingpin until now." Princess Amy tells Jaleel, "When is Robbie going to be here, we have to be at Abda Electronics nearly an hour." Jaleel tells Princess Amy, "He'll be here in a hour to pick you up." Princess Amy tells them, "Well, I better get dressed. I don't want to see me looking like this." Princess Amy gets up from his chair and goes upstairs to change. Newton tells Jaleel, "I think she has a crush on your partner Robbie. I think I never seen act like this before." Jaleel tells Newton, "What are you talking about, she must have dated a lot of guys and or a prince. I don't think she would fall for a guy like Robbie?" Newton tells Jaleel, "Princess Amy is always been busy working with her father oil business, studying really hard in college and she reads a lot of comic books and watches a lot of movies and tv. She hasn't had a lot of time for dating." Jaleel tells Newton, "Why, she looks like a supermodel. Their was like a million guys would line up to date her. How come she never had any time to date?" Newton tells Jaleel, "She is kind of shy with other guys. She never actually barely said a word to any guy ask her out. Besides she likes to date a guy, who likes her who she is not what she can offer." Jaleel tells Newton, "That's true." Newton tells Jaleel, "She always wish their was a right guy for her to date. But she never found it." Jaleel tells Newton, "Well Newton, no offense to my partner and Robbie is my best friend. Amy is a princess and looks like a supermodel. Their is no way she would date a guy like Robbie." Newton tells Jaleel, "We'll never know, who knows maybe opposites can attract." Jaleel tells Newton, "Well, I'm going to say this one time to Robbie. Good luck.: Newton tells Jaleel, "He's going to need it." The doorbell rings and Jaleel tells Newton, "I'll get it." Jaleel gets up from his chair and answers the front door. Jaleel head to the front door and opens it. Jaleel opens the door and it's Robbie. Robbie is really dressed wearing a suit and a briefcase. Jaleel tells Robbie, "Robbie nice suit, is that Armani?" Robbie tells Robbie, "Yeah, it is! Jaleel tells Robbie, "That suit is really expensive, how did you afford a buy a suit like that." Jaleel sees the Ferrari FF GT4 outside his house and tells Robbie, "And that Ferrari. Did you win the lottery or something?" Robbie tells Jaleel, "Of course not, I want to look good going undercover, Nigel the hotel manager of Four Corner's Hotel got some great deals on the Ferrari and the suit when I told them I'm going to undercover on a huge case. So, he helped me out to look the part." Jaleel tells Robbie, "Wow, it's looks like you owe Nigel big." Robbie tells Jaleel, "Yeah, I do. I promise something big for him if he helps me out with this favor." Jaleel tells Robbie, "So, what's the favor?" Robbie tells Jaleel, "Not right now, I'll tell you later." Jaleel tells Robbie, "Okay, you can tell me later. Come on in, dude. I got some fresh donuts and some hot coffee with your name on it." Robbie tells Jaleel, "Jaleel, tell me you have the glaze?" Jaleel tells Robbie, "It's on the kitchen table." Robbie tells Jaleel, "Thanks man, you're a great friend." Robbie goes inside the house and Jaleel closes the door. Robbie and Jaleel enter the kitchen and sees Newton eating a glaze donut and drinking some coffee. Jaleel sees Newton and is about to introduce him to his best friend. Jaleel tells Newton, "Hey Newton!" Newton sees Robbie and Jaleel and looks at Robbie for a minute. Robbie is not what he expected to be. Newton whispers to himself, "What is wrong with Princess Amy?" Jaleel tells Newton, "Newton this is my best friend and partner Robbie Champberg." Jaleel breathes for a minute and tells Robbie, "Robbie this is Newton, Amy's butler." Newton gets up from his chair and shakes Robbie's hand for a minute. Robbie tells Newton, "It's a pleasure to meet you, Newton." Newton tells Robbie, "It's also a pleasure to meet you Agent Champberg." Robbie tells Newton, "You can call me, Robbie." Newton tells Robbie, "Okay Master Robbie." Robbie whispering to Jaleel, "Master Robbie." Jaleel whispering to Robbie, "It's a British custom and plus we want to get in good with this guy. So, he can call you anything you want. If you're thinking about dating her." Robbie whispering to Jaleel, "Point taken." Newton tells Robbie, "The princess told me a lot about you." Robbie tells Newton, "I hope good things I hope." Newton sarcastically tells Robbie, "Some are bad and some are good. But you sound like a nice guy and I think I can trust you with Princess Amy." Robbie tells Newton, "I appreciate that Newton. So where is Amy?" Jaleel tells Robbie, "She's upstairs in her room, getting ready." Robbie tells them, "I hope she hurry's up, we have to be Abda Electronics half an hour." Newton tells Robbie, "Well Master Robbie, why don't you sit down and have some donuts and coffee with us. Until she gets here." Robbie tells Newton, "You ready my mind." Robbie and Jaleel sits down in their chairs and Robbie grabs a glaze donut and starts eating it. Robbie tells himself, 'The best cop food in the world, glaze donuts and coffee." While Robbie, Jaleel and Newton starts eating donuts and coffee on the kitchen table, Princess Amy comes down from the stairs wearing her business suit and carrying a briefcase head to the kitchen. Princess Amy is also wearing some make up and looks really beautiful. Princess Amy sees Robbie, Jaleel and Newton eating some donuts and drinking some coffee in the kitchen table. Princess Amy tells them, "Hey guys." The guys tell Princess Amy, "Hey Amy!" Princess Amy tells Robbie, "So Robbie are you ready to go?" Robbie forgot about his meeting with Yorkshire this afternoon. Robbie tells himself, "Oh, I know forgot something." Robbie gets up from his chair and tells the guys, "Jaleel remember go back to the library and find any information about...?" Jaleel interrupts Robbie for a minute and tells him, "Find any information on the Israeli Terrorist team that Alden and Yorkshire is going to do business with." Robbie tells Jaleel, "Exactly, I don't want Newton to get board all day. So, why don't you take him with you and help us with this investigation. Since he is part of the Secret Room and he knows everything about us and we know a lot about him. I think he make a good asset for the team." Jaleel tells Robbie, "Plus he complimented you a lot. So, that makes him a good asset for the team." Robbie tells Jaleel, "That too." Jaleel tells Newton, "Come on, Newton. Were heading to the library, since you're one of us now." Newton tells Jaleel, "Do I really have a choice?" Jaleel tells Newton, "Nope!" Newton tells Jaleel, "I got one thing say to you. I'm in." Robbie tells them, "Will give you a call after our meeting with Yorkshire." Newton tells Robbie, "What if he recognizes you or something goes wrong." Robbie tells Newton, "Will worry about that when the time comes Newton. Besides, I'm a trained FBI agent, I will keep the princess safe. Come on, Amy." Princess Amy tells Robbie, "Sure thing, Robbie." Robbie and Princess Amy exits the kitchen and head to Robbie's rental car. Newton looks at Robbie and Princess Amy, "That guy who is protecting the Princess Amy. Boy are we in trouble." Outside of Abda Electronics parking lot where Robbie parks his rented Ferrari FF GT4 in the parking space. Robbie and Princess Amy exits the car and carrying their briefcases. Princess Amy is wearing her Ray Ban sunglasses. Princess Amy tells Robbie, "Okay, let me do the talking. Since I'm the one made the appointment and had the idea." Robbie tells Princess Amy, "So, I have to follow your lead." Princess Amy tells Robbie, "Yes, but no argument. We don't have time for this. My father life is depending on this moment." Robbie tells Princess Amy, "I wasn't planning on it. But I will follow your lead." Princess Amy tells Robbie, "Good, follow me." Princess Amy and Robbie head to Abda Electronics main entrance. The secretary who is working on the front desk is on the phone and Princess Amy and Robbie enter the lobby and sees the secretary in the front desk. Princess Amy and Robbie goes over talk to the secretary. Princess Amy and Robbie waits for the secretary to finish her call. The secretary who is on the phone tells the person, "Okay bye!" The secretary hangs up the phone and talks to Princess Amy and Robbie. The secretary from the front desk tells Robbie and Princess Amy, "Hi, can I help you?" Princess Amy tells the secretary, "Hi, my name is Amy Greenly. I'm here to see Contel Yorkshire today." The secretary tells Princess Amy, "Is he expecting you?" Princess Amy tells the secretary, "Yes, I made an appointment with him today for an investment I'm about to make with him." Robbie tells the secretary, "Is Mr Yorkshire is in today?" Secretary tells Robbie, "I'll check to see if he's in his office today?" Secretary grabs her phone and makes a call. Robbie whispers to Princess Amy, "You think she will by it." Princess Amy whispers to Robbie, "I'm hoping Yorkshire bys it's right now." Secretary is on the phone with Mr Yorkshire secretary and tells Yorkshire secretary, "Okay thank you bye!" Secretary hangs up her phone and tells Princess Amy and Robbie tells them, "Mr Yorkshire is in today and he's ready to see you now." Princess Amy tells the Secretary, "Thank you, ma'am." Robbie try to remember something and figures it out what it is. Robbie tells the secretary, "What floor is Mr Yorkshire office is in?" Secretary tells Robbie, "His office is at fifteenth floor and the elevator is over their." Secretary points to the elevator to the right section and puts her arm down. Robbie tells the Secretary, "Thank you, Ma'am. I appreciate that." The secretary tells Robbie, "You're welcome." Robbie and Princess Amy heads to the elevator and the door is still open. They both get inside the elevator and Princess Amy tells Robbie, "Just in the nick of time." The elevator starts ringing on the sixteenth floor near Yorkshire's office and the elevator door opens. Robbie and Princess Amy exits the elevator and Princess Amy tells Robbie, "I just hope Yorkshire doesn't recognize me." Robbie tells Princess Amy, "Were about to find out in a minute." Yorkshire is working in his office. Contel Yorrkshire is in his early forties. He is British, distinguished and handsome. Yorkshire is still working in his desk, until he hears an intercom button buzzing. Yorkshire turns on the intercom and tells his secretary, "What is it, Penelope?" Penelope tells Yorkshire, "Miss Amy Greenly and Mr Robbie Champberg is here to see you." Yorkshire tells Penelope, "Send them in." Penelope tells Yorkshire, "Yes sir." Yorkshire turns off the intercom button. The door opens and it's Robbie and Princess Amy. Yorkshire gets up from his chair and is about to greet Robbie and Princess Amy. Robbie and Princess Amy goes over to greet Mr Yorkshire. Princess Amy tells Yorkshire, "Mr Yorkshire, I'm Amy Greenly from Greenly Investments and this is my associate Robert Champberg." Yorkshire shakes Princess Amy's hand and tells Princess Amy, "It's a pleasure to meet Miss Greenly." Yorkshire let's go of Amy's hand and shakes Robbie's hand and let's go. Yorkshire tells them, "I wondered if I could offer you anything?" Robbie tells Yorkshire, "Well, I wondered if you have any Diet Pepsi around?" Yorkshire tells Robbie, "Mr Champberg, we have a vending machine at the end of the hall. I'll have my secretary to go their to get you some Diet Pepsi." Princess Amy looks at Robbie and Robbie sees her expression to stick to business. Robbie tells Yorkshire, "Right now, I'm not thirsty. But thanks anyway Mr

Yorkshire." Yorkshire tells Robbie, "Hey, it's okay." Princess Amy tells Yorkshire, "Mr Yorkshire let's get down to business." Yorkshire tells Princess Amy, "Yeah, I forgot why you guys came her here?" Yorkshire, Robbie and Princess Amy sits down in their chairs. Robbie and Princess Amy put their briefcases down and they're about to talk about their investment that Princess Amy is going to make. Princess Amy tells Yorkshire, "I'm sure, Mr Abda told you why I'm here for?" Yorkshire tells Princess Amy, "You are here to make an investment in our company." Princess Amy tells Yorkshire, "Yes, that's why were here. I read your financial portfolio that you Mr Abda's company just offered a huge three hundred million dollar account with British Knight Shoes." Yorkshire tells Princess Amy, "Were about to close the deal on this account in a couple of days. The people who invest in my company, your stock will skyrocket in a minute when you invest with us." Princess Amy tells Yorkshire, "My father sent me here to make an investment to your company. Were looking around other companies, but something drew him when he read your portfolio?" Yorkshire tells Princess Amy, "Really, what drew him to his company Miss Greenly?" Princess Amy tells Yorkshire, "Mostly I can tell you the business terms. But I won't bore you with that. He likes how you drive this company to succeed and push to the limit. One thing I always learned in salesmanship. When you sell a product, were not buying the product." Robbie tells Yorkshire, "Were buying them." Princess Amy tells Yorkshire, "That's what I look into your company, get to the bottom line. That's why we want to invest in your company." Yorkshire looks at these two and they are very serious and investing in this company. Yorkshire tells Princess Amy, "How much are you willing to invest Miss Greenly and Mr Champberg?" Princess Amy tells Yorkshire, "I think were willing to invest a willing sum over a hundred million dollars." Yorkshire tells them, "A hundred million dollars to invest on our company." Robbie tells Yorkshire, "Well Mr Yorkshire, a hundred million dollars is small change to us. But I think we can go a little bit higher." Yorkshire tells Robbie, "How higher?" Robbie tells Yorkshire, "Over a five hundred million dollars." Princess Amy tells Yorkshire, "I think that sums it up. Besides it's double what you're getting this account." Robbie tells Yorkshire, "That will make you and this company a lot more richer when we invest in this company." Princess Amy tells Yorkshire, "So, we do we have a deal?" Yorkshire tells them, "I got one thing say to you.

You have a deal." Princess Amy grabs her briefcase and takes out her financial portfolio and gives it to Yorkshire. Princess Amy tells Yorkshire, "Here is our financial portfolio, Mr Yorkshire. A binding contract and a account number so we can transfer five hundred million dollars to your company's account." Princess Amy gives the financial portfolio to Yorkshire and Yorkshire starts reading the account. Yorkshire tells them, "Thank you, Miss Greenly. I really appreciates what you're doing for this company." Princess Amy tells Yorkshire, "I'm sure Mr Abda will be proud of what you're doing for his company. Who knows he may leave you the company to run someday." Yorkshire whispers to himself, "Or I can take over his company." Princess Amy tells Yorkshire, "I beg your pardon." Yorkshire tells Princess Amy, "Oh nothing just thinking out lately." Yorkshire thinking for a minute when he looks at this financial portfolio. Yorkshire grabs the contract from his desk drawer that he opens and closes it. He gives the contract to Princess Amy and Robbie to look over and signed. Yorkshire tells them, "Here is your contract to invest in Abda Electronics, once you signed it. You'll have one hundred million shares of our company and we will wire your money to our account as soon as the contract is signed." Robbie tells Yorkshire, "Without our signature, you can authorize to transfer any of our money to your account." Yorkshire tells Robbie, "Exactly Mr Champberg." Princess Amy tells Yorkshire, "We can't sign anything right now. Until my father looks at it. He's in his hotel room. So, will take the contract to him and get his signature. He's the one who can authorize the deal." Yorkshire tells them, "No problem. Our deal will only last in two days. Tell your father, to sign that contract when he finishes looking at it tonight." Robbie tells Yorkshire, "Once Mr Greenly signs the contract, will give you a call and give you the contracts tomorrow." Princess Amy tells Yorkshire, "You can tell us when or where you want to give you the contracts tomorrow." Yorkshire tells them, "Sure thing, I appreciate that." Princess Amy tells Yorkshire, before we go. Their is something we want to talk to you about." Yorkshire tells Princess Amy, "Sure go ahead." Princess Amy tells Yorkshire, "We read an article on the San Francisco Chronicle about some middle eastern drug runners. I have no idea who they are or where they from." Robbie tells Yorkshire, "I think they might be from, I'm going to take a wild guess here. Probably somewhere around Jerusalem or Israeli. I heard these guys pay a lot of money for heroine to a top drug kingpin." Princess Amy tells Yorkshire, "I heard it might be some British lord who might be frontrunner for Prime Minister election and owns a billion oil company and runs a huge drug lab somewhere around Fisherman Wharf." Yorkshire starts laughing about this rumor and tells them, "You can't believe everything you read in the Chronicle. I heard they're just about rumors they want to get people thinking." Princess Amy tells Yorkshire, "Kind of like tabloid, where woman carries an alien baby." Robbie tells Yorkshire, "Even the rumor, that this British lord is stealing oil from a British duke oil wells and trying put him out of business so he can make more money. Get the duke to sign a merger agreement and trying to take over his company." Princess Amy tells Yorkshire, "Put a lot of people out of work. You know the weird thing about this English lord who is stealing this guy oil?" Yorkshire is getting a little suspicious but goes along with the ploy and tells Princess Amy, "What is the weird thing about this British lord?" Princess Amy tells Yorkshire, "I think he's hiding heroine inside oil barrels, so they can take the scent off. So, no K-9 can track it down." Yorkshire is still laughing for a minute and he stops. Robbie tells Yorkshire, "I also heard this British Lord, I still couldn't figure out what is name is. Let me think." Robbie thinking for a minute and tells Yorkshire, "Alten, Aldren, Alto." Princess Amy tells Robbie, "I think it's Aldo." Robbie tells Princess Amy, "No, I don't think that's not it. Oh Alden. Like Lord Randall Alden." Yorkshire tells Robbie, "Yeah, that's him. What makes think Lord Alden, might be stealing a British Duke oil supply and selling drugs to a top drug runner in Israeli terrorist?" Robbie tells Yorkshire, "It was just a rumor that I read on the Chronicle that Lord Alden had a partner who used to work for MI6 who was selling trade secrets to some Israeli drug lords." Yorkshire tells Robbie, "You don't say?" Princess Amy tells Yorkshire, "I heard it was some deadly plants that scientist found somewhere around Jerusalem. Those plants can actually make heroine, but it also might be a deadly explosive. Kinda of like...?" Robbie interrupts Princess Amy and tells Yorkshire, "Like TNT. Mr Yorkshire, you know what TNT is do you?" Yorkshire tells Robbie, "We know it's not a tv channel, I know it's some kind of explosive." Robbie tells Yorkshire, "Exactly, MI6 send some scientist to dispose, but the plants were gone. I think some dug up those plants to start making heroine out of it. This person who worked for MI6 was suspected of selling those trade secrets to a Israeli terrorist. They never had any proof that he's was connecting selling those secrets to them." Princess Amy tells Yorkshire, "I heard after that, he left the agency and start working for Lord Alden. With MI6 connections, he found a way to cover his tracks with Scotland Yard and Interpol." Yorkshire tells Princess Amy, "Really, I couldn't believe it either." Robbie tells Yorkshire, "The biggest rumor I read about this ex British spy works for Abda electronics and probably using this company as a cover. They'll probably use Mr Abda as a scapegoat, in case if he ever meddles in their drug deal. But that's just a rumor. I'm sure nothing like that happened." Yorkshire tells them, "Of course not, you can't believe everything you read." Princess Am tells Yorkshire, "Exactly, just ordinary rumors. I guess we have to go now." Princess Amy, Yorkshire and Robbie gets up from their chairs and shakes Yorkshire's hand and let's go. Yorkshire tells them, "Don't forget to tell you father to sign that contract today. Before you wire your money to the company account." Princess Amy tells Yorkshire, "Don't worry, Mr Yorkshire I'll make sure father will sign the contract indefinitely. Bye Mr Yorkshire" Robbie tells Yorkshire, "See ya!" Princess Amy and Robbie grabs their suitcases and exit Yorkshire office. Yorkshire sits back down in his chair. Princess Amy and Robbie are walking in the hallway and head to the elevator. Robbie tells Princess Amy, "You think he bought it." Princess Amy tells Robbie, "I don't know, were about to find out." Back in Yorkshire's office, Yorkshire calls somebody on the phone and tells this stranger, "Patrick, do you have a security camera monitoring my office. Okay, listen I need you to send a DVD of the footage to my office right now. Okay, thank you bye. Yorkshire hangs up his phone and tells himself, "He's not going to like this when he hears about when he sees that DVD." Robbie is driving his rented Ferrari FF GT4 downtown Mountain View. Where Robbie and Princess Amy are wearing their Ray Ban Sunglasses, Robbie is behind the wheel driving and Princess Amy is in the passenger seat. Robbie and Princess Amy is still trying to figure out where Lord Alden drug deal is a. Robbie tells Princess Amy, "We still have to figure out who these Israeli terrorist are and we still have to find Alden's drug lab is at and still figure out when and where he's going to make his drug deal with those guys?" Princess Amy tells Robbie, "It could be anywhere and my father's company and his health is on the online here." Robbie tells Princess Amy, "Well, you don't have to tell me twice." Princess Amy tells

Robbie, "Man, I wish we knew somebody that can help us find Alden's drug lab and figure out when or where his drug deal going to be?" Robbie tells Princess Amy, "You mean like a source." Princess Amy tells Robbie, "Yeah!" Princess Amy remembers something and tells Robbie, "I forgot you have a source. He's the guy who gave you the tip that Lord Alden was the drug kingpin and he might be the running his heroine dealing here?" Robbie tells Princess Amy, "That's right. I forgot about him." Princess Amy tells Robbie, "How come he never told you it was Alden running the drug deal?" Robbie tells Princess Amy, "We never asked him about that, we just asked him where this drug lab is at. But he never gave out a location or an address. Because Alden is been covering his tracks and my source got shot last week by him. We were back at square one. That's why we been here for a month and couldn't find anything." Princess Amy tells Robbie, "Let me guess, he was about tell you, who was running the show and when and where the drug deal is going to take place." Robbie tells Princess Amy, "My source was killed by Alden before he gave us the information on his whereabouts." Princess Amy tells Robbie, "I guess were back at square one. Man, I wish he was here. We could have really need him." Robbie tells Princess Amy, "Actually he can." Princess Amy tells Robbie, "What do you mean, he can still help us. You told me he was murdered by Lord Alden before he gave you anything?" Robbie tells Princess Amy, "He is, but he has a friend who he would trust with his life on the information that he has on Alden. In case he ever dies. If Alden killed my informant, Alden never got the files or info on him or drug deal. But the person he would mail it to and has same connections as my source is his friend." Princess Amy tells Robbie, "Robbie who is his friend, you think he might be in town or something?" Robbie tells Princess Amy, "Actually Amy, he is in town and I know where to find him." Princess Amy tells Robbie, "I just hope Alden doesn't find this guy before we do. Or were going to be in big trouble." Robbie tells Princess Amy, "Tell me about it." Robbie and Princess Amy makes a left in downtown Mountain View California and finds Robbie informant's friend. The limousine enters outside of Lord Alden's warehouse with the garage door opens and the limo stops. The limo driver exits the limo and opens the limo door from the back door and it's Yorkshire who comes out of the limo. Yorkshire exits the limo and the limo driver closes the door. Yorkshire is carrying a DVD that had a security camera monitoring his office while he was talking to Princess Amy and Robbie. Yorkshire sees the office door upstairs where the managers office is at. Yorkshire heads upstairs and sees Lord Alden's workers working in a heroine lab putting heroine in plastic bags and hiding them in oil barrels. Lord Alden is talking to Rutherford and Alberto about this big meeting. Alberto tells Lord Alden, "When is Yorkshire arriving, my lord?" Lord Alden tells Yorkshire, "He said to be here in a few minutes sharp. He has something to show us that is really important." Rutherford tells them, "Whatever it is, it must be really important that he would come down here." somebody is knocking on the door and Lord Alden tells the person who is knocking on the door, "Come in." The door opens and it's Yorkshire. Yorkshire enters the manager's office and closes the door. Yorkshire tells Lord Alden, "My lord we have a problem?" Lord Alden tells Yorkshire, "What is it Yorkshire. You called us out here nearly an hour when you told us this was a big emergency." Yorkshire tells Lord Alden, "I think you should take a look at this." Lord Alden seeing the DVD that Yorkshire has in his hand and tells them, "If you're here call us all here to watch Dr Who again with you. Now is not the right time, were busying making this huge deal our clients are coming in Saturday Night. Their expecting the merchandise here pretty soon." Yorkshire tells Lord Alden, "Lord Randall, this is not a Dr Who dvd. Besides you promise we can watch it together back home after the deal is done with our clients." Lord Alden tells Yorkshire, "Just tell us what brings all the way here Yorkshire?" Yorkshire tells Lord Alden, "Yes sir!" Yorkshire sees the tv set and DVD and VCR player. Yorkshire turns on the tv set and puts the DVD in the player. Yorkshire starts the DVD and Lord Alden and his associates sees the security footage of Princess Amy and Robbie talking to Yorkshire in his office. Yorkshire pauses the DVD for a minute. Yorkshire tells them, "This is the major emergency I called you here Lord Randall!" Lord Alden, Rutherford and Alberto gets up from their chairs and sees the footage. Alberto tells Yorkshire, "What's the emergency anyway?" Yorkshire tells them, "Their were two people who claimed to be investors, who wanted to invest in Abda electronics since Abda landed a huge account for British Knight shoes." Alberto tells Yorkshire, "If they're not investors, who are they?" Lord Alden recognizes Princess Amy on the security footage, but he doesn't recognize the guy who is with her. Yorkshire tells them, "I don't know, but they were asking me questions about our heroine deal, where our drug lab is at and our heroine dealing with our clients who are Israeli drug runners. The worse part, they knew I used to worked for MI6 and how I got fired when I sold top secret documents to our clients." Alberto tells them, "About those deadly plants the Israeli's found outside Jerusalem." Yorkshire tells Alberto, "That's the one." Lord Alden is angry and grabs Yorkshire by the nose. Yorkshire nose is hurting and Lord Alden tells Yorkshire, "Did you tell them about our heroine dealings and where it's going to be and who are clients are?" Yorkshire tells Lord Alden, "I swear my Lord, I didn't tell them anything. That you stole your competitors oil to put them out of business and use them smuggle your heroine inside their oil so you can sell to our clients who are Israeli terrorist who are willing to pay top dollar for your heroine. Not only that, you hired me to cover your tracks with Interpol and Scotland Yard in case they come after us. I did that." Alberto tells Yorkshire, "We also helped you update your resume to get you high executive job in Abda Electronics as a cover, so Interpol or Scotland Yard can track us down." Rutherford tells Yorkshire, "We also sent in that invitation to Computer conference to Abda so he can leave and so he can put you in charge in his company. So you can help us finish our deal with our clients." Yorkshire tells Lord Alden, "I did all that, you guys asked. So, we have nothing to worry about." Lord Alden let's go of Yorkshire nose and punches him in the stomach. Lord Alden tells Yorkshire, "We have a lot to worry about, because why these two guys are asking you questions about our heroine deal with our clients?" Yorkshire is groaning a little but he's fine and starts explaining to Lord Alden about this predicament. Yorkshire tells Lord Alden, "Do you recognize any of these two my Lord?" Lord Alden sees Princess Amy and Robbie in the security footage and I think he recognizes Princess Amy. Lord Alden tells Yorkshire, "I know who she is. It's her, the Princess." Rutherford tells Lord Alden, "Amy Greenly, thee Princess Amy Greenly. The Duke's daughter the one you were supposed to marry if her father doesn't sign the merger agreement." Lord Alden tells Rutherford, "That's her. I knew Maddie told me was true. But we got her exactly where we got her." Alberto tells Lord Alden, "What do you mean, sir?" Lord Alden tells Alberto, "Simple my friend, I asked Lindy to spy on Amy and her father and figure out what they're up to. She also got on board The Duke's jet to see what they're up to. When Maddie told me, they're were investing Abda electronics and they land a huge shoe account. That's where I step in and planned the whole thing." Alberto tells Lord Alden, "So what is this major plan to get the princess to marry you Lord Alden." Lord Alden tells Alberto, "I always been making heroine deals with my client for a year in San Francisco. I was about to take over Abda Electronics too, so I updated Yorkshire resume to be qualified enough to be an executive. Earned Abda Jr trust, to watch over the company while he's out in his computer conference. Just in case, Amy was trying to save daddy's company, Yorkshire would take that money and wired it into my account and block British Knight Shoe account. Not only will I take over two companies, The Duke will have no choice to get Amy to marry me. She will make a great trophy wife and I will double my profits with my client in Saturday Night." Yorkshire tells Lord Alden, "Well Lord Alden, our plan is working out just the way we want. We have a bigger problem, the guy that she is with. Who do you think he is?" Rutherford tells them, "I don't know who he is. Yorkshire he told you he was asking you questions. Like he was some kind of cop. You think he might be Scotland Yard?" Yorkshire tells Rutherford, "He's not Scotland Yard, he's American. It's true he might be a cop, but not in Scotland Yard." Lord Alden tells them, "We have to find out who he is. I don't want this fat loser, near my fiancée." Alberto tells Lord Alden, "fiancée!" Lord Alden tells Alberto, "She will be, once her father will have no choice to sign the merger agreement. Alberto come here for a minute." Alberto tells Lord Alden, "Yes Lord Alden." Lord Alden elbows Alberto in the ribs and tells him, "Never doubt me when I can't do something. Like when I marry Princess Amy. Okay." Alberto scared of Lord Alden and tells him, "Yes sir Yes Sir, it won't happen again." Lord Alden tells them, "Good back to business. I need to find out who he is. I know who to call." Lord Alden head to his desk and sits down in his chair. Lord Alden picks up his phone and makes the call." Lord Alden tells the person on the phone, "Maddie, listen I need a favor." Robbie and Princess Amy enter Luigi's Pizza. Princess Amy tells Robbie, "So who was this guy that your contact send all the info on Alden." Robbie tells Princess Amy, "He owns this Pizzeria. He has a lot political strings with the Pentagon and DOJ." Princess Amy tells Robbie, "So, how do you know him?" Robbie tells Princess Amy, "Around." Princess Amy looks at Robbie for a minute and tells her, "My classmate Cal Zona from Caltech worked on the R & D department in the pentagon after graduation. He has tons of connections with us and DOJ, he was my contact on any cases that I need help with the FBI." Princess Amy laughs for a minute and tells Robbie, "Cal Zona, that's unusual name. It's sounds like a sandwich than more than a name." Robbie tells Princess Amy, "Actually it's called Calzone. Sometimes my friend's name is really funny sometimes. Even though he is sensitive about that." Princess Amy tells Robbie, "Anyway about Cal, being your contact with the FBI. I know Cal was killed by Alden, because he was about to tell you where Alden drug lab is at and his Israeli clients that he is going to sell his heroine too." Robbie tells Princess Amy, "Before he was killed, he knew somebody was watching him. He knows he couldn't mail me the information, Alden would send some of his guys to come after me. Their is only one person he trust." Princess Amy tells Robbie, "Who did he mail the information too?" Robbie tells Princess Amy, "His cousin Lou Zona." Princess Amy tells Robbie, "Lou Zona." Robbie tells Princess Amy, "It's short for Luigi." Princess Amy tells Robbie, "The guy who owns the pizza place." Robbie tells Princess Amy, "Exactly. But he won't help us, as long we don't order anything." Princess Amy tells Robbie, "Really!" Robbie tells Princess Amy, "No, I was just hungry. It almost lunch time." Princess Amy tells Robbie, "So am I." Robbie tells Princess Amy, "What is your secret, you eat like me. You look so fit?" Princess Amy tells Robbie, "I do a lot of martial arts." Robbie tells Princess Amy, "That explains a lot." Princess Amy tells Robbie, "I hope Lou is here today." Robbie tells Princess Amy, "Trust me, he's here. It's twelve o'clock, rush hour. Let's go!" Robbie and Princess Amy heads to counter and sees the waitress working on the register. Robbie and Princess Amy goes over talk to her. Waitress tells Robbie and Princess Amy, "Hi, can I help you?" Robbie tells the Waitress, "Is Lou Zona here?" Waitress tells Robbie, "Yeah, he's in his office. May I ask who it is?" Robbie tells the Waitress, "Tell him, Robbie Champberg is here to see him?" Waitress tells Robbie, "Sure, I'll go get him." The Waitress leaves the counter and head to kitchen to find Lou. Robbie tells Princess Amy, "I think I'm going to go for the beef and pepperoni. What about you?" Princess Amy tells Robbie, "I'll take the same." Robbie looks at Princess Amy for a minute and starts falling in love. Robbie snaps out of it, until Lou enters the counter. Lou is a fat guy with a beard wears jeans and a gray t-shirt and wearing an apron. Lou goes over talk to Robbie and

Princess Amy. Lou tells them, "Robbie is that you." Robbie tells Lou, "Hey Lou what's up." Robbie fist bumps Lou for a minute. Robbie tells Lou, "How are you feeling since you know what happened to Cal." Lou tells Robbie, "It's been a month since he died. I really miss the guy. I wanted to go after the guys who killed them. But, I can't because he was being chased by assassins. If I go after them, they'll go after me too." Robbie tells Lou, "Well Lou, I have good news. I might know who killed them. Do you still have the package that Cal gave you." Lou tells Robbie, "The information that got Cal killed. Yeah, I still have it. It's in my safe where I keep my petty cash." Robbie tells Lou, "Lou that information that Cal had, might be the key to find his killer and put him away for good." Lou tells Robbie, "So, who is the guy? I want to get my hands on him." Robbie tells Lou, "You leave that to me, but this information will give you the justice for your cousin." Lou tells Robbie, "Okay, who is he?" Robbie tells Lou, "His name is Lord Randall Alden, he is a British lord, who is a drug kingpin. He's selling heroine to some middle east terrorist. I know he has a drug lab somewhere around San Francisco. But we have to know where it is and who is middle east clientele is." Lou tells Robbie, "I remember Cal told me about a British lord trying to kill him. I guess it was too late for him and he paid for it with his life. So, what can I do for you to help you guys out?" Robbie tells Lou, "The information that Cal gave you about all the files he have on Alden, his client and his drug lab. Do you still have it." Lou tells Robbie, "Yeah, I still have it. It's in my safe. Luckily for me my contact from DOJ helped me blocked all traces from my computer so Alden couldn't track me down. I'm the one who got Cal the job with DOJ after he left the army." Robbie tells Lou, "Do you have a pen and paper." Lou tells Robbie, "Hang on a second." Lou takes out a notepad and a pen behind the counter and is about to start writing it. Lou tells Robbie, "Here it is." Lou gives the notepad and pen to Robbie and starts writing the email address to Jaleel. Robbie gives Jaleel email address to Lou and tells him, "This is my favor, the information you have on Lord Alden. I need you to email the information that Cal gave you to my partner Jaleel Brown. This is his email address." Lou tells Robbie, "Sure, no problem. I guess were even." Princess Amy tells Robbie, "What do you mean, you guys are even." Robbie tells Princess Amy, "I loaned him the money to start his pizza business here." Lou tells Princess Amy, "Thanks to Robbie's connection

with the FBI and his friend in the hotel business, business been booming."
Princess Amy looks at Robbie and sees why she fell in love with him.
Robbie tells Lou, "Lou before we leave my usual and double for her." Lou
tells Robbie, "No problem, two large beef and pepperoni pizzas New York
Style and two bottles of diet Pepsi coming right up." Princess Amy tells
Robbie, "You remembered." Lou tells Robbie, "First, let me email this to
your friend and I'll get your pizzas right away." Robbie tells Lou, "Okay."
Lou exits the computer and goes to his office and email the information
on Lord Alden to Jaleel." Robbie takes out his cell phone right pants pocket
and makes a call to Jaleel. Robbie tells Jaleel on the phone, "Hey Jaleel.
Good news, I have the info on Lord Alden. The information will be
emailed in a couple minutes. Me and Amy will be in the library half an
hour, okay bye." Robbie hangs up his cell phone and Princess Amy looks
at Robbie for a minute. Robbie tells Princess Amy who is camera shy,
"What!" Princess Amy tells Robbie, "Nothing." Princess Amy can't stop
smiling so is Robbie. Back in Lord Alden's office, where Yorkshire, Lord
Alden, Rutherford and Alberto are sitting down in their chairs waiting for
the phone to ring. The phone rings and Lord Alden picks up the phone.
The person on the phone that Lord Alden is expecting is Maddie. Lord
Alden talks to Maddie on the phone, "Yes Maddie, you got it. Okay. Bye!"
Lord Alden hangs up the phone and tells them, It was Maddie, he got the
information on the guys that was Amy Greenly in your office." Yorkshire
tells Maddie, "Whoever this guy is, you think we should be worried about
him." Lord Alden tells Yorkshire, "Don't worry Yorkshire, I seen that guy
in that security footage. He's not but a fat loser. He's not goanna slow us
down, were going to speed him up." Yorkshire tells Lord Alden, "So who
is he?" Lord Alden tells Yorkshire, "Maddie is going to fax us the information
right now." The fax machine started and Maddie just faxed the information
on Robbie right now. Yorkshire tells Lord Alden, "Speak of the devil."
Yorkshire, Alberto, Rutherford and Lord Alden gets up from their chairs
and head to the fax machine. Yorkshire grabs the information on Robbie
and starts reading it. Lord Alden tells Yorkshire, "So, who is fat geek
running around my business deal and trying to steal my fiancée." Alberto
tells Lord Alden, "Your fiancee, my lord." Lord Alden tells Alberton, "She
will be once my heroine deal is done." Yorkshire looks at information on
Robbie and is now to start worrying. Yorkshire tells Lord Alden, "Lord

Alden, you're not goanna like who this guy is?" Lord Alden tells Yorkshire, "So, who is he?" Yorkshire tells Lord Alden, "He's more than a cop, he's FBI." Alberto tells Yorkshire, "FBI." Yorkshire tells them, "Yes, he's FBI. His name is Agent Robert Champberg, he's an outstanding and top FBI agent and detective in the field." Lord Alden tells Yorkshire, "Come on, how good is this Champberg guy anyway? He's just some fat loser I can take out in three seconds." Yorkshire tells Lord Alden, "This man took down a couple of top drug lords and shut down ten drug labs in a couple of years. He and his partner Jaleel Brown are high decorated FBI agents." Lord Alden tells Yorkshire, "Not on my watch, I'm going to make sure that chubby loser doesn't stick my nose in my business." Yorkshire tells Lord Alden, "What are we going to do, my lord." Lord Alden tells Yorkshire, I'm going to show what I am going to do Champberg." Lord Alden elbows Yorkshire by the stomach and flips him from the floor. Lord Alden punches him in the face too." Lord Alden tells Yorkshire, "That's exactly what I'm going to do, when I see him. Get up Yorkshire, I don't pay you lie around the floor." Yorkshire tells Lord Alden, "Yes, Lord Alden." Yorkshire gets up from the floor and he is hurting. Alberto tells Lord Alden, "So, are you going really do that to Champberg, Lord Alden." Lord Alden tells Alberto, "If he gets in my way I will. But I have another way, were going to kill him." Yorkshire tells Lord Alden, "But sir, we don't know where he Champberg and the princess is. They could be anywhere." Lord Alden tells them, "Yorkshire, what else can you tell me about Champberg?" Yorkshire looks at his file in the fax machine and it also has an account number and credit card information in his file when he reads it. Yorkshire tells Lord Alden, "I think I might know where they are." Lord Alden tells Alberto, "Alberto get on the phone and call some of our men and tell them I have mission for them to do." Alberto tells Lord Alden, "Yes sir, what do we call it." Lord Alden tells Alberto, "Operation kill Champberg." Alberto tells Lord Alden, "I'll get on the phone and call them." Lord Alden tells Alberto, "Alberto one more thing." Alberto one more thing?" Alberto tells Lord Alden, "What is that, sir?" Lord Alden tells Alberto, "I want Princess Amy alive in one piece. Once you finish with Champberg, bring the princess here. I have a little arrangement for her." Alberto tells Lord Alden, "Yes sir." Alberto picks up the phone and starts dialing. Lord Alden tells Yorkshire, "Yorkshire go to your laptop and give me a location where they are, it's time we deal with Champberg personally." Yorkshire tells Lord Alden, "Yes, my lord." Lord Alden watching Alberto and Yorkshire working hard to take down Champberg personally. Robbie and Princess Amy are eating their pizzas and drinking their bottles of diet Pepsi in their table at Luigi's Pizza. Princess Amy tells Robbie, "Robbie, I know this is none of my business. Can I ask you something." Robbie tells Princess Amy, "Yeah, go ahead." Princess Amy tells Robbie, "How come you don't have a girlfriend. A guy like you must have been a lot of dates." Robbie tells Princess Amy, "I wish I had a girlfriend. But I guess my job keeps me busy, I guess I don't have time to date." Princess Amy tells Robbie, "It must be lonely." Robbie tells Princess Amy, "I'm not alone, I have Jaleel. He is like family to me. Ever since my parents died." Princess Amy tells Robbie, "I'm sorry what happened." Robbie tells Princess Amy, "Well, I was born and raised in Boston. They died on a car crash, while trying to get to my high school graduation. They saw a dog in a middle of a bridge and got side swiped and crashed and fell off a bridge and died." Princess Amy tells Robbie, "That must be really painful." Robbie tells Princess Amy, "I never got out of bed all week. But my big brother Jack, snapped me out of it and my parents gave me a letter before they died." Princess Amy tells Robbie, "What is it say?" Robbie tells Princess Amy, "My parents tells me, if anything ever happened to us. I want you to fulfill your destiny and don't waste time mourning us forever." Princess Amy tells Robbie, "What was your destiny?" Robbie tells Princess Amy, "They wanted me to change the world someday. The only way I can change it, is when me and Jaleel joined the army. I guess we both wanted to make a difference." Princess Amy tells Robbie, "Really." Robbie tells Princess Amy, "Plus, I watch a lot of action movies, I thought if we join the army. We can change things for the army. After me and Jaleel left the army, we got recruited to join the FBI and the rest is history. I knew we change things and someday we can be great detectives like our hero Inspector Harry Callahan AKA Dirty Harry." Princess Amy tells Robbie, "Dirty Harry was your hero?" Robbie tells Princess Amy, "Yes and so is Batman in the comic book genre." Princess Amy tells Robbie, "You are one crazy dude, Robbie Champberg." Robbie tells Princess Amy, "You are one weird princess Amy Greenly. I wanted to ask you something?" Princess Amy tells Robbie, "Amy, you are a princess right and a girl." Princess Amy sarcastically tells Robbie, "Gee, I never noticed. Because I wouldn't wear somebody underwear for no reason." Robbie laughs for a minute and tells Princess Amy, "Why is a beautiful, rich and a girl who is way out of your league be interested in a guy like me." Princess Amy tells Robbie, "I beg your pardon?" Robbie tells Princess Amy, "Wants to be a guy like me. You know, I'm not the guy who can pass as Prince Charming." Princess Amy tells Robbie, "Well, that's true. You may not look like Prince Charming, but you have the heart of Prince Charming. That's why I fell for you." Robbie tells Princess Amy, "Really, I always kind of knew you have to kind of this little vibe when you see me. Just like I have a vibe for you." Princess Amy tells Robbie, "You know it's true, girls who are like me, would end up dating guys like Robert Pattinson or Taylor Lautner. But that's not me, I like to date a guy who likes me for who I am. Not just a date, who would treat me like a girl who is trophy they would put on a mantle. That's one reason, why I would never date Lord Alden." Robbie tells Princess Amy, "I get Lord Alden, has the perfect qualifications to date you. So, give me one good reason, why you hate that guy?" Princess Amy tells Robbie, "He doesn't want to date me because he was in love with me. He doesn't know anything about me. All he cares about his fortune and his title. If I marry him, I'll end up like his trophy wife who will be one close to stepford." Robbie tells Princess Amy, "We don't want that. I guess why you hate him. I can see why I take that guy out myself. I can see why I am in love with you. I think I been waiting for you my whole life." Princess Amy laughs for a minute and tells Robbie, "Even though I only know you for nearly a day Robbie, I think I'm in love with you too." Princess Amy looks at Robbie for a minute and starts to kiss for a minute and stops. Robbie tells Princess Amy, "Sorry about that. I didn't...?" Princess Amy tells Robbie, "I'm sorry too. I didn't know what I was thinking. I came here to help my father. I forgot why I'm here. Right now, I have to concentrate on my father's business and his estate. His life depends on it." Robbie tells Princess Amy, "Yeah, I forgot why I'm here. I just on a drug case with Jaleel, I also have to stay focus too." Princess Amy tells Robbie, "If it was different circumstances you and I would be dating now. But right now, we have to concentrate on your case and trying to save my father's business first." Robbie tells Princess Amy, "Yeah, I know." Princess Amy and Robbie look at each other again and they're about to kiss again. Until Alberto enters the pizzeria out of nowhere, goes over talk to Robbie and Princess Amy. Robbie tells Alberto, "Excuse me, can I help you." Alberto tells Robbie, "Yes I'm Alberto Rodriguez I'm Mr Yorkshire personal assistant, he wants to see you two right now. He said it's very urgent." Princess Amy tells Alberto, "What do you mean, it's urgent." Alberto tells Princess Amy, "Will Miss Greenly, Mr Yorkshire have some important news that he wants to share with you. It's something do with your investment of our company." Princess Amy tells Alberto, "I hope it's not bad." Alberto tells Princess Amy, "Nothing bad, he has another business contract he need your father to sign for his authorization to wire his money to our company saving's account. Princess Amy tells Alberto, "Why didn't he just email the contract to my father's address." Alberto tells Princess Amy, "No, it has to be done in person. He was going to stop by here and get something to eat while he was on the way to his hotel room. But we saw you guys and decide to give you the other business contracts for him to sign." Princess Amy tells Alberto, "So do you have it, I'll give it to my father when I see him at the hotel." Alberto tells Princess Amy, "I don't have it, but Mr Yorkshire has it. He's waiting for you outside to give you the other business contracts." Robbie tells Alberto, "Since, he's here will pick the business contracts." Alberto tells them, "follow me." Robbie and Princess Amy gets up from their chairs and Alberto shows them where Yorkshire is at. Princess Amy tells Robbie, "I think we have to be careful, it might be a trap." Robbie tells Princess Amy, "I know, but we have expect the unexpected. Whatever happens I have your back." Alberto shows Robbie and Princess Amy to the back of the parking lot. The back door opens and it's Alberto, Robbie and Princess Amy. Alberto shows Robbie and Princess Amy the back door where they expect to meet Yorkshire. But their is no Yorkshire, but six of Lord Alden's men who are wearing suits and their is a limousine in the back too. Alberto tells them, "Right this way." They all stopped for a minute and Robbie tells Alberto, "Mr Rodriquez, where is Mr Yorkshire. I don't see him anywhere." Alberto tells Robbie, "He's not here, but we are." Alberto and six of Lord Alden's men takes out their Glock 19 G19 Semi-Automatic guns in back of their left jacket pocket and aims the gun on Princess Amy and Robbie. Princess Amy tells Alberto, "I knew this was a trap. This was a setup." Alberto laughs hysterically for a minute and tells Princess Amy, "Of course this is a trap. You're majesty. Oh I have one more surprise for you Oh Maddie!"

The back door of the limousine opens and it's Maddie the flight attendant who was with Princess Amy and Newton on their private jet. Maddie exits the limousine and wearing Louis Vuitton sunglasses and a black business suit and carrying a Beretta M9 and aims it on Princess Amy. Maddie tells Princess Amy, "Hello Amy, I've been expecting you." Princess Amy tells Maddie, "I know you, you're the flight attendant in my father's jet." Maddie laughs a little and tells Princess Amy, "Yes, I've been working with Randall near a year long. I really do love that man. But, he is in love with you and I have to respect that. If it was me, I would kill you myself. You're coming me, Lord Randall is expecting you right now." Princess Amy tells Maddie, "I'm not going anywhere." Maddie tells Princess Amy, "Actually' you're going somewhere. To Lord Randall office. He has a little surprise for your father." Princess Amy tells Maddie, "What surprise is that Maddie? Or should I say wicked witch of the west." Maddie is a little upset and goes over to Princess Amy and slaps her in the face. Princess Amy didn't feel anything for a minute and tells Maddie, "Good comeback, I thought you didn't have any heat on you. But I do take it back. You're not the wicked witch of the west. You're the wicked witch of the North." Maddie is more upset now and starts to punch Princess Amy in the face, but Alberto blocks his punch and tells Maddie, "Lord Randall wants her alive. We have to respect that." Maddie resultantly tells Alberto, "Fine, but I hope Randall kills this little tart pretty soon." Alberto tells Maddie, "If she refuses to marry him. Which I hope so." Princess Amy tells them, here is my word I could give Randall. No!" Maddie slaps Princess Amy in the face again and holds the gun to her head. Maddie tells Princess Amy, "I don't know why he has a crush on you. But I don't care. You're coming with us." Princess Amy tells them, "Look, I'm not going anywhere you can tell Randall, if he wants to marry me. He'll have to knock me out and drag me to the altar before he pushes me to this marriage." Maddie tells Princess Amy, "If I have to." Maddie knocks out Princess Amy with her gun to her head and she is out cold. Robbie tells them, "Hey, leave hear alone you jerks." Robbie is about to make a move, until Alberto still holds his gun to Robbie's head and tells him, "Don't move." Maddie tells them, "Guys, take the princess to the limousine and Alberto you and the guys finish off this fat moron who calls himself a federal agent. Which I'm shivering." Maddie laughing a little and Alberto tells Maddie, "Sure thing." Alberto is laughing a little and two of Lord Alden's men grabs Princess Amy and takes her to Lord Alden's limousine. Princess Amy is unconscious and goes inside the limo and the two of Lord Alden's men go back and holds the gun on Robbie. Maddie goes inside the limousine and tells Alberto, "Alberto, honey. Make sure you give our little FBI agent a little send off. For our boss Lord Randall." Alberto tells Maddie, "Sure thing, Madeline." Maddie closes the door and the limousine exits the parking lot. Robbie mad and tells Alberto, "Alberto, Anything happens to Amy, I'm coming after you. You can tell that to Lord Alden too." Alberto tells Robbie, "I'll make sure I'll tell him that. Too bad you'll be dead before I give him that message." Alberto tells Lord Alden's man 1, "Jax search Champberg and checked to see if he's not armed." Jax tells Alberto, "Okay Alberto." Robbie tells them, "Trust me, guys I'm not armed. You can search me all you want. But I'm not armed." Alberto tells Robbie, "Will see about that." Alberto looks at Jax for a minute and still tells him, "Jax go search him." Jax goes over to Robbie and searches him from head to foot. Jax tells Robbie, "Turn around." Robbie tells Jax, "Okay, but I don't think you should touch my back for a minute." Jax tells Robbie, "Why because you're gun is in the back. Don't worry, I'll take it out of you, before we kill you. Turn around." Robbie tells Jax, "Okay, but I warn not to touch my back." Robbie turns around and Jax searches him in the back. Jax sees something and that might be Robbie's gun. Jax tells Robbie, "Looks like I found your gun, by the way, Dummy. What do you say, if I touch your back." Robbie tells Jax, That I would do this. "Robbie stomps on Jax's foot and elbows him to the ribs. Jax stomach is hurting and Robbie turns and takes out his Beretta M9 from back of his pants and fires his gun. Three bullets comes out of his gun and hits Jax in the stomach and dies. Alberto tells them, "Shoot him." Robbie tells himself, "I wondered if it's a good time to wear a vest right now." Alberto shoots his gun, one bullet comes out of his gun and hits the floor near Robbie's foot and misses him. Robbie tells himself, "Yeah, it's definitely a good time." Robbie dives down on the floor to the right and after three bullets comes out of nowhere when Lord Alden's Man 3 fires his gun. Robbie dives down on the floor to the right and rolls down near three barrels to hide. Lord Alden 2 fires his gun, three bullets comes out of his gun and hits the wall near Robbie and misses him. Robbie aims his gun on Alberto, fires his gun and two bullets comes out of his gun and hits the wall near him and misses him. Robbie fires his gun again and he's out of bullets and removes the clip. Robbie takes out another clip behind his back and loads it. Robbie aims his gun on Lord Alden 4 and fires his gun. Three bullets comes out of his gun and hits him in the chest and dies. Lord Alden 5 fires his gun, one bullet comes out of his gun and hits the box and misses Robbie. Robbie tells himself, "Time to do a little break dancing." Robbie fires his gun, one bullet comes out of his gun and hits Lord Alden Man 6 foot and misses him. Lord Alden Man 6 jumps a little bit and stops. Robbie fires his gun, two bullets comes out of his gun and hits Lord Alden Man 6 in the chest and dies. Lord Alden Man 3 fires his gun and two bullets comes out of his gun and hits the door and misses Robbie. Alberto tells the guys, "This fat loser is still trying to piss me off." Robbie aims gun on Lord Alden Man 3 and one bullet fires his gun. One bullet hits Lord Alden Man 3 in the right leg and he is soaring. Robbie fires his gun, two bullets comes out of his gun and hits Lord Alden Man 3 in the stomach and dies. Robbie aims his gun on Lord Alden Man 2 and fires his gun. Three bullets comes out of his gun and hits Lord Alden's Man 2 in the chest and dies. Lord Alden Man 5 fires his gun and two bullets comes out of his gun and hits the wall near Robbie and misses him later. Robbie tells himself, "Time for the pick and roll." Lord Alden Man 5 fires his gun and two bullets comes out of his gun and hits the door near Robbie and misses him. Robbie takes out his cell phone and turns on the alarm on his phone really loud. Lord Alden Man 5 can't concentrate on that buzzing and tries to cover his ears. Lord Alden Man 5 tells Alberto, "I can't hear anything or trying to see where that fat fool is." Robbie comes out of the barrels and aims his gun on Lord Alden Man 5 and tells him, "I'm right here Metal head or should I say bullet head." Robbie aims his gun on Lord Alden Man 5 and fires his gun and four bullets comes out of his gun and hits Lord Alden Man 5 in the foreheads and dies. The alarm on Robbie's cell phone went off and two bullets comes out of nowhere and hits the wall near Robbie and misses him. Robbie fires his gun and one bullet hits the wall near Alberto and misses him. Robbie start running and tackles Alberto to the floor and both of them drop their guns. Robbie is about to arrest Alberto and tells him, "I guess you will be coming with me quietly." Alberto tells Robbie, "Not today, Champberg!" Alberto kicks Robbie in the groin and gets up from the floor and punches him in the stomach. Alberto tells

Robbie, "Lord Alden is right about you, you are a fat loser than I thought and too easy to beat up." Alberto punches Robbie in the face, but Robbie blocks his punch and knees him in the stomach. Robbie kicks Alberto in the face and Alberto falls down on the floor. Robbie grabs Alberto by the shirt and tosses him to the floor. Robbie sees Alberto's gun and grabs it from the floor. Robbie goes over to Alberto and starts to arrest him. Alberto sees Robbie's gun and grabs it and aims his gun on Robbie. Alberto tells Robbie, "I guess you're a little big boy." Robbie fires his gun, one bullet comes out of his gun and hits the floor near Alberto and misses him. Robbie aims his gun on Alberto, "Nope, I'm a little faster little boy." Robbie fires his gun and three bullets comes out of and hits Alberto in the chest and dies before he fires his gun. Robbie tells himself, "Who said, never gets exciting in Silicon Valley." Lou comes out of the pizzeria and goes over talk to Robbie. Lou is a little frightened and tells Robbie, "Are these guys...?" Robbie interrupts him and tells Lou, "Yes, too bad Jaleel will be disappointed in this." Lou tells Robbie, "Why would he disappointed." Robbie tells Lou, "Their was a fire fight, he's miss the action." Lou tells Robbie, "Boy will he be pissed off." Robbie tells Lou, "I'm going to get my phone over the trash cans and calls this in." Lou tells Robbie, "Where is Amy?" Robbie tells Lou, "Long story and don't ask. Boy, this is going to be a long day." Robbie goes over to the trash can to get his cell phone to call the director to call this in to remove the dead bodies in this fire fight. Back in Lord Alden's warehouse where he is sitting in the manager's office where Rutherford, Yorkshire are waiting for Alberto and Maddie to bring in Princess Amy. The door opens and it's Maddie and Princess Amy. Maddie and Princess Amy enters Lord Alden's office and Maddie is holding Princess Amy at gunpoint and making her a hostage. Lord Alden is pleased that Maddie did a good job brining Princess Amy here. Lord Alden tells Princess Amy, "Hello Amy, long time no see." Princess Amy tells Lord Alden, "Save it Randall, I'll be seeing you in a long time where you'll be going when the feds come after you." Maddie tells Princess Amy, "Sit down. Rutherford tie her up." Rutherford tells Maddie, "Sure thing Maddie." Princess Amy sits down in the chair and Rutherford ties both of her hands on arm chair. Lord Alden tells Maddie, "Maddie, I hope our arrangement worked out well." Maddie tells Lord Alden, "You got that right, Randall." Princess Amy tells Lord Alden, "What arrangement?" Lord Alden tells Princess Amy, "Well Amy, you just fell into our little trap." Princess Amy tells Lord Alden, "What trap?" Yorkshire tells Princess Amy, "I am the one who put the article that Abda Electronics is seeking new investors after closing a deal with British Knight Shoes." Lord Alden tells Princess Amy, "I knew that article and that website would bring you here, so we grab you and hold you ransom for the Duke." Princess Amy tells them, "So, this was a set up. Abda Electronics never land an account with British Knight shoes and are not looking for investors." Lord Alden tells Princess Amy, "That stuff was true, Abda was looking for investors after he close a deal with British Knight shoes. I knew you were desperate to save your father's company. We set up that article for you to look to come here and we got Yorkshire a job in this company with an impressive resume and knowledge of computer to hack into Abda mainframe so he can be hired and sent Abda to computer conference call in Chicago all week that we arranged just to see you." Yorkshire tells Princess Amy, "Once that settled, we knew we can ransom you from your father." Maddie tells Princess Amy, "I knew your father would never give up his crown or his oil company. So once we hijack your father oil from his wells, we knew we can make more money with this company." Lord Alden tells Princess Amy, "Not only I will make more money, he will be out of business soon and he will have no choice to sign the merger agreement so I can take over his company and put him out of the street and you would marry me pretty soon that came with our agreement." Princess Amy tells Lord Alden, "Let me guess Randall, if I refuse my father would have to pay the dowry and that would nearly bankrupt my father's fortune and he would lose everything. I know that part, but this wasn't about money was it." Lord Alden tells Princess Amy, "This was about you. I wanted you all to myself and your father's title. I was looking forward to heir to the throne of England. Since I can't buy my way in the Prime Minister election. But I have something bigger for your father. It was all going to go well, until you brought that FBI moron here to interfere in my heroine dealing and my big plan. But that will be dealt with in a minute." Princess Amy tells Lord Alden, "I knew you guys kidnapped me, but what did you guys did to Robbie anyway." Lord Alden tells Princess Amy, "My associate and right hand man Alberto is taking care of your fat little friend. He will be tasting bullets in a few seconds when he's done with him. I don't have to worry about Champberg ruining my heroine dealing with my Israeli clients. But I have a bigger purpose with your father that he will give me." Princess Amy tells Lord Alden, "What purpose is that." Lord Alden tells Princess Amy, "Simple I'm going to ransom you, when I tell your father that he has until Thursday to give up his crown and his fortune to me or I would kill you." Princess Amy tells Lord Alden, "I thought you cared about me." Lord Alden tells Princess Amy, "Oh, I do. But their is something bigger than you. Is your father's crown and his fortune that I wanted so badly. Marrying you would get me that wealth and power. Since I have you, I no longer need you." Princess Amy tells Lord Alden, "Gee Randall, I thought we had something going." Lord Alden tells Princess Amy, "I still love you, baby. Like I said, I only care about one thing is your crown and your wealth. But I would love to leave you a consolation prize." Lord Alden makes out with Princess Amy and stops for a minute. Lord Alden tells Princess Amy, "What do you think honey. Am I great or not." Princess Amy tells Lord Alden, "I think you're an arrogant jerk and you are a lousy kisser." Lord Alden is upset right now and tells Princess Amy, "Maybe you should kiss this right now." Lord Alden slaps Princess Amy in the face. Lord Alden tells Princess Amy, "You know Amy, we were going to have great plans together. But know I'm going to kill you whether you father pays me your ransom." Princess Amy tells Lord Alden, "Randall, what makes you think my father would pay my ransom. My family doesn't negotiate with terrorist. Trust me, you fit the bill." Lord Alden tells Princess Amy, "Trust me, he will once I have you. I'm going to make the call." Lord Alden sits down in his chair and picks up the phone and starts dialing. Lord Alden calls the nurse at the hospital on the phone and tells the nurse, "Nurse can you get me Nivel Greenly, the duke of Granwich room." Robbie enters the FBI Secret Room and head to the computer room where Jaleel and Newton are waiting for him. Jaleel and Newton look at Robbie and it doesn't look good. Jaleel and Newton get up from their chairs and Jaleel ask Robbie, "Rob, where is Amy and what happened. You don't look so good." Robbie is upset right now and punches the wall. Robbie tells them, "I want to find Alden and Yorkshire, I want to take them down all of them and their empire. I want to wipe them all out." Newton tries calm Robbie down and tells him, "Robbie, calm down. Please calm down. Just tell us what happened." Robbie is a little frustrated and sits down in his chair and calms down for a minute. Robbie tells them, "It's Amy, Alden took her. He was watching us all day." Newton is not frustrated too and punches the wall and sits down in his chair. Newton tells himself, "I failed him, I failed her. The Duke, what is he going to say. He was just feeling better and now I lost his only daughter to that maniac." Robbie tells Jaleel, "So Jaleel, anything else that can get worse." Jaleel tells Robbie, "I already know Amy is kidnapped, because I got a call from the director. He is really upset with us." Robbie tells himself and Robbie, "It got worse. How upset is he?" Jaleel tells them, "Lord Alden called up for a ransom to the Duke, he is asking him to forfeit his estate and his crown in 24 hours. Or he's going to kill her." Newton tells them, "24 hours, that's Thursday and that's tomorrow. Does the FBI knew it might be Lord Alden who is the mastermind behind this heroine dealing and the Princess kidnapping?" Jaleel tells them, "I don't think so, the FBI couldn't trace the cell the phone or their cell phones. I think they're covering tracks really well." Robbie tells them, "Since Yorkshire is an ex MI6 agent and a top computer hacker. They covered their tracks really well, since they don't know it's Alden is the mastermind behind this. Their is no way the Duke is going to negotiate with Alden, rule number one, we don't negotiate with terrorist." Jaleel tells Robbie, "Sorry Robbie, but Amy's father is making a deal with Lord Alden. He'll give up the crown and his estate to him on Thursday as long he doesn't hurt her daughter. He was already emailing the deed to Newton email account right now for Lord Alden to sign." Newton tells them, "I better check my email." Newton gets up from his chair and goes to the FBI computer and checks his email. Robbie tells Jaleel, "Come on, Amy's father can't do this. Does he even know it's actually Lord Alden speaking too." Jaleel tells Robbie, "Not yet, since he's sick. He's not thinking seriously right now. Besides, he even called us their is no way, the FBI can find him and getting back his daughter is the only thing he cares about right now." Robbie tells Jaleel, "What about the director, how mad is he at us?" Jaleel tells Robbie, "The Director is not just mad at us, he's totally steamed. The Duke ask the FBI stepped down and he will ask Newton to give Alden the deed where he is at, to get his daughter back." Robbie tells them, "This stinks." Jaleel tells Robbie, "Well, it's going to stink a lot worse on us. The Director asked us back in Washington. We can forget about the review board, were going to be fired when we get back home." Newton prints out the deed from the printer, takes it out and sits back down stairs. Newton reads the deed that Nivel signed and needs Lord Alden's signature to give the entire estate and his crown to him. Their is also a ransom note where to drop off the deed and where to pick up Princess Amy. Robbie tells Newton, "Newton what is it?" Newton tells them, "I reading the ransom note where Lord Alden wants me to hand the deed to him." Jaleel tells Newton, "Where?" Newton tells them, "615 west avenue. That's where Lord Alden wants to give them the deed and he's going to release the Princess. This address around Midnight." Robbie tells them, "615 West Avenue, that's near Fisherman Wharf. I think I might know where Alden's drug lab at. I also forgot Lou emailed you all the information that Cal sent him. I ask Lou to email you." Jaleel tells Robbie, "Oh yeah, I have the files that I printed in the computer desk. Hang on a second." Jaleel goes over to the computer and sees the file and grabs it. Jaleel goes back to his seat and show the file of the information that Cal has on Lord Alden's drug operation, his associate and his israeli clients to Robbie. Jaleel tells Robbie, "Here it is." Robbie reads the information on Lord Alden and tells them, "I think I'm right. It is in Fisherman Wharf and the drug operation in 612 West Avenue. About a few blocks where Newton make the drop at." Newton tells them, "Since we know where Randall is drug operation is at, any idea where he might be holding his heroine dealing with his Israeli clients?" Robbie tells Newton, "I don't think so Newton, that's one place Cal could never find. But I think I know who is clients are?" Jaleel tells Robbie, "Who are they?" Robbie tells them, "Their called Yasmina Group, their were ex Israeli special forces led by Colonel Abu Yauba. Yaba and his troops are Interpol Most Wanted and Yauba is the number drug runner in the middle east. These guys were tried to overthrow the Israeli government and trying to assassinate the Israeli Prime Minister in the Embassy when he visited London two years ago. MI6 almost captured them, they're were rumors that they have a MI6 agent helping them escape, cover their tracks and the one who provided all the funding for their terrorism." Jaleel tells them, "Let me guess, that's Contel Yorkshire." Robbie tells them, "You betcha Jaleel, he's the one who is working with Yasmina Group. Guess who is the one funded their terrorism and the one who helped that group make a lot of money?" Newton tells Robbie, "Lord Randall Alden." Robbie tells them, "That's right Newton, not only stealing oil from Amy's father business, running a heroine lab in Fisherman Wharf. Is not only his only hobby. His biggest pride and joy is funding off the books terrorism with Colonel Yauba's troops the Yasmina Group." Jaleel tells them, "Too bad we wish we knew when or where Alden is going to sell his heroine to Yauba's troops. They could be anywhere." Robbie tells them, "I think I might know when they will arrive, FBI was working on a huge drug bust around Saturday night around 10 pm. But they couldn't find the location, one location they checked was an abandon warehouse about twenty blocks from Fisherman Wharf. But the place stripped clean. Their was a same drug bust that happens every month in a year in that same warehouse around Saturday night around 10 pm." Newton tells them, "I think Lord Alden must have an informant, when he was tipped off when the police or the FBI was arriving in their drug operation." Jaleel tells them, "That informant must be Yorkshire, he's the one who tipped off Alden about the cops arriving. That explains why the FBI and SFPD couldn't find anything on Alden, Yorkshire or his clients." Robbie is reading something else in the file and snaps his fingers and tells them, "The drug deal that Alden will be having Yasmia Group won't be on Saturday night at ten. It might be tomorrow, because Cal heard some rumors their rescheduling Thursday night. After Yasmina Group finishes their heroine dealing with Alden, he is still planning on overthrowing the government by assassinating the Israeli Prime Minister that will be in San Francisco tomorrow night at 11 pm." Newton tells them, "Wait a minute, the Israeli Prime Minister is here in town?" Robbie tells them, "He is in town for a speaking engagement on a new trade agreement with the Mayor in Moscone Center at 11 pm tomorrow night." Jaleel tells them, "If Yauba takes out the Prime Minister, the whole Israeli government and economy will collapse and Yasmina could take over the government with an iron fist." Robbie tells them, "He will be a like middle east Hitler in Israeli." Newton tells them, "Not only Yauba will have power, so will Lord Alden and Yorkshire, when the duke gives up his crown and his wealth to them. They will have more power in England than they ever did. Pretty soon, he will take the throne of England pretty soon once he gets Yauba to assassinate the royal family once he's finish the Israeli Prime Minister. Robbie tells them, "Only were not going to let that happened. If we can find the heroine dealing, we can find Alden and Yorkshire. We also can find his heroine dealing, Amy father's stolen oil and Yauba and his troops, once we find them, we will have enough evidence to put them for good and save Amy's father company and his crown." Jaleel tells Robbie, "Robbie we still don't know where the heroine deal is at?" Robbie tells them, "You right, Jaleel, we still don't know where it is. We got 24 hours to find it or were going to lose our jobs." Jaleel tells Robbie, "We don't have 24 Robbie, we already fired." Robbie tells Jaleel, "Were not fired yet. I call the director and tell him to give us 24 hours to find Lord Alden drug deal. If we don't were fired and Amy will be dead in 24 hours and her father will be out in the street and lose his crown if we lose." Jaleel tells Robbie, "You think the boss will give us all day to turn this around." Robbie tells Jaleel, "Were about to find out." Robbie takes out his cell phone from his left pants pocket and makes the call to the director. Robbie calls the Director and tells him, "Excuse me, sir. Can I have a moment." Robbie holds the speaker from his right hand and tells them, "This is going to take a while." Robbie takes right hand off the speaker and continues talking to his boss. Back in Lord Alden's warehouse finishes the call with his Amy's father and tells him by raspy voice, "You got 24 hours goodbye." Lord Alden hangs up his phone and sees Rutherford, Yorkshire and two of his men guarding Princess Amy will be tied up in the chair. Rutherford tells Lord Alden, "So what happen you think the Duke doesn't know it's you?" Lord Alden tells Rutherford, "My phone is on a scrambler, he doesn't know it's me. Luckily for me, Yorkshire help me block out the trace and dubbed my voice when he was working with MI6." Yorkshire tells Lord Alden, "My lord do you think the Duke will give us what we want." Lord Alden tells Yorkshire, "Of course he will give us what we want. He loves his daughter and he just did. He's already faxing the contract to give up his crown and his wealth to me. Once we return back to London, were going to be walking home in a red carpet with the Duke's throne and his estate. Sometimes, I love being me." Yorkshire tells Lord Alden, "What are we going to do we the princess Lord Alden." Lord Alden tells Yorkshire, "Simple Yorkshire, once we finish our heroine dealing and get our money with Colonel Yauba tomorrow night, well finish her off." Rutherford tells Lord Alden, "Gee my lord I always thought you were in love with the Princess you been in love with her all your life." Lord Alden tells them, "I was, she was beautiful and made a great trophy wife. I thought her father would pay me her dowry if she refuse or get her father to sign a merger agreement with me. But ever since she got here and her fat loser boyfriend interfered in our drug dealings. I had take matters in my own hands. Besides, I only cared about her father's wealth and his crown more than her. Since Champberg is dead, no one else can not even the FBI could stop me." Lord Alden sees Princess Amy gagged with scotch tape and tied up. He goes over to Princess Amy and remove the scotch tape out of her mouth and tells her, "I just want you to hear your words, Amy. That my right hand guy Alberto rubbed out your boyfriend or soon to be boyfriend nearly an hour ago after my heroine dealing with the Yasmina Group you'll be next. I like to see the look in your father's face you'll be a corpse next to your fat boyfriend that failed to protect you once we finish you off tomorrow night. I just want to hear your beautiful words, that what were going to do to you tomorrow night. I hope I could get a last kiss from you, before we kill you." Princess Amy tells Lord Alden, "I rather kiss my fat boyfriend, than some amateur drug dealer that thinks my father would ever give up his crown or his estate to you." Lord Alden gets upset and slaps her in the face again. Lord Alden tells Princess Amy, "That will teach you respect little girl, never call me an amateur drug lord." The door opens and it's Maddie, Maddie enters the manager's office and informs Lord Alden what's going on. Rutherford tells Maddie, "Hey Maddie, how is our little friend Champberg, is he eating dirt yet and where is Alberto?" Maddie tells them, "That's what I want to talk to you about?" Lord Alden tells Maddie, "What is it, Maddie?" Maddie tells them, "I got a report with the FBI and SFPD, Alberto, Jax and six of our men are dead. Champberg took them all out. He is still alive." Lord Alden is upset and tells them, "What!" Lord Alden goes over to his desk and removes all the papers out of his desk really hard. That he is upset. Rutherford tells Lord Alden, "Well great my Lord. That FBI fool Champberg is still alive. I bet he is already informed his partner Agent Brown about us and I bet theyre still coming after us." Lord Alden looks at Rutherford for a minute and he is not a good mood what Rutherford said to him. Lord Alden tells Rutherford, "Rutherford come here." Rutherford tells Lord Alden, "Yes sir, you think we should call off our heroine dealing with General Yauba since the FBI are tracking us down?" Lord Alden tells Rutherford, "First of all, Rutherford. Never talk back to me when I'm upset or when I have an idea. You know why, I don't like people talking back to me." Rutherford is little frightened and tells

Lord Alden, "Why sir?" Lord Alden tells Rutherford, "Because I would do this." Lord Alden kicks Rutherford in the stomach and punches him in the face and falls down on the floor. Lord Alden tells Rutherford, "Don't ever talk back to me when I'm upset." Rutherford tells Lord Alden, "Yes Lord Alden, I'll remember that sir." Lord Alden tells Rutherford, "Get up, you're way more pathetic lying on the floor." Rutherford tells Lord Alden, "Yes sir." Rutherford gets up from the floor and Lord Alden tells them, "By the way Rutherford, were not going to cancel our heroine dealing with Yauba. I already rescheduled this huge deal with him tomorrow night at ten. Luckily for me he's in town with business with Israeli Prime Minister right after we conclude our huge heroine dealing tomorrow night." Yorkshire tells Lord Alden, "What about Champberg, you think we should go look for him and Brown and still kill them. Before they look for us or drug deal?" Lord Alden tells them, "I love to find them and kill them myself. We don't have time, General Yauba and his Yasmina Group are going to be in town for one night. Were almost finished the last supply of heroine before the big day starts." Maddie tells Lord Alden, "So what about Champberg and Brown, they'll running around Silicon Valley looking for us." Lord Alden tells Maddie, "Relax Maddie, once we finish our heroine dealing with the Yasmina Group. Well find them and kill them right after we kill Amy." Lord Alden is thinking for a minute and tells them, "Maddie tomorrow night before we head to our heroine deal with General Yauba, The Duke is going to send his personal assistant to give us the Duke's contract for me to sign. I already told them when and where to meet him, So I want you to wait for him and give us the contract right before our deal starts. Once we finish, will meet back here and I'll sign the deed and will all go back to collect our riches." Maddie tells Lord Alden, "What is if it's a trap, the Duke is not stupid as you think." Lord Alden tells Maddie, "We have nothing to worry about, the Duke is a broken man now. Since we have his daughter, if he is setting us up. He won't try anything, since we have some of our men watching our backs and we have a van out back that is untraceable to track us down. So we have nothing to worry about." Maddie tells Lord Alden, "What a relief." Lord Alden tells them, "Come on guys we have a lot of work to do. Maddie re tape her mouth, I need some quiet time before our heroine deal starts. Maddie tells Lord Alden, "Yes, my lord." Maddie sees the scotch tape on the file cabinet, grabs it and tapes Princess Amy mouth again. Lord Alden looks at Princess Amy and tells her, "Looks like we have to kill your boyfriend again. This time were going to do it right. I'll be the one to finish him off." Lord Alden leaves the warehouse and Princess Amy is a little teary once he heard the man he loves and is going to be pretty soon. Lord Alden exits the manager's office and sees his men finishing heroine dealing in his warehouse. Lord Alden smiles for a minute and everything will go smooth sailing. Back in FBI secret room in Mountain View Public Library where Robbie is talking to the director in his cell phone with Jaleel and Newton sitting down in their chairs in the meeting room. Robbie tells the director on the phone, "Thank you sir. Bye!" Robbie hangs up phone and talks to Jaleel and Newton. Jaleel tells Robbie, "What happened?" Robbie tells Jaleel, "I have some good news and some bad news?" Jaleel tells Robbie, "What is the bad news first." Robbie tells Jaleel, "We still don't know where Lord Alden heroine dealing with Yasmina Group is at?" Jaleel tells Robbie, "And the good news is?" Robbie tells them, "I called the director, he's giving us twenty-four hours to find Lord Alden, Yasmina Group and to find Amy. If we fail, you and I are fired. Amy will be dead and his father and Newton will be out in the street twenty four hours." Jaleel tells Robbie, "All right, we got twenty-four hours. If we find the heroine deal, we just need another lead." Robbie tells Jaleel, "Jaleel, I think I have something. While I was on the phone with the director, I just got an email from Lou about the girl who works for Lord Alden and the one who took Amy from behind his Pizzeria parking lot and knows where to look for her?" Jaleel tells Robbie, "Who is she?" Robbie tells Jaleel, "Her name is Madelyn Swift, she used to be an ex special forces for the British army. She was high trained Krav Maga and Kung fu and she was thrown out for high brutality and abuse with fellow soldiers. After leaving the British Army, Lord Alden heard about her and hired her as a body guard and personal assistant to him. With her military contacts, she can get a hold any drug runners around the world. That's how Lord Alden got his business deal with General Yauba and the Yasmina Group, because of Swift military contact." Jaleel tells Robbie, "If she is Lord Alden right hand woman, maybe she can help us find his heroine dealing. Too bad, I wish we knew where she is?" Robbie tells Jaleel, "I think I know where she is. I found out she hangs out in a night club called Club Red. She goes their around 9:30 pm on Thursday." Newton tells Robbie,

"That's Thursday." Robbie tells Newton, "That's right Newton." Newton tells Robbie, "I just got an email from Duke Greenly from the phone, he told me go to Club Red to meet Maddie their at 9:30 pm tomorrow night to give her the contract for Lord Alden to sign. Once Lord Alden signs it, Nivel's estate and his crown will go to him if he wants Princess Amy back." Jaleel tells Newton, "You think Alden is going bring Amy back just like that." Newton tells Jaleel, "Of course not, I'm know guys like Alden. Amy is a huge witness, she saw the whole thing. Of course they won't give her back." Jaleel tells Newton, "I don't make this worse Newton, they're going to kill her after Alden signs the contract and finishes his deal with General Yauba's troops." Newton tells them, "I'm not going to let that happened, I'm not going to let her die out their. I made a promise to her father, I protect her. I will." Robbie tells Newton, "Of course not Newton, neither are we. We made a promise to protect her too. Were not going to let that happened too." Jaleel tells them, "The only way to get Amy back and keep our jobs, is to find Alden heroine deal. We still don't know where it is." Robbie tells them, "We don't need to find it, Alden's guys will help us find it. I know how. Newton you're not going to meet Maddie at Club Red tomorrow night." Newton tells Robbie, "I'm not." Robbie tells Newton, "Me and Jaleel are going to meet her tonight. Were going to ask her where the deal is tonight." Jaleel tells Robbie, "What is she doesn't tell us." Robbie tells Jaleel, "If she doesn't tell us, will just arrest her or beat the snot out of her until she tell us. Newton you are one of us now. Were making you an honorary FBI agent. Welcome to the team." Newton tells Robbie, "I'm very honored Robbie. I appreciate this." Robbie tells Newton, "Just don't let it go to your head." Newton tells Robbie, "I won't." Robbie tells Newton, "Just in case, if Maddie won't tell us where the deal is going down. Newton, I want you go to Alden drug lab. he has a limousine parked out front. I need you to put a tracking device behind the limousine trunk." Newton tells Robbie, "What tracking device ?" Robbie gets up from his chair and goes to the computer and takes out a watch from the desk drawer that he opened and closed. Robbie sits back down in his chair and gives Newton the watch that is a tracking device." Newton tells Robbie, "This looks like an ordinary watch." Robbie tells Newton, "It may look like an ordinary watch, when you press the red button, the tracking device is on when you wear it on your wrist or leave it any place. We can monitor it on the laptop or my computer. Cal has a friend Lucas and his contact who is head of the R&D department in the pentagon. He can get any hands of equipment we need on cases like this. That's where Cal and Lou got a lot of intel from the Pentagon and got Cal in the job in the Justice department." Jaleel looks at the watch and tells Robbie, "This watch is pretty neat. Any other stuff that Cal sent us." Robbie tells Jaleel, "In the glove compartment in the car, I only use that for emergencies. We got one day to find Lord Alden's drug deal, Jaleel you and I will start training to get ready for the fight of our lives. Newton I need start practicing the tracking device, my laptop is on the desk. All you have to do, press the enter button and the tracking device will start. You have a big night for you tomorrow. It's time for Princess of Silicon Valley." Jaleel tells Robbie, "Princess of Silicon Valley?" Robbie tells Jaleel, "That's code for operation rescue princess. You guys are in, if you're not I understand. This is a big mission, I know were going to die out their." Jaleel tells Robbie, "You had us, when do we start." Newton tells Robbie, "I made a promise the Duke that I protect her daughter, I'm going to do that. I'm in too Robbie." Robbie tells them, "It's time to begin." Robbie, Newton and Jaleel start their fist bumps and let's go. Robbie and Jaleel start traning, Jaleel starts punching and kicking in the punching bag. Robbie starts flipping Jaleel on the mat." Newton places the watch outside the FBI secret room and starts the tracking device on the laptop. Jaleel starts shooting five bad guys with his fake video game gun in a warehouse. Robbie starts firing his gun and three bullets comes out of his gun and hits the target in the firing range. Jaleel spars with Robbie and flips to the mat. Newton starts the laptop tracking device again and sees the watch at the children reading room section on the table. Robbie fires his video game gun and shoots three bad guys in the harbor. Jaleel starts practicing in the firing range, five bullets comes out of his gun and hits the bulls eye of the target. Newton starts the laptop tracking device again and this time the watch is in on the table in the poetry section. Newton gives them a thumbs up. Robbie starts firing his gun again and four bullets comes out of his gun and hits the bulls eye at the firing range. Robbie starts smiling and tells himself, "I think were ready." Robbie parks his Ferrari FF GT4 on the curb right outside Club Red. Robbie and Jaleel exits the car and goes inside Club Red. Jaleel is carrying the yellow open envelope that carries the contract to Princess Amy father sent in his right hand. Robbie tells Jaleel,

"The deal is going down around ten. We got thirty minutes to find it, so Jaleel remember the game plan." Jaleel tells Robbie, "We find Maddie, bring her in and gently tell her where the deal is going down." Robbie tells Jaleel, "Were going in and get out." Jaleel tells Robbie, "You don't have to ask me twice Robbie." Inside Club Red, the club is getting really busy and Robbie and Jaleel enter the club. Robbie sees the bartender and goes over talk to him. Robbie tells the bartender, "Excuse me?" Bartender tells Robbie, "Hi, can I help you?" Robbie tells the Bartender, "Were looking for Maddie Swift, is she here?" Bartender tells Robbie, "That depends?" Jaleel tells the Bartender, "Depends on what?" Bartender tells them, "I know where she is, but I'm not going to tell you anything unless you order something." Robbie tells the bartender, "I'll take a bud light." Jaleel tells the Bartender, "The same!" Bartender opens the fridge and gives them two bottles of bud light." Bartender tells them, "Six bucks!" Jaleel takes out his wallet and gives him the six bucks. Bartender takes out the bottle caps and Robbie and Jaleel grabs their beer. Bartender tells them, "She is at VIP room right over their." Jaleel and Robbie starts drinking their beer and the Bartender points to the VIP room at the right and stops. Bartender tells them, "What do you need to see her for?" Robbie tells the Bartender, "Let's just say we owe her money." Jaleel tells the Bartender, "She called us here to give it to her. So, we're going to come in and come out after were done." Bartender tells them, "Good luck guys." Robbie tells them, "Were going to need it." Robbie and Jaleel put their bottles of beer on the table and goes to the VIP room where Maddie and five of Lord Alden's men are enjoying the night. Robbie and Jaleel enters the VIP room and Robbie tells Maddie, "Hello Maddie, Newton was going to arrive with here tonight. He was under the weather, so we decide to give you the contract ourselves." Maddie recognizes these guys and Robbie tells Maddie, "The envelope is empty because we forget the contract. I guess we left at home. I wondered if you give us nearly half an hour to get it back." Maddie tells Lord Alden's men, "It's them too shoot them." Maddie and Lord Alden's men take out their Glock 19 that is taped underneath the tables and took it out and aim their guns on Robbie and Jaleel and gets up from their chairs. Maddie fires his gun and two bullets comes out of his gun. The two bullets hits the sofa and misses Robbie. Robbie tells Jaleel, "Get down." Jaleel tells Robbie, "You don't have to ask me twice." Robbie and Jaleel dives down on the floor where two bullets comes out of nowhere and hits the table near Jaleel and misses him. Robbie and Jaleel dives down on the floor rolls over to the right, where three bullets comes out of nowhere and hits the floor near Robbie and misses then. Robbie and Jaleel rolls over to the sofa and hide behind it. Robbie and Jaleel takes out their biretta 92 behind their backs and Jaleel fires his gun, three bullets comes out of his gun and hits Lord Alden man 5 in the chest and dies. Robbie fires his gun, two bullets comes out of his gun and hits the floor near Maddie and misses her. Lord Alden man 1 and 2 fires their guns and two bullets comes out of their guns. One bullet comes out of Lord Alden Man 1 and one more bullet comes out of Lord Alden Man 2 gun. Robbie sees Lord Alden Man 3 and aims his gun on his left leg. Robbie fires his gun, one bullet comes out of his gun and hits Lord Alden Man 3 in the left leg. Lord Alden Man 3 left leg is hurting and Robbie fires his gun again and three bullets comes out of his gun and hits Lord Alden Man 3 in forehead and stomach and dies. Jaleel fires his gun, two bullets comes out of his gun and hits the table near Maddie and misses her. Jaleel takes out his clip and gets another one behind his and reloads his gun. Jaleel fires his gun and three bullets comes out of his gun and hits Lord Alden Man 4 in the chest and dies. Lord Alden Man 2 fires his gun, three bullets comes out of his and the floor near Robbie and misses him. Robbie sees Lord Alden Man 2, takes out a quarter out of pocket and flips it to distract Lord Alden Man 2. It does distract him for a minute, Robbie fires his gun and two bullets comes out of his gun and hits Lord Alden Man 2 in the chest and dies. Jaleel tells Robbie, "We have to get out of here." Robbie tells Jaleel, "Were going to need a create a diversion. I know how." Robbie takes out another quarter and flips it hard and Jaleel fires his gun and three bullets comes out of his gun and hits the floor near Maddie and misses her. Maddie is a little distracted and frightened. Robbie and Jaleel gets up from the sofa and exits the VIP room. Maddie gets upset and tells Lord Alden Man 1, "Get those morons. I don't want to leave out here alive." Lord Alden Man 1 tells Maddie, "Got it Maddie." Outside of Club Red, Robbie and Jaleel exits the club and head their car. They both go inside their car and exits the parking and head to the highway. Lord Alden Man 1 and Maddie exits the club too and sees Robbie and Jaleel leaving. Lord Alden Man 1 is upset and tells Maddie, "They got away, we don't know where they're going to go." Maddie tells Lord Alden Man 1, 'I know where they are, follow me." Robbie is driving his Ferrari in the Mountain View highway with Jaleel sitting in the passenger seat. Inside the car, Jaleel tells Robbie, "You think we lost them." Robbie hears a bullet coming out of somebody's gun out of nowhere. Robbie tells Jaleel, "I think not." Jaleel looks out in the window and sees Lord Alden Man 1 carrying a Franchi SPAS 12 gun out of the window of Black SUV van and shots his long gun again. Two bullets comes out of his gun and hits the road and misses the Ferrari. Jaleel gets back down from the window and tells Robbie, "We got some company. Lord Alden Man 1 fires his gun and three bullets comes out of his gun and hits the Ferrari taillight and misses them. Robbie tells Jaleel, "Stall them, were going to have lose them." Jaleel tells Robbie, "How!" Robbie tells Jaleel, "I know a short cut." Jaleel sees his gun on the dash and grabs it. Jaleel goes out of the window and sees the Black SUV van where Lord Alden Man 1 and Maddie are driving. Jaleel fires his gun and two bullets comes out of his gun and two bullets hits the hood. Lord Alden Man 1 fires his gun, two bullets comes out of his gun and hits the license plate. Lord Alden Man 1 fires his gun again and one bullet comes out of his gun and hits the road and misses the Ferrari. Jaleel fires his gun, one bullet comes out of his gun and hits the hood again. Robbie tells Jaleel, "Fasten your seat belt Jaleel, it's going to be a bumpy ride." Jaleel tells Robbie, "I hate where this going!" Robbie sees road closed high way from the right, crashes Road Closed sign and that's nearly halfway constructed bridge. Jaleel tells Robbie, "This is a short cut!" Robbie tells Jaleel, "Fire dummy now" Jaleel tells Robbie, "If I die I'm taking you with me." Jaleel gets up from the window and aims his gun on Lord Alden Man 1. Jaleel fires his gun, two bullets comes out of his gun and hits the signal light and misses them. Lord Alden Man 1 fires his gun and three bullets comes out of his gun and hits the trunk of the Ferrari. Lord Alden Man 1 fires his gun and one bullet comes out of his gun and hits the rear view mirror that breaks it off. Jaleel gets out of the window and tells Robbie, "We need to lose them. Robbie tells Jaleel, "You see those two grenades and three dvd holders!" Jaleel tells Robbie, "Yeah!" Robbie tells Jaleel, "Throw the Grenade first, then throw two DVD holders." Jaleel tells Robbie, "Compliments from our friend Cal." Robbie tells Jaleel, "Hang on, were going to swirl and slide." Robbie swirls and slides his car to right and goes loop to loop once and Robbie sees Black SUV van and throws the grenade on the Black SUV van. But the grenade doesn't works. Lord Alden Man tells Maddie, "We gotta get out of here, we got a grenade on us." Robbie swirls and slide on the car once and Jaleel throws the DVD holders three times on the Black SUV van and the DVD holders explode with Lord Alden Man 1 and Maddie and dies in the explosion. Robbie stops the car for a minute and they both exit the car and sees the explosion. Jaleel tells Robbie, "What happened, that grenade was a dud. Why did the DVD holders explode." Robbie tells Jaleel, "Simple the grenade is a fake. I needed them to distract them for a minute, before you threw the DVD holders on them." Jaleel tells Robbie, "Those weren't ordinary DVD holders were they Robbie?" Robbie tells Jaleel, "Those were three pounds of heavy explosives on those holders. They only work when you toss them at something." Jaleel tells Robbie, "I don't think Maddie is going to tell us where the heroine deal is anytime soon. I guess were back at square one." Robbie tells Jaleel, "That was a Plan A. We have Plan B. I just hope that works out well, were out of plans." Jaleel tells Robbie, "I know Plan A went into flames, I just hope Newton puts that tracking device on Alden's limo pretty soon." Robbie tells Jaleel, "Yeah, me too." Newton is taking a taxi behind Lord Alden's warehouse and sees his limousine parked outside the warehouse. Newton tells the Cab Driver, "I'm just going to be in and out for a minute." Cab Driver tells Newton, "Well hurry up, the meter is running." Newton exits the cab and sees the scotch tape and the watch. Newton grabs the watch and Scotch Tape and closes the cab door. Newton walks slowly to Lord Alden's limo and sees his trunk and tapes the watch in back of the trunk. Lord Alden runs back to the cab and goes inside for a minute and tells himself, "That was close." Lord Alden sees the laptop and starts it. Lord Alden sees Lord Alden limo, two Black SUV vans and three trucks exits the warehouse. Lord Alden presses enter on the laptop and the tracking device is on. Lord Alden tells himself, "I'm in!" Lord Alden takes out his cell phone from his right pants pocket and makes the call to Robbie and Jaleel. Robbie and Jaleel are in the highway driving the Ferrari and Jaleel cell phone rings. Jaleel tells Robbie, "It's mine." Jaleel takes out his cell phone from his right pants pocket and answers it. Jaleel tells Newton who is on the phone, "Hello!" Newton voiceover tells Jaleel, "Jaleel, it's me Newton. Good news, I put the watch in back of Lord Alden's trunk. I know where he's going." Jaleel tells Newton on the phone, "That's great

Newton." Newton voiceover tells Jaleel, "He's going I-12 make it right." Jaleel tells Newton on the phone, "Hold on a minute." Jaleel tells Robbie, "Robbie, it's Newton. He put the tracking device on Alden's limo. Go to I-12 right." Robbie tells Jaleel, "No problem." Lord Alden's limo, two Black SUV and three trucks are on the San Francisco highway. Jaleel tells Robbie on the phone, "West 15!" Newton tells Jaleel on the phone, "Make a left and hit East 145." ." Lord Alden's limo, two Black SUV and three trucks are on the San Francisco highway again. Jaleel tells Robbie on the phone, "East 113!" Lord Alden's limo, two Black SUV and three trucks are on the San Francisco highway again. Lord Alden sees the tracking device and knows where Lord Alden going and where his heroine deal is at. Lord Alden tells himself, "So their you are." Lord Alden calls Jaleel on the phone, "I know where he is and where is his heroine deal is at. It's at South Beach Harbor in San Francisco Bay it's about ten miles from here. Okay, I got it." Jaleel tells Robbie on the phone, "Robbie we found it." Robbie tells Jaleel, "So where the deal going down?" Jaleel tells Robbie, "South Beach Harbor, it's ten miles from here. I already told Newton to call the Director and tell him where we are." Robbie tells Jaleel, "We better get going. Just hope Newton got back up here in time." Jaleel tells Robbie, "Me too." Newton is on the cell phone with the FBI Director and tells him, "Sir, send in two SWAT vans and two boats and three helicopters waiting. Hurry, the Princess life is depending on us. All right bye!" Newton hangs up his cell phone and tells the Cab Driver, "Jack, take me to South Harbor Beach. I'll double the fare if you get me their." Jack tells Newton, "No problem." Inside South Beach harbor abandoned warehouse where Rutherford, Lord Alden and two of his men are tying up Princess Amy to the chair of the office. Princess Amy is wearing a tight gray tank top and blue jeans. Rutherford tells Lord Alden, "I'm done, my lord." Lord Alden tells Rutherford, "After were done, will finish her off. I just hope Maddie got the contracts for me to sign before we head back home." Rutherford tells Lord Alden, "We better hurry up, sir. General Yauba and his men will be here in a minute." Lord Alden tells Rutherford, "We better get ready." Lord Alden looks at Princess Amy, "I always thought their would be something between us. You would've made a great wife for me. Not anymore. Oh by the way." Lord Alden kisses Princess Amy in the lips for a minute and stops. Lord Alden tells Princess Amy, "I did promise you that kiss Amy. Too bad you had to die for it. I hope you remember that in eternity." Princess Amy spits on Lord Alden and tells him, "I hope you remember that in eternity." Lord Alden slaps Princess Amy in the face hard and tells him, "We would have been so happy together. Not anymore. Let's go!" Lord Alden, Rutherford and two of Lord Alden's men exits the office and get ready for the deal. Robbie parks his Ferrari across the street of the South Beach Harbor warehouse. Robbie and Jaleel exits the car and tells Jalele, "I hope Nigel has insurance for the Ferrari." Jaleel opens the trunk and takes out two Biretta 92 out of the trunk and gives it to Robbie. Robbie also takes out another Biretta 92 from his trunk. Jaleel tells Robbie, "How long before back up arrives." Robbie tells Jaleel, "It's going to take them a few minutes to get here. Alden and his guys will be out of warehouse in no time before they get here." Jaleel tells Robbie, "I guess were going to have to stall them when they get here." Newton taxi arrives and parks right outside the street of the warehouse. Newton exits the cab and goes over talk to Robbie and Jaleel. Jaleel tells Newton, "Newton what are you doing here?" Newton tells them, "I thought I could back you up. Where's backup." Robbie tells Newton, "It's going to take a while for them to get here. Were going to stall them before they arrive." Newton tells them, "That's the reason, why I'm here I thought I can back you guys up here." Robbie tells Newton, "We appreciate that Newton, but were FBI agents and what were doing is dangerous." Newton tells them, "I know dangerious, I used to be in the special forces in British Army before I was the Duke's butler and I did sign a release forum, before I did this mission with you guys." Robbie tells Newton, "Well that's true." Newton tells them, "Besides I promise Duke Greenly, that I protect her daughter. I'm going to do that." Robbie tells Newton, "Okay Newton, just be careful out their." Jaleel tells Robbie, "So Robbie, what's the plan." Robbie tells Jaleel, "I'm going to give them a little distraction." Robbie gives Newton a gun and Newton takes the gun from him. Inside the South Beach Harbor warehouse where eight barrels of Duke Greenly's oil are in the warehouse and Lord Alden, Rutherford, Yorkshire and eight of Lord Alden's men are here to make a deal with General Yauba and six of his men who are the Yasmina Group. General Yauba opens the two briefcases of five million dollars each on the table. Lord Alden nods his head to Yorkshire to get the bags of heroine out of the barrel of oil. Yorkshire grabs the bag of heroine out of Nivel's oil barrel and puts it on the table and wipes the oil off the bag. The bag of heroine that General Yauba sees that makes him happy. Before the deal was concluded, Robbie enters the warehouse and tells them, "Excuse me. I'm a little bit lost. I was suppose go to a boat tour of San Francisco Bay, you know where it is. Hey are you guys working on a huge business deal here. Are you guys trading flour for money. Man, you guys are weird business men. It must be a lot of money on flower huh." Lord Alden recognizes Robbie and tells his men, "Kill him!" Lord Alden, eight of his men, Yorkshire, Rutherford, General Yauba and six of his men takes out their Glock 19 guns from their right gun holder behind their jackets and aims their guns on Robbie. Three bullets comes out of Lord Alden's gun and hits the floor near Robbie and misses him. Robbie takes out his Biretta 92 back of his pants and fires his gun. Three bullets comes out of his gun and hits General Yauba in the chest and dies. Two more bullets comes out of nowhere and hits the floor near Robbie and misses when he dives down on the floor. Robbie dives down the floor and rolls over to the three boxes to the right and hide. Robbie sees Lord Alden Man 3 and aims the gun on him. Robbie fires his gun, three bullets comes out of his gun and hits Lord Alden Man 3 in the chest and dies. Robbie fires his gun again, two bullets comes out of his gun and hits Lord Alden Man 1 in the stomach and dies. Newton and Jaleel sneaks in the warehouse with their guns and Newton fires his gun, three bullets comes out of his gun and hits Yamina Group Man 1 in the chest and dies. Jaleel fires his gun and two bullets comes out of his gun and hits Yasmina Group Man 4 in the chest and dies. Jaleel and Newton hide two boxes and a barrel to the right. Yorkshire fires his gun, three bullets comes out of his gun and hits the box near Robbie and misses him. Robbie fires his gun, two bullets comes out of his gun and hits the near Rutherford and misses him. Jaleel aims his gun on Rutherford, fires his gun and three bullets comes out of his gun and hits Rutherford in the chest and dies. Newton fires his gun, two bullets comes out of his gun and hits Yasmina Group Man 5 in the chest and dies. Robbie fires his gun, three bullets comes out of his gun and hits Yasmina Group Man 4 in the chest and dies. Lord Alden Man 2 fires his gun and one bullet comes out of his gun and hits the wall near Newton and misses him. Jaleel fires his gun, two bullets comes out of his gun and hits Lord Alden Man 2 in the chest and dies. Robbie sees Lord Alden Man 7, aims his gun on and fires his gun. Three bullets comes out of his gun and hits Lord Alden Man 7 in the chest and dies. Jaleel fires his gun, two bullets comes out of his gun and hits Lord Alden Man 6 in the chest and dies. Lord Alden is pissed off and fires his gun really hard. Six bullets comes out of his gun and hits the wall near Robbie and misses him. Newton fires his gun, three bullets comes out of his gun and hits Yasmina Group Man 3 in the chest and dies. Jaleel fires his gun and two bullets comes out of gun and hits the wall near Yorkshire and misses him. Robbie fires his gun again, two bullets comes out of his gun and hits Lord Alden Man 8 in the chest and dies. Jaleel fires his gun, four bullets comes out of his gun and hits Yasmina Group Man 6 in the stomach and dies. Newton fires his gun, two bullets comes out of his gun and hits Lord Alden Man 5 in the stomach and dies. Yorkshire fires his gun, four bullets comes out of hits the barrels near Jaleel and misses him. Robbie looks at Jaleel and Newton and tells them, "Cover me, I'm going in!" Jaleel and Newton nods their heads and Newton fires his gun, one bullet comes out of his gun and hits the floor near Yorkshire and misses him. Robbie comes out of the barrel and run for his life to tackle Lord Alden. Five comes out of nowhere and hits the near Robbie and misses him. Robbie tackles Lord Alden to the table and both of them falls down on the floor. Both of them drop their guns. Robbie and Lord Alden is about to get up from the floor. Lord Alden kicks Robbie in the face and Robbie falls down on the floor. Lord Alden picks up from Robbie's jacket and toss him to the office next door where Princess Amy is tied up on the chair. Lord Alden goes over to the office and sees Robbie beaten up. Lord Alden kicks Robbie in the stomach and grabs him by the jacket. Lord Alden punches him in the stomach twice and punches him in the face. Lord Alden let's go of his jacket and punches him in the face again and Robbie falls down on the floor. Jaleel fires his gun, two bullets comes out of his gun and hits the floor near Yasmina Group 2 and misses him. Yasmina Group Man 2 tells Yasmina Group Man 3, "Come on let's get out of here." Yasmina Group Man 3 tells Yasmina Group Man 2, "We can escape from the back." Yasmina Group Man 2 and 3 are about to exit the warehouse until, Jaleel fires his gun and one bullet comes out of his gun and hits Yasmina Group Man 2 in the left leg. Yasmina Group Man 2 left leg is soaring. Jaleel fires his gun again, three bullets comes out of his gun and hits him in the chest and dies. Yasmina Group Man 3 sees his friend dies, he doesn't have doesn't have any time to be upset right now. Like I said, only the strong survives. Yasmina Group Man 3 is exiting the warehouse. Lord Alden continues punishing Robbie. Lord Alden kicks him in the chest and goes near his face and punches him in the face again. Lord Alden tells Robbie, "So Champberg, you think you could stop me. I was wrong. What makes you think Amy would pick you over me. Huh." Lord Alden kicks Robbie in the stomach and tells Robbie, "I can't hear you, why did she pick me over you. Answer me, you fat moron!" Lord Alden kicks Robbie in the stomach, but Robbie blocks his kick. Robbie gets up from the floor and punches him in the groin. Robbie let's go of Lord Alden's foot, knees him in the kick and give him a roundhouse kick in the face. Robbie gets Lord Alden up from the floor and picks up by the shirt and punches him in the stomach three times. Robbie lets him go and punches him in the face three times and gives him another round house kick to the face. Lord Alden falls down on the floor. Robbie tells Lord Alden, "You wanna know why Amy picked me over you. I treat her with respect and you treat her like a trophy wife. Does that answer your question." Lord Alden tells Robbie, "Not but this does." Lord Alden kicks Robbie in the groin and gets up from the floor and punches him in the face twice. Robbie falls down on the floor and Lord Alden picks him up on the floor and flips him across the floor. Princess Amy is a little hurt seeing Robbie being defeated like that. Lord Alden sees their guns on the floor their and goes over to pick them up. Yasmina Group Man 3 exits outside the warehouse and tells himself, "Only the strong survives. I guess I make myself General." Three FBI Members and two FBI SWAT vans are outside the warehouse and both of them are carrying his SPAS 12 gun. FBI SWAT 1 tells Yasmina Group Man 3, "Hands up, You're Under Arrest!" FBI SWAT 2 tells Yasmina Group Man 3, "Their is no escape, it's over." Yasmina Group Man 3 tells them, "Their is one escape and it's time to get your hands up big men!" Yasmina Group Man 3 fires his gun and three bullets comes out of his gun and hits the FBI SWAT van and FBI SWAT 1 fires his gun, four bullets comes out of his gun and hits Yasmina Group Man 3 in the chest and dies. Lord Alden sees his gun and Robbie's grabs them and head back to the office. Yorkshire fires his gun, three bullets comes out of his gun and hits the wall near Jaleel and misses him. Jaleel tells Newton, "Cover me, I'm going in." Newton tells Jaleel, "What do you want me to do?" Jaleel takes out a quarter and gives it to Newton and tells him, "Toss it in the air and it will distract him. While I will do my thing." Newton tells Jaleel, "What thing that will be?" Jaleel removes the clip out of his gun and takes out another one and reloads it. Three more bullets comes out of nowhere and hits the wall near Jaleel and misses him. Yorkshire is upset and tells them, "Come on boys, come out come out wherever you are!" Newton flips a quarter in the air while Yorkshire gets a little distracted and Jaleel dives down on the floor out of the box and gets up from the floor and aims his gun on Yorkshire. Jaleel tells Yorkshire, "Heads I win!" Jaleel fires his gun, three bullets comes out of his gun and hits Yorkshire in the chest and dies. Newton comes out of the box and Jaleel tells Newton, I better go check on Robbie and see if he's okay. Lord Alden enters the office and sees Robbie being beaten on the floor. Lord Alden tells Robbie, "Look what I have here, two guns and one of them is yours. You want it come and get it Champberg. Lord Alden tosses Robbie's gun on the floor. Robbie tries to get up a little and Lord Alden takes the scotch tape out of Princess Amy's mouth and tells Robbie, "You know I want to see the look in her face when I kill you. I was planning on killing her after my heroine deal comes through. But after you killed my clients!" Lord Alden kicks Robbie in the stomach again and tells Robbie, "And my killed my crew and ruin my deal that cost me money. Not tonight, I thought it would be fitting that she watches you die first. When I kill you!" Princess Amy cries a little and tells Robbie, "Robbie get up, please. Randall please let him go I'll do whatever you want. Just let him go!" Lord Alden tells Princess Amy, "Too late for that Princess. Don't worry you two will have plenty time to mourn him right after we kill him." Princess Amy tells Lord Alden, "Please, just don't hurt him!" Lord Alden tells Robbie, "Like I said, Champberg. I always been better!" Jaleel enters the office and throws the explosive DVD cover on the desk and it explodes. Lord Alden tells himself, "What the!" Robbie gets up from the floor and grabs his gun from the floor. But Lord Alden sees him carrying his gun and Lord Alden fires his gun, one bullet comes out of his gun and hits Robbie near the shoulder and Robbie is a little hurt for a minute. Robbie tells Lord Alden, "Not tonight, consider this your abdication!" Robbie aims his gun on Lord Alden that he is a little distracted for a minute and Robbie fires his gun. Three bullets comes out of his gun and hits Lord Alden in the chest and dies. Robbie shoulder is still hurting, he and Jaleel unties Princess Amy and while she is loose. She tries to hug Robbie and he is a little soar. Robbie tells Princess Amy, "Easy baby, I'm a little soar." Princess Amy tells Robbie, "I thought I lost you." Princess Amy makes out with Robbie for a minute and let's him go. Robbie tells Princess Amy, "I'm fine honey, just a flesh wound and plus I'm wearing a bulletproof vest." Jaleel tells Robbie, "Like I said always wear a vest." Jaleel and Princess Amy helps Robbie get back outside where the squad cars and ambulance are outside. The Paramedic leaves while Robbie is sitting back in the ambulance van where Jaleel and Princess Amy are waiting. Newton comes over to the van and tells them, "Good news the director called, he is really proud of what you guys did and you recovered all the heroine and the stolen oil from this drug bust. He almost commended you two for taking Interpol Most Wanted terrorist and a top drug lord and a corrupt MI6 agent. You two guys will receive the FBI Medal of Honor for what you guys did and a raise." Robbie tells them, "All in good work." Jaleel tells Robbie, "Well Rob, I guess we get to keep our jobs." Newton tells them, "You're majesty, I got a call from the hospital. You're father is feeling better and he'll be out in the hospital in no time. Since we recovered all the stolen oil, the money that Lord Alden made will go to us and double what your father makes. So you're father's company is safe." Jaleel tells Princess Amy, "I'm sorry, you never had a chance to invest in Abda electronics. Since you're father's business and wealth restored. I guess you don't have to make that investment after all. Even if you wanted to save your father's company." Newton tells them, "I don't think we have to worry about that, you're father while he was recovering, he got a hold of Mr Abda and investing a hundred million dollars in his company. After they closed the British Knight Shoes account. The stock hit the roof and making more money for this company. Will be enough to build Abda electronics factory in Granwich. Princess Amy tells them, "That sounds great. I guess me and Newton did what we had to do. What about you guys?" Robbie tells them, "Since the case is closed and we still have our jobs, me and Jaleel will head back to Washington for another case." Princess Amy tells them, "I guess this is goodbye. I'm really going to miss you guys." Jaleel tells Princess Amy, "Were going miss you too." Robbie tells Princess Amy, "So am I!" Princess Amy hugs Robbie and Jaleel for a minute and let go. Newton tells Princess Amy, "Come on, you're majesty our limo is here. All our stuff is packed up. We have to be London at tomorrow. That's when you're father will check out in the hospital." Princess Amy tells them, "Bye guys!" Princess Amy and Lord Alden goes inside the limo and exits the warehouse and head to the airport. Robbie tells Jaleel, "I really do love her." Jaleel tells Robbie, "You should go after her man." Robbie tells Jaleel, "Were FBI agents, I don't think I can't just pack up and go follow her to London." Jaleel tells Robbie, Louise will follow me at the ends of the earth. No matter where I go, I think Amy would follow you anywhere too. But right now, I think it's time you follow her to end of the earth. Just for a week, you have some vacation it's time you use it." Robbie tells Jaleel, "Okay but one condition, you're coming with me." Jaleel tells Robbie, "Okay!" Back in Royal London Hospital where The Duke is in the wheel chair and Newton and Princess Amy is pushing him out of his room. Newton tells the Duke, "It's just procedure sir, when we leave the hospital." Princess Amy is a little heartbroken that he couldn't see Robbie again because of his job and she still loves him. Nivel tells Princess Amy, "You okay honey." Princess Amy tells Nivel, "I'm fine Dad." Nivel tells Princess Amy, "I know everything is back to normal. My business is saved and I get to keep my dukeship and my workers still have their jobs. I had to thank you're two American friends who are from the FBI for their help. But are you sure their is nothing bothering you." Princess Amy tells her father, "I'm fine, really!" Nivel tells Newton, "Newton, why don't just give us a minute." Newton tells Nivel, "Yes, you're majesty." Newton exits the lobby and goes to the waiting room. Nivel tells Robbie, "You're friend you talk about you really do love him." Princess Amy tells Nivel, "What makes you think that?" Nivel tells Princess Amy, "I can tell, I think you should go after him." Princess Amy tells Nivel, "Father he is an american and an FBI agent. I'm a princess, plus he lives in American and I live here. It won't work." Nivel tells Princess Amy, "You maybe Princess by title and by blood. But you became more than that. When you went to America, I think you became an American too. Besides you maybe a princess, wherever you go. You're still a princess and I like to appoint as my ambassador of Granwich. I need you to represent us in America. They need a princess to look after them and protect them." Princess Amy tells Nivel, "I don't know father, but what about you. I can't leave you behind." Nivel tells Princess Amy, "I have a new heart and I can outlive anyone ten or twenty years. So, I'll be fine. So, take my offer be an ambassador to Granwich wherever you and your friend go." Princess Amy tells Nivel, "I will, I love you Dad!" Princess Amy hugs her father for a minute and tells her, "I love you too!" Princess Amy let's goes of her father for a minute and sees Robbie and Jaleel for a minute that came to see her and her father. Princess Amy is a little teary and goes over to hug him and make out with him. Nivel is happy that his daughter has found true happiness. One year later Robbie and Princess Amy are married and live in the same house where Jaleel rented and now is owned by them. Robbie and Jaleel are part time FBI agents and moonlights as co head librarians in Mountain View California. Princess Amy is now ambassador in California and represents her town Granwich with Newton as their bodyguard and personal assistant. Robbie, Jaleel, Newton and Princess Amy are in the kitchen leaving for their jobs. Robbie tells Princess Amy, "Me and Jaleel, will be busy in this huge case. So were going to be late in the office." Princess Amy tells Robbie, "Are you sure, you guys need my help?" Robbie tells Princess Amy, "I think were going to be fine." Princess Amy tells Robbie, "I thought I could ask. Besides, me and Newton have an important speaking engagement for Abda Electronics in Moscone Center. I promise Carmelo that we attend the event. Bye Honey." Robbie makes out with Princess Amy and let's go. Robbie tells Princess Amy, "I'll see you tonight at seven. Bye honey." Princess Amy tells Robbie, "Bye baby!" Robbie tells Jaleel, "Come on, Jaleel we don't want to be late." Jaleel tells Robbie, "I'm coming, I'm coming!" Robbie and Jaleel exits the kitchen and Newton tells Princess Amy, "Come on, you're majesty the limo is here we don't want to be late." Princess Amy tells Newton, "Just a second Newton." Princess Amy sees her laptop on and tells herself, "Time to logout!" Princess Amy logouts of her computer and they live happily ever after.

The End.

The Princess of The Water

Plot Summary: The Princess of the Water opens up with a flashback of JACK KOUFAX as a nine year old boy in Los Angeles. It is during this flashback that the audience learns about his tight knit family and the heroism of Jack's DAD, a rescue swimmer for the Coast Guard. The story then moves to present day New York City where a twenty-something Jack is now head librarian at the New York Public Library. Misfortunate in love, Jack tries repeatedly to woo the opposite sex, but to no avail. BOBBY ROMANO, Jack's best friend since youth teases Jack about his failed romantic endeavors, but he and his wife SARAH ROMANO want to see Jack in a happy romantic situation. Bobby Romano mentions to Jack that he has won free swimming lessons for two weeks at the Lorelai Rosenberg Recreation Center. Unable to attend the lessons due to a meeting with a party planner, Bobby gives the lessons to Jack. Jack goes to the swimming lessons, hesitatingly, until he meets the Olympic gold medalist and supermodel LORELAI ROSENBERG, his swim instructor for the next two weeks, a striking woman in her late twenties and wealthy. They call her the Princess of the Water, she scored a few gold medals in Swimming in the Olympics and she makes more money in Endorsements and modeling gigs than no swimmer ever had. Jack is instantly intrigued. After Jack's first lesson there is a flashback to Jack as a nine year old boy. The flashback is of the telephone call that Jack's MOM received telling of her husband's death during a heroic rescue attempt. This flashback explains Jack's fear of the water. After the flashback the story returns to the present day, to the Lorelai Rosenberg Recreation Center where Jack is taking swimming lessons. Very interested in Lorelai, Jack asks her out on a date for ice cream. On this date he learns that she is engaged. Nevertheless they have a great time and end up planning a double date, in spite of the fact that Jack does not have a girlfriend. It is on this date that Jack meets COLIN, Lorelai's fiancé. After the double date, Jack continues his swimming lessons. After one of his lessons, Jack asks Lorelai to dinner with him, Bobby, and Sarah at the Ritz-Carlton Atelier, much to the chagrin of Colin. Jack finally reaches the final lesson and says goodbye to Lorelai. The story then moves to the anniversary party of Bobby and Sarah at the Ritz-Carlton. As this scene is unfolding the story cuts to Lorelai's wedding day. As Lorelai prepares for her wedding too her fiance Colin. Will Lorelai will take the plunge and marry Colin, for somebody she is not in love with or decide to take the plunge and be with his true love Jack. Only time Will tell.

Once upon a time their was a regular everyday man Jack Koufax who is in his late twenties who is nerdy and childish is sleeping in his bed at his apartment wearing his pajamas. Jack wakes up in the middle of the night tossing and turning in his bed. In a clumsy fit he decides to sit up and turn the TV on for a little bit; right as the TV is turned on he notices it's an episode of Scooby doo on. This makes Jack smile and think about his past as he lays back down. Jack flashes back when he was a child watching the same cartoon when he was a kid. Young Jack who is nine years old, looking like a nerdy kid who loves to watch a Scooby-Doo cartoon with his MOTHER on the couch in his living room. Young Jack tells his Mom, "Do you think Scobby-Doo will catch the monster again?" His Mom tells him, "In a heartbeat Jack, sometimes you'll have to go with the same instincts he always uses." A commercial for the Coast Guard interrupts cartoons.

Young Jack tells his mother, "Dad is really awesome, saving people's lives every day. He's like Superman out there. You think I can be Superman, like him someday?"

His Mom tells him, "Well, if you put your mind to it. You can do anything, but remember Superman was born in the planet Krypton. He didn't have the powers on accident, he was born with them. But if Superman didn't have any powers He'd still goes out there every day to help. Young Jack tells his mother, "I guess that's like what Dad does, well Dad found his way to be like Superman. I hope my passion will make me like Superman too.

Jack's Mom thinking about the question that he asked her, she told him, "I hope so, to honey." Mom kisses Jack in the forehead. Then she hears somebody coming down the stairs again. Jack's Mom tells her son, "I guess you're Dad is going back to work again. Young Jack is thinking about his father and tells her, "Does he have super hearing when somebody cries for help like Superman does?"Jack's Mom explains to him, "Actually his phone works as his super hearing." Jack's Father, whose wearing his Coast Guard Uniform, carries his work duffle bag and heads into the living room. Jack's Father greets his son and daughter before he goes to work. Jack's Father tells them, "Hey kid, hey Honey." Young Jack tells his father, "Hey Dad." Jack gets up from the couch, goes over to his Dad to hug him. Young Jack continues telling his father, "I've missed you, Dad. You've been gone for fifteen hours last time and you finally got back home just now. I've been waiting for us to watch Scooby-Doo together." Young Jack let's goes of his Dad. Dad starts laughing. Jack's father tells his son, "Well, I don't want to miss this one. This is the episode, where Scooby, Shaggy and the rest of the gang stops a major counterfeiting operation in a puppet theater." Young Jack tells his father, "I'm glad you're here Dad. We didn't want you to miss the rest of the episode." His father didn't want to miss this episode too. Jack's father tells him, "Jack, I can't stay and watch right now, I have another emergency call that just came in. I have to be on the plane in a few minutes." Young Jack tells his father, "I understand Dad, but couldn't you stay and watch Scooby-Doo with me for a few more minutes?" His father wishes that he could still watch the rest of the episode in a few minutes. Jack's father tells him, "Not right now, kiddo. But I have the episode on tape, so we don't have to worry about missing it again." Mom goes over to Jack and Dad. Jack Mom's tells her husband, "So, how long is the emergency this time?" He tells her, "There's a huge rainstorm tonight, a few ships are sinkin and people are running out of time. So, I can't guarantee

I'll be back in a few hours. It's going to take some time to rescue those people from their ships. Mom kisses Dad in the lips. Jack's Mother tells him, "Don't worry, honey. Those people need you out there; they need my Superman out there to save the day." Young Jack tells his dad, "Yeah Dad, they need you. Good luck and be careful. Jack's father tells him, "Don't worry, Jack. I'll try to do my best to make you proud and be back to you guys as quick as I can." Young Jack ask his father, "Dad, you're coming to my Variety Show tonight right? I'm doing my stand up comedian routine of Eddie Murphy tonight.

Jack's Father tells his son, "Don't worry kiddo. I'm not going to miss for the world. Come here. Dad hugs Young Jack. Jack's Father tells him, "Do you know how I am proud of you, son. There are a lot of people who would love to have a great son like you someday, I know I'm blessed." Young Jack is pleased when he told them that. Young Jack tells him, "There's a lot of kids out there would love to have a great Dad like you, I guess I was lucky too. It's like I won the lottery. Jack's Father tells his son, "Someday, you're going to make a difference in the world like Superman. I know you will son." Young Jack tells his father, "I promise, I won't let you down Dad. I'll make a difference."

Jack's Father tells his son, "Whatever you want to do that makes a difference, Jack. It will be just fine with me." Young Jack tells his father, "Thanks Dad." Young Jack let's goes of his Dad, then Dad kisses Mom on the lips and hugs her tight. Jack's Mom tells her husband by whispering, "You come back home to us, okay." Jack's Father whispers back to his wife and tells her, "I will, honey." Dad let's goes of Mom and looks at Jack for a minute. Jack's Father tells his son, "Don't worry, Jack. I won't miss you're variety show."

Young Jack tells him, "I know you won't, Dad." Young Jack's Father says goodbye to his wife and his son and tells them, "Bye, honey. Bye kid." Dad leaves the living room and head to the front desk. Both of them say goodbye back. Young Jack's Mother tells her husband, "Bye, Honey." Young Jack says goodbye to his father too and tells him, "See ya." Young Jack thinks for a minute and hears a voice. The Adult Jack wakes up and he's back in the present where Jack is sleeping in his bed in his apartment in New York City. Jack is sleeping in his bed wearing his pajamas. Jack is narrating his story about how he met his true love and he found her an unusual place is in the water. Jack's voiceover tells himself, "This is me, Jack, a nice guy who was born in L.A. but moved into my grandmother's house with my mom in Queens's right after my father died when I was only nine." The alarm clock is going off, Jack wakes up and turns off his alarm clock. Jack gets out of bed sees his glasses on the nightstand, puts it on and heads to the bathroom. Jack's Voiceover continues telling himself about his day, "I'm the kind of guy that tries so hard but seems to have nothing going right. Some things have to change. World here I come." Jack is wearing a jeans and t-shirt, he takes out of the pot of coffee and pours it in his mug. Jack's Voiceover tells himself about who he is, "Doctors, lawyers, police officers, and firemen seem to have the more exciting jobs in the world. But I can't complain, I feel I have the most exciting job of them all." Jack sees the cream and sugar on the table, Jack grabs the cream and sugar and pours it on the coffee mug. Jack's Voiceover tells himself, "I'm a head librarian; I know it sounds like a boring job but it's me making my difference in people's lives. I have the power of books at my fingertips." Jack puts the cream and sugar back on the table, puts the coffee pot back in the coffee maker, grabs his mug and sits down on his table. Jack put his coffee mug on the table, sees a box of glaze donuts and grabs one of the donuts and starts dunking it in the coffee. Jack looks out the window from the kitchen table and ponders over his previous relationship. Jack tells himself, "There has to be somebody out there for me. I don't know who but I'll find her, and I'll be her prince charming… Yeah. It has to happen sooner or later, right?" Jack is a little out of it; and accidentally pours some hot coffee on himself and burns his crotch. Jack feels something burning and tells himself, "Ah, aah, ow!" Jack gets up from his chair, accidentally drops his coffee mug on the floor and the mug near brakes. Jack's right foot slips on the split coffee on the floor when he tries to pick up the coffee mug. Jack tells himself, "Whoa, whoa!" Jack trips on the floor again, and is about to get up from the floor and hits his head on the table and he is aching. Jack tells himself, "Ow!" Jack gets up from the table and covers his head with his right hand. Jack's Voiceover tells himself, "Oh Man. Welcome to a little routine of mine. You can see why I don't drink coffee much. Well I'll

just water the plants and get off to work after. That's where I really shine."
Jack goes over to the window to water the plants. He is about to water his
plants, until he sees a pretty girl walking on his sidewalk out of his window.
Jack starts day dreaming and pours the water on his pants instead of the
watering the plants. Jack looks at his pants when he stops looking out the
window. Jack is not concentrating again and tells himself, "What the, oh
man. Not again. I just got these babies, I don't have any time to change I
have an appointment in a few minutes. This is terrible. Alright, think…
Okay I got it. I'll tell everyone that I was blasted by a sprinkler on the walk
to the library. Oh man, that'll never work. Jack puts the huge glass of water
on the table and heads out the door. Jack's best friend and co-worker in
New York Public Library, Bobby is on the front desk reading a F.H.M.
magazine. Bobby tells himself, "How does Scarlett Johansson have a rack
like this? I do know if they're real but hey they're not perfect like Kristen
Stewart' though." Jack enters the front desk for a minute and goes over talk
to Bobby. Bobby sees Jack and tells him, "Hey Jack! Whoa buddy, what
happened to you? Did you piss your pants?" Jack tells Bobby, "Hey Bob,
Oh no I was walking here and there was a sprinkler and I turned around
and… you get the point."

Bobby kinda of understood and tells him, "Oh yeah. Those downtown
New York sprinklers get me every time. Nice try piss pants. How do you
feel about Scarlett Johansson's rack?" Jack answers that question and tells
him, "She can't compete with Michelle Pfeiffer in my book." Bobby is still
asking this question and tells Jack, "I don't know about Michelle Pfeiffer.
But the winner as always is Pamela Anderson." Jack tells him, "Oh, Pamela
Anderson. I know girls that have a better rack than Pamela Anderson:
Dyan Cannon and Diane Keaton." Bobby tells him, "WHAT?! Dyan
Cannon, wasn't she married to Cary Grant?" Jack answers that question
and tells him, "Yeah. That's her."

Bobby tells Jack, "And you wonder why the girls aren't all over you? Jack,
here I got an idea. Why don't you start trying to flirt with the girls that
come in the library?" Jack feels like he can't except Bobby's challenge to
ask out a girl. Jack tells him, "What? I'm not that desperate thank you

very much. But this morning I was feeling pretty good about myself till the sprinkler got me, so how hard can that be. This is just for fun though.

Bobby admires Jack's confidence and tells him, "Oh look at you. Mr. Big shot. Well start strong, look at this girl who just walked in." An attractive brunette in her late 20's walks into the library and starts heading towards the front desk. Jack being rushed to walk towards her by Bobby meets her about half way. Jack talks to the girl and tells him, "Um, Hi. Can I help find something today? Do you even need help?" Jack bows back and spins around to try to walk away immediately due to how nervous he is but then he hears the woman say something. Young Woman tells Jack, "Excuse me sir." Jack turns around as if he just arrived and didn't just speak to her. He points to himself to make sure she is talking to him and she nods. Jack tells her, "Yes, do you need help finding anything? I'm Jack by the way." Young Woman tells Jack, "Ok, Jack, I don't care what all that was about but can you point me towards the newspaper archives?" Jack is thinking about asking her out, but he answers her question first and tells her, "Of course. Oh that? It's just my friend made me come over here to talk. I didn't even know if you needed help. I just love reading up on the newspapers. There's just so much news to be found in those papers. Oh I almost forgot there on the second floor in the back left corner Ms...? I didn't get your name." Young Woman tells Jack, "No you didn't, because I didn't give it." The woman walks up the stairs with an attitude looking back at Jack and whispers to herself. Jack stands there alone and a little stunned at what just happened. He felt as if things were going good. He tried to make small talk and with how she left he feels doomed still. He decides to lie to Bobby about what happened with the woman. Jack starts walking back to the front desk as if everything went great. Jack tells Bobby, "Hey Bobby. I love this experiment, that woman couldn't get enough of me. Bobby isn't buying it. Bobby tells Jack, "Really? It went that well? Jack she looked great and she was interested in you? Great, what's her name?" Jack kinda panicked and Jack tells Bobby, "Her name? It was very European. I don't want to butcher trying to pronounce it." Bobby tells Jack, "Oh, come on. It's not like she's here to hear you mess it up. Take a stab at it." Jack realizing he is going to have to fabricate some name to tell Bobby to fully convince him that everything when well. He looks around the walls of the library quickly looking for anything he could use. Jack tries to wing it and tells Bobby, "Her name was Victoria."

Bobby tells Jack, "No way. That's as European as French fries. You have no idea what her name is do you?" Jack continues fabricating the story and tells Bobby, "No, I don't know her name. But you're just as terrible with woman though you just found Sarah and were let off the hook." Bobby gets a little upset. Bobby tells Jack, "That's cold man. I'm afraid I'm going to have to kick your butt for that." Jack starts to laugh at the fact Bobby is so flustered. Jack tells Bobby, "I know you to well Bob. We go back to when we were little kids on the playground. And back then it was always me kicking your butt." Bobby is laughing and less upset. Bobby tells Jack, "Haha well then I better even things up and whoop your ass now." Jack continues tells Bobby, "Hey, I still got it." Bobby Sarcastically tells Jack, "Yeah, Funny. Panic Jack!" Bobby looks at Jack's pants for a minute and he's seeing that his crotch is still wet. Bobby tells Jack, "Oh my bad. I didn't know you still did that. I was just playing you earlier." Jack tells Bobby, "I beg your pardon. Do what?" Bobby points at Jack's pants. Jack looks down at his pants and sees an embarrassing puddle on his crotch. Jack tells Bobby, "Oh that? That was just the darn water fountain. I should get it fixed pretty soon." Bobby Sarcastically tells Jack, "The water made you pee your pants? Or the fountain sprayed you?" Jack tells Bobby, "Both! But shh don't worry I don't think not anyone is going to notice anyway." Bobby looks at Jack and is thinking the exact opposite. Bobby whispers to Jack, "Good Luck with that." Jack's Voiceover tells the audience, "Man, Bobby thinks I'm desperately trying to find a girl. He's giving me advice already. I mean I'm not that bad with women am I?" Bobby and Jack are still working in the library, Bobby sitting down in his chair in front desk reading his F.H.M. magazine talking to Jack, until Bobby's wife SARAH, an attractive woman in her twenties, goes over to Jack and Bobby and talk to him. Bobby talks to wife and tells Sarah, "Hey Sarah!" Jack also greets her and tells Sarah, "Hey Sarah!" Sarah greets them back and tells them, "Hey guys." Sarah opens her purse, takes out seats for the New York Knick's game to Jack. Sarah tells Jack, "Here are the tickets to for the Knick's game, Jack. Jack grabs the three tickets from Sarah and really please she got the tickets he was waiting for. Jack tells Sarah, "Thanks

Sarah for waiting in the line for me, I have a lot of work to get done sooner than later. Like finding a date for this game." Jack, Bobby and Sarah start laughing. Bobby tells Jack, "So Jack, are you going to help us out with the invitations for our anniversary party tonight?" Jack tells Bobby, "I wish I could, but I have stay pretty late already. I'm sorry I'd still like to help another time maybe?" Bobby tells Jack, "Don't worry about it Jack. You've helped tons already. Do you still plan to make the toast at our party next Saturday?" Jack tells Bobby, "Wouldn't miss it Bobby. I can't believe you guys have been married for a year already. It feels like just the other day when Sarah was starting here. And I gotta ask when you two first looked at each other was it love?" Bobby and Sarah interrupt Jack. Bobby and Sarah tells Jack, "Love at first sight!" Jack tells them, "I envy you guys, I wish I could have something like what you two have. It's just beautiful." Sarah tells Jack, "Thanks Jack, we appreciate that." Jack tells them, "Hey, no problem." Bobby gives Sarah a kiss on the lips. Bobby tells Jack, "Jack, you have to give a tour for some kid's field trip in 15 minutes." Jack tells Bobby, "Thanks for the heads up. I'll keep these little guys in line this time." Sarah tells Jack, "Go get'em Jack." Bobby tells Jack, "Yeah, show them the real Jack Koufax is not afraid." Jack agrees with them and tells them, "Let's see if I have a magic touch, bye guys." Bobby tells Jack, "Bye Jack." Sarah says goodbye to Jack and tells him, "See ya." Jack leaves the front desk and heads to the common room. Jack comes out from behind the front desk to meet an elementary class accompanied by the teacher and a few parents. Jack meets the teacher and tells her, "Hi I'm, Jack Koufax, the head librarian. You must be Ms. Robertas who called last week. It's nice to meet you."

Jack and Ms. Robertas shake hands. Ms. Robertas tells Jack, "It's a pleasure to meet you as well Mr. Koufax. I'm sorry were a little late but I would like to get the tour started as soon as we can. Jack tells Ms Robertas, "Oh sure. Well if you'd like to gather up your class and follow me into the main room I'll start the presentation as soon as I can."

Ms. Robertas tells Jack, "Thanks. Okay class lets follow the nice librarian." Ms. Robertas looks back at Jack after addressing her class and smiles. Jack smiles back being very excited at the idea of things going so well with the teacher without him trying. He gulps and waves, feeling added pressure to not mess up now. The tour continues with more positive non-verbal cues from the teacher. It picks back up with the class and Jack standing by a floor to ceiling old world map. Jack tells the group, "This map we have here is our largest; it also it one of the biggest in the world. It depicts the modern world of the 1500's. It's this kind of exciting stuff that gets me out of bed in the morning eh kids?"

A kid in the group then raises his hand to ask Jack a question. Jack then calls on him to answer him. Jack answers the question that kid raised and tells him, "Yes, What's your question kid?" Kid tells Jack, "Excuse me, Are there any Harry Potter books in this Library?" Jack answers the kids question, "Yeah it's in the children section."

Kid ask another question to Jack and ask him, "What floor is that on?" Jack answer the kid's question and tells him, "The second floor." Kid ask another question to Jack and tells him, "When are we getting to that part of the tour?" Jack answers another question and tells him, "Not for another half hour." The kid is about to start asking another question but he is interrupted by Ms. Robertas. Ms. Robertas tells the kid, "Cory, What did we talk about on our last field trip?" Cory tells Ms Robertas, "About asking too many questions." Ms. Robertas apologizes to Jack and tells him, "Sorry about that Mr. Koufax. He always has so many questions to ask where we go." Jack tells her, "Hey, it's ok. I work at a library; I'm use to answering a lot of questions." Ms. Robertas sarcastically tells Jack, "You have to forgive him he was dropped on his head when he was little." Jack sarcastically tells Ms. Robertas, "Yeah, I think my friend Bobby was dropped one too many times on the head." Ms. Robertas starts laughing. Jack tells Ms. Robertas "Okay, if there's no more questions. Lets continue with the tour." After Jack finishes the tour school field trip, she meets with Bobby and Sarah. Sarah tells Jack, "How'd the field trip go? They seemed to leave a little rushed." Jack tells Sarah, "Oh yeah don't ask, There was one kid who reminded me of Bobby when he was little." Sarah tells Jack, "Let me guess, he asked too many questions to the teacher and would allows get through out. But Jack I'm got something I've been meaning to ask you." Jack tells Sarah, "Ha that was it alright. Ok, what is it?" Sarah tells Jack, "If you're not busy today, that is." Jack sarcastically tells them, "That depends what you call busy. I planned on hittin' up the clubs later, you know, dancing, drinking." Bobby and Sarah are laughing. Sarah tells Jack, "Haha well it's nothing like that, Do you remember that raffle contest that Bobby entered? The one all those people came to the library to enter. Well he ended up winning the grand prize.

Jack tells them, "Yeah, it was last week or something? Bobby won? That's great. What's he get?" Sarah tells him, what Bobby won, Well the grand prize is two weeks of free swimming lessons at Lorelai Rosenberg Recreation Center. The lessons are today in about an hour, right after your meeting with the book club and we have an anniversary party to plan. Our first meeting is with the Concierge at the Ritz today." Jack tells Sarah, "So, you're asking me go the Rec Center and ask tell them you're not goanna make it?"

Bobby suggest and ask Jack, "We thought you could take the lessons for me; we have the tickets you might as well. Just tell them I have a previous engagement and that you're filling in for Mr. Romano who is planning his anniversary party at the Ritz Carlton."

Jack ask Bobby, "They'll actually believe that? But even if I do go what makes you think I want to take these lessons?" Bobby explains to Jack, "Because you're my friend and I really need to be in that hotel right now, before we lose the rather expensive deposit. I don't want the tickets to go to waste. I'm just trying to help you out. Maybe you can start getting back in the water?" Jack tells Bobby, "But it's been a long time since I've been in the water, ever since…?" Bobby interrupts Jack and tells him, "I know, this is very last minute but please do this for me. Maybe this time you could take a chance and go back in the water. Deep down he would want you to overcome this and take the lessons. Don't just forget his memory." Jack looks at Bobby for a minute and can't resist.

Jack tells them, "Okay, I'll do this just for you. Only because my old man would've wanted me to, when do I suppose to be there?" Sarah was relieved and tells Jack, "In an hour." Bobby tells Jack, "Thanks for helping me out, Jack. I really appreciate this."

Sarah also tells Jack, "Yeah, thanks Jack." Jack tells them, "Anything for my only great and loyal friends. Bobby sees the raffle tickets on the front desk. He grabs the raffle tickets and gives them to Jack. Jack puts the raffle tickets in his pocket after reading them. Jack sarcastically tells them, "If I end up drowning at these lessons it's your fault." Bobby tells Jack, "Don't worry, Jack you're going to be fine. There's nothing in the water at the center I swear. Just think no matter what it's not Hurricane Katrina." Jack tells them, "There's only one way to find out I suppose, bye guys." Sarah tells Jack, "Bye Jack." Bobby also says goodbye to Jack and tells him, "See ya."

Jack leaves the front desk, carrying his file and the raffle tickets in his right hand and heads to the common room. Jack enters the lobby and goes over to the front desk where a woman is working in the LORELAI ROSENBERG RECRATION CENTER. Jack is carrying his bag on his left shoulder that his pool gear is in and the raffle tickets from the right hand. Jack tells the secretary, "Excuse me; I'm looking for the pool." Secretary answers Jack question and tells him, "It's up to the right of the lobby; men's locker is in the left hand corner." Jack tells the secretary, "Thanks. One more thing, I'm Jack Koufax, my friend Bobby Romano won free swimming lessons in a raffle last week. Do I need to verify anything?" Secretary ask Jack, "The librarian who was the big winner last week, how come he isn't here?" Jack tells her, "He and his wife Sarah are planning a wedding anniversary in two weeks at the Ritz Carlton. They have an appointment with the Concierge and the lessons are right now. Since he can't be everywhere at once and if he misses this appointment he might lose his deposit for the banquet hall. He asked me to fill in for him, until they finish planning the party." Secretary tells Jack, "Let me see the tickets." Jack gives the tickets to the secretary, the secretary inspects the tickets from Jack, approves and hands them back to him. Secretary tells Jack, "You remember where the locker room is?" Jack answers the Secretary question, "Yeah." Secretary tells Jack, "Your instructor will be out in a few minutes, so in the mean times enjoy our lessons and the day at the center." Jack tells the Secretary, "Thanks, I appreciate that ma'am."

Secretary tells Jack, "No problemo." Jack ask one more question to her and tells her, "The Pool is...?" The Secretary receives a call and interrupts Jack while holding the phone away from her mouth and points. Secretary tells Jack, "Over there to the right of the lobby." Jack whispers to himself, "Thanks a lot." The secretary continues on with the phone conversation while Jack leaves the front desk and makes a right up the lobby.

The Men's Locker Room door opens and it's Jack. Jack closes the locker room door. He is very pale wearing his old school blue swimming trunks, carrying a towel in his right hand and takes a look at the pool for. Jack's Voiceover tells the audience, "Wow, it looks like something I've only seen on TV for the Olympics. I don't know if I'm cut out for all this but I've already come this far I guess. I hope your with me Dad I'm going to need you out here." A whistle comes out of nowhere and Jack looks around to find where it's coming from. Jack tells himself, "What the...? "Female Swimming Instructor enters the Pool, she is carrying a whistle around her neck and wearing a dark blue one piece bathing suit. Jack looks at her like he has never seen a woman like her before. This Female Swimming Instructor is a brunette, an attractive woman who is in her late twenties and looks like a supermodel. Female Swimming Instructor goes over talk to Jack. Female Swimming Instructor tells Jack, "Hi." Jack spaces off just dazed that such an attractive woman is talking to him. Female Swimming Instructor tells Jack, "I'm looking for Jack Koufax." Jack tells her, "That's me, I'm Jack. So you're the...? Female Swimming Instructor interrupts Jack and tells him, "The Swimming Instructor." Jack tells her, "It's a pleasure to me...eeet you?" Female Swimming Instructor shakes Jack's hand.

FEMALE SWIMMING INSTRUCTOR tells Jack, "Lorelai Rosenberg." Jack tells Lorelai! "Please to meet you, Miss Rosenberg." Jack let's goes of the Lorelai's hand.

Lorelai tells Jack, "Call me, Lorelai." Jack wakes up from his little shy trance. Jack tells Lorelai, "Oh wait, Lorelai? Lorelai Rosenberg? The great

Olympic swimmer?" Lorelai tells Jack, "That's me, I started this promotion would spark a lot of interest when I bought this place a year ago and I heard the raffle had a lot of entrees when they want to meet me. This place is where celebrities like to play, work out or swim when they hear about me. That's why it's the number one celebrity hang out." Jack tells Lorelai, "Yeah, the library was a little extra busy for a few days but I didn't know it was because of you.

I a little shocked, sorry. But where's everyone else?" Lorelai tells Jack, "Who are you talking about?" Jack ask the question again and tell her, "The other people are taking these lessons?" Lorelai answers Jack's question and tells Jack, "I guess you haven't read the raffle tickets that closely yet, these lessons are private. So you have me for the next two weeks." Jack is a little shock and tells Lorelai, "Wow, you and me. That sounds kind of nice and not so bad. So what do I do, do you start me out in the kiddie pool, because I don't mind starting out there." Lorelai tells Jack, "Haha let's just try getting in the water first." Jack tells Lorelai, "Oh well there is something you should know first. I have a little problem with water." Lorelai tells Jack, "What kind of problem?" Jack tells her, "Going into any kind of large body of water like a lake or ocean scares me." Lorelai tells Jack, "Let's take one step at a time, see those stairs in the pool, you can it one step at a time on those steps in the pool and make you feel the water first. Let's not worry about swimming yet. Just getting your feet wet. That can't be too bad huh?" Jack tells Lorelai, "Yeah, but the steps are in the pool, I'm scared to get in the pool." Lorelai tells Jack, "Here, I'll go in first and you follow me, ok?" Jack sarcastically tells Lorelai, "Okay, just hope you are ready see my lunch again?" Lorelai sarcastically tells Jack, "It won't be the first half digested lunch I've ever seen." Lorelai and Jack are laughing. Lorelai takes off her whistle across her neck, goes into pool and steps in and comes down into the pool.

Lorelai tells Jack, "See, nothing to worry about. Now come on in, one step at a time."

Jack tells Lorelai, "You think so?" Lorelai sarcastically tells Jack, "Actually, it's freezing so hurry up." Jack tells Lorelai, "Ha, I'm not getting tricked so easily. I need get into the mood first." Lorelai sarcastically tells Jack, "What mood you trying to get into?

Come on!" Jack tells Lorelai, "I'm just doing a little breathing exercise. I'll begin my decent down the stairs shortly. You just wait." Lorelai tells Jack, "Jack puts both of his hands together and starts breathing like a Chinese breathing exercise." Jack is breathing and tells himself, "Hmm, Hmm!" Jack starts breathing a lot harder during his Chinese breathing exercise. Lorelai sarcastically quietly tells Jack, "Hey, tough guy while were you young?" Jack breathes a lot harder in this Chinese breathing exercise once more, he takes one step but there is a slippery puddle outside the pool and Jack slips on the puddle. Jack slips into the pool, starts screaming and thinks he is drowning. He proceeds to splash pool water with both of his hands and legs clumsily in a panic. Jack yells at himself, "Help, I'm drowning. I'm drowning, where is David Hasselhoff when you need him!"

Lorelai starts laughing at Jack's tumble. Jack tells himself, "I'm drowning and I'll never make it alone. Help!" Lorelai sarcastically tells Jack, "Jack, you do realize were in a shallow pool. Not the Atlantic Ocean." Jack realizes the pool is shallow and stops kicking the water and stands up. Jack tells Lorelai, "Man, I saw my life flash before my eyes or something." Lorelai swims across to Jack and starts talking. Lorelai tells sarcastically tells Jack, "That's what all my students usually say when they first step in the water." Jack tells Lorelai, "Being in the shallow water isn't that bad I guess but I don't want a repeat entrance like that." Lorelai tells Jack, "That was my first lesson, getting in the pool is one thing. Teaching you how to swim will be another. But admitting you're fear is not the water. Your problem is what you associate with the water." Jack tells Lorelai, "How do you know that stuff since it's the first time you've been in the water with me?" Lorelai tells Jack, "You're not the first student I've known, that lost a loved one or had a bad experience with water." Jack tells Lorelai, "So, how do you let make them face...?" Lorelai interrupts Jack and tells him, "Face their fears? One day at a time. That's includes our first lesson today, which is getting them in the water. Then progressing them to the Freestyle, buts our second lesson for tomorrow."

Jack tells Lorelai, "So, that's it for today?" Lorelai tells Jack, "Well since I got you in the water you should try to go underwater, watch me." Lorelai holds her breath and goes underwater for a minute. Jack looks at her and sees that it looks hard. Lorelai comes up from the water and starts breathing. Lorelai tells Jack, "Just do what I did and you'll be fine. Come up if you get scared." Jack tells Lorelai, "You must be crazy or there something in this water if you think I'm going under." Lorelai starts laughing.

Lorelai tells Jack, "All you have to do is hold my hand then we both go underwater and come up. Once you master it with me, you'll be ready to go solo." Jack tells Lorelai frightened tells Lorelai, "Couldn't I just get a rain check on this?"

Lorelai tells Jack, "Come on, you'll be fine Jack." Jack tells Lorelai, "I doubt that."

Jack and Lorelai are holding hands together, start breathing, they both go underwater. Jack and Lorelai both hold their breath underwater, Jack lets go of Lorelai's hand and floats towards the stairs and ends up hitting his head underwater. Jack tells Lorelai while he was gurgling water, "Ow!" Jack puts his left hand on top of his head, and opens his eyes in panic underwater which leaves him a little blinded. Jack comes up from the water, covers his eyes with his left hand. Jack tells Lorelai, "I can't see." Lorelai comes up from underwater and sees Jack covering his eyes. Lorelai tells Jack, "Hang on a second, I'll be right there. Don't move." Jack starts heading to the steps for and covering his eyes.

Jack tells Lorelai, "What? I can't hear you!" Lorelai tries to make it to Jack, but too late Jack tries to make it up the stairs and falls down back into the water. Jack tells himself, "Oh man!" Jack looks at the stairs with angry squinted eyes as they start burning from the chlorine. Jack tells himself, "My eyes are burning, Lorelai where are you my eyes are burning!" Lorelai tells Jack, "Hang on a second, don't move!" Lorelai swims across the pool where Jack is and grabs him again before he goes underwater. Jack is sitting down on the bench of the men's locker room and Lorelai is putting eyes drops in his eyes to help his redness and blindness from the pools. Lorelai tells Jack, "Okay, these should help a ton. Just give them a few minutes to work." Jack starts blinking again and sees really clearly. Jack looks at Lorelai for a minute. Jack tells Lorelai, "What happened? I remember hitting my head. And my eyes, Oh my eyes, they still hurt." Lorelai tells Jack, "You were underwater for a couple minutes, hit you're head on the stairs and you couldn't see anything. You tripped walking on the stairs, you're eyes got a lot of chlorine in them, when you tried get up from the stairs, you fell back into the pool." Jack tells Lorelai, "Really? That's a memory I'm glad I won't remember for a while." Lorelai sarcastically tells Jack, "It would make a great bit for my blooper reel." Jack tells Lorelai, "Ha I don't doubt that. So, what was that stuff you put in me eyes? Lorelai tells Jack, "My magic eye drops, I had a friend in the Olympics who was a physician and an Optometrist and he gives me these eyes drops every time one of my students have red eyes or blinds themselves when they were in my pool." Jack tells Lorelai, "I feel like I have to apologize for all the panic for the first day. I'll have to get more comfortable with the water sooner than later." Lorelai tells Jack, "Don't worry, you're not the first of my student who does the reenactment of a drowning victim and blinds themselves. Just sit and relax a few more minutes." Jack tells Lorelai, "Alright. Well thanks for saving me countless times already." Lorelai tells Jack, "Don't worry, we have a long two weeks to go. Just watch for the puddles tomorrow." Jack tells Lorelai, "Oh don't you worry, I can only get better from here." Lorelai laughs for a minute. Lorelai tells Jack, "See ya, Jack." Jack tells Lorelai, "Bye Lorelai." Lorelai leaves the locker room; Jack gets up from the bench and opens his locker. Back in the New York Public Library where Sarah is sitting down in the front desk and reading a Vogue magazine. Customer enters the front desk and goes over talk to Sarah. Bobby heads to the front desk. Bobby goes inside the front desk and sits down in his chair. Bobby tells Sarah, "Hey Sarah!"

Sarah tells Bobby, "Hey Babe, how did the caterers go?" Bobby tells Sarah, "I've got an estimate around five thousand." Sarah tells Bobby, "And the other one?" Bobby tells Sarah, "Around nine thousand big ones!" Sarah tells Bobby, "We'll take that then."

Bobby tells Sarah, "Whoa! You sure about this? That would use up the last of wedding and inheritance money babe." Sarah tells Bobby, "Trust me they're really good it'll be worth it. And by the way we have talk to the florist tomorrow too." Bobby tells Sarah, "Okay, I'll call them back but this means we'll have to cut back our spending somewhere." Jack enters the front desk for a minute and goes over talk to Sarah and Bobby. Jack tells them, "Hey guys." Sarah tells Jack, "Hey Jack." Bobby tells Jack, "Hey Jack." Sarah ask Jack, "How did the lessons go?" JACK sarcastically tells them, "Let's see, I was trying to reenact a drowning victim in the Titanic and thought I drowned. I slip on a puddle and fell in the pool twice; then I hit my head in the edge of the pool. After that I fell on the stairs and I blinded myself for a minute. Few more seconds I would be able to play piano like Ray Charles." Sarah tells Jack, "That bad, huh!" Jack tells them, "The one good thing was meeting the swim instructor; she was very understanding." Bobby sarcastically tells Jack, "I was always thought you would have gone for one of back up dancers for Liza Minneli." Jack sarcastically tells them, "I asked one of them out but she stood me up." Sarah tells Jack, "Oh don't listen to him Jack. I'm glad you have a new friend to talk to." Jack tells Sarah, "Thank Sarah. Well I'm going to go get some work down before my next lesson I'll see you guys in a little bit." Bobby tells Jack, "Later." Sarah takes out a Cosmopolitan magazine from the front desk. Jack enters the front desk carrying his swim bag. Jack tells Sarah, "Hey Sarah." Sarah tells Jack, "Hey Jack." Jack tells Sarah, "Where's Bobby?" Sarah tells Jack, "The Party Planner called a few minutes ago, they needed to see him right away about the invitations."

Jack tells Sarah, "Thanks for covering my shift. But I'm off to the pool for my second day of these lessons." Sarah tells Jack, "What about this instructor that you have a crush on, what's her name again?" Jack tells Sarah, "Lorelai." Sarah ask Jack, "Jack, all I'm saying is if you really like her I think you should take a chance soon before it's too late."

Jack tells her, "You've got a point. I just don't know what to say around her." Sarah tells Jack, "Jack, whatever happens. Good luck." Jack tells Sarah, "Thanks Sarah, see ya." Sarah tells Jack, "Bye." Jack makes a left and heads to his office to get his bag. Jack comes out of his locker room, wearing the same blue swim trunks he was wearing yesterday and stops to look at the pool. Jack thinks for a minute. Jack flashes back when he was nine years old. The phone rings in the house and Jack's mother picks up the phone. She instantly gets a worried face. She starts yelling at the person on the other line.

Mom quivering and ask the Coast Guard on the phone, "Is he okay? Just tell me if he's alright. No please, tell me he's going to fine. You tell me he'll be home soon. You just say it." Jack's mom collapses to the floor crying leaving the dial tone to ring out on phone. Jack stops to watch TV and walks over to his mom. She starts wiping her tears away and still is quite shaken. Young Jack ask his Mom, "Mom, who was it? Why are you crying?" Mom tells Jack, "Jack, come here. You know your daddy had to go help those people? Well he saved everyone. He was such a Hero, but the cable broke. The helicopter didn't have enough gas and to save everyone else they had to leave your Dad behind." Young Jack tells Mom, "The ocean it, it took him? But he'll be back after that though right?" Mom tells Young Jack, "No, Jack. Daddy won't be back. He's up above now, looking over you with every waking second, I know it." Young Jack looks up to the ceiling of the room to try to see his Dad. Back in the present and Jack wakes up from his day dream looking saddened, turns around and sees Lorelai. Lorelai is wearing a dark black color bathing suit with her whistle above her neck and carrying her clipboard in her right hand. Jack tells Lorelai, "Oh, oh. Sorry!" Lorelai ask Jack, "Jack, you okay?" Jack tells Lorelai, "Yeah, just been out of it lately." Lorelai tells Jack, "If you want talk about it, my door is always open." Jack tells Lorelai, "Thanks, but I'm good for now. So what kind of lesson do you have for me today?" Lorelai tells Jack, "Your first goal is to breathe underwater for a minute, now let's trying diving into the water first. Just watch me then you can try." Lorelai puts down her clipboard on the floor, takes off her whistle and puts it down on the floor. Lorelai tells Jack, "Which dive do you want to do first, the usual half-gainer or the cannon ball?" Jack sarcastically Lorelai, "I was never much of a half-gainer type but I could give the cannon ball a try." Lorelai tells Jack, "Alright, Cannon ball it is." Jack sarcastically tells Lorelai, "I would challenge you to a splash contest but I don't know what to do." Lorelai laughs for a minute. Lorelai tells Jack, "Just do exactly what I do." Jack sarcastically tells Lorelai, "Anything you say, miss all knowing.

Lorelai turns around to give herself some room to do the cannon ball dive and stops. Lorelai runs as fast as she can and cannon ball dives in the pool and makes quite the splash before coming up for air. She yells back to Jack from the pool." Lorelai tells Jack, "Now, you do it!" Jack tells Lorelai, "All right, that didn't look too hard. Here I come!"

Jack turns and stops. He is thinking really hard over his falls from yesterday. Jack's Voiceover tells the audience, "Okay, I can just jump in I think. I'll just jump closer to the shallow end just in case. Now let's get into this pool with some style." Jack runs as fast as he can for his cannon ball, there's some water near the pool from Lorelai's dive a few minutes earlier. Jack is about to dive in the pool, when his right foot slips on the water, and he falls into the pool again but this time head first. Jack resurfaces kicking his legs, arms and starts screaming. Jack ask Lorelai, "Help, help. For the love of Pete I can't swim!" Lorelai looks at Jack, and with a sarcastic sigh she starts swimming over to Jack. Jack tells Lorelai, "Help me. This falling stuff is getting old." Lorelai goes over to Jack and talks to him. Lorelai tells Jack, "Jack, you do realize you're panicking in shallow side of the pool?" Jack stops kicking and screaming and looks around him. He looks down at the water for a minute and remembers the pool is shallow. Jack tells Lorelai, "Wow. You could've fooled me. I thought I was a goner." Lorelai tells Jack, "Are you sure you don't want talk about what it is that is bothering you?" Jack tells Lorelai, "No, I'm sorry it's personal. But hey, now that I've successfully got in the pool for the second day what do you have to teach me? Lorelai tells Jack, "First were going to start with the basic freestyle technique, at least for today." Jack tells Lorelai, "Freestyle? No offense but I can't rap. If you're trying to get me to rap and swim I might as well quit now." Lorelai starts laughing. Lorelai tells Jack, "No, the freestyle swim technique. It's one of the most basic but they have been doing it in the Olympics for years. It's where you use both arms to swim while kicking your legs." Jack tells Lorelai, "Alright, sounds pretty difficult." Lorelai tells Jack, "Watch me, do what I do. Remember don't think about it, just swim. If you think you might be tasting chlorine before you know it, so just swim and relax. Don't worry about the change in depth once you get out there. You won't sink underwater unless you try to." Jack tells Lorelai, "Wait one second, were talking about swimming from the beginning to the end of the pool?" Lorelai tells Jack, "You betcha, don't worry Jack. You'll be fine. Wish me luck." Jack tells Lorelai, "I'm the one who needs the luck." Lorelai sarcastically tells Jack, "If I'm not back in twenty minutes call the National Guard." Jack tells Lorelai, "You know, you gotta stop joking. I am going to need them sooner than later." Lorelai starts swimming freestyle across the entire pool and Jack watches her go down to the end and stop. Jack is amazed at how fast she just swam down the length of the pool and he yells out to her. Jack sarcastically tells Lorelai, "Are you related to Aquaman?" Lorelai sarcastically tells Jack, "Not that I know of, but he did teach me how to swim in the pool. Do you think you're ready?" Jack sarcastically tells Lorelai, "Ready as I ever will be, just hope I don't drown in the second day." Lorelai sarcastically tells Jack, "Just look at it like the worst thing that could happen is you die." Jack tells Lorelai, "Hey, I'm standing right here even if I am standing in a pool." Lorelai laughs for a minute. Lorelai tells Jack, "Oh sorry. I can't really hear you, you have to swim down here." Jack tells Lorelai, "Ha, Real funny. Wish me luck." Jack starts swimming freestyle all the way to the other end of the pool; Jack starts to think about Lorelai and how he's going to ask her out. Jack's Voiceover tells the Audience, "Okay, after these lessons I'll ask her to ice cream or something. Even if she doesn't like me, who doesn't like ice cream. Well then its, set I just have to survive through this lesson. Wait, I had a thought. Shit!" While Jack is thinking to himself he forgets about the swim technique and starts to slow down in the deeper portion of the pool. This realization starts to make Jack panic. He goes down underwater, tries to get up for air and Lorelai is about to save Jack... again. Jack's Voiceover is Gurgling and telling the audience, "Remember don't think, just swim." Jack closes his eyes and uses his arms to push him back up for air. He starts swimming freestyle again and Lorelai is shocked to see he is no longer in distress. Jack continues swimming, or a poor excuse of swimming, and gets back to Lorelai exhausted. Lorelai tells Jack, "That's my boy." Jack is gasping and tells Lorelai, "I can't believe, I actually did it. I swam from there to here. I can't believe it. And you wanted me to go back? Ha you're crazy." Lorelai tells Jack, "I told you could do it. As long as you are calm and just swim.

You'll be fine." Jack tells Lorelai, "Thanks Lorelai. Today was big day in the water for me. I owe you." Jack hugs Lorelai and they both realize it's awkward after a few seconds and let go quickly to act as if they weren't hugging. Lorelai tells Jack, "Uh, don't worry, it's part of the job." Jack tells Lorelai, "Yeah, I can't believe I actually was swimming. I didn't even hit my head though I was in the middle of a pool." Lorelai tells Jack, "I know, well that is something to build off of." Jack tells Lorelai, "Can you believe it? It's been so long since I've done my last stupid thing in this pool." Jack is breathing slowly and looks down at the water while resting on the ledge. Lorelai notices Jack isn't paying attention and tries to spook him. She puts up both her arms and yells.

Lorelai tells Jack, "Ahhh!" Jack tells Lorelai, "Ahh Man!" Lorelai starts laughing. Lorelai sarcastically tells Jack, "Oh man I got you good. Are you going to be alright?"

Jack's accidentally pees his pants unknowingly. There is a pause in the conversation till both Jack and Lorelai realize the "warm spot" in the pool. Lorelai looks like she doesn't want to acknowledge the fact. Jack looks very embarrassed. Jack tells Lorelai, "Oh, yeah. Uh that's my bad." Lorelai tells Jack, "Oh god, you had to mention it. Well I guess that's it for the day; let's get out of the pool." Jack and Lorelai exit the pool and head to their respective Locker rooms. Jack in the Men's Locker room and puts his shirt on, and there is a knock at the door. Jack tells the person who is knocking on the door, "Come in."

The door opens and it's Lorelai. Lorelai enters, closes the door, and goes over to Jack.

Lorelai tells Jack, "Hey sorry about earlier, you okay? Jack tells Lorelai, "I'm really sorry too about that little incident. I knew I shouldn't have that fifth diet coke.? Lorelai tells Jack, "Hey, it's okay. Don't be embarrassed." Jack tells Lorelai, "That's impossible but Thanks. So, you think I have a chance to be a mirage of Aqua man someday??

Lorelai sarcastically tells Jack, "Not unless, you lay off Diet Coke once in a while."

Lorelai and Jack start laughing for a minute. Jack tells Lorelai, "Ha, I do suppose that would be a good start." Lorelai tells Jack, "Bye Jack." Jack thinks about asking Lorelai out as she is walking out and he musters up enough courage to at least say something to get her attention. Jack tells Lorelai, "Hey just wait. I feel terrible about what happened today. The least I could do is take you to cream some ice? Uh, I mean ice cream. Could I buy you some ice cream?" Lorelai tells Jack, "Uh well. Yeah I guess all the stress you put me through, I could go for some ice cream. I'll go change and meet you in the lobby in ten minutes, ok?" Jack sarcastically tells Lorelai, "Okay, I'll try not to mess up in the mean time." Jack and Lorelai meet up in the lobby of rec. Center. Lorelai looks even beautiful even after a full day of work in the pool. Lorelai is wearing a tight black tank top, blue jeans, a black leather jacket and Ray Ban Sunglasses. Jack on the other hand looks more thrown together though he is in his work clothes from earlier. They walk to a local ice cream shoppe a few blocks away. Jack and Lorelai are eating ice cream at Mike's Ice Cream Parlor. They are both sitting in the booth in shoppe. Jack is eating a large cup of chocolate ice cream while Lorelai has a huge waffle cone with multiple scoops that is Chocolate Chip and Chocolate. Jack tells Lorelai, "I know I've already apologized but I'd like to say I'm sorry one more time. Hope this cream will help cool things over." Lorelai tells Jack, "Really, don't worry about it. I wouldn't mind if you messed up so much if it results in ice cream. You found one of my weaknesses here. When I trained for the Olympics I had to work extra hard cause I couldn't give this up."

Lorelai takes a huge lick off the cone. Lorelai tells Jack, "So Jack, the head librarian who can't swim, are you married?" Jack tells Lorelai, "Nope I never got around to that.

What about you, do you have a significant other of some sorts?" Lorelai tells Jack, "Yeah I do, His name is Colin. And I'm actually engaged to get married to him in two weeks. Things have so good but lately it's been a bit rocky. But hey what couples don't go through that you know." Jack tells Lorelai, "Oh that's great. You're lucky, relationships don't seem to last these days." Lorelai tells Jack, "Thanks. But we aren't without bumps in our road. I just hope things get smoother after the wedding. Things are just so stressful lately." Jack tells Lorelai, "Well then I feel even more terrible about being such a hassle during the lessons. Without you though I would have to say things would be even worse. You're quite the instructor." Lorelai tells Jack, "Don't worry about any of that, you're fine. I am curious though what is it that bothers you so much about the water?" Jack tells Lorelai, "I don't really like to talk about it but I guess you should know. Well for starers my father was in the Coast Guard as a rescue swimmer." Lorelai tells Jack, "Oh wow. Those guys are so brave. What happened?" Jack tells Lorelai, "When I was nine, he was received a call to help rescue a cruise ship that was shipwrecked by a storm. He got all the people out of the boat alive, but he didn't make it. He was stranded on a cable wire, trying to rescue one of the last swimmers, he got'em back in the helicopter, then the cable and the hook broke. He fell into the ocean, and the helicopter was running out of fuel so they needed take the swimmers back to the shore and he died out at sea." Lorelai tells Jack, "Oh Jack, I'm so sorry to hear that. He's probably very proud watching over you conquering your fear."

Jack tells Lorelai, "Thanks Lorelai. It's nice to get that off my chest. I'm usually not as scared as I am around you but you've only seen me around water. I hope this helps explain my apprehension." Lorelai tells Jack, "I never knew that the water was so terrifying to you. But I have to say you are doing pretty well; it has to take a lot of guts to get in that pool." Jack tells Lorelai, "Yeah, that's a good way of looking at. But hey I'm done with my ice cream, do you want to go?" Lorelai tells Jack, "Sure. I could go for some fresh air." Jack and Lorelai walk out of ice cream shoppe. Jack tells Lorelai, "So which way you headed?" Lorelai tells Jack, "Well I have to pick some things up on the way home. But thanks for the conversation and ice cream Jack. I guess I'll see you tomorrow for the next day of lessons." Jack tells Lorelai, "No problemo. See ya tomorrow." Jack starts walking in the opposite direction of Lorelai towards his apartment.

Jack's Voiceover tells the audience, "I should've known that she was taken. I mean she's getting married two weeks for crying out loud. But she's so easy to talk to and hey she did still say yes to the ice cream. Oh who am I kidding? I'm a lost cause." Jack enters the first floor, goes over to the table and talk to Bobby and Sarah. Bobby doesn't see Jack come in. Bobby tells

Sarah, "You think Jack asked her out? No offense to Jack but she's out of his league." Sarah tells Jack, "Hey Jack." Jack tells Sarah and Bobby, "Hey Sarah. And you know what Bobby I did ask Lorelai out last night." Bobby tells Jack, "What? No. You sly devil you. Where'd you go?" Jack tells them, "Well after the lessons I asked her out for some ice cream." Bobby tells Jack, "Oh man, you're a player. How'd it go?" Jack tells Bobby, "It went really good. You know I shared to her why I have my fear of the water. Um she told me she's getting married in two weeks. We had some ice cream and then we went our separate ways." Sarah tells Jack, "No way, you mean…?" Jack tells them, "Yeah, she has a fiancée. His name is Colin, a Wall Street broker and looks like a Abercrombie And Fitch Model I bet. And who am I to be able to compete with that?"

Bobby tells Jack, "Well sounds like quite the challenge. Do you like her more than friends?" Jack tells them, "I don't know though I think I…? Bobby interrupts Jack. Bobby tells Jack, "That you like her?" Jack tells Bobby, "I don't know, but she's my instructor. It makes me think about dating a teacher in high school like Mrs. Rustle or something." Bobby shrugs and grosses himself out at the thought of Mrs. Rustle.

Bobby tells Jack, "Hey, don't ever mention her again. Besides, I think you could do better than Mrs. Rustle." Jack tells them, "Thanks for the confidence. She kind of made out with me once though." Sarah is shocked and ask Jack, "What?! You made with Mrs. Rustle? Bobby tells Jack, "Oh my god. That's nasty." Jack tells them, "This information doesn't leave this library, okay?" Bobby tells Jack, "No problem, we'll pretend we didn't hear it. Ha, so what happened?" Jack tells them, "After graduation, I was going to get a drink of water. Mrs. Rustle was kind of drunk; I remember she stored bottles of wine in her office. I think she had a couple drinks, she saw me when I was taking a drink of water and after I was done. Mrs. Rustle made out with me for a few minutes, then she left and starting puking in the bathroom. That was my first kiss; I have never brought it up since." Bobby tells Jack, "Man, having a first kiss with a teacher who drank too much is totally crazy." Jack sarcastically tells them, "I always thought I was a lousy kisser. Because every time somebody makes out with me they always end up puking in the bathroom." Sarah tells Jack, "I'm sure that didn't happen last time when you were with Alyson." Jack tells them, "Actually it happened twice, but she had five hot dogs when were watching the Mets game. The second time I would like to refrain from saying." Bobby tells Jack, "I don't even want to ask, but for a much needed subject change what's your instructor like?" Jack tells Bobby, "Well for starters she's young and pretty. I might also add that she was an Olympic swimmer and a supermodel on the side. Back in the Olympics they called her the Princess of the Water that the media called her when she won her first event in the Olympics. "Bobby tells Jack, "Why they call her the Princess of the Water." Jack tells Bobby, "She won six gold medals at six events in the Olympics and her father runs a huge corporate law firm that her great grandfather founded in 1920 and the Rockefellers were their first clients in that time. Not only that she lives off her family billion dollar fortune and her grandfather from her mother's side of the family is a British Duke and she is sole heir to the throne Duke of Abbey throne. Since her family are British royalty." Bobby tells Jack, "Wow, that explains a lot, why the call her the Princess of the Water." Bobby is thinking for a minute and tells Jack, "Whoa. The only swimmer that comes to mind is, No! Lorelai Rosenberg herself is teaching the lessons?" Jack tells Bobby, "Yeah and think they could have been your lessons. The even raffle says I get an exclusive two week session of swim lessons from her." Sarah tells Jack, "So, do you really like her or you going to let her go by like all the other ones?" Jack tells Sarah, "Hey, I'm standing right here. And she's just doing her job; I'm out of her league so I'm not going to do anything. Girls like her are not going to be lonely for long, as long as there are pretty boy wannabes trying to date her. I have no problem with it so I'm going to stick with my swimming lessons that just it. She's been nice so far and asking her out would just make things awkward." Bobby tells Jack, "Come on Jack, Take a risk. Ask her out for real like dinner or something." Jack tells them, "She would say no without blinking. I'm not trying to deliberately get rejected."

Sarah tells Jack, "How do you know if you don't ask?" Jack tells them, "Cause she is getting married and said she loved him. I don't want to make it weird between us. Thanks for the talk but I have to go." Sarah tells Jack, "Bye Jack. Just relax." Bobby tells Jack, "Yeah stay calm man." Back in the Swimming Pool at the rec center. Jack is waiting for Lorelai to arrive when he looks at the pool. Lorelai tells Jack, "Hey Jack."Jack tells Lorelai, "Aah!" Jack turns around and sees Lorelai. Lorelai tells Jack, "Sorry." Jack tells Lorelai, "Jeezes, I almost peed my pants again." Lorelai sarcastically tells Jack, "If you are planning something like that again you better go to the bathroom first." Jack sees Lorelai as she takes off her towel to get in the pool wearing a black two piece bikini, a whistle around her neck, and holding a clipboard in her right hand. Jack is a caught up in how great Lorelai looks and zones out. Jack Out Of It tells Lorelai, "My, my....My Mista.....ke!" Lorelai tells Jack, "Haha well it's nice to see you too." Jack whispering to himself, "Remember she's taken, oh geez." Jack looks down away from Lorelai and more at the pool for asecond. Jack tells Lorelai, "So, Lorelai. What's with MTV Sprink Break look?" Lorelai is confused and ask Jack, "What?" Lorelai looks at what she's wearing and she get's Jack's question for a minute. Lorelai tells Jack, "Oh, I had a modeling shoot for F.H.M. I forgot my bathing suits are being washed, this is only one that was clean, so it's either that or go commando." Jack thinks about that for a minute. Lorelai smacks Jack in the left arm with a clipboard. Jack tells Lorelai, "What?" Lorelai tells Jack, "Don't even think about." Jack tells Lorelai, "What, I was kidding and I wasn't thinking. I swear." Lorelai glares sarcastically at Jack to try to intimidate him. Jack tells Lorelai, "Whoa killer. Can we just continue with today's lesson?" Lorelai tells Jack, "Ok, the goal for today is to learn the breast stroke." Jack tells Lorelai, "The breast stroke, what's that?" Lorelai tells Jack, "Here watch the way I move my arms." Lorelai moves her arms like a frog." Jack tells Lorelai, "I think I can do that." Jack moves his arms like a frog for a minute, like Lorelai did. Jack tells Lorelai, "That's pretty easy; I want to see if I can try it when I get into the pool." Jack moves his arms like a frog, Jack moves close to the pool for a minute and doesn't see that he's to close. Jack's Voiceover tells the audience, "Oh that was close, I was worried that I was going to slip again." Lorelai tells Jack, "Jack, wait?" Jack tells Lorelai, "You can tell me after finish one more, Lorelai."

JACK'S Voiceover tells the audience, "I knew I had to learn my balance around this pool soon or later." Jack steps back into the pool and intentionally falls in while looking at Lorelai. Lorelai starts giggling at

Jack for a minute. Jack resurfaces faking some sort of injury. Lorelai tells Jack, "You okay?" Jack sarcastically tells Lorelai, "Yeah, it's a lot nicer to enter this pool under my own will." Lorelai tells Jack, "Since you're in the pool, I think you're ready for the breaststroke. Hang on a second." Lorelai takes off her whistle from her neck, puts her clipboard on the floor and dives down the pool. Lorelai goes over to Jack and starts talking to him. Lorelai tells Jack, "You ready, ?" Jack tells Lorelai, "Ready as I will ever be. Lead the way, Obi Wan." Lorelai tells Jack, "Just watch me and go with the flow." Lorelai starts swimming the breaststroke all the way to the other end of the pool and stops. Lorelai looks back at Jack and starts waving. Lorelai does another breaststroke and goes back to the pool where Jack is. Jack tells Lorelai, "I think I got it, wish me luck." Jack starts doing the breaststroke all the way to the other end of the pool, Jack swims the breaststroke halfway and stops for a minute. Jack accidentally drinks some of the pool water. Jack tells Lorelai, "Oh god, that's terrible." Lorelai tells Jack, "You okay?" Jack tells Lorelai, "Yeah I just swallowed some water." Jack goes back to swim the breaststroke again all to the end of the pool and stops. Jack looks at the end of the pool and thinks if he can make it back. Jack's Voiceover tells Lorelai, "Let's see if I can make it all the way back." Jack swims down the last part back to where Lorelai is standing in the shallow part of the pool. Jack tells Lorelai, "How about that, I didn't even get hurt." Lorelai sarcastically tells Jack, "Jack, that's amazing. I can't believe you conquered one swimming technique without getting hurt." Jack tells Lorelai, "Let's test how lucky I am and go conquer those stairs." Lorelai tells Jack, "Knock yourself out, Jack. Watch out for the hand rail." Jack tells Lorelai, "Don't worry, Lorelai. I'm feeling a lot better about it today." Jack swims to the stairs and stops for a minute. Jack looks at Lorelai and gives her a thumbs up. Lorelai gives Jack a thumbs up back again too. Jack starts to walk up the stairs but loses his balance again, slips underwater again and hits his head on the bottom. Jack gets up from the water for a minute. Jack tells himself, " Ow." Lorelai looks at Jack like he didn't just get hurt again. Lorelai is thinking and tells Jack, "I hate when he does this." Lorelai tells Jack, "Hang on a second Jack, I'll be right there." Jack puts his right hand on his head for a minute. Jack tells Lorelai, "

I don't think I can see anything again. I'm just going to sit down and wait."Jack bumps his head the hand rail on the way down. Jack angry whispers to himself, "Ow!" Lorelai tells herself, "I wondered if the Coast Guard ever had to save the same guy this many times." Lorelai starts swimming and gets Jack out of the water again. Back in the Men's Locker Room. Jack puts his right hand on top of his head for a minute. Jack Out Of It and tells himself, "I wonder how I got so messed up because my head is killing me."

The door opens and it's Lorelai. Lorelai closes the door and is carrying an ice pack in her right hand. Lorelai goes over to Jack. Lorelai tells Jack, "Here's you're ice pack, Jack."

Jack grabs the ice pack from Lorelai with his right hand, observes the ice pack and puts the ice pack on his head. Lorelai tells Jack, "I've never seen somebody bump their head so many times as you have." Jack tells her, "Yeah, I thought I was doing so good today. I don't know how much more I can't take. Maybe my dad doesn't want me swimming." Lorelai tells Jack, "You know, Jack. I never met your father, but he never asked you to stop swimming in the pool or the ocean. I think he would want you to honor him and keep on going. To swim in the pool or the ocean and don't push him away. It makes his memory a lot more alive." Jack tells Lorelai, "You've got a point, Lorelai. When I was swimming for the last three days, I felt I could hear him with me. Like he was alive again, that's all I've wanted to do is to keep his memory alive." Lorelai tells Jack, "Well that's great, we should continue." Jack tells Lorelai, "So now that I've opened up, I gotta ask what's the deal with you and Colin? You don't look like a girl who would go for the bad boy type." Lorelai tells Jack, "I met Colin at one of the parties that Donald Trump had in Trump Tower Penthouse 18 months ago, when I first saw him and he told me his profession. I was pretty bored at first but he has worked hard to win me over. I just feel like I have to date someone that the tabloids approve of you know?"

Jack tells Lorelai, "If he was boring why'd you go out with him?" Lorelai tells Jack, "Well when he asked me out, I said yes. I hadn't had a date for a couple weeks from when my last boyfriend and I broke up; I guess I caught up in the excitement. Now things are different though, we've been through a lot already and I love him. I'm sure." Jack tells Lorelai, "So, how did he propose to you?" Lorelai tells Jack, "Did it like any other celebrity proposal I guess, put it in Wall Street Journal and said will you marry me?"

Jack tells Lorelai, "You actually said yes? When you read it in the Wall Street Journal?"

Lorelai tells Jack, "Of course I said yes. He is an attractive and successful man that I love. To mention it I think you guys could get along great together." Jack tells Lorelai, "Yeah I don't know about that. I've never had many guy friends besides Bobby over the years." Lorelai tells Jack, "Hey I got an idea, would you like to go on a double date with me and Colin? I don't know if you're dating anyone but I think it could be fun. It'd be nice going out with some other people. What do you say?" Jack tells Lorelai, "Oh yeah no problem, I have someone in mind I could ask." Lorelai tells Jack, "Oh that's great. How about we meet at that little Chinese restaurant around the corner from here, say around 8?" Jack tells Lorelai, "Sounds great, I'll see you two there." Jack enters the lobby of the library looking quite frantic. He rushes over to the front desk where Sarah is sitting reading a magazine waiting to closing things done thinking Jack would be at his lessons.

Jack tells Sarah, "Sarah. I've been looking all over for; could you do me a huge favor?"

Sarah tells Jack, "Yeah Jack what is it?" Jack tells Sarah, "Okay, I know this is going to sound a little crazy at first but just listen. Lorelai invited me to a double date with her and her fiancée; and to cut a long story short I need a date. Sarah starts laughing looking at Jack as if he must be joking. Sarah tells Jack, "So wait. You accepted an invitation to a Double Date without actually having a date?" Jack tells Sarah, "Well that's one way of putting it I guess." Sarah erupts into laughter again. Sarah holding back laughing and tells Jack, "Sorry. Ha I wish I could help you but I have an anniversary meeting with Bobby at the Ritz tonight." Jack tells Sarah, "Man. What do I do? I can't show up to a double date alone. I'm supposed to meet them in less than hour." Sarah tells Jack, "I don't really know what to tell you Jack. Why did you even say yes to the date?"

Jack tells Sarah, "I'm not sure. I thought it would be a great way to hang out with Lorelai outside of the rec. center. Now the plan has backfired but if I stand them up I'll never have a chance with her." Sarah tells Jack, "Um, Jack. You remember she's engaged."

Jack tells Sarah, "Oh yeah there's still that. I just don't know I have a feeling she's special. I don't think I'm ready to give up just quite yet. Well thanks for the talk Sarah, but I have figure a way to get to that double date. See you tomorrow." Jack starts rushing quickly out of from the front desk towards the main doors of the library. Sarah tells Jack, "Good luck." Back in the Chinese restaurant. Jack is at the bar by himself drinking a beer and repeatedly looking up at the clock to check the time. Its ten minutes till eight and Jack starts playing different scenarios through his head. Jack's Voiceover tells the audience, "Okay I could act like she was suppose to meet me here and I got stood up. Unfortunately I think I could act pretty convincing at being stood up by someone. "Jack takes a huge chug of beer and with a face of disgust takes a big gulp. Jack's Voiceover tells the audience, "Oh who am I kidding? Why am I even here, I should just leave before it's too late. Or maybe they just won't show up and I'll be off the hook. Yeah, they just won't show up and I'll say how sad I was they couldn't make it." Jack takes another swig of beer and looks up at the clock and its now five minutes to eight. Jack's heart pounds with each tick of the second hand until it gets louder and faster and drowns out the sounds of the bar. At the peak of the heart beats Jack looks over to the door and sees Lorelai in an evening dress accompanied by her fiancée. Jack's Voiceover tells the audience, "Well escaping is no longer an option. Looking like the victim of being stood up is my terrible last resort.(gulp) Here goes nothing." Jack finishes his beer gets up to head over to where Lorelai and her fiancée are waiting to be seated. Lorelai sees Jack from a distance walking to where she is standing and waves to him. Lorelai tells Jack, "Hi Jack. It's great to see you. Where is your date? I'd like to meet her." Jack tells Lorelai, "Hey Lorelai. Well I wish I could tell you where my date was. I've been waiting over that at the bar, she said she'd just meet me here after work." Lorelai tells Jack, "Oh no that's awful. Oh where are my manners. Jack this is my fiancée Colin, Colin this is Jack the winner of the lessons raffle." Colin tells Jack, "Real nice to meet you Zach." Jack tells Colin, "Nice to meet you to Colin. But the way my name is Jack." Colin tells Jack, "Ok. Whatever. Hey babe why did you pick this shitty restaurant to eat at? We can do a lot better than this." Lorelai tells Jack, "Oh come on this isn't that bad. Hey Jack we'll go get a table if you want to wait at the bar a little longer for your date." Jack tells Colin, "Thanks that'd be great. I'll just meet you guys at the table in fifteen with or without my date." Colin whispering to Lorelai and tells her, "I got an idea, why don't get go get a table somewhere else?" Lorelai and Colin start walking in the direction of an open table. Jack on the other hand heads back to the bar and orders another beer. Lorelai tells Colin, "We're already here just get use to it. And this is a new friend in a time when I don't have very many so try to be nice to him alright?" Colin tells Lorelai, "What? He's a weird duck I can't help it." Lorelai tells Colin, "Please just try limit being a jackass for one night." Colin tells Lorelai, "Alright, alright. I'll give him a chance."

Lorelai find an open table and sit themselves. They then tell the waiter they are waiting for two and to come back in a little while. Jack is sitting by the bar drinking his beer, worried to go talk to Lorelai and Colin. Jack's Voiceover tells the audience, "Man how did I even believe I could compete with someone like Colin? He even is he a jerk to go with the whole pretty boy look. And now they've seen me, they expect me to eat dinner with them." Jack finishes his beer looks at the clock and realizes it's about time to head back to where they are sitting. Jack's Voiceover tells the audience, "Just think I can do this. Worse case scenario I can get through this date. Oh man, what've I gotten into?" Jack walks to the back part of the restaurant to a booth where Colin and Lorelai are seated. Jack tells them, "Hey guys. Sorry but I think she's going to be a no show. I don't want to infringe on just you two, it would just be weird." Colin tells Jack, "You got that right. "Lorelai glares at Colin. Lorelai tells Jack, "Oh Jack, don't be silly. We'd enjoy the company. You have to be hungry at least." Jack tells Lorelai, "Really? Well thanks. A dinner out would be a nice change." Jack slides into the other side of the booth. The waiter then comes up to deliver the menus. Waiter tells them, "Hey everyone. Here are your menus; oh I thought there was going to be four of you?" Jack tells the Waiter, "Yeah once of us couldn't make it." Waiter tells Jack, "Ok, that's no biggie. Can I get you all started with some drinks? Maybe an appetizer?" Colin tells the Waiter, "Yeah can I get a beer? Or whatever you people call it." Lorelai tells Colin, "Could I get a glass of champagne please?" Waiter tells Jack, "And for you sir?" Jack tells the Waiter, "I'll just have a beer. Thanks." The waiter leaves to go get the drinks. Colin tells Jack, "You're not one of those book reading hippies are you?" Jack tells Colin, "No. I'm just a head librarian, nothing too fancy." Colin tells Jack, "Okay good. I'm just making sure you're not some radical crazy." The waiter returns with the drinks. Lorelai tells Jack, "Sorry this is just his way of getting to know someone. So Jack how did you become a head librarian? You look too young for that to me." Jack tells Lorelai, "Well I always use to help out when my Uncle Pete was the head librarian when I was little. Then this past year Uncle Pete retired and moved down to Florida, so it just kind of made sense for me to fill in for him. I don't mind it but it makes me feel a little older each day." Lorelai tells Jack, "Yeah were not getting any younger." Colin tells Jack, "I feel in my prime I don't know what you two are talking about." Jack tells Colin, "Yeah I'm not surprised you feel that way. Working on Wall Street has to be exciting for you." Colin tells Jack, "Yeah my Dad got me the job. I guess it's something to do. It works well with the ladies if you know what I mean." Everyone starts laughing, though Jack seems to laughing just to go along. Lorelai tells Jack, "Ha yeah right he wishes. But I have to use the ladies room, I'll be right back." Lorelai gets up and leaves Colin and Jack at the table alone.

Jack tells Colin, "Good work, that girl is a keeper." Colin is off starting at some girl in a tight dress walking through the restaurant. Colin tells Jack, "Oh yeah you can say that again man. Oh you mean Lorelai? Yeah she's pretty good." Jack tells Colin, "Man you are just Joe cool? How do you do it?" Colin tells Jack, "You just have to play the field; every girl likes getting swept off their feet. I'm just the one who does it." Lorelai returns to from the bathroom and sits back down in the booth. Colin tells Lorelai, "Hey sweetie, you ready to order? Cause I could use another beer." Lorelai tells Colin, "Yeah, I'm starving." Colin waves the waiter over. He takes their orders and their menus. The conversation picks up with everyone getting their food. Jack tells them, "So I've never been married, I got to ask what's it like to take the "plunge"?" Lorelai tells Jack, "Oh it's great. I've been dreaming out planning a wedding since I was a little girl. Everything feels a little surreal to me right now." Colin tells them, "It's the right move I think. It's just time to get married and have that family base at home." Lorelai tells Jack, "Since you brought it up, why haven't you ever been married? Don't you want to settle down?" Jack tells Lorelai, "Oh gosh. Well relationships never worked out for me when I was younger. Now I've got my career and I don't get out much besides that." Colin tells Jack, "That's rough buddy, stick in there. Hey waiter, can I get another beer over here?" Waiter shows up with another beer for Colin. Lorelai whispers to Jack, "Sorry he's not usually like this." Jack whispering back to Lorelai, "Don't worry; it has lead to an interesting night." Jack, "So Colin, when did you know Lorelai was the one?"

Lorelai tells Colin, "Oh I'm curious to hear this one." Colin tells Jack, "Well once we dated for about 6 weeks I knew she was different. I couldn't really put my finger on it but she just understood me. We went so well together I just had to propose to make sure she didn't slip away." Colin smiles at Lorelai and kisses her in between drinks of beer. Lorelai tells Colin, "Aw that's so sweet." Colin tells Jack, "So Jack, Lorelai said you scared of the water? What's all that about?" Lorelai tells Colin, "I didn't say he, I didn't say you scared of the water Jack." Jack tells Colin, "Well that's alright; and yes I have to say I have a fear towards the water. But Lorelai is helping me tons in our lessons; she really has a passion for swimming and I think it's rubbing off on me." Colin tells Jack, "Yeah she really does love all that swimming alright. I don't get it." Jack tells them," Oh a different subject the dinner was very good. I've never been here before." Lorelai tells Jack, "Thanks, it's one of my favorite little places. The service isn't the best though." Colin tells them, "You can say that again. Waiter, can I get another beer?" Lorelai tells Colin, "Are you sure you want to keep drinking honey?" Colin tells Lorelai, "I'm fine; I could just go for another beer. Waiter!" The waiter shows up with two beers. Waiter tells Colin, "Here's an extra you drunk. Now stop yelling in the restaurant." Colin tells the Waiter, "Whoa, little guy relax." The waiter storms off whispering stupid Americans under his breath. Colin tells them, "Whoa baby, what was that guys problem?" Jack sarcastically tells Colin, "I haven't a clue. You couldn't have been in the wrong." Lorelai starts laughing. Lorelai sarcastically tells them, "Yeah he must've been just having a bad day." Colin tells Lorelai, "Yeah he must have. Well once I finish these beers you wanna get out of here?" Lorelai tells Colin, "Yeah, I'll have to get a to-go box with the check. Jack do you think you could get the waiters attention this time just in case." Jack tells the Waiter, "Ha yeah of course. Excuse me sir.

Sir, excuse me." The flustered waiter returns to the table at the request of Jack calling him over. Waiter tells Jack, "Sir, if you demand a beer I will remove you from this restaurant myself. That being said how can I help you?" Jack tells the Waiter, "I was just wondering if we could get the check please. And I think she would like a to-go box." Lorelai tells the Waiter, "Yes please.?" Waiter tells them, "Okay, let me go get that and be right back." Colin drinks the last of the two beers, burps, and goes to raise his empty to signal for another. Lorelai forces his arm down. The waiter returns with the check, a to-go box, and two fortune cookies. Lorelai tells Jack, "Thank you. I'm so sorry for my fiancée." Waiter tells them, "It's okay he'll be gone soon." Colin tells the Waiter, "Hey. Hey, where's my fortune cookie china man?" Waiter tells Colin, "That's the last straw sir. You're leaving this restaurant now, or I will make you leave." Colin tells the Waiter, "Yeah right you'll get me out of here by yourself." Waiter sarcastically tells Colin, "Well you probably know how good we all are at karate. Do you really want to find out? Jack tells them, "No one is karate fighting anyone. Here, I'll just pay the tab.

Lorelai you should go walk Colin out and start trying to call a cab. I'll be out there soon if you need any help." Lorelai tells Jack, "Thanks Jack. Alright you heard the man, let's get you outside." Colin slurred and tells them, "Thanks for the beers bookworm." Jack calms down the waiter by paying the bill and getting outside as soon as he can. Lorelai throws one of Colin's arms over her shoulder and walks him out as he drags along. Outside the Chinese Restaurant, Lorelai still has Colin slouching half on her and she tries to way her arm to call a cab. A cab sees the two and starts to pull up to the curb. Jack comes out of the restaurant at the same time the cab shows up. Jack tells Lorelai, "You need any help getting him in there?" Lorelai tells Jack, "No, the pool keeps me strong enough to take care of guys this size." Jack and Lorelai start laughing. Then Lorelai opens the cab door and dumps Colin into the back seat and pushes him up right. LORELAI tells Colin, "Hey just sit tight. I'll be in a second and we can get you home." COLIN slurred tells Lorelai, "Man, I'm fine. Don't baby me." Lorelai ducks to get her head back out of the car to talk to Jack. Lorelai tells Jack, "But thanks for everything tonight. It was nice not seeing you fall in the pool for a change. I'm sorry your date couldn't make it." Jack tells Lorelai, "Hey, things like this happen don't worry about me. Well you have your hands full with taking care of him so I'll just be heading home." Lorelai tells Jack, "Yeah you're probably right. See you at the lessons tomorrow right?" Jack tells Lorelai, "Yeah I'll be there." Lorelai goes in for a good night hug and it catches Jack off guard. At first he just tightens up and locks his arms. Once he realizes it's a hug he tries to play it off cool, so when he hugs Lorelai back he gives her the buddy pat of the back. She pulls back looking a little confused by the whole event. Jack tells Lorelai, "Uh, well yep. See you tomorrow." Jack's Voiceover tells the audience, "Idiot. Could that have ended any worse. Besides picking up the bill, which was a lot more than expected, I was as smooth as sand paper. I don't think that Colin is much to compete with though. He came off as a real jerk." Jack turns around and starts quickly walking in the direction of his apartment. Lorelai still looks quite confused starts to laugh about the whole thing and climbs into the cab and it pulls away from the curb. Back in the pool, Jack and Lorelai look at the pool. Lorelai is wearing her black one-piece bathing suit, wearing her whistle in front of her neck and holding a clipboard in her right hand. Lorelai tells Jack, "You ready for another great day in the pool." Jack tells Lorelai, "I wanna apologize for the way things ended last night. I didn't really expect it, I panicked. I know this apology is even a little awkward but I'm just nervous around you still." Lorelai tells Jack, "Well I'm flattered, but what do you say to getting back to the pool?" Jack tells Lorelai, "Yeah let's do it." Lorelai blows her whistle and scares Jack into the pool. They both start laughing and Lorelai starts teaching Jack a new swim technique. Bobby and Sarah are talking to the Party Planner at a table in the Ritz in the library. Jack and Lorelai are in the pool, where Lorelai is wearing a dark red one-piece bathing suit. Jack is swimming freestyle again all the way to the end of the pool. Jack looks at the pool and throws up in the pool. Lorelai swims freestyle over to Jack and avoid the area he threw up in. Jack is working around the library giving a tour to a few people and cataloging new books. Jack and Lorelai in the pool, Lorelai is wearing a blue one piece bathing suit again. Jack swims the backstroke all the way to end of the pool. Jack looks at Lorelai and gives her a thumbs up. Lorelai looks at Jack and he sees some chlorine red eyes on him. Lorelai laughs and Jack doesn't know what's going on. Lorelai and Colin are getting some coffee and Colin is flirting with the barista. Lorelai is wearing jeans, t-shirt and a jacket and looking at her wedding dress held in front of her in the mirror in her Penthouse apartment. Jack is eating a cheeseburger and drinking a can of Diet Pepsi and watching Everybody Loves Raymond on T.V. in his bed. Something comes on about swimming and he thinks about Lorelai in his bedroom at his apartment. Jack and Lorelai in the pool, they start splashing and flirting with each other in the pool. Colin and Lorelai argue back and forth till Lorelai storms out of the room at her Penthouse apartment. Jack and Lorelai look at the pool. Lorelai is wearing her black one-piece bathing suit, wearing her whistle in front of her neck and holding a clipboard in her right hand. Jack tells Lorelai, "Wish me luck."

Lorelai tells Jack, "You'll be fine, you already gotten through all the lessons. It's time we see how much you've learned this past week. You're going to be okay right?" Jack tells Lorelai, "I'm good, I don't have to worry about the puddles again. This time I'm going in, without their help." Lorelai tells Jack, "Let's see what you have, kid." Jack tells Lorelai, "This is for you, Dad." Jack dives into the pool looking quite like a more confident swimmer. He swims freestyle down and back. He pauses and holds one finger up. Jack tells himself, "One!" Jack swims the breaststroke all to the end of the pool and back. Jack holds two fingers at Lorelai. Jack tells himself, "Two!" Jack swims butterfly all the way to end of the pool and back. Jack holds three fingers at Lorelai. Jack tells himself, "Three!" Jack swims backstroke all the way to end of the pool and back pool. Jack holds four fingers at Lorelai. Jack tells himself, "Four!" Lorelai tells Jack, "I knew you could do it, congratulations!" Jack tells Lorelai, "I can't believe it, I conquered the water. Man, I wish my Dad was here." Lorelai tells Jack, "I wish he was here too, he would have been proud of you. I know I am."

Jack tells Lorelai, "Thanks Lor, Let's call it good before I go and get hurt again. What do you say?" Back in the Men's Locker room. Jack is putting his jacket on for a minute, closes his locker and hears a door knock. Jack tells the person, "Come in." The door opens and it's Lorelai. Lorelai enters the men's locker room, closes the door and goes over talk to Jack. Lorelai tells Jack, "Hey, How's it feel to get through these lessons? How's you're heading doing from all of it?" Jack sarcastically tells Lorelai, "I'm think I might have a concussion, I think I better go talk to my Neurologists." Lorelai tells Jack, "You have to lay off the sarcasm a while Jack. All your falls have me worrying. How are you really?" Jack tells Lorelai, "I'm good, really good for the first time in my life. I think I can go in the water, without worrying about the past." Lorelai sits in the bench with Jack for a minute. Lorelai tells Jack, "No matter where he is or where he goes, he's still in part of you, right here." Lorelai points at Jack's heart and Jack smiles back at Lorelai. Jack tells Lorelai, "I never did ask you this and I knew you probably would turn me down. My friend Bobby and his wife Sarah are having dinner at the Ritz Carlton, the same place of their anniversary party. I was wondering if you like to come with me to it, but just as friends. If you don't I understand." Lorelai laughs for a minute. Lorelai tells Jack, "I'll definitely come with you Jack, not because I have to. But I could go for a night out." Jack tells Lorelai, "I appreciate that." Lorelai tells Jack, "You think so?" Jack tells Lorelai, "I don't know yet, but I think deep down, you guys will make the right decision." Lorelai tells Jack, "Thanks for believing in me Jack, I better go change. Which car you want us to take, mine or…?"

Jack tells Lorelai, "My car will be okay." Lorelai tells Jack, "I'll meet you at the front entrance." Jack tells Lorelai, "Sure thing, Lorelai!" Lorelai gets up from the bench, head to the door and stops. Lorelai turns around and looks at Jack for a minute. Lorelai tells Jack, "Jack, you did great out there." Jack tells Lorelai, "Thanks." Jack's Voiceover tells the audience, "I should have learned to swim so much sooner." Lorelai opens the door and exits the men's locker room. When Lorelai and Jack meet up outside Colin is there to pick up Lorelai. Colin tells Lorelai, "Hey sweetie. You ready to go?" Lorelai tells Colin, "Hey. I wasn't expecting you here." Colin tells Lorelai, "I know I probably should have told you but I wanted it to be surprise. Oh hey Zach didn't see you there." Jack tells Colin, "Hey Colin, I almost didn't recognize you without all the beers." Colin jokingly tells Jack, "Oh look at this guy. Good thing you're a funny man. So you ready to go?" Lorelai tells Colin, "Well I didn't know you were coming and I said I'd go meet some of Jack's friends at the Ritz with him." Colin tells Lorelai, "Wait, so I come and surprise you; now you're going to the Ritz with him? Don't even bother. Whatever I'll see you tomorrow I guess.

Colin peels out and drives away. Jack and Lorelai both look shocked Jack and Lorelai enters the Atelier Restaurant in the Ritz Carlton too attend Bobby and Sarah wedding anniversary. Jack and Lorelai enter and sit down at Bobby and Sarah's table. Bobby looks at Jack and Lorelai. Jack tells them, "Hey guys." Bobby tells Jack, "Jack, it's great to see you." Bobby looks at Lorelai like he has a crush on her and can't seem to look away Bobby tells Jack, "And you are?!" Jack tells them, "Oh, where are my manners." Jack starts laughing for a minute. Jack introduces them to Lorelai and tells them, "Bobby, Sarah. This is my friend and my swimming instructor Lorelai Rosenberg." Lorelai tells them, "It's a pleasure to meet you Bobby, Sarah." Lorelai shakes Sarah's hand for a minute. Sarah tells Lorelai, "It's a pleasure to meet you, Lorelai. Jack has told me lots about you." Lorelai tells Sarah, "I hope its good things. This place is amazing, how could you guys afford all this?" Sarah tells Lorelai, "Bobby still has from money due to family inheritances. We feel so fortunate." Lorelai tells them, "Well congratulations. I wish me and Colin would have thought to look here to host our reception." Lorelai let's goes of Sarah's hand and shakes Bobby's hand. Bobby is blushing and in awe.

Bobby tells Lorelai, "It's a pleasure to meet you, Lorelai. I gotta ask did you really pose nude in Playboy last year?" Bobby let's goes of Lorelai's hand for a minute. Sarah smacks Bobby on the head when he sits down. Bobby tells himself, "Ow!" Sarah tells Lorelai, "Sorry about that, my husband is a little bit out of it for the moment. Sometimes, I forget he is just another stupid perverted guy. Lorelai tells Sarah, "No worries over it. I always have to put up with nerdy perverts being in the limelight from time to time."

Jack and Lorelai grab a menu and figure out what they're having. Sarah tells Lorelai, "So, Lorelai how are the lessons with Jack going?" Lorelai tells Jack, "Oh he's getting more comfortable in the water with everyday so I'd say there going great." Jack tells Lorelai, "Yeah they sure are." Bobby tells Lorelai, "I also heard you're engaged Lorelai? Congrats." Lorelai tells Bobby, "Oh thanks Bobby. Yeah his name is Colin, what'd Jack tell you about him?" Bobby tells Lorelai, "Nothing big just a couple things about him, he's a Wall Street broker and looks like an Abercrombie And Fitch Model."

Lorelai tells Bobby, "That's him alright." Jack, Sarah and Bobby are laughing Bobby tells Lorelai, "Well good for. Marriage is a big step, I'm happy for you."

Lorelai tells Bobby, "Thanks, Bobby." The waiters enters the table, carries her notepad and pen in her right hand. Waiter tells them, "Hi, I'm LINDA. I'll be server for today and I want to say welcome to Ritz-Carlton Atelier. What is it you folks would like to order?" Jack tells Linda, "I'll take the twenty-four oz sirloin steak, with some homemade gravy and a diet pepsi." Lorelai tells Linda, "Could I get the T-bone and a Coors?" Linda tells Lorelai, "Would you like a draft or bottle?" Lorelai tells her, "Bottle please." Bobby tells Linda, "I'll have the prime rib and mushroom stew with a Coors light." Sarah tells Linda, "I'll take a Beef Short Rib, and some water." Linda finishes writing all the orders in her notepad with her pen. Linda tells Sarah, "Water, is there anything else I can get you folks?" Jack tells her, "I'd like to have some, A1 Steak Sauce with my meal please." Linda tells Jack, "Sure, coming right up." Linda recognizes Jack and Lorelai for a minute.

Linda tells Lorelai, "Excuse me, are you…?" Lorelai tells her, "That's me." Linda tells Lorelai, "Their is no way, I'm actually meeting an Olympic Gold Medalist/model here in my restaurant. I can't believe it!" Lorelai tells Linda, "Would you like an autograph?"

Linda tells Lorelai, "Oh, my god. Lorelai Rosenberg's autograph? Yes please, if it's not a hassle or anything." Lorelai tells Linda, "It's no trouble, I get this a lot. Here just let me borrow your pad and pen." Linda tells Lorelai, "Sure, sure! Hang on a second." Linda gives Lorelai the notepad and pen. Lorelai signs her autograph and when she's finished she gives it back to Linda. Linda tells them, "I was going to ask you, are you two together?" Jack tells Linda, "Oh, no. Just friends!" Linda tells them, "Oh ok, I'll get your drinks out here in a couple minutes." Linda leaves the table. Jack tells Lorelai, "Wow she thought we were together. That's silly." Lorelai tells Jack, "Yeah, can you believe she thought we were a couple!" Jack tells Lorelai, "Come on, that's ridiculous. It's not like I fell for you, when I first saw you in the pool." Bobby looks at Jack like he's lying through his teeth with leads to an awkward silence Jack tells the, "Well I'm starving; let's bring out the food." Flashes forward to Jack, Lorelai, Bobby and Sarah eating their dinner. Jack is drinking his diet pepsi from a glass with a straw, Sarah is eating her Beef short ribs, Bobby is eating his French fries and Lorelai is drinking her Coors Light. Lorelai tells Bobby, "I'm just saying I was so relieved when the buzzer stopped; I won the first event by only a few tenths of a second. And that's when I got my second gold medal and was began my shot at stardom in modeling." Bobby tells Lorelai, "I almost peed my pants when you won. I thought you were about to lose it by a hair." Lorelai tells them, "Yeah that was too close of a race. But the time doesn't really matter in the end; as long as you have the heart and determination to win." Sarah tells Lorelai, "That's what I thought too; when I use to win swim meets back in high school." Lorelai tells Sarah, "You used to swim in high school?" Sarah tells Lorelai, "Yep state champ, back in my more fit days of course." Lorelai tells Sarah, "Oh stop it. How come you never went to Olympics?"

Sarah tells Lorelai, "Ha I wish; I torn ligament in my knee when I was 19. But at least I know I went out of top in a way." Lorelai tells Sarah, "Yeah, that's a good way to look at it. I'm was fortunate to continue my success in the pool after winning a few state championships when I was younger. I was so amazed when I was giving a bid for the Olympic team, which has led to bigger and better things for me. So how do you guys know each other?" Jack tells Lorelai, "We met in fourth grade, when me and my mom moved to grandparents house in Queens right after my father died. I didn't think I would have any friends, until I met Bobby and Sarah. They came up to me when I was the new kid and were my only friends. Now I can talk to these guys about anything and they'll understand. And you stick with friends that you've known for that long. We all went to college together and have been working here at the library that my Uncle use to run. The rest was history so to speak." Lorelai looks at Jack like she's in love with him, grabs her of Diet Pepsi, accidentally spills the Diet Pepsi in her lap and gets up from her chair. Lorelai tells Jack, "Whoa." Jack tells Lorelai, "Lorelai, you okay?" Lorelai sarcastically tells Bobby, "It looks like I peed my pants. I guess I wasn't supposed to drink it." Bobby sarcastically tells Lorelai, "I think you should use a straw next time." Lorelai grabs a napkin, tries to wipe out the diet pepsi stain from her lap. Lorelai tells them, "I think I better…?" Jack interrupts Lorelai and tells them, "Sarah, why don't you go with her and help her for a minute." Sarah tells Lorelai, "Sure, come on Lorelai." Sarah gets up from her chair and goes over to Lorelai. Sarah tells Lorelai, "Let's get you dried off." Lorelai and Sarah leave the table and head to the bathroom. Lorelai sarcastically them, "I hope I don't get funny looks on the way to the bathroom." Sarah tells Lorelai, "You'll be fine, just walk closely behind me." Jack and Bobby are laughing at the formation of Lorelai and Sarah going to the bathroom. Bobby tells Jack, "So, that's the famous Lorelai Rosenberg?" Jack tells Bobby, "That's her alright; she's one of a kind." Bobby tells Jack, "Tell you the truth, the way I see it. I think she's really in love with you. Hell she at least has to like you." Jack tells Bobby, "You can tell that?" Bobby tells Jack, "Well for starters she came out to this dinner with you." Jack tells Bobby, "I know, but I'm out of my league and she's marrying this Colin Farrell wannabe. I don't think I can break up that relationship." Bobby tells Jack, "Why not? You're crazy about this girl and she at least likes you. You have to make a move and not just because it's the Lorelai Rosenberg." Jack tells Bobby, "Oh come on, I don't see her like that." Lorelai and Sarah comes out of the Women's Bathroom. Sarahheads to the table and Lorelai looks at Jack like she's in love with him. The dinner continues and everyone is laughing having a good time. Lorelai tells them, "Hey, Thanks again for the dinner. It was great to meet you guys." Bobby & Sarah tells Lorelai, "It was nice to meet you too. Bye." Jack and Lorelai walk out of the Ritz." Lorelai tells Jack, "Jack, do you think you I could use your phone?" Jack tells Lorelai, "Well I have to admit, I don't have a cell phone. We'd have to go back to my place."

Lorelai tells Jack, "Oh that's no biggie." Back in Jack's Apartment, the door opens, it's Jack and Lorelai and Lorelai is holding her purse in her right shoulder. Jack and Lorelai enter the living room and Jack closes the door. Jack tells Lorelai, "The phone is right here." Lorelai tells Jack, "Thanks, but I don't think I will need it." Jack tells Lorelai, "Why, I thought you locked yourself out of your apartment. Don't you need to call your doorman to get a key?" Lorelai takes the purse out of her right shoulder, opens it and takes out the keys from her purse. Lorelai shows Jack her keys. Lorelai tells Jack, "They were in my purse the whole time." Jack tells Lorelai, "Wow, so why'd you come up?" LORELAI sarcastically tells Jack, "Oh no particular reason." Jack tells Lorelai, "Well I don't think you have to be in a hurry to go home right now, there's no rush. You can always leave later." Lorelai tells Jack, "Well thanks for the invitation but that's what I was planning on." Jack tells Lorelai, "Oh really?" Jack and Lorelai are about to making out, but Lorelai threw up and passes on the floor and Jack was relieved that he wouldn't do something he regret. The sun rises in the window and shines on Lorelai's face and when she wakes up and she is wearing the same clothes while she was sleeping in Jack's bed. Jack enters the bedroom and tells Lorelai by whispering to her on while he was lying on the bed. "Jack's Voiceover tells Lorelai, "I don't know, how or why, but I think I can do this. I need to thank this great girl for giving me something to believe again. I've always worked really hard at relationships, but they never seemed to work out. You have saved me an in the water so many times too and I think I love her. Jack kisses her on the forehead. Jack is making scrambled eggs at the stove in his pajamas in his kitchen, until Lorelai enters the kitchen with a long silk white bathrobe and sees Jack. Lorelai looks at Jack and smiles at him. Lorelai tells Jack, "Good Morning!" Jack accidentally grabs the potholder and burns his left hand. Jack tells Lorelai, "Ow, aah ow!"

Jack goes to the sink, turns his faucet on and cools off his left hand, Lorelai laughs for a minute and Jack turns off the faucet. Lorelai goes over to Jack, hugs him in the back and Jack turns around sees Lorelai. Lorelai tells Jack, "Hello." Jack tells Lorelai, "Hey you."

Lorelai tells Jack, "What happened?" Jack sarcastically tells Lorelai, "Hey, we don't want your fiancée to get jealous. "Lorelai sarcastically tells Jack,

"Don't worry; he's probably drunk too." Jack and Lorelai are laughing; Lorelai goes to get the pot of coffee and fills up a mug off the table. Jack gets ready to dish the eggs up on the plates at the table but he pauses. Lorelai tells Jack, "What happened? I couldn't remember anything." JACK tells Lorelai, "I think you too much too drink, You were looking for your keys, but it was in the apartment, you passed out and threw up on the floor. I cleaned up the floor and put you into my bed and...?" Lorelai interrupts Jack for a minute. Lorelai tells Jack, "Did we...?" Jack interrupts and tells her, "No, I slept on the second bedroom and that's it."

Lorelai tells Jack, "Thanks Jack. I didn't want do something I regret." Jack tells Lorelai, "Neither did I. I'm not that kind of guy who would take advantage of a drunk beautiful girl coming on to me, I have thought about it, but I wouldn't do that to you. Lorelai tells Jack, "I don't know what I'm going to say to Colin, but I've been on this roller coaster with him for eighteen months. I don't know how much more I can handle." Jack tells Lorelai, "Whatever you tell Colin that's up to you. I don't want to be the reason for."

Jack puts his scrambled eggs on his plate that already has buttermilk pancakes, bacon and sausage links just like Lorelai's plate. Lorelai tells Jack, "No, don't think that. It's just I'm not even the one who's been around. Do you know how many women Colin has been with?" Jack tells Lorelai, "A hundred?" Lorelai starts laughing. Lorelai tells Jack, "Too many to count but there was at least one more after we started dated. It's like he is juggling our relationships and still going after girls." Jack finishes pouring Lorelai her scrambled eggs. Then he heads to the sink where to puts the pan. Jack tells Lorelai, "So, why did you two want to get married if he was still running around another girl when you guys were dating?" Lorelai tells Jack, "I figured he wasn't going to run around with both of us forever. At least so he told me; but then he proposed to me. So, after I said yes he went to the phone to end whatever it is he had with her." Jack head to the kitchen table and sits down in his chair next to Lorelai. Jack tells Lorelai, "You really think he ended it with her? I barely know him and would guess..." Lorelai interrupts and tells him, "He ever ended it, no he never did. Cause I've seen him at Cafe Napoli with her." Jack tells her, "I'm sure it was a misunderstanding; maybe they were ending it there instead over the phone?" Lorelai tells Jack, "It's one thing to end a relationship but if they broke up she shouldn't have gave him some tongue and cheek in public." Jack looks at Lorelai for a minute. Lorelai tells Jack, "The Hotel Clerk called me a couple hours earlier and let me know my fiancée's presidential suite is already booked for him and his fiancée for the day. Guess what, the fiancée they were talking about was not me, but for…?" Jack interrupts Lorelai for a minute. Jack tells Lorelai, "NO! He didn't? The ex?" Lorelai tells Jack, "You guessed it. I still can't believe it. It's bad enough he was cheating on me for three months, but lying about ending it and still running around with his playmate after he proposed." Jack tells Lorelai, "Oh my. I never knew things were so bad between you two." Lorelai tells Jack, "I've made a bad choice too and I still love him. Even no matter what dumb things we do, we still love each other. I'm not going to mess with that, no matter what the relationship between us is." Jack tells Lorelai, "No one can talk you out of anything you want to do." Lorelai smiles at Jack for a minute. Lorelai tells Jack, "Thanks, if I ever have a chance to marry again someday I want it to be with you. You were too late but being with you is the best thing that ever happened to me and you're the kind person I never want to let go. Bobbby tells Jack, "I appreciate that. Why don't we finish eating and we'll get dressed. I'll see you in the pool like nothing happened if you'd like." Lorelai tells Jack, "Yeah. Okay." Jack grabs his fork and eats his scrambled eggs. Lorelai looks at Jack watching him eat and gets a big smile on her face. Lorelai and Jack are back in the pool and starts his final lesson. Lorelai tells Jack, "What do you want to do for your last day of lessons?" Jack tells Lorelai, "I'd like to challenge you to another splash contest. It'll be a way of signifying I'm comfortable in the water." Lorelai tells Jack, "Sure, but I have to say I'm going to win again. Oh and Would you want come to the wedding tomorrow? We have an extra seat in the bride section." Jack tells Lorelai, "I don't think I could, the anniversary party is in Ritz Carlton Banquet Hall tomorrow, I promised I be there and make the toast." Lorelai jumps in the pool making a pretty large splash that even gets Jack a little wet. Jack then jumps in like a cannonball and lands square on this back. Jack tells Lorelai, "Oh man. I should have figured that would happen." Lorelai tells Jack, "Ha I'll give you the win, for moral support." Jack tells Lorelai, "Oh thanks." Back in the Men's Locker Room, Jack looks at Lorelai for a minute realizing the lessons are over and she is to get married the next day. Jack tells Lorelai, "Well I'm always in your debt. You helped me conquer one of my fears a child and I'll never forget it." Lorelai tells Jack, "Oh I'll never forget you and your falls either. But this seems like goodbye." Jack tells Lorelai, "The library is always open if you need a book or anything." Lorelai tells Jack, "I'll be sure to stop by. Tell Bobby and Sarah, congratulations." Jack tells Lorelai, "I'll make sure to tell them." Lorelai tells Jack, "Bye Jack." Jack tells Lorelai, "Bye Lorelai." Jack leaves the lobby with giving Lorelai a hug and walks out. She watches him for some time thinking about their last two weeks together. Bobby and Sarah's Anniversary Party at banquet hall where Jack is watching, Bobby and Sarah are slow dancing in their formal dress. Bobby looks around the Ritz to all the friends and family enjoying themselves on the dance floor and at the dinner tables.

Bobby tells Sarah, "This anniversary is the second best thing that ever happened to us."

Sarah tells Bobby, "What was the first?" Bobby tells Sarah, "You are honey, happy anniversary." Bobby kisses Sarah in the lips. Sarah tells Bobby, "Happy Anniversary babe!" Bobby tells Sarah, "I hope Jack hurries up, he's has to make his anniversary toast soon." Sarah tells Bobby, "Don't worry, honey. Jack will be here. He'd never miss this."

Sarah looks as Jack enters the banquet hall looking handsome in a full three piece suit.

Sarah tells Bobby, "See what I mean." Bobby tells Sarah, "I guess I better go see him. He looks like shit besides the suit. Right now I think he needs me."

Bobby goes over to Jack to see what's wrong. Bobby tells Jack, "Hey Jack." Bobby hugs Jack for a minute. Jack tells Bobby, "Hey Bob." Bobby let's goes of Jack. Bobby tells Jack, "How'd the last lesson go?" Jack tells Bobby, "Let's see, We said our goodbyes and she's still getting married to Colin." Bobby tells Jack, "That bad, huh!" Jack and Bobby see some empty seats and a table. Jack tells Bobby, "Yeah." Bobby tells Jack, "Come on." Jack and Bobby sits down in their chairs and finish talking. Bobby looks at the waitress to catch her attention. Bobby tells the Waitress, "Excuse me." Waitress tells them, "Can I help you?" Bobby tells the Waitress, "Two shots of the strongest liquor you got." Waitress tells Bobby, "Coming right up Mr. Romano!" Waiter leaves the table, Bobby and Jack continue talking. Jack tells Bobby, "You know what the worse part of this is?" Bobby tells Jack, "That you had to let go of somebody you really love?" Jack tells Bobby, "Yeah, I mean shit. With all my luck in the world I will never meet anyone like her again." Bobby tells Jack, "I guess deep down, she has feelings for Colin. I think you just not need to get too dragged down by all this. She was engaged to him when you met her for crying out loud." Jack tells Bobby, "Well that's not very comforting. I think I'm just going to be in funk for a little bit." Bobby tells Jack, "Sorry Jack. I'm glad you still made it here." Jack tells Bobby, "No offense but I wish I was on that altar with her today instead." Bobby tells Jack, "You'll get your chance soon enough. Maybe not this time but now you're ready for when the time does come." Bobby and Jack look at Sarah dancing with her father. Bobby and Jack wave their right hands to Sarah. Jack tells Bobby, "Thanks Bobby, I think there is hope for me I just don't know how many more chances I'll get." Bobby tells Jack, "Just stick in there. You deserve a girl who wants to be with you. No matter the situation." Lorelai enters the Main Room at the Cathedral Of St. John The Divine wearing a beautiful Vera Wang white wedding dress and sees his father in the hallway for a minute. Lorelai tells her father, "Hey Daddy!" LORELAI'S DAD hugs Lorelai for a minute. Lorelai's Dad tells her daughter, "Hey hon, you ready. It's the big day." Lorelai tells her father, "I think I'm ready pop, have you seen Colin?"

Lorelai's Dad tells Lorelai, "Honey, you do realize about tradio….?" Lorelai interrupts his Dad. Lorelai tells her fahter, "I just want to know where he is." Lorelai's Dad tells Lorelai, "I think he's still in his room." Lorelai tells her father, "Thanks Dad." Lorelai enters the doorway of Colin's changing room. Lorelai knocks on his door. Lorelai tells Colin, "Colin, I think we need talk." Colin's Voice tells Lorelai, "What?" Lorelai is still knocking on his door. Lorelai thinks she hears a girl's voice. Lorelai tells Lorelai, "Colin, I think we need to talk for a minute." COLIN'S Voice, "I'm kind of busy, Lorelai. But, I'll be there in a minute." COLIN'S GIRLFRIEND'S

VOICE tells herself, "Oh Yeah!" Lorelai looks upset for a minute. Lorelai tells Colin, "Who's in there?" Colin's Voice tells Lorelai, "There's no one in here but me." Lorelai whispering to Colin, "Were about to find out." Lorelai opens up the door after violently jiggling the door knob loose. Lorelai enters the Colin's Changing Room, seeing Colin bare chested with his pants at his ankles and his old girlfriend for the last three months, who is a blonde and wearing short black low cut dress. Lorelai looks upset. Colin looks kind of frightened and trying out how to figure this. Colin let's goes of his old girlfriend for a minute and goes over to Lorelai for a minute. Colin tells Lorelai, "Honey, I can explain." Lorelai sarcastically furious tells Colin, "Spare me. Explain what? That her tongue was in your mouth."

Colin tells Lorelai, "You're right I can't explain that." Lorelai tells Colin, "I can't believe I was this close to marrying you. I would have regretted it till I died. You know why?"

Colin tells Lorelai, "Why's that?" Lorelai tells Colin, "This!" Lorelai punches Colin in the face. Lorelai tells herself, "What a, I doing here? I've should've listen to him. I knew this would happen." Lorelai takes off her wedding ring from her finger and throws it on the floor. Lorelai tells Colin, "I'm leaving you Colin. Hope she knows about all your STD's. Well have a good wedding you two!" Lorelai exits Colin's Changing Room and leaves the church running still wearing her wedding dress. Lorelai exits the church, sees a cab driver a block away and Lorelai raises her hand. The cab stops in the main entrance of the church, Lorelai gets in the back of the cab and closes the back door. Cab Driver tells Lorelai, "Where to ma'am?" Lorelai tells the Cab Driver, "Ritz-Carlton, hurry!"

Cab Driver tells Lorelai, "Sure, no problemo. Is it too bold to ask or Are you getting cold feet about a wedding?" Lorelai tells the Cab Driver, "Shut up and drive. I'll give you an extra 10 to step on it." Cab Driver tells Lorelair, "Okay ok. I'm on it." The cab driver speeds out of the the main entrance of the church and heads to the Ritz-Carlton. The main table at the banquet hall where Bobby and Sarah are sitting at, Bobby is standing up and proposing a toast with his champagne glass up in the air. Bobby tells his guest, "A toast to my loving wife Sarah. Here's to one good year and many ahead of us. The cab driver is driving and Lorelai in the backseat stops for a minute when the cab driver comes to s stop when he sees a red light. Lorelai looks agitated in the back seat but can only hurry so much. The main table at the banquet hall where Bobby and Sarah are sitting at, Bobby sits back down in his chair after the toast. Jack is sitting down near the main table, grabs a fork and taps on his champagne glass. He puts down the fork, lifts his champagne glass high and gets up from his chair. Jack tells the guest, "Hi everyone, I'm Bobby and Sarah's best friend since when we little. Since I was Bobby's best man, they asked me to make a toast. No promises but this is the best I got. For five years, this couple has surprised us a lot. We thought it wouldn't last six months or one year. Hope you didn't have a twenty on it." Everyone, Sarah and Bobby are laughing. Jack continues telling the guest, "I've seen true love pass me by whole life, and I've known these guys long enough to see what they have is true love. From the time when we were fourteen and Bobby looked at Sarah and way back then it was like they were meant for each other. I always envied them for that. When they got married, I had a best friend Bobby. I also added a best friend-in-law Sarah. I said I'd triple their salaries if I cried so give me a second here." Everyone, Sarah and Bobby are laughing. Jack continues telling the guest, "To my best friend. To my best friend in-law. I'm honored to give a toast at your first anniversary but will be glad to come back to the many more anniversaries expect from you two. Here's to many more years of great things from this couple. Cheers." Bobby and Sarah are crying Jack raises his champagne glass and so does everyone else. EVERYONE'S VOICE tells Bobby and Sarah, "To Bobby and Sarah Romano! Jack sits back down in his chair, everyone is applauding and Jack looks around and sees Bobby's relatives sitting right next to him."

Jack tells Bobby and Sarah, "I have to go. Tell Bobby and Sarah congratulations and that I've left. They'll understand." Bobby's Relative tells Jack, "Sure, I'll tell him." Jack gets up from his chair, head to the door that open and leaves the banquet hall. The Cab stops for a minute in the front entrance, the back door opens and it's Lorelai. Lorelai exits the back door and says good-bye to her cab driver on the run. Lorelai tells the Cab Driver, "Thanks a lot." Lorelai closes the back door and goes inside the Ritz Carlton. Everyone is dancing in the dancing floor in the banquet hall,

Sarah and Bobby are dancing in the banquet hall and Bobby turns around for a minute sees Lorelai for a minute entering the banquet hall. Bobby tells Sarah, "Honey, I'll be right back." Sarah tells Bobby, "I'll go with you." Bobby and Sarah stop dancing and head to where Lorelai is standing in her wedding dress. Bobby tells Lorelai, "Lorelai!" Lorelai tells them, "Hey guys, I told you I'd make it. Sorry about this dress. I had to rush." Sarah tells Lorelai, "Oh don't you worry. I'm glad you came." Lorelai hugs Sarah for a minute. Sarah tells Lroelai, "It's great to see you Lorelai." Lorelai tells Sarah, "It's great to see you too, Sarah." Lorelai let's goes of Sarah and Lorelai hugs Bobby. Bobby tells Lorelai, "I'm really glad you here, Jack really miss you." Lorelai tells them, "I miss him, too." Lorelai let's goes of Bobby for a minute. Sarah tells Lorelai, "Lorelai, weren't you suppose to be get married in Colin right now?" Lorelai tells Sarah, "Change of plans." Bobby tells Lorelai, "What happened to Colin?" Lorelai tells them, "Ancient history, I was going to ask you do you know where I can find Jack?" Bobby tells Lorelai, "He left party a couple minutes ago; I think he was going somewhere important." Lorelai tells them, "Like the library." Sarah tells Lorelai, "No, I doubt he would leave to go to work." Lorelai thinks about where Jack could be and she think she thinks she figured it out. Lorelai tells herself, "I think I know where he went, congratulations you two." Lorelai starts leaving the banquet hall, until she hears Bobby's voice. BOBBY'S VOICE tells Lorelai, "Lorelai!" Lorelai stops and turns around. Bobby tells Lorelai, "Good luck." Sarah tells Lorelai, "Go get 'em Lorelai."

Lorelai smiles at Bobby and Sarah and continues exiting the banquet hall. Jack looks down at the pool, Jack takes a ring from his right pants pocket and observes it. The Rec Center door opens gently and it's Lorelai. Lorelai sees Jack but he didn't hear her come in and goes to talk to him. JACK whispering to himslef, "I did it Dad." LORELAI'S VOICE tells Jack, "Jack." Jack turns around and sees Lorelai in the Rec Center. Jack tells Lorelai, "Hey Lorelai!" Lorelai tells Jack, "Hey Jack, what are you doing here?" Jack tells Lorelai, "You're secretary let me in, when my father died out in sea we had a funeral and I said my good-bye. But I was just a kid, I wanted to tell him goodbye on my own terms. I had this ring that belonged to him once; I wanted it to throw it in the water to honor him. I never had a chance too, because…?" Lorelai tells Jack, "You're fear of the water." Jack tells Lorelai, "Yeah, But now that you've helped me conquer it at least for a couple weeks. I think I'm ready to say good-bye, and it fitting because today is also the anniversary of his passing. Lorelai tells Jack, "He would have been proud of you, let's say good-bye together." Jack tells Lorelai, "Thanks, Grab on the ring." Lorelai grabs Jack's father's ring. Jack silently tells himself, "This is for you Dad." Jack and Lorelai throw Jack's father's ring in the pool and watch it slowly sink to the bottom. Jack tells Lorelai, "What are you doing here; I thought you and Colin were getting married?" Lorelai tells Jack, "Change of plans, I always knew it was a big mistake marrying the wrong kind of guy. When I looked at him today I knew he wasn't the one for me, the one person I wanted is right in front of me. That's the person, I was in love with and I never wanted to let go." Jack tells Lorelai, "I never want to let go of you either. How about for good old times we take a dive together, what do you say?" Lorelai tells Jack, "In a heartbeat." Jack and Lorelai hold hands dive into the pool and Jack and Lorelai go underwater and then resurface. Jack tells Lorelai, "What'd you think of that dive?" Lorelai tells Jack, "The best dive I've taken so far. Jack and Lorelai start making out." Jack wakes up from his day dream in front of his computer at the library at the computer room and hears a knock at the door. Jack tells the person, "Come in." The door opens and it's Bobby. Bobby tells Jack, "Hey Jack. You okay? I haven't seen you all day." Jack tells Bobby, "Yeah I'm fine. I just must have fallen asleep in front of the computer." Bobby tells Jack, "Did you have a late night with Lorelai?" Jack tells Lorelai, "Yeah we just got back from a great weekend away." Bobby tells Lorelai, "What are you doing coming into work already for?" Jack tells Lorelai, "Just figured I would get this speech for the book fair coming up next week out of the way." Bobby tells Jack, "Lorelai called here looking for you. I didn't think you came in today, I told her to stop by. She sounded pretty worried."

Jack tells Lorelai, "Oh I'll call her and let her know I'm here." Jack and Bobby hear another knock on Jack's office door. Lorelai tells Jack, "Hey you! I've been looking all over for you. You really need to get a cell phone. Wanna grab some dinner?" Jack tells Lorelai, "Sorry I didn't call; I fell asleep on the job. Dinner sounds great let's go. I'll see you tomorrow."

Bobby tells them, "Sure thing guys: I better lock up and get back home to Sarah before she starts getting worried too. Jack tells Bobby, "Oh don't worry about that Bob, I got it. Just head on home, and we'll see you in the morning." Bobby tells them, "Bye guys." Bobby leaves the computer room. Jack shuts down the computer and starts gathering up his things. Jack tells Lorelai, "You ready?" Lorelai tells Jack, "Yeah let's get out of here. What do you want tonight?" Jack tells Lorelai, "I could really go for some Italian." Lorelai tells Jack, "I know just the place that makes the best New York style pizza. Let's go call a cab." Jack tells Lorelai, "Sure thing, we can go there next week after your lessons." Lorelai tells Jack, "I think I could squeeze you in. You don't need any more lessons do you?" Jack tells Lorelai, "I think I've learned everything you can teach me." Lorelai tells Jack, "Oh yeah, well there's a lot more I could teach you." Jack tells Lorelai, "Yeah, what's that?" Jack and Lorelai starts making out. Jack and Lorelai exit the library. They spot a cab and start to flag it down. Jack's Voiceover tells the audience, "People always said there something magical about the water; that there is something in the water that makes you feel at peace, calm." The cab pulls up to the curb. Jack's Voiceover continuing telling the audience, "Well now look at me. I got the girl and I can now successfully fall into a pool whenever I need to. Things are looking pretty good. I think my Dad would be proud." Jack opens the door, Jack and Lorelai get inside the cab and Lorelai closes the door. Jack and Lorelai start making out as the cab leaves down the street into the horizon. Jack's Voiceover tells the audience, "To answer a broad question of is there true love. Well Bobby and Sarah just celebrated another anniversary and Lorelai and I aren't far behind. Just stick to what feels true to you and you will never be let down. Live life with as little regret as possible and always remember what conquering a fear can encompass. Jack and Lorelai lived happily forever to my Princess of the water."

The End.

Final Word

Thank you for reading the four princess series. I hope you enjoy reading them. Who knows maybe I can come up with another Princess Story in another time. This is my sixth book that I turn third princess stories in one book. See you next time and my castle door is always open. Goodbye!